FLIGHT TO
PARADISE

Thank you for you
Support —

M___ Coe
PROV 13:12

*In loving memory of Martha
My Mother*

DEDICATION

To my wife, for showing me the way to paradise
To my God, for leading me to my wife

* * *

*Paradise is found when love is given; love can only be
given when it is understood as an act of the will rather than a
response of the emotions.*

FLIGHT TO PARADISE

A novel by
Mike Coe

Four centuries ago, John van Linschoten (1563-1611) wrote about the beautiful birds of Paradise (God's birds) during his voyage to the East Indies. He wrote, ". . . no one has seen these birds alive, for they live in the air, always turning towards the sun, and never alighting on the Earth till they die."

The Malay Archipelago
by Alfred Russell Wallace,
1869

Chapter 1

Nine years earlier—Saturday, June 23, 1974
Buckhead, Georgia

"The South—where roots, place, family, and tradition are the essence of identity." Carl N. Degler (Social Historian)

The hot shower poured over Keri's naked body, engulfing her in a therapeutic cocoon, numbing her thoughts to everything but the pain deep within her heart, in her bones, in her head. For months she had begged God to do something—anything—to stop it, but He'd done nothing.

Imprisoned by her youth in a society of economic rules and social etiquette, she saw no escape. Nothing short of a miracle could free her from the unavoidable sentence of four painful years of separation from the one she loved.

Ryan Mitchell was her prince. The thought of him made her tingly all over. When they were together, nothing else mattered. The world even looked different: pinks were pinker, blues were bluer, and her favorite foods were yummier. He fulfilled her every dream about love, and more. But how could she ensure time would not change the man she believed to be her soul mate, robbing her of her dreams?

Ryan's acceptance to the United States Naval Academy meant tonight was their last date of the summer. Tomorrow he would be gone. Keri couldn't blame him for her pain. She wanted him to have his dreams and be happy, but the thought of not seeing him or being with him—possibly losing him forever—was more than she could bear.

Stepping from the shower, she wrapped herself in an Egyptian cotton towel and cleared the condensation from the fogged mirror above the vanity. Taking her comb, she worked the tangles free from her shoulder-length brunette hair. Her thoughts turned to her mother, and resentment boiled in her chest.

Only yesterday her mother was planning the wedding, but with the death of Ryan's father and Ryan's subsequent change in socio-economic class, things changed. Ryan Mitchell was struck from the Hart's studbook of acceptable prospects faster than the coronary had choked the life out of Mr. Mitchell. The way Barbara Ann saw it, the Southern culture consisted of two classes: Us and Them, and Ryan Mitchell was now a Them.

At first, Keri tried to blame Ryan's father. Mr. Mitchell never exercised and should have taken better care of himself. In addition to his poor personal habits, he died with no life insurance and no money. He left Martha Mitchell broke, with no way to pay the mortgage on their Buckhead house or the tuition for Ryan to continue attending the private school on West Paces Ferry Road. His death forced Ryan and his mother to move into a small rental house in a much-less prestigious area of Atlanta. Ryan transferred to a nearby public school.

Unable to find satisfaction blaming the dead, Keri turned her resentment toward God. If God had not let Ryan's dad die, her life would still be perfect—Ryan would *still* be living in Buckhead attending her private school; they'd *still* be attending the same college as planned; and she'd *still* be having her fairy tale wedding after college. Ryan would fly jets in the Navy, eventually landing his dream airline job, and they'd both live happily ever after—traveling the world and eventually starting a family.

But blaming God didn't help, either. It was her mother's fault. After Mr. Mitchell's death, her mother insisted that Keri stop dating Ryan. She said it would never work—he'd never make her happy. Arguing with her mother only made things worse, pushing her outside her country-club-cool comfort zone. Surprisingly, Ryan's acceptance to the Naval Academy caused her mother to back off from her "dump Ryan" campaign.

But Keri wasn't buying her mother's fake change of heart. She knew the idea of Ryan being locked up in a military academy over six-hundred miles away was why she'd, so willingly, decided to call off the dogs. Whatever the reason, she and Ryan were able to spend the last few months together in peace.

With her hair wrapped around pre-heated rollers, Keri moved to her dresser and selected a bra and a matching pair of lace panties. She had preselected and laid out everything she planned to wear, days before.

As she let the towel fall to the floor, the wall of mirrors revealed a beautiful young woman with a proportioned body. She stood five-six, was full-breasted and had a flat abdomen. Her toned legs and arms reflected the results of years of dance, gymnastics, and cheerleading.

She slipped into a silky pink bathrobe and strode into her bedroom filled with memories of her last two years with Ryan. Every item held special significance, from the movie-ticket stubs from their first date to the now-wilted mum she'd worn at the senior prom. Sitting at her dressing table, she began applying her makeup.

Keri dreamed of the fairy-tale wedding set in a romantic location surrounded by all who were dear to her. She imagined the reception would be the best night of her life, filled with dancing and being admired by everyone. Her mother fueled Keri's dreams with promises of her having a wedding Atlanta would never forget. However, with every storybook image of a glorious wedding came the usual undertones laced with warnings concerning *whom* she would marry. If Keri had heard it once, she'd heard it a million times: "Now Sugah, when you get *married*, you must remember that you're not just marrying a *man*, you're marrying the *family*." Her mother had made it clear that Keri was to set her sights on marrying up, never down, and God *forbid* she should marry a Yankee. Barbara Ann Hart was emphatic in her belief: "It's all about roots—Southern roots."

Raised as a privileged child in Buckhead—the trendy, upscale section of downtown Atlanta—Keri had been schooled by her mother in the importance of pedigree. When Keri was younger, her mother would say, "Now Darlin', you should always remember, golf and tennis are good, but huntin'-n-fishin' are bad. Those that kill the little animals are cruel. We call them rednecks."

Barbara Ann ensured that Keri was seen in all the right places. Every outfit was selected for her. Potential friends—and their parents—were pre-screened. In her subtle yet manipulative way, she coerced Keri throughout her childhood, usually against her will, to participate in a pre-selected menu of activities designed for one sole purpose: preparing her to become Atlanta's most desirable catch.

Each activity—ballet, dance, gymnastics, piano, voice, beauty contests, cheerleading, and especially that ridiculous four-week finishing school in Virginia—was undoubtedly a concerto conceived in her mother's mind and carefully orchestrated long before Keri's birth. For eighteen years, Keri had been nothing more than a puppet dangling from the strings of a masterful puppeteer.

Keri asked herself why she'd let it happen and submitted that it was the child in her trying to earn her mother's approval. She wanted her mother to love her and was afraid that if she didn't do exactly as she insisted and listened to every word she spoke, she wouldn't love her—something Barbara Ann had proven to be true.

A light knock came on her bedroom door. "You busy?" The door eased open. "So, are you and Ryan doing anything special tonight?"

"Not really… other than saying our good-byes." Keri knew her mother loved hearing that. "I'm not sure when we'll see each other again."

"Darlin', that's what I wanted to talk to you about."

Chapter 2

Keri's mom crossed the bedroom and sat on the bed. Bed talks always ended ugly. "What did you want to talk about?" She braced for her mother's words.

"I…well, actually, your *father* and I… think tonight would be a good time for you and Ryan to say your good-byes."

She struggled to process the *exact* meaning of her words—then it hit her. Like a hammer, pounding a spike into her heart. She faced her mother. "What are you talking about?" Finally the truth: her dating privileges with Ryan had been granted in exchange for his exile to the Naval Academy—and now, from her life.

"You can tell him you think it would be best for both of you not to be tied down during college. I'm sure he'll understand."

"Best for both of us! Understand! You're asking me to dump him the night before he leaves, and you think he'll understand!" She stood from her dressing table and paced the room—her heart pumping red into her face; her jaw locked. Tonight of all nights—her last night with Ryan. Now she had to deal with *this*.

"We just don't think it's a good idea for you to tie yourself down at such a young age."

Keri stopped and spun toward her mother. "We? What do you mean 'we'? That's not it at all! *You* never have liked Ryan! Admit it! He's not good enough for you! It's not Daddy! It's *you*! *You're* the only one who hates him!" Tears filled her eyes.

"Listen, it's just not time for you to get serious, especially with a boy going off to the Army and—"

"Come on Mom, it's not about that! I know you hate Ryan… and he's *not* going into the *Army*!"

"While you're at college, you need to be free to date other boys."

"Did you hear me? It's not the army! It's the United States Naval Academy—a *big* difference! Obviously, you don't have a clue. Ryan is very smart. Over fifty thousand applied and only two thousand were selected."

"Yes, Dear, but for goodness sake, he's going to be in the service and you deserve more than a military man. That life is not for you. I think—"

"How do you know what kind of life is right for me?" Keri snapped.

"Sugah, I've known those kinds of people and—"

"What do you mean? Those kinds of people? What do you think he is? You can't do this! It's not fair! Ryan is a fantastic person and is going to do great things with his life—you'll see." She continued pacing.

"Well, to be honest... we didn't raise you to go off with some soldier."

"He's not a *soldier*! How many times do I have to tell you? He's going to be a pilot!"

Her mother stood. "Keri, why are you acting like this? You know this boy is no good for you. Haven't I taught you anything? If you were to marry a man like this, you'd regret it for the rest of your life. You'd end up working in some pathetic job just to survive. Look around you. Don't you want a nice life?"

"You don't get it!

Keri knew it was all about Barbara Ann's image—what her gossipy lady friends would think if she had to confess her daughter was dating some poor boy whose mother worked as a retail clerk. It was not exactly the kind of stuff that would win gawking affection from her card-playing huddle of gold-digging has-beens.

Her mom had forgotten what it meant to be in love. Keri watched how she treated her dad at home. They rarely touched each other. However, when they were in public, Barbara Ann always painted a rosy picture of marital bliss. Her dad played along, as Barbara Ann made sure all her so-called "friends" had no reason to think she did not absolutely adore her husband.

Her mother walked over to the door, turned, and looked at Keri. "Darlin', it's for your own good. Trust me, you don't love this boy."

"Trust you? Why should I trust you? What do *you* know about love? You and daddy don't even sleep together anymore."

"Keri, Honey, I'm trying to help you." Her mother walked over to her and placed her hands on Keri's shoulders. "Look at me, Darlin'."

Keri turned, reluctantly, and looked at her through watery eyes.

"I don't hate Ryan. But for now, you don't need ties in your life, especially to someone you'll only see once or twice a year. You're too young for that. You need to be free."

Free? What is she thinking? The only one I need to be free of is her!

"But Momma, I love him, and I don't want to lose him. Why can't you understand?"

"I know, Dear. If it's meant to be, it'll all work out *after* you both finish school." She stopped a tear from running down Keri's cheek. "Honey, you know your momma just wants you to be happy. You need to trust me." She hugged Keri. "I know it's not easy, but I want you to end it tonight. After he's gone, you'll see I was right." She left, pulling the door closed behind her.

Keri threw herself on the bed and burst into tears. She knew her mother despised Ryan—not because of who he was but because of what he had.

Why would God do this? Why couldn't her mom be more like Ryan's mom: someone who understood her and loved her? It was times like this when she would go to Martha Mitchell. Martha always knew what to say.

Lifting her head from the pillow, she checked the time. Ryan would be there soon. She wiped the tears from her cheeks, walked over to her dresser, and stared into the mirror—her eyes red and puffy.

I can't let him see me like this.

Her hands trembling, she began unrolling her hair. She breathed deep and exhaled slowly, trying to calm her nerves. If she did what her mother asked, it would crush Ryan; if she didn't, her life would be miserable. Either way, she would lose—like a rat, she was trapped.

With all emotion drained from her heart, she began considering the unthinkable:

Four years is a long time; a lot can happen in four years; Ryan will be totally consumed at the academy; he needs to focus on his school; if we are meant to be together, it will work out.

The forbidden thoughts brought a strange calm—an acceptance, of sorts.

After taking the last curler from her hair, she took a piece of paper and started to write.

June 23, 1974

Dear Ryan,

> *I believe if we are meant to be, nothing can keep us apart. As long as I live, I will patiently wait on each sunrise and follow each sunset into tomorrow, for I believe it is the path of the sun that will lead us to our hopes and dreams. Promise me that you will never lose hope in tomorrow.*

I love you,
Keri

Chapter 3

Later that night, Ryan and Keri sat in his 1965 four-door Chevrolet Impala parked in her driveway; a place they'd spent many Saturday nights after dates.

"I'm going to miss you," he said, his back resting against the car door, while she sat close to him in the middle of the bench seat.

How can I tell him it's over?

"I know you'll do great." She tried not to think about what she had to say. Taking his hand, she gently rubbed it, thankful the darkness hid a tear spilling from her eye. She always liked his hands. They made her feel safe. She was happy for him and wanted to be strong. He had worked hard. She forced her thoughts into the hopeful, yet distant future. The pain swelled even more.

Ryan pulled her close, kissing her on the forehead. She looked up at him. "Don't cry," he said. He kissed her softly on her lips. "What's wrong? You act like your best friend just died."

She snuggled under his arm as they quietly embraced their last intimate moments. She wished time would stop. Her words would change everything. Feeling like a crazed killer about to commit a premeditated murder, in a matter of minutes, she would drive her words—like a dagger—deep into his heart.

"Keri, you know I love you, don't you?" She sniffed as fresh tears streamed from her eyes.

"Yes," she whimpered, her head still tight against his chest.

He swept a loose strand of hair back behind her ear. "I want you to remember, no matter what, I will always love you."

She squeezed her eyes tight; the tears stinging. Her chest and throat tightened. She did all she could to keep from bursting. For the past two years, hardly a day had gone by they had not been together, and now this. It would be months before they touched—maybe years, if at all.

It's time. Do it! Do it now! Don't forget the note.

She hugged him one more time and slipped the note into his shirt pocket; something she had done many times before at the end of their dates: simple messages of encouragement, love, or, at times, just a funny quote. However, this note would be her last. Keri looked at him; his face mostly darkened by shadows. She saw a twinkle in his eyes as he smiled.

"What is it?" he asked, seeming to detect her words before they came. "What's wrong?"

She swallowed, took a breath, exhaling slowly. "Ryan, you're not going to understand what I'm about to say, but I truly believe it is the right thing for you. I don't want anything to get in the way of you reaching your goals. I've thought about it for a long time and... and... I think...." The words wouldn't come. She paused, then forced the dagger into his heart. "I think we need to break up." The darkness couldn't hide the shock on his face.

"What? What are you talking about? No! Don't say that!"

"When you leave, I don't want you to have to think about me," she lied.

"How can I *not* think about you?"

Like a heartless wooden puppet in the lap of a ventriloquist, her mouth opened and repeated the words of her mother. "You need to be free."

I can't believe I said that!

He fought to hold on, denying her words. "But I don't *want* to be free."

What do I say now?

She twisted the lie in another direction. "Ryan, the only way I can know if we are truly meant to be together is to let you go."

"But we're *supposed* to be together. Nobody knows you like I do. Nobody sees you like I do. We *belong* together. I love you... I *love* you, Keri. Why are you doing this?"

He won't let go.

"I'm sorry. This is something I have to do, Ryan." She lied again. Her mouth released words that were not her own. "I need to date other people."

I hate her for making me do this!

His eyes revealed the finality of her blow; a mix of shock, denial, and helpless acceptance. She'd killed him.

She wanted to tell him it was all a lie. She wanted to tell him she loved him and would never leave him; that she would write him every day.

"I need to go," she said.

"Please don't do this!"

"Ryan, you're going to do great." She got out of the car, closed the door, and didn't look back; hurrying into the darkness, glad he couldn't see her anguish. Her heart wrenched in pain, seeking a safe place to release its cries. Her emotions exploded. The reality of what she'd done came crashing down on her shoulders.

Once inside, her mother, an image of the Devil, stood waiting to see if she had sold her soul as instructed. Keri paused, her heart beating wildly in her chest. "I did it! I hope you're happy!"

Her mother moved toward her with open arms. "Darlin' it's gonna be alright."

Keri stepped back. "Get away from me! I hate you! It won't be alright!"

"Honey, God has someone better for you."

"God? If this is what God wants, I hate Him, as much as I hate you!" She ran to her bedroom, threw herself on the bed, and cried, releasing the pain and regret. The words replayed in her mind like a curse: *You need to be free. I need to date other people.* How could she have said those things? She hated herself.

She cried into the night until there were no more tears to give. Wrenched and emptied of all emotions, she turned on her side and stared out her window. A full moon stared back, encircled with a misted halo, hiding its normally brilliant glow. All she could think about was Ryan. Her heart ached knowing how confused he must be. She wanted to take it all back; to tell him how sorry she was for hurting him. She never should have listened to her mother.

A glimmer of hope lifted her spirit when she realized that in a matter of weeks, once she left for college, she would be free from her mother. Then, after college, she could do anything she pleased; live anywhere she wanted.

When I graduate, I'm never coming back here. I'm moving as far away from her as possible.

Continuing to gaze into the black sky, her thoughts brightened as she recalled the many nights she and Ryan had stared up at the same sky together. She would listen while he carried her on a journey, mapping their future across the black canvas, jumping from star to star—the Naval Academy; their wedding; flight school; the airlines. Dreaming of a life filled with romantic adventures, he continued his game of naming the stars—London, Paris, Rome, Hawaii, Greece, and more.

She couldn't lose him. She must keep the dream alive. Regardless of what her mother said, it could work. She would write him often, telling him everything, making sure they stayed connected—every thought. She smiled.

* * *

Ryan heard the door to her house close. He sat alone, his mind grasping for answers while the sounds of the summer night engulfed him: cicadas and tree crickets. Her words rang in his mind: *I need to date other people.* It didn't make sense. Yesterday, everything was fine as they dreamed about their future together—now this.

He started the car, backed out of the driveway, and drove away. The neighborhood streets were quiet. The night's events replayed in his mind much like a television network might broadcast a shocking clip of a disaster on the evening news.

The note!

He pulled the car to the curb, snapped on the overhead light, and pulled the folded note from his pocket.

June 23, 1974

Dear Ryan,

I believe if we are meant to be, nothing can keep us apart. As long as I live, I will patiently wait on each sunrise and follow each sunset into tomorrow, for I believe it is the path of the sun that will lead us to our hopes and dreams. Promise me that you will never lose hope in tomorrow.

I love you,
Keri

Chapter 4

The next morning—Sunday

Ryan's senses stirred to life with the smell of bacon frying. With each waking moment came the ugly realization of last night. Keri dumped him. Her stupid idea of wanting to date other people made no sense at all. Only yesterday, she said she could never be with anyone else.

"Breakfast is ready!" his mother called out, her voice easily heard through the thin walls of the small two-bedroom house.

"Coming," he said, as though he were talking to someone in the same room.

He flung the covers back, willed his muscular six-two frame to its feet, and headed for the bathroom. Half-naked, standing sleepily over the toilet, he relieved himself, flushed, and stepped to the sink. The blemished mirror reflected a confused and abandoned face.

Why'd she do it?

Exclusive for the last two years, everyone viewed them as the perfect couple; hardly ever referring to one without the other.

"Ryan! I don't want your breakfast to get cold."

"Coming!"

He pulled-on a pair of faded jeans and headed down the hall to the kitchen.

His mother kissed him on the cheek. "Good morning, Sweetie." She placed a plate on the small wooden table—scrambled eggs, cheese grits, and three slices of bacon.

"Morning," he growled.

The squeak of the oven door produced the smell of homemade biscuits. A jar of his favorite Mayhaw jelly waited in the center of the table.

"You sleep well?"

"I guess."

"Sounds like you need one of your momma's hot biscuits and some Mayhaw jelly," she said, placing a plate of steaming biscuits on the table. "That ought to fix you right up." She poured a cup of coffee, took a seat, and watched him spread butter and jelly on a biscuit while she fiddled with a tiny cross hanging from a thin silver chain around her neck.

"So, how did your date go last night? I'll bet it was hard for you to say good-bye to my sweet little Keri."

"She dumped me."

"What do you mean, 'dumped you'?"

"Some crap about wanting me to be free and her needing to see if she loves me. If you ask me, it sounds like some of her mother's brainwashing. That woman has the evil eyes for me."

"Now, that doesn't sound like *my* Keri."

"Ever since Dad died, and we left Buckhead, Mrs. Hart has treated me like ghetto trash."

"Don't you worry about Barbara Ann. She's even given *me* the cold shoulder a time or two. I don't let her bother me. When it comes to people like that... all you can do is love 'em. I know for certain Keri loves you more than her own skin. Not only does she tell me, she practically glows when she's around you."

"Yeah? Well, it looks like her mom controls that light switch now. It's just hard to understand how her mother can have such a strong hold on her."

She took a sip of coffee. "Give her some time. If it's meant to be, it'll work out. You'll see. Not even Barbara Ann can stop it." She handed him a napkin from the stack in the plastic holder on the table.

Ryan took the napkin and crunched it in his hand before closing the biscuit on his plate. "So, I'm supposed to believe, if she goes off and meets somebody else, it was meant to be?" He carefully lifted the jelly-packed biscuit to his mouth with both hands, making sure not to let a drop of the Mayhaw jelly escape.

"You know you *could* give up your appointment to the Naval Academy and go to school with Keri."

"Impossible! Without a scholarship, I can't afford college, and I'm definitely not going to be strapped with a bunch of student loans after I graduate."

After a moment of silence, she said, "I can help."

He shook his head. "What are you talking about? You barely make enough to pay the bills."

"I've got a little saved up."

"Forget it… not gonna happen."

"Just trying to show you that you always have a choice."

"Well, that's not one of them."

She held the cross between her fingers, sliding it back and forth. "Ryan, you're going to have to trust God with this one. If it's what He wants for you and Keri, it'll work out. Have a little faith."

Managing a mouth full of biscuit, he said, "Yeah... maybe I'll have more faith after her mother's dead."

"I'll bet once Keri gets out from under her mother and all settled into her new life at college, you two will be back on go."

"Maybe, but four years is a long time. Need I remind you, Keri is a beautiful girl and about to be dropped into the middle of a public university with thousands of hormone-charged dogs thinking of only *one* thing… you do the math. Oh, I almost forgot; her parents are gazillionaires. I'm sure her mother won't have any trouble finding her an *acceptable* mate—someone Barbara Ann can use for breeding *acceptable* grandchildren."

She fingered the cross again. "I'll tell you what you need to do."

"What?"

"I think you should just let her go."

"Do I have a choice?"

"That way you'll both know if you are truly meant to be together."

"Now you're starting to sound like Keri." It reminded him of Keri's painful words: *Ryan, the only way I can know if we are truly meant to be together is to let you go.* He looked at his mother. "So, just like that... I'm supposed to forget about her and see where she lands?"

"I believe when two souls are meant to be together, nothing can keep them separated. Eventually they will find each other. And to be perfectly honest, I believe you and Keri are meant for each other."

He chuckled. "Glad somebody has it figured out, because from where I'm sitting things don't look so good. And what did you mean by 'Eventually'? Is that before or after she's been married and divorced? I guess I'm supposed to think my Polaroid taped to her dorm-room mirror is going to be enough to keep her hanging on—especially with her mother working overtime to find her a breeding partner. I'm no fool."

She got up and cleared the dishes from the table. Ryan turned his glass up, finishing the last of his orange juice.

After rinsing the dishes off in the sink, she dried her hands. "Let's go in the den."

She took her favorite spot in the worn chair where she spent hours most evenings, reading or creating one of her cross stitch tapestries. Ryan sat on the couch.

"Ryan, you're young, and I know you love Keri, but the time is not right." She reached beside the chair for a small brown paper bag full of embroidery, fished out her needle, and began working the thread with practiced fingers.

"So, let me get this straight. You're saying I should just forget about her and move on?" Ryan scooted to the end of the couch and laid back, propping a pillow under his head. They still had almost a half-hour before they needed to get ready for church.

"Not completely. Keri was your first love. Nothing will ever compare to a first love. In time, you will know if she's the one." Head down, her lips moved without sound. After counting her stitching, her fingers went back to work on the canvas.

"How much time?"

"For now, I suggest you focus on your school work. Keri is not going anywhere. She and I are close. I'll be sure she keeps up with everything you're doing. You will see each other when you come home on breaks."

She adjusted the angle of the canvas while she talked. "To be honest, I'm more worried about you than I am Keri. You're the kind of man *many* women would love to get their hands on—smart, attractive, ambitious."

"Says who? My *mother*. I don't think that counts."

She stopped stitching; her eyes peered over her half-glasses. "Do you know what I pray for the most?"

He waited silently, knowing she would answer her own question.

"I pray you will learn how to listen to your heart; something most men never learn to do. It has taken me a lifetime to learn that the deepest desires of the heart can only be satisfied when love is given; that's what the heart was made to do." She paused. "Also, as a man, you must learn the difference between love and lust and not go chasing the first pretty little girl that blows you a kiss."

"Gross, Mom."

"Ryan, God made men differently than he did women."

"Mom, where are you going with this?"

"A man is aroused—"

"Please, Mom!" He put a pillow over his face.

"Let me finish. A man is aroused by his eyes. Most young men don't understand women, they only respond to them. Women know how to trap innocent men, simply by their look. I'm sure you remember the story of David and Bathsheba? All it took was one look. Before you know it, he slept with her, got her pregnant, and had her husband murdered. It all started with one simple look."

"Are we done, yet? I don't like where this is going."

"I just don't want some cute little girl, who is only thinking of herself, to come along and sweep you off your feet, and later, for you to wake up and realize you've made the biggest mistake of your life." Her eyes lowered back to the canvas, putting the needle in motion." That's my greatest fear for you."

"What makes you think I'd be so stupid?"

"You're a man, aren't you?"

"No woman, I don't care how hot she is, will ever sucker me into her trap."

"I just don't want you to get hurt."

"Did you forget? In a matter of days I'll be locked up with a bunch of men for the next four years? I don't think I'll be doing a lot of serious dating at the academy. I'll be lucky to even see a woman." He sighed. "I'm tired of talking about this. I don't need girls."

"Okay, we have a few more minutes. So, what else is on your mind?"

He looked around the small den with its modest furnishings. Compared with their Buckhead house, it was a miserable hovel. "I know one thing for sure; when I'm on my own, I'm going to have nice things. I don't care what it takes. I want to be rich, like Keri's dad."

"Ryan, you know money and the things it buys—alone—will never make you happy. Trust me, I've seen both sides."

"You trying to tell me you're happy living in this dump?"

"When your father was alive, we had plenty of money. We lived in the best homes money could buy, but I couldn't say I was happier then, than I am now."

He opened his arms wide. "How can *this* make you happy?"

"Ryan, what you give your love to has a way of becoming your most valued treasure. Always remember your momma told you this: money and the things it buys can't love you back. You'll never be happy, and you'll never have enough."

He sat up on the couch. "How can you say that?"

"It's basic human nature. You'll always be in *pursuit* of happiness instead of enjoying it."

"So, I shouldn't try to make anything of my life… just give up and plan to live in a dump? *That's* supposed to make me happy?"

Her voice calm, her stitching steady. "No. I think you know what I'm talking about. Of course you should use all your gifts and abilities to do the best you can in life. Always keep learning and pushing yourself to do better. You need to keep your dreams alive. What I'm saying is simple. You will find your treasure where your heart is. Know your heart, and you will be happy."

"What can make me happier than money? I know for sure it's not women."

"Most people spend their lives wanting more because they think they have too little. In so doing, they end up overlooking what's most important in life."

"And that is?"

"People. Your heart was made to love people, and once your heart is satisfied, everything else will work itself out. By the time most people figure it out—if they ever do—it's often too late." She tugged on the edges of the canvas and turned it toward Ryan. "What do you think?"

Almost complete, it was a late-afternoon beach scene, the sun three-quarters below the horizon, and the silhouette of a bird in flight headed toward the setting sun. Two empty Adirondack chairs, side-by-side, faced the ocean. Three phrases were stitched into the fabric—one below the horizon: LEARN FROM THE PAST; one on the horizon, next to the sliver of orange sun: EMBRACE THE PRESENT; the third above the horizon against a canvas of purple-blue sky: HOPE IN THE FUTURE.

"I like it," he said. "Who's it for?"

She folded the embroidered canvas and tucked it back into the paper bag. "I think I might keep this one for myself. It has a special meaning." After returning the bag beside her chair, she stood. "We can continue this later. We need to get ready for church." She patted his shoulder. "Remember, life is all about learning to love others. If you miss that, you will miss life. So, know your heart and guard it. It can lead you to great happiness or great sorrow. Now let's get ready so we won't be late."

He followed her down the hall, mulling over her words. Her words threatened his big dreams, yet, on another level, they satisfied his soul.

She doesn't understand. Her life is almost over. Mine is just beginning...

Chapter 5

Friday, May 13, 1983

After four grueling years at the U.S. Naval Academy, and five tumultuous years on active duty, Ryan felt like he had lived two lives.

From 1979 to 1981, he flew the Navy F-14 based at Naval Air Station Oceana in Virginia, with Fighter Squadron 41—the "Black Aces." Navy life as a fighter pilot was anything but stable, being called to perform missions around the globe with little notice.

His first of many deployments came in September 1979 aboard the USS Nimitz. During the Iranian hostage crisis, the nuclear-powered supercarrier was dispatched to increase the U.S. Naval presence in the Indian Ocean. The Nimitz became the launch pad for "Operation Evening Light", an attempt to rescue 52 American embassy workers being held hostage in Tehran. During the cruise, VF-41 chalked-up 144 continuous days at sea; the squadron's longest period at sea without a break since World War II.

His commanding officer quickly recognized Ryan's potential to become an exceptional instructor pilot. His natural stick-and-rudder abilities, along with his being articulate, intelligent, and having a strong work ethic, won him an assignment to the prestigious Navy Fighter Weapons School "TOPGUN", an intense six-week course designed to sharpen the air-to-air skills of the Navy's best fighter crews.

In August 1981, after his tour at TOPGUN, Ryan rejoined the Black Aces aboard the Nimitz for another deployment to the Mediterranean.

On the morning of August 19, while flying combat air patrol over the Gulf of Sidra, radar spotted two Libyan, Soviet-built Sukhoi Su-22 Fitters. The Fitters had launched from nearby Okba Ben Nafi Air Base, headed his way. Within minutes, the lead Fitter fired a heat-seeking missile. After evading the missile, Ryan and his wingman, Rex Dean, engaged and returned fire using AIM-9 Sidewinder missiles, shooting down both Libyan fighters. The incident marked the first Navy air combat confrontation since the Vietnam War, and the first ever for the F-14 Tomcat.

Ryan's final assignment with the Navy, which began in 1981, was a three-year tour at the Fighter Weapons School at Naval Air Station (NAS) Miramar, San Diego, California, as a TOPGUN instructor. With only fourteen months left, his goal was to land an airline job after leaving the Navy.

While at the Naval Academy, he'd lost contact with Keri Hart—something he now regretted. At first, she'd written him almost daily. His sporadic and infrequent responses had not been enough to keep the relationship alive. He was certain she had moved on. How could he blame her? His mother mentioned her in one of her letters, but never said anything about her love life.

Friday afternoon, May 13, Ryan arrived home—earlier than usual. The condo was empty. He glanced at his watch—four thirty—seven thirty Atlanta time. His mom would be expecting his call. He always called her on her birthday, regardless of where he was in the world. He imagined her sitting in her favorite chair, working her needle like a skilled surgeon, bringing a drab piece of canvas to life with one of her heart-felt scenes—each with its own special meaning about life.

After changing into his workout shorts and running shoes, he grabbed a bottle of water from the fridge, took a seat on the couch in the den and dialed her number.

"Hello?" she said.

"Happy birthday, Mom!"

"Ryan, so happy to hear your voice! How are you doing?"

"Good. You having a good day?"

"Well, at my age, they're all good." She chuckled.

Ryan pulled the phone over by the couch, leaned back, and propped his feet up.

"Guess who I got a birthday card from yesterday?" She asked.

"Who?"

"Keri. She always remembers my birthday."

"Keri Hart?" Ryan sat up. "What did she say?"

"Not much. Just that she loved me, missed me, and wished me a happy birthday. She's so sweet."

"Where is she now?"

"She's in Florida... Ft. Lauderdale. Did I tell you she's a flight attendant?"

"Yeah. You mentioned it in one of your letters."

"I wish you two could get together."

Ryan remembered the dreams he and Keri shared when they were younger. He loved the game they played of naming the stars, letting them represent the cities they planned to visit. The vastness of the sky reminded him of the unlimited possibilities life holds. But things had not turned out the way they'd planned.

"Me, too, but I'm sure she's met someone by now. Does she ever ask about me?"

"I keep her up to speed with what's going on in your crazy life. We don't see each other much anymore; just a few letters every now and then. Do you remember that night before you left for the academy?"

"How could I forget? She dumped me cold. I still think it had to be her mother."

"I never told you, but the next day she came over and we had a long heart-to-heart talk. I'd never seen her so sad. She was a mess. And you were right, Barbara Ann *did* encourage her to break up with you."

"I knew it!"

"She hated herself for doing it but felt trapped. The poor little thing was so confused. But there was no doubt she loved you more than life itself. She said she would do anything to take back that night. That's when I told her not to give up, that you would understand. She decided to write you every day. But you know, it takes two to keep a relationship alive and you weren't exactly the best at writing."

"You don't have to rub it in, but in my defense, they were busting my chops. I barely had time to brush my teeth."

"Ryan, you could have—"

"Okay Mom, I know. I blew it... should've written her more... I screwed up. Nothing I can do now."

"Why don't you write her now? She knows you're in California. I think it would be nice. I know she would love to hear from you." A moment of silence followed.

Ryan shook his head. "She's probably dating someone... might even be engaged."

"Don't you think she would have told me? And besides, what does it matter if she is dating someone?"

"Do you have her number?"

"No. We agreed not to call, only write, because I really can't afford long distance, and I don't want her wasting her money. Let me give you her address."

He grabbed a notepad and a pen. "What is it?" He scribbled it down, then said good-bye.

The thought of talking to her excited him. He remembered the note she slipped in his pocket that night:

In time, we will know if it's meant to be.

He still had it somewhere. Staring down at the white paper, he wrote:

Dear Keri,

His mind went blank.

What do I say? How do I start? Do I tell her I still love her? How about: Remember when you dumped me? Write something—anything.

After five crumpled pieces of paper, he finally had something.

Friday, May 13, 1983

Keri,

  It's been a long time. I learned from Mom you're living in Florida. She tells me you're a flight attendant. Sounds exciting. I also hope to be hired by the airlines, once I complete my commitment to the Navy. Probably next summer.

  The Navy keeps me busy and out of touch with everyone. Even Mom complains. I'm ready for a change.

  Maybe we can talk sometime and do some catching up. Mom didn't have your number. Mine is 619-231-1515. Please give me a call or write. I'm living with a Navy buddy in Del Mar, a small beach community north of San Diego.

He stopped.

How should I sign it? Love, Ryan, or just Ryan? Love is too much. How about sincerely? No. Just put Ryan, then wait and see how she signs hers when she writes back—if she writes back.

He signed the letter: Ryan.

As he licked the stamp, he heard the condo door close. "What's up Buddy?" Rex called, as he made a beeline for the fridge.

Rex Dean was the perfect poster boy for a Southern California travel magazine: blond, tanned, and athletic-looking. Raised in an upper-class family in the prestigious La Jolla, near San Diego, and a graduate of the University of Southern California, Rex was a member of a select group of persnickety Southern California families who pridefully wore their net worth on their sleeves. His parents typified the "be" in "wannabe." They weren't *striving* to keep up with the Joneses; they *were* the Joneses.

Ryan met Rex while assigned to VF-41. They'd attended TOPGUN together. After the incident with the Libyan fighters, the Navy sent them to NAS Miramar as TOPGUN instructor pilots.

Their extreme personality differences made them a perfect team. Rex, the extrovert, amused Ryan, while Ryan's more reserved personality fit the bill perfectly in Rex's search for a social wingman.

When it came to women, Rex lived and breathed by a self-made philosophy he called "Rexology": women are to be used, not loved, and they existed solely to satisfy and serve men. He'd once said, "Women are disposable items, much like the bones from a juicy, succulent, rib dinner."

He strategized that single women normally run in pairs, so a wingman was essential. "You get synergistic effects from teamwork: mass firepower; different sensors looking in different places; and better self-protection." For Rex, everything related to the kill—always striking first, leaving Ryan to pick-up the "sister ship"—one of his many code phrases. With his target acquired, Rex announced "YOYO," meaning, You're On Your Own. Ryan's underdeveloped social skills and reserved personality made Rex shine which he used to his full advantage.

Ryan strutted into the den, eager to share his good news with Rex. "You won't believe this! Did I ever tell you about Keri Hart?"

Sprawled out on the couch, half-way through his first beer, Rex said. "Not sure."

"Hang on." Ryan rushed off to his bedroom, returning with a picture. "Check it out."

"Gnarly, Dude! This girl looks like she's in high school. Who's that punk with her?" He brought the picture closer to his face. "Is that *you*?" He laughed. "You look like you're twelve!" He handed it back to Ryan. "Dude, you can do better than that."

"You don't understand." Ryan stared at the picture.

"Let me see her again." Rex looked at the photo for a minute. "I guess… put a few years on her… it's possible. Got a better picture?" He took a gulp from his can of beer, followed by an unrestrained belch.

"No, that's it. I haven't seen her since we split up back in high school."

"Hey Dude, you'd better be careful. No telling what she looks like now. She could be bald, bucktoothed, and the size of a baby whale—a real swamp donkey."

"You're crazy. I'm sure she's drop-dead gorgeous."

"Not worth the chance. Too many babes out there for you to waste your time thinking about some woman you might not be able to recognize on a beach full of sea lions. Yo, mate, let me grab my harpoon."

"Funny. I thought I might try to contact her," Ryan said.

"Man, what am I going to do with you? I hope I don't have to rescue you from yourself. Really, Dude, I think you're headed for the rocks."

"Can't hurt to write her a letter."

"Just remember, the Rexter tried to warn you." Rex picked up the TV remote and started surfing.

Ryan took the photo back to his room, returned with his letter to Keri and dropped it on top of a stack of outgoing mail by the door. "I'm going for a jog. You want to come?"

"I'm noodled. I need to fuel up for tonight. You *are* going out tonight, aren't you?"

"Yeah, I'll go."

"Awesome! I'm afraid to leave you home alone with that picture. I'd have to hide all the lube." He chuckled. "No telling what you might do."

"Funny."

"Yo! Dude! Before you go, how 'bout grabbing me a brew."

Ryan detoured back to the kitchen, pulled a can of beer from the fridge and handed it to Rex. "Enjoy."

"S'later, Brah," Rex said.

* * *

When Ryan closed the door, Rex popped up off the couch and headed for the stack of outgoing mail by the front door. He grabbed the envelope addressed to Keri Hart. With a sharp knife, he surgically opened it, slipped the letter out, and studied it. "Ryan... Ryan. Dude, I can't let you do it to yourself. If you get mixed up with this chick, I'll lose my wingman."

He took the letter to his bedroom and rolled a fresh piece of paper into his typewriter. Trying to duplicate Ryan's handwriting would be too risky. With a small bit of doctoring, he spun-out a letter guaranteed to get the job done. "Don't worry, Dude, I got your back."

The letter read:

Friday, May 13, 1983

Keri,

> *It's been a long time. I learned from Mom you're living in Florida. She tells me you're a flight attendant. Sounds exciting. I also hope to be hired by the airlines once I complete my commitment to the Navy. Probably next summer.*
>
> *Have you met anyone special? I'm sure, by now, you have. I met a wonderful woman here in San Diego. We've been talking about getting married. If we do, I hope you will come to the wedding.*
>
> *Keep in touch and drop me a note sometime.*

Ryan

Rex slipped the new letter into the original envelope and sealed the flap with glue. "Buddy, I just saved your life. You can thank me later." He placed the envelope with the outgoing mail by the door and flopped back on the couch.

All he had to do now was wait for Keri's letter, intercept it, rewrite it, and stick it back in her original envelope. Then everything would be back to normal.

Chapter 6

When Keri saw Ryan Mitchell's name in the return address her heart fluttered. She'd always believed they'd one day get back together. For nine years, she hoped and prayed he hadn't forgotten her. The thought of losing him was unbearable.

The first year he was at the academy she wrote daily receiving only sporadic responses. Then, for no reason, he stopped writing, as if he had died. After he graduated, trying to revive the relationship seemed futile. His being either at sea on a multi-month cruise or involved in some military exercise on the other side of the globe made even the thought of reviving the relationship tiring.

While in college, Keri made a special effort to return home to Buckhead on weekends to visit Martha. Being with Martha and seeing pictures of Ryan around the house gave her hope that all was not lost. Her mind often played tricks on her, imagining he was in another part of the house and might walk around a corner any minute. The thought of them married and home visiting her mother-in-law was a dream her mind brought to life. Giving in to the charade helped her avoid the haunting voice of reality reminding her that he was gone forever.

She studied the unopened envelope. She suspected, one day, a letter would arrive from Martha delivering the dreaded news: Ryan is getting married. The thought of a wedding invitation crossed her mind, but why would he invite her to his wedding? Hopefully, this letter contained better news.

Sitting on the couch, her little West Highland terrier, Bill, peered up at her from the floor, his ears perked, as if anxious for her to open the envelope and see what was inside.

Keri knew Ryan was in San Diego and would be separating from the Navy next August, just over a year from now. Her transfer request to LA had been approved for July—two months away. Perfect timing, she'd thought. She dreamed of moving to the West Coast and reconnecting with Ryan—picking up where they'd left off. She gazed at the letter again. Perhaps Martha had secretly told him of their many talks and relayed to him her haunting regrets and bottled passions.

"Let's see what's inside," she said to Bill. He barked. She tore open the envelope and read.

> *Friday, May 13, 1983*
>
> *Keri,*
>
> > *It's been a long time. I learned from Mom you're living in Florida. She tells me you're a flight attendant. Sounds exciting. I also hope to be hired by the airlines once I complete my commitment to the Navy. Probably next summer.*

She clung to every word, her mind racing ahead as she imagined how wonderful it would be to see him again. A warmth spread over her as she analyzed the intent of each phrase.

> *It's been a long time.*

Finally he was ready—ready to start his new life with her.

> *I just learned from Mom that you're living in Florida.*

"That is so sweet." In his search to find her, he'd contacted Martha. Her prayers had finally been answered.

> *She tells me you're a flight attendant. Sounds exciting. I also hope to be hired by the airlines*

once I complete my commitment to the Navy. Probably next summer.

She detected nervousness in his words reminding her of his tender heart; something she found attractive.

Have you met anyone special? I'm sure, by now, you have.

She chuckled, as though he were sitting with her. "Are you kidding?" She read on, savoring each word.

I met a wonderful woman here in San Diego. We've been talking about getting married.

Her heart stopped. She looked away from the letter. "Married?" The blood drained from her head. Her chest tightened. She re-read the sentence to be sure.

I met a wonderful woman here in San Diego. We've been talking about getting married.

Tears spilled from her eyes onto the paper. "No! You can't do this!" Grief knotted her stomach, ripping at her heart. Pins and needles ran up the back of her neck and a lump in her throat threatened to choke her. Panic took over. The little Westie looked up at her and whimpered. Bile rose to her throat. She ran to the bathroom, collapsed to her knees in front of the toilet, and vomited.

Why God, why? It's not fair.

Hugging the toilet bowl, she continued to sob. She'd lost him. Her nightmare had become her reality. After all the years of waiting, hoping, and praying—the worst happened. Alone and forgotten, all that was left was a bundle of memories promising to torment her for the rest of her life. Bill pawed at her leg and whimpered, obviously sensing things were not right.

Keri flushed the toilet. Shivering from the coldness of the tiled floor, she shakily steadied herself to her feet. Braced on the vanity, she stared into the mirror at her pitiful state, and burst into tears.

What did I do to deserve this?

She never doubted he loved her, but as she'd feared, time robbed her; it clouded his heart and twisted his mind.

This can't be happening! It must be a mistake!

Wiping the tears from her cheeks, she turned on the water in the sink, and washed her face. The warm water refreshed her and with it came a new sense of purpose. She dried her face on a hand towel and glanced up at her reflection in the mirror—her eyes puffy and red. As if a switch had been thrown in her mind, her self-pity turned into desperation. "Married!" Bill let out a bark.

She returned to the den and recovered the letter. After a quick check of the words, she hurled the paper into the air. As if a thief had broken into her house and robbed her of her most valuable possession, she felt violated. She had waited; why couldn't he?

Now what? I'm moving to California in two months, and for what?

The transfer couldn't be stopped. In addition, because it was a voluntary request, she would be locked-in for a minimum of a year.

Her thoughts ricocheted back in time, rewinding to every possible mistake, searching for *something* or *someone* to blame. She first blamed herself. If only she'd been more persistent in writing him. Why hadn't she hunted him down after he left the academy? All those times Martha mentioned to her where he was, she could have gone to him. Why had she been so stubborn? Then her thoughts returned to that night; the night she told him they needed to date other people; he needed to be free. "How stupid! What was I thinking?" As she replayed the details of that night in her mind, her eyes narrowed. She screamed out, "Mother! I hate you!"

She needed to talk to Martha. Surely she would have more information. She could call her and get Ryan's address—better yet—his telephone number.

That's it, I'll call him. If he knows how I feel, I know he'll break it off with that woman.

She picked up the receiver and started dialing Martha's number and then hung up.

I can't just call him. I have to see him in person.

She could hop on a plane and be in San Diego in a matter of hours, but she needed his address.

The envelope!

She scrambled for the envelope, finding it wedged behind a cushion in the sofa. The return address said Del Mar, California. She hesitated.

What am I going to do? Fly to San Diego, drive to his house, walk in and find him with that woman. After not seeing him or communicating with him in years, I'm going to prance into his life, tell him I love him, and demand he marry me. How stupid!

Scooping the letter off the floor, she read it again.

> *I met a wonderful woman here in San Diego. We've been talking about getting married.*

The words popped off the page:

> *...talking about...*

Talking? Wait a minute. He's not engaged—yet! He's only talking about getting married!

I'll write him. When he sees how I feel, he'll know we're supposed to be together. She ran to her bedroom, pulled out her stationary, and took a deep breath.

May 27, 1983

Ryan,

I received your letter. It was sweet of you to write. I'm glad to hear you are doing well. Knowing how dangerous your job is, I never stopped praying for you.

I must be honest, when I heard you met someone, it broke my heart. I have always thought that we would one day be together, but I would never stand in the way of your happiness.

In July, I will be transferring to California. I would love to see you.

Don't feel like you need to write back. After I move, I will forward my new address to your mother. If you feel like talking, please call me. (954) 122-1977.

Love,
Keri

P.S. I adopted a Westie (West Highland White Terrier) to keep me company. I named him Bill, after the Naval Academy mascot. He doesn't look much like a goat, but he is cute. In a special way, he reminds me of you. I never stopped thinking about you.

Chapter 7

A week later—Friday, May 27, 1983

The minute Ryan walked into the condo, Rex said, "Hey Buddy, did you have a good day?"

Ryan headed for the kitchen. "I'm beat."

"Dude, I put the mail on the bar. You got a letter from that chick... Karen? Kathy? Oh frap, man, I forget her name."

"Keri?"

"Yeah, that's her."

Ryan flipped through several bills before seeing it. The address on the front of the envelope was definitely her handwriting

"Is that the one?"

"Finally."

"Great! I'm going to jump in the shower."

When Ryan opened the letter, he expected a hand-written note, but instead, it was typed.

May 27, 1983

Ryan,

> *I received your letter. It was sweet of you to write. I'm glad to hear you're doing well. Knowing how dangerous your job is, I never stopped praying for you.*
>
> *It has been a long time and many things have happened since we last saw each other— good things. After I graduated from college, I decided to apply for a job with the airlines. I thought it would be fun to travel.*

Ryan, I met someone. He is a very special man. His name is Bill. I am sure you will approve. We have been dating for about two years and are seriously talking about marriage. He is an airline pilot.

I wish you the best and am sure the perfect girl is out there for you. The next time I'm in California, I'll give you a call. It would be great to catch up. I also can't wait for you to meet Bill.

Tell your mom hi for me.

Love,
Keri

He read the letter a second time, pausing in spots.

...many things have happened since we last saw each other—good things... I met someone... We have been dating for about two years and are seriously talking about marriage.

He crumpled the paper into a ball and tossed it in the trash. "I *knew* I should have never contacted her. What was I thinking?"

Rex appeared with only a towel wrapped around his waist. "Dude, did she send us a picture? Should I get my harpoon?"

"I should have known. She's dating someone... has been for the past two years. She's talking about getting married."

"I'm sorry, Dude." Rex walked over and patted him on the back. "Hey Buddy, it's just one chick. Hundreds of gorgeous babes are out there begging you to give them a chance." His tone lifted with enthusiasm. "Listen, tomorrow I'm going to take you to my favorite beach. It's a magical place. Dude, you won't *believe* the babes!" He smiled. "Your good buddy Rex is gonna take care of you. Trust me. Before the sun sets tomorrow, you'll have forgotten all about Keri. She's no good for you.

Dude, look at me." He stepped back and pointed at himself with both hands. "The Rexter knows."

Ryan stared at Rex. What was there to lose? He needed to forget Keri. If there were anything there, she would have waited for him, even though he had been a jerk for not keeping in touch. "Yeah, sure. Why not?"

Rex patted him on the back. "That's my man."

Ryan went into his bedroom and stretched out on the bed. His mind repeated Rex's words: *Before the sun sets tomorrow...* He couldn't stop his thoughts from journeying into the past. He remembered the note Keri stuffed in his pocket that night—their last night together.

He had kept it... but where? His Bible!

He sprung up, trying to remember where he might have put his Bible. He seldom read it, but his mother had given it to him when he was in high school. He kept it for sentimental reasons.

He rummaged through a box of books in his closet and found it. He fanned the thin pages releasing several pieces of paper to the floor. It only took a glance to spot the note, folded just as Keri had done before slipping it into his pocket that night. The sight of it flooded him with memories—good and bad.

June 23, 1974

Dear Ryan,

I believe if we are meant to be together, nothing can keep us apart. As long as I live, I will patiently wait on each sunrise and follow each sunset into tomorrow, for I believe it is the path of the sun that will lead us to our hopes and dreams. Promise me that you will never lose hope in tomorrow.

I love you,
Keri

He re-read:

> *As long as I live, I will patiently wait on each*
> *sunrise and follow each sunset into tomorrow,*
> *for I believe it is the path of the sun that will lead*
> *us to our hopes and dreams...*

His mother's words echoed in his head, "Two souls that are meant to be together can never be separated."

He put the note back in his Bible, tossed it into the box, and slammed the closet door closed.

"Well, Mom, I guess it just wasn't meant to be."

Chapter 8

Saturday, May 28, 1983

Behind the wheel of his red, 1983, Porsche cabriolet, Rex exited Interstate 5 and joined Route 75, launching them onto the two-mile-long, award winning, San Diego-Coronado Bridge.

The distinctive curve and soaring sweep ascended the Porsche two hundred feet above San Diego Bay, high enough for even the tallest of the Navy's ships to pass under.

While in the curve, at the top of the bridge, Rex yelled out over the wind and wail of the engine, "You see the big building with the red shingled roof?"

"Yeah."

"That's the Del."

"Nice." Ryan nodded. The distinctive architecture of red-tiled cupolas and turrets rising from the water's edge invoked the grandeur of a European fairy-tale castle to ensure upper crust guests from around the world felt at home.

They joined the quiet beach town on 3rd Street, turned left on Orange Avenue, and cruised through the exclusive and affluent downtown area to the ocean's edge before turning into the entrance to the hotel.

"Just remember… blend," Rex said. He downshifted the Porsche, raising the hum of the engine an octave, and wheeled under the protective cover. Valets rushed to both sides of the car.

"We're meeting some clients," Rex told the attendant. "Should only be a few hours."

"Yes sir."

They proceeded up the steps to the grand hotel, each carrying a small bag containing the essentials for a day on the beach. A refreshing breeze circulated throughout the large lobby. A three-tiered chandelier hung from the ceiling, two levels high. The second level was open to the lobby, bordered by a dark wooden balcony rail, matching the masterfully crafted ceilings and paneled walls. A birdcage elevator with brass telescoping doors, hand-operated by an attendant, gave the modern day Victorian hotel a feel of the past. The charm of the old hotel made it easy to picture its storied and romantic past; a favorite spot of presidents, royalty, and celebrities, for more than 100 years.

Rex strutted through the lobby as if he owned the place. "Follow me. We can change in the men's room down the hall."

After changing, he picked up a couple of towels embroidered with the hotel crest and name. He tossed a towel to Ryan. "Dude. Throw that over your shoulder. Makes us look like guests." They headed off through a set of double doors at the rear of the hotel opening to an adjoining terrace overlooking the grassy expanse of Windsor Lawn; the Pacific Ocean as the backdrop.

Just as Rex had promised, the broad white beach was "target rich". They stood a minute in the sand and surveyed the area—doubles everywhere. "Dude, what'd I tell you?" Rex reached up and pivoted his sunglasses from atop his head to the bridge of his nose. "Follow me."

After walking a few hundred feet, Rex stopped and put his hand on Ryan's shoulder. "Now, Buddy, I want you to forget about that chick in Florida ... Carol."

"Her name is, Keri."

"Whatever, you don't need her." He turned and continued to plod through the sand toward the ocean. "Today is your day, and your life is about to change. I'm going to find you the hottest babe in SoCal."

It didn't take Rex long to spot his first two targets. "Over there ... two o'clock... a blond and a brunette... late twenties. Watch the master work."

Rex used his God-given attributes to his advantage: from his "pretty-boy smile" to his quick humor. But sadly, at times,

Ryan would embarrassingly watch, as Rex teased the less-attractive girls with his flirtatious advances, simply for sport. The poor girls didn't have a chance. Rex viewed it as human target practice, like a gunnery range for testing new ammunition. Masked with a deceptive facade, he fleeced the wavering emotions of his, not so beautiful, young victims, and left them violated and brokenhearted.

With each step closer, his heart pounded louder. What would he say? That's when he found security in Rex as his lead-man. He was smooth. He had heard him use the same lines hundreds of times before, but only on rare occasion was he not able to have the girls eating out of his hand in a matter of minutes. Like a skilled magician, he captivated his audience with ease.

This particular time, Rex used what he called his "stealth approach". With both girls on their backs "sunny side up"—as Rex would say—and eyes closed, he eased up close enough to block the sun, casting a shadow on their faces. He then stood quietly while looking out at some imaginary object in the ocean.

"Hey. You're blocking the sun," the blond said.

"Oh. I'm sorry," Rex said, stepping aside. "I thought I saw a shark's fin about a hundred feet offshore. It looked big!" The brunette sprang up, shading her eyes as she searched the surface of the ocean. Rex squatted next to the blond and pointed, trying to show her where to look.

"I don't see it," said the brunette. Rex stood and walked over beside her. Pointing with one hand, he placed his other hand on her shoulder and guided her to move over a few steps. A good head taller than the girl, Ryan could see Rex was more interested in his bird's-eye view, than the imaginary shark.

"I still don't see it," she said.

"Maybe it's gone. It was a big one. They've spotted great whites out there before. They love the cold water and the seals. I don't think I'd go swimming."

I don't believe it, Ryan thought. *As easy as that, and we're in. How does he do it?*

"I'm Rex, and this is my buddy, Ryan." The brunette returned to her towel on the sand.

The blond said, "Hi. I'm Emily and this is Kate."

"You girls from around here or just visiting?" Rex asked.

"We live in the area," Kate said. "How about you guys?"

"We just came out to the beach for a little sun," Rex said. He worked his way over by Kate and sat down beside her on the sand.

"You work here in San Diego?" Emily asked.

"We're Navy pilots. Based over at NAS Miramar," Rex offered.

"Pilots?" Kate asked, seeming to be impressed.

"Yeah. We're both fighter pilots," Rex said.

"Wow. That's cool," Kate said.

Seeing Rex favor Kate, Ryan knew his job was to entertain Emily. Both girls were stunning and Ryan was more than happy to pair up with Emily. Her blond hair, shapely figure, and bubbly personality captivated him. She didn't appear to fit the stereotypical "party animal", but was a far cry from the "cute-homely" type he often had to babysit after one of Rex's "YOYO" calls.

Rex stood and helped Kate up. "We're going up to the hotel and grab something to drink. You guys want to come?" Rex asked.

Ryan defaulted to Emily. "I think I'll stay down here and work on my tan," she said.

"We'll be back in a few," Rex said. He waited for Emily to turn her head, then lifted his glasses and winked at Ryan.

Rex and Kate walked off through the sand toward the hotel. "Your friend is something else," Emily said.

"Yeah... he's a real piece of work—good guy, though."

"How long have you known each other?"

"Almost five years."

"Where do you boys call home?"

"Rex is a California boy and I'm from Atlanta.

"I *thought* I detected a Southern accent."

"Yeah. Can't seem to shake it."

"I think it's cute." She reached over and squeezed his leg.

Her flirtatious giggles and little touches attracted him almost as much as her stunning physical attributes. "Where are you girls from?"

"I was born here in San Diego and Kate is from Iowa. We were roommates at San Diego State. After we graduated, we got jobs with the same company and decided to get an apartment together. A year later, here we are."

"Think you'll stay in the area?" Ryan turned to put the sun more behind him, giving him a better view of Emily's face.

"Hope not," she said, rolling her eyes.

"What's wrong? You don't like paradise?" He laughed.

"California's home, but I want to travel and see the world." She looked out at the vast ocean and proclaimed with outstretched arms, "I want to see it all!"

"Here comes Rex," Ryan said.

"Hey, guys. You seen Kate?" Rex asked.

"Maybe the big shark swallowed her up," Emily said. She glanced at Ryan and smiled.

"What's wrong, you lose her?" Ryan said.

"Dude, she vanished. I went to the bathroom and when I came back, she was gone. No sign of her anywhere. I thought she was out here."

"She did say her brother was coming to the hotel later," Emily said. "She planned to get a ride home with him. Maybe he showed up early."

"Seems funny she wouldn't, at least, hang around to tell me she was leaving."

"Yeah, that's not like her. I'm sure there's an explanation," Emily said.

"No big deal," Rex said. "Ryan, you ready to go?"

"I guess." He turned to Emily and asked, "You ever been up to the Old Lighthouse on Point Loma?"

"Many times."

"Think I could hire you to give me a tour. I've read about it, but haven't made it up there yet."

"My services don't come cheap, you know."

"How about dinner anywhere in San Diego?"

"I'll have to check my schedule. You got a pen?"

Ryan pulled a pen from his bag and handed it to her. She took his hand, flipped it over, and wrote her number on his palm. "Call me."

Chapter 9

The warm sun, the rhythmic pattern of the waves lapping against the shore, and the smell of salt air drifting across the sand lulled Emily into a near hypnotic state. She'd never met a man so attractive, yet without an attitude. She felt relaxed around him, comfortable.

"That was creepy," Kate said.

Emily opened her eyes and saw Kate spreading her towel, preparing a place next to her.

"What happened?" Emily asked.

Kate sat down on her towel. "Typical, egotistical jerk."

"I figured when you asked him to go back to the hotel you were going to dump him. He was a bit much, if you ask me."

"Yeah, I'm glad we had a plan." Kate peeled-off her T-shirt and rubbed lotion on her front.

"With all the military guys around here always hitting on us, we'd be stupid not to have an escape plan."

Both lying on their backs with their eyes closed, they continued to talk. "This guy was your typical fighter jock," Kate said. "But I'll have to hand it to him, he had balls. You won't believe what he did!"

"What?"

"First, he made sure I knew he came from money—born in La Jolla… USC grad… you know the type. He played down the Navy, saying the only reason he joined was for the free ticket to an airline job."

"What's so bad about that?"

"Then, he started getting touchy-feely"

"*Really*? What did he do?"

"We were sitting on one of those couches. You know, the ones just off to the side of the bar?"

"Yeah."

"That's where he made his move. First, he put his arm around me. Then, he tried to kiss me, right in front of a woman and her three kids. I had to practically shove him off me."

"Good Lord! You just met the guy, like… thirty minutes ago."

"When he went to the bathroom I left. I hid out by the pool like we had talked about. I had a great view of the beach. When I saw the guys leave I came out."

"Dogs with one track minds—all of them," Emily said.

"Yeah, isn't that the truth?" A calming silence allowed Kate to catch her breath, and then she said, "But isn't it great?" They laughed.

"And how about that shark thing? What a loser."

"I actually thought it was a nice touch." Emily said. They laughed again.

"What did you think of Ryan?"

"He's dreamy. A little on the shy side, but that makes it easier. At least I don't have to worry about him trying to grope me on the first date."

"So, I guess you're planning to see him again?"

"Why not? I figure he's good for at least a couple of free dinners. He asked me to show him the Old Lighthouse up on Point Loma in exchange for a free dinner—I get to choose the place."

"Go girl! Give me five." Kate raised her open palm in the air and Emily slapped it. "If you need any help thinking of a nice place for dinner, just let me know."

"I'll try to be easy on him the first time. I don't want to scare him off, too fast."

"Rex was prime, but I can't imagine trying to hold him off for an entire evening."

"I'm not sure I would write him off so fast. From what you say, he sounds like he's worth more than a few dinners. You know the guy is a trust fund baby—probably loaded. He's hot, too."

"I don't know," Kate said.

"Listen, it's hard to find 'the perfect package'. I don't even know if it exists. They either come from money and are spoiled brats, or they're great guys and broke. You have to decide if you're going to marry for money and tolerate the man or marry for love and hope for the money. I personally think it's easier to go for the money. You can always find love on the side."

"Whatever. I don't think I'm ready yet to sell myself for a free dinner."

"One thing is for certain, I'm not going to sit around and do nothing. Who knows, after I finish with Georgia boy, I might even take the Trojan for a spin. I could do a trustee... no problem." She turned to Kate. "Assuming you're not interested."

"Go for it, girl. He's all yours. Good luck."

Chapter 10

Rex was stone quiet, but Ryan could tell he was pissed. After storming off the beach and tipping the valet, he burned rubber back to the interstate. Rex rarely got snubbed by the ladies. However, if he did, he was quick to slug an overdose of denial and return to his place of control.

With each exchange of clutch and accelerator, he pushed the RPM to the red-line. Jerking the shifter from "second" to "third", "third" to "fourth", and "fourth" to "fifth", the Porsche launched out ahead of light traffic, cruising well above the posted speed limit.

With the powerful engine purring and Rex hopefully feeling some sense of restored control, Ryan wrapped himself in the solitude of the steady rush of wind and drone of the engine. He couldn't get her out of his mind. Everything about her was perfect. He imagined how she would look the next time he saw her, and how she would act toward him. Would she still be interested?

I wonder if she felt the same way I did.

He tried to recall the tone in her voice, the way she'd laughed, her attentiveness, and the way she'd touched him freely. It gave him assurance that she must have felt something. He glanced down at his hand. One of the numbers on his palm had smeared but was still legible.

Don't lose that number. It's all you've got.

He looked around for paper, but remembered the pen was in his bag, in the trunk.

Keep your hand open and don't touch anything.

Then a horrid thought crossed his mind.

Maybe it's a bogus number. She could have given me the number to her hair salon, or even a pizza delivery service.

He replayed the scenes from the beach.

She wouldn't do that. What am I thinking?

They arrived back in Del Mar faster than he had expected. The electric door on the garage was already on its way up when it came into view. Rex timed it perfectly. It was a game he played. Just prior to the door being fully retracted, he would press the button to lower it. The car had to be sufficiently in the garage to ensure the door didn't hit it. Rex often referred to it as the "bat cave".

Once the front half of the car rolled into the garage, with one fluid motion, he reached up, tapped the button on the transmitter, and turned the ignition off. Still rolling, the Porsche swallowed its growl and the garage door started down.

"One day it's gonna bite you," Ryan said.

"I don't think so, Robin."

"Are you ever going to grow up?"

"Probably not," Rex said, closing the door to the Porsche.

Rex wasted no time heading to the bathroom, while Ryan was more interested in dialing the number written on his palm.

The nicely furnished luxury apartment was not typical for a couple of Navy pilots who spent most of their time at sea. Well beyond Ryan's budget, Rex had worked out a deal to rent him a room at a relatively low price, splitting the utilities. They each had their own bedroom and private bath with a smaller third bedroom they shared as an office.

Returning from the bathroom, Rex said, "Wow! That feels better." He walked over to the refrigerator, got a beer, twisted the top off, tossed it in the trash, and headed for the den. "You call Blondie yet?" He plopped down on the couch and took a long draw from the bottle of beer.

"Yeah, but no answer."

"Dude. Probably not her number."

"The answering machine message sounded like her. Must still be at the beach. I left a message."

"She's pretty hot. I knew I should've taken her and given you mystery woman, but what are friends for? I told you I'd take care of you today."

"By the way, how *did* it go with Kate?"

"It was going great until she disappeared. I think she had the hots for me."

"How could you tell?" Ryan sat in the soft leather chair by the couch.

"Just instinct. I sensed her sending me signals. You saw how she reacted when she heard we were fighter pilots; she dug it."

"I'm glad you think so."

"I might hook-up with her later, or, better yet, once you get to know Blondie, you can get her to set us up. Then again, I wouldn't be surprised if she calls me first. They usually do."

Chapter 11

"Georgia boy beat us home," Emily said, seeing the flashing red light on her answering machine. She hit the replay button on her way to the kitchen for a bottle of water.

The digital voice said, "You have one message..."

"Hi, this is Ryan." Emily glanced over at Kate.

"That was fast," Kate said.

Emily moved closer so she could hear every word. "I was just calling to tell you I enjoyed meeting you today and look forward to my guided tour of the Old Lighthouse."

"How sweet," Kate said. "And listen to that accent."

"You're probably still at the beach. Feel free to give me a call, 755-3599, or... ah... I'll just call you back later. Talk to you soon."

"Based on the time of the message, that boy went straight home," Kate said. "I think if you play this one right, you might get more than a *couple* of free dinners."

"He's a sweetie," Emily said. "Think I should call him back?"

"Now, if it were 'lover boy', I'd make him beg. I might even wait for his *second* call. But I think you're safe with this one."

Emily replayed the message and wrote down his number. She put the phone on speaker and dialed.

"Hello," Ryan said.

"Hi, Ryan. This is Emily. Remember me?"

"Absolutely. I guess you got my message."

"Yeah. You ready to book that tour?" She looked at Kate and raised her eyebrows.

"Sure. When can you work me in?"

"How about next Saturday?"

"Sounds great! What time?"

"Three o'clock too early?"

"No. That's perfect."

"Good. The park closes around six, so that should give us enough time. The sunsets are to die for. I'll even introduce you to a good friend of mine, J.R. Cabrillo." Kate rolled her eyes.

"Who's that?"

"I'll let it be a surprise."

"I like surprises," Ryan said. "Also, don't forget, you need to be thinking of where you'd like to eat dinner."

"Oh, don't worry, I'll pick out a good place," she said, looking over at Kate with a sly grin. "Listen, I need to go. Call me later this week and I'll give you directions to my place."

"Okay. Talk to you later."

"Emily Anderson... you are *so* bad," Kate said.

"Yeah, don't you love it?" This guy had something intriguingly different going on—something she liked. Perhaps it was his innocent Southern charm, or his overly sensitive attentiveness. Whatever it was caught her off guard and she liked it.

Chapter 12

Six months later—Saturday, December 22, 1983
San Diego, California

Ryan was smitten. Emily Anderson had won his heart in only six months. Thoughts of Keri had grown foggy with time, however, like an unwelcomed ghost in his mind, her many special qualities haunted him at times—tempting him to question his love for Emily. He learned to push them away, convincing himself they were only the remaining fragments of a childish infatuation. He was happy for her and Bill. If it didn't work out, he knew she would eventually make someone a great wife.

He and Emily had grown inseparable—romantic dinners, walks on the beach at sunset, and weekends filled with impulsive adventures from morning until night. He lost himself in her playful and carefree spirit. Her uninhibited affection kept him in an almost constant state of arousal.

With only six months remaining in the Navy and knowing an airline job would take him away from San Diego, he feared losing her, much like he'd lost Keri; the result of his not acting on his feelings. Marriage—a topic they frequently discussed—was a possibility but he wished for more time. He desired to know *everything* about the woman he planned to spend the rest of his life with. However, the thought of leaving her behind was unbearable. He'd already blown it once.

Emily made life exciting both in private and in public. As they walked together in crowded places, heads turned and followed them like fields of wheat blown by a gentle breeze. He often met the glazed stares of gawking men with a proud sense of ownership, thinking:

Eat your heart out boys; she's all mine.

Although he found no fault in her physical beauty, other areas of her life screamed out "danger ahead". Her undisciplined use of credit became apparent. Her credit cards were often refused by merchants, stating, "I'm sorry, but this card was declined." As quickly as the words rolled off the merchant's lips, she would produce a second card—a third if necessary. With each confrontation, she appeared shocked the card's limit had been reached. His momentary waves of embarrassment would quickly vanish when she wrapped him in one of her playful hugs.

Overall, her many attractive qualities outweighed his few concerns, allowing him to compromise his worries. Once married, he could teach her about money, and together they would build a solid financial life.

However, something in his core haunted him. He remembered his numerous Sunday morning talks with his mother. When the subject of qualifying a woman as a potential wife came up, she would say, "Now Ryan, you can always tell what kind of wife a woman will make by the relationship she has with her father. Often, a woman's idea of men is synonymous with her image of her father."

The distant relationship Emily had with her alcoholic father concerned him. The few occasions he had seen them together they barely talked. And her mother, a shy, quiet woman seemed to live in fear, as if a prisoner sentenced to a life of solitary confinement. Although a part of him was suspicious, he believed that once they were married, these issues would not present any long-term threats.

After talking with several major airlines, they all seemed very interested in offering him a job after he separated from the Navy.

He wondered if he could support a wife on the first-year airline probationary salary. If Emily worked, they might be able to squeeze out enough to afford a cheap one-bedroom apartment in Texas. Then he remembered the time he asked Emily how she felt about working after they married. She'd scrunched-up her nose and said, "I don't mind waiting a few months."

He knew it would be more like a year—probably longer. A year was a long time, and she was a beautiful woman. It didn't take a genius to put two and two together; the second part of the equation being a never-ending batch of fresh, young, fighter-pilots, most of them like Rex, combing the beaches for hot girls. One look at her in her bikini and they would be all over her.

He remembered his mom telling him, "Learn to listen to your heart". Well, his heart was crying out for Emily, and he didn't want to lose her. Time was running out. He would soon be leaving the Navy and California. He needed to know if she was willing to give up everything to go with him. He planned to find out today. Every detail had been meticulously planned. The ring was in his pocket. Today was the day he hoped to ask Emily Anderson to be his wife.

Chapter 13

Two o'clock in the afternoon

Ryan pressed the small white button mounted on the wall beside her apartment door. A faint chime sounded inside. In his arms he cradled a long white box wrapped with a wide red ribbon and a large red bow.

The sound of steps grew louder. The peephole in the center of the door flickered dark seconds before the door opened. "Happy anniversary!" he said, offering the white box to Emily.

"You are so sweet!"

Her look of excitement was priceless. Wrapped in a white bathrobe, no makeup, and her hair in a towel, she was still gorgeous.

"Come in." She took his hand and guided him into the apartment, closing the door behind him. "Am I late?" She turned his arm slightly to get a better look at his wristwatch.

"No. You're fine. I wanted to surprise you." He'd planned a night filled with surprises. He only hoped she would be as excited later when he presented her with the biggest surprise of them all.

"What did you bring me?" She carefully removed the red bow and ribbon from the box then slipped the top off. "Oh!" She folded the thin paper away. "Roses! They're beautiful."

She leaned down and breathed-in the mesmerizing fragrance. A small white card caught her eye. She placed the box of flowers on the table by the door, took the card, and started reading it silently. Her eyes grew watery. Quickly wiping them, she handed the card to Ryan. "Would you read it for me? I don't think I can."

"My dearest Emily,

With these roses I give you my love. I chose thornless red roses because of what they symbolize:

Red roses to symbolize romance, love, beauty, and courage: A romance between us I hope never ends; My love for you that has overtaken every corner of my heart; Your beauty which words cannot describe; and my wish for the courage to make the changes in my life that will allow you to love me more."

He took one rose from the box and handed it to her.

"The thornless stems signify that the first time I saw you; it was love at first sight. Thank you for the most wonderful six months of my life.

I love you more than you will ever know.

Ryan."

He looked into her eyes and softly said, "I love you."

She wrapped both arms around his waist and hugged him; her cheeks still wet with tears. "I don't deserve you."

He leaned down and kissed her. With excitement in his voice, he said, "I've got a big night planned, but we're on a tight schedule. So you'd better get ready."

"How exciting!" She removed the towel from her head and shook her slightly damp hair. Taking both hands, she slowly pulled it back and twisted it into a ponytail. With her arms raised and her hands behind her head, the front of her robe accidentally opened, exposing her bare breasts. His eyes dove uncontrollably to take in the view. His heart rate spiked. Time froze, like an out-of-body experience.

Reluctantly, he forced his eyes to their previous orbit—hoping she had not noticed. She smiled, making no attempt to pull her robe closed.

"Like what you see, sailor?" She took his arm and led him to the nearby couch, encouraging him onto his back. Slipping the robe from her shoulders, she straddled him and began unbuckling his belt.

"We'd better not," he said. "I don't think we have time."

She chuckled seductively. "There's always time for me to show you how much I love you." With his pants unbuckled and zipper down, she smiled and said, "Looks like someone down here didn't get the memo about being on a schedule."

As she reached for him, he grabbed her hand and pulled her down on top of him. Face-to-face, he said, "Emily, now is not the time." He kissed her. "I have something very special to show you, and, if we don't go now, we might miss it." He kissed her again.

"Okay, sailor, but it better be good." She sat up.

The sight of her made him think hard about going anywhere. He glanced at his watch—almost two thirty. "It's a surprise you're going to love."

"If you say so." She slipped into her robe. "I'll only be a minute."

She called out from the bedroom, "I don't know if I can handle all these surprises."

"Me neither," he said, zipping his pants.

Chapter 14

"Wow!" Ryan said. "You look gorgeous!" He stood from the couch taking a moment to arrange the pillows before walking over to Emily.

"You're sweet." She kissed him on the cheek. "Oops." With her finger, she attempted to remove the lipstick. "There... that'll give you a nice rosy look." She patted his butt.

"Thanks." Ryan said. He looked at his watch—two forty-five.

"Are we on schedule, Captain?" She smiled and gave him a wink.

"Yes, ma'am, right on schedule."

Beneath his disciplined military shell, Ryan was a full-blown romantic. Although he didn't wear his emotions on his sleeve, he understood the sensitivities of a woman—something he attributed to his mother's long talks. His love for Emily had grown deep and he feared time was running out.

He'd planned the evening to perfection, much like one of his military missions. His sights were aimed at Emily's heart. After leading her through his masterfully planned journey, the day would end with an amorous evening at the Del; what he hoped would be the perfect romantic setting to solidify their commitment to a future together.

"I'm so excited!" she said. "You make life so much fun." He reached over and took her hand.

The day was clear with an average temperature for December of sixty-four. Ryan brought along an extra jacket for Emily. The daily closing time for the park was adjusted seasonally to correspond with the breathtaking sunsets; one of the main reasons for visiting the park. Today, sunset was forecast to be at 4:57 p.m.

A few miles after turning onto Catalina Boulevard, the scenic drive took them to Fort Rosecrans National Cemetery; Ryan's first planned stop.

It was beautiful, yet sobering. The two-lane road divided tens-of-thousands of unpretentious white grave markers spreading over acres of meticulously manicured lawns. Many of the gravesites were dressed with Christmas wreaths and grave blankets from loved ones; seasonal gifts of respect and love.

As he turned into the cemetery, she said, "I never expected our romantic date to include a visit to a graveyard."

He smiled, but offered no response. A feeling of quiet reverence permeated the silence.

"Look," she said. An older couple was placing a wreath on a grave. "That could have been their son."

"Might even be a father or grandfather," he added. "Some of the graves here date back to the battle of San Pasqual in 1846." He pointed off to the left across the green lawn and rows of white markers. "Do you see that large boulder?"

"You mean that big rock in the middle of the cemetery?"

"Yeah. It was brought here in 1922 by the San Diego chapter of the Native Sons and Daughters of the Golden West. A plaque is attached to the face of the stone listing the names of those who died in the battle."

"How do you know all this stuff?"

"I love military history."

Although Ryan enjoyed reading about military history, the details of the Rosecrans National Cemetery were mostly uncovered in his research and preparation for his date with Emily. He hoped a short drive through the cemetery would allow him to point out, in a visual way, the brevity of life and the need to live each day to the fullest—something he had embraced since the death of his father. The trip to the cemetery served two purposes: to see how she would respond to a more serious side of life and to encourage a sense of urgency to take their relationship to the next level—marriage.

They drove slowly along the smooth, black lane as it wound through the acres of white grave markers. Wind rustled the leaves as a single crow cawed. The eerie quiet held the voices of the decaying bones and mortified flesh of lives once lived, as if to the visitors they said: "embrace the present—make each day count".

The markers were identical except for the chiseled inscriptions listing the specifics of the deceased: name, dates, branch of service, home state, and more. Emily read the states as they drove by: "Alabama, Virginia, Tennessee, Texas, California...."

Occasionally they would drive by a marker with freshly turned dirt at its base; the sign of a new grave.

He pulled the car to the side of the narrow road, rolled down his window, and turned off the engine. Whispering winds rustled the branches of the towering trees. A crow cawed, breaking the silence.

Without saying a word, he pointed out beyond the front of the car at a small gathering of people seated in front of casket. He and Emily sat quietly and watched.

Three Navy soldiers dressed in dark uniforms stood at attention beside the casket. While two of the soldiers held a stiff salute, the third soldier raised a bugle to his lips and played "Taps"; the smooth, tender, touching farewell, lasting less than a minute.

When the bugler lowered his bugle, the other two soldiers marched to a point in front of a woman dressed in black. One soldier presented the woman with an American flag, neatly folded in the shape of a triangle. A brightly polished wooden casket—the eternal bed for a brave soldier—rested on the sturdy straps of a grave-lowering device.

Emily whispered, "Makes you wonder what happened. I mean, why they died and how old they were."

"Yeah. When I see things like this, I think about the people who loved that person. How painful it must be for them to live with the loss and separation." Ryan paused in silence for a moment, remembering the grief that followed the death of his father. "I'm reminded of my dad. I wish I had spent more time with him before he died."

He had not talked much about his parents with Emily.

"Were you and your dad close?"

"Not really. He wasn't much of a family man. I think that's why I wound up an only child. Mom said he never wanted children."

"What about your mom? Is she still alive?"

"Yeah. She lives near Atlanta. We have always been close... that is... until I left home."

"What happened?"

"It's mostly my fault. I've never been good at writing." The thought of Keri popped into his mind. He had lost her for the same reason—not writing. "I guess I should call her more."

Since leaving for the academy, his communication with his mom had waned. During the six months since he'd met Emily, he had stopped writing her completely. He hadn't even told her about Emily.

Deep down he knew she would not approve. He didn't want to deal with her probing questions, starting with her family: "Ryan, does Emily come from a good family?" He could only imagine his response. "Not really, Mom. Her dad is an alcoholic and her mom is a recluse. And I'm not sure, but I think her mom might even have a drug problem, nothing illegal, just the run-of-the-mill sedatives and tranquilizers."

Next, she would surely ask if Emily had brothers or sisters. Again, he imagined himself telling her, "Her older sister is a stripper in Seattle, and her younger brother is in prison for selling drugs—the not-so-legal kind."

He loved Emily and wanted to marry her regardless of what his mother thought.

"You should call her more often," Emily said. "I'm sure she misses you."

"Yeah, I know. I'm sure the lack of contact has changed things... hard not to. Even though we both know we love each other, over time the relationship is destined to take-on a whole new dimension."

Emily sat quietly in thought. He hoped his words made her think about how devastating a separation would be to their young relationship.

"Ready to go?" he asked, reaching for the key in the ignition. They needed to stay on schedule. Seeing an actual service in progress had provided an effect he had not expected.

"Ready," she said.

"I always see life differently after I attend a funeral, or even when I visit a cemetery."

"How can you not?" she asked.

"I think it's important to be reminded of the brevity of life."

After a moment of silence, she responded, "I agree."

Hearing her words gave him hope.

He left the cemetery, and within minutes they were parked in the lot next to the visitor center.

He jumped out and raced around the car, hoping to open her door. She beat him to it. She looked up at him and jokingly said, "What's a lady got to do around here to get a little respect these days?" They both laughed.

A cool breeze reminded him to grab the extra jacket.

"First, let's go take a look at the lighthouse," he said. He took her hand.

Not only did the lighthouse offer an unbelievable 360-degree view from the highest point on the peninsula—422 feet above the water—it was his second visual illustration.

As they walked up the paved pathway to the lighthouse, he heard the roar of a military jet departing from the North Island Naval Air Station, just below Point Loma on the tip of Coronado Island. He turned, watching it climb-out over the Pacific.

"You gonna miss it?" Emily asked, looking up at the jet streaking through the sky.

"Some things I'll miss, but it's time to move on. The Navy has been good to me. I don't know where I would be today if it weren't for the Navy."

The thunderous sound of the jet subsided.

"I'll bet you can't guess the one thing the Navy gave me that I am most thankful. I call it my pearl of all pearls."

"What?"

"You." He looked at her and smiled. She smiled back, putting her arm around his waist and pulling him close while they walked. "If it weren't for the Navy, I never would have found you."

The old Point Loma lighthouse was originally built in 1854, but in the 1960's the National Park Service refurbished the interior to its historic 1880's appearance, as a reminder of a bygone era.

The lighthouse had a short life. The seemingly good location concealed a serious flaw: fog and low clouds often obscured the beam. When it was decommissioned in 1891, a new light station was built at the bottom of the hill.

It was not the lighthouse Ryan wanted Emily to focus on but rather the life of the "keeper" of the house and his family.

Climbing the steps and entering the front door of the small, white, two-story house took them back in time, over 100 years. Life for the keeper and his family was simple and lonely.

A descriptive message mounted on the wall behind a protective layer of acrylic stated that it was not uncommon for several weeks to go by between visits to town by horse-and-buggy over steep and rutted dirt roads.

The keeper's school-age children attended Mason Street School in town, the first public school in Southern California. But instead of being picked up by a local "buggy pool", the five-mile journey was made across the San Diego Bay in a rowboat. While away at school, the children would stay with relatives who lived in town.

The raw simplicity experienced by the keeper and his family presented a sharp contrast to modern day life, especially to the life Emily had grown accustomed. Ryan used the visit to the lighthouse to encourage Emily to focus on the simple and lonely life the keeper and his wife had *willfully* accepted—a life he would soon ask Emily to accept as his wife.

"You've seen all this before, haven't you?" he asked. He was specifically talking about the interior of the lighthouse where the keeper and his family lived.

"It's been a long time. The few times I've come up here, I mostly walked the trail or hung-out over by the monument. You know... with my good friend J.R." She smiled, nudging him with her elbow. "But to be honest, the time you and I came up here on our first date six-months ago, that was the first time I'd seen this place in years."

"Really?"

"It's just no fun coming up here unless you're with someone special."

He wondered how many other guys she had introduced to J.R.

"It's always fun to bring someone up here for their first time, like you." She gently poked her finger into his stomach followed by a hug.

It was as if she could read his thoughts. It gave rise to an unjustified premonition. Could she possibly know his motives and just be playing along? Surely not. He dismissed the presage and continued with his plan.

"Do you think you could live like this?" he asked, looking at the simple, tiny room: a fireplace beneath an oak mantle; a wooden rocker sitting ghostly to one side; thin translucent drapes covered the small window diffusing the light.

"This would be a prison," she said, looking around the room. "How could anyone live out here on this rock in total isolation from the rest of the world for weeks at the time?"

Not exactly what I had hoped to hear, but at least she is being honest.

They climbed the spiral stairs in the center of the small house. Two bedrooms were located on the second level; one at each end of the house. The cozy master bedroom had a double bed with a solid oak headboard and a barley-twist footboard. A homemade quilt was spread atop a thin mattress with two white pillows. A fireplace, similar to the one in the downstairs den, sharing the same chimney flue, took up most of the far wall. A light blue drape was pulled back from the window revealing a spectacular view of the ocean.

She slipped her arm around his waist. "If I were up here living with the person I loved and had everything I needed, well... I can see where it might not be so bad... maybe even a good thing," she said.

His ears perked up. Maybe it was the intimacy of the bedroom that sparked her romantic reflection. He could only hope.

She said, "When I think about it, these folks had a good thing going up here. They could sleep as late as they wanted; their kids were off at school living with relatives in town; her husband was always at home. The more I think about it, it looks more like paradise than a prison. To answer your question, yeah, I think I could do this." She looked up at him and smiled. "If I were with you."

He wasn't sure how to interpret her comments. He heard two undertones in her response—one good, one not so good. She wanted to be with him; that was good. But how could she be happy sending her children off to live with relatives? He was certain she would think differently if they were her children.

For the time being, he concluded the trip to the lighthouse had served its purpose. Time to move on to his third and final visual: the monument of J.R. Cabrillo.

They walked back down the hill toward the visitor's center. Sunset was thirty minutes away. Perfect timing, he thought. The view out over the ocean and toward Coronado Island would be spectacular.

The temperature had dropped a few degrees as the sun lowered in the sky. He cloaked the extra jacket across her shoulders helping her slip her arms into the sleeves.

"Did you bring that for me?" she said, snuggling in the new-found warmth.

"I thought you might need it."

"You are so thoughtful."

The jacket hung down below her waist with her hands hidden in the sleeves.

The last object was the Cabrillo National Monument which was built in memory of Juan Rodriguez Cabrillo: the first European to set foot on the West Coast of, what is now, the United States. He set out on his epic voyage fifty years after Columbus landed in America on the opposite coast.

Holding hands, they walked out to where the monument of Cabrillo was located. The view was breathtaking: San Diego harbor, the skyline of the city, and Coronado Island with the Hotel Del Coronado in the near distance.

"There's your good buddy J.R.," he said, attempting to remind her of the first time they talked on the beach, when she had agreed to give him a tour of Point Loma. She had jokingly mentioned in a later phone call that she wanted to introduce him to her good friend, J.R. Cabrillo—who lived up on the hill. It didn't dawn on him until they were standing in front of the monument for the first time that, "good old J.R." was a block of stone.

"Yeah, J.R. and I go way back. I think he's ashamed of himself."

"Should he be?" They stood in front of the statue looking up at his face, some fourteen feet above them.

"See how he has his head turned. He just can't look me in the eye. I can't stand it when a guy can't look me in the eyes. And I never have understood why he has his back turned to the ocean. Shouldn't he be looking out for a new place to go conquer? He even looks like he's hiding behind that pole."

"Wow, you sure are being hard on the poor guy."

"Like I said, we go way back. I'm sure he understands."
Still holding hands, they circled the base of the statue observing
the lifelike details of the stone carving.

"Did you ever think about the risk he took to accomplish
what he did?" Ryan was trying to turn the conversation toward
his third point.

"What do you mean?"

"I really respect those early pioneers. They launched-out
into uncharted waters in tiny ships and would be gone for years
at the time. They took chances few men would take today."

"Why do you think they were willing to do that?" she
asked.

"I don't know. I guess it was the promise of a better life, or
maybe just the thrill of an exciting adventure. One thing is for
sure, they weren't afraid to pursue what they believed in—
regardless of the risk."

"I guess if you want something badly enough, it's worth the
risk," she said.

Her words struck home in Ryan's heart. Logically, he knew
it would be best if he *did* wait a year or so to get better
established before committing to the responsibilities of being a
husband. But like J.R., he felt the risk was worth taking.

He put his arm around her and walked over to the edge of
the lookout. Pointing across the water, he said. "You see the
Del, over there?"

"Yeah. The red roof makes it easy to spot. It's my favorite
place in all of San Diego."

"Tonight, that's where I'm taking you to celebrate our six-
month anniversary. The same place where we first met."

"Really?" She turned and hugged him. "That sounds
wonderful! I can't wait!" She reached up and kissed him. "You
are so romantic." She kissed him again, then snuggled up close
to his side. "I can't wait. It should be absolutely beautiful with
all the Christmas decorations."

"We're going to have the most romantic dinner ever. As long as I live, I will never forget how I felt that day. Tonight is the perfect night to celebrate," he said.

Noticing she was chilled, he turned her around, put her back up against his chest, and wrapped his arms around her. Her body was warm and soft. They faced toward the ocean, watching the sky begin its evening performance of colors.

He hoped the three illustrations would settle into the fertile fabric of her emotions: the brevity of life and the urgency to embrace the present; the importance of relationships over places and things; and when faced with the unknown, willing to embrace the driving power of adventure and discovery.

Down the cliff toward the water, he noticed four people standing on one of the lower viewing spots overlooking the entrance to the harbor. He watched as they took turns casting their arm up in the air releasing a fist-full of white chalky dust which quickly dispersed into the breeze. He surmised the chalky dust to be the cremated remains of a loved one.

The contrast was sobering. A life from the past was slipping through the fingers of loved ones while he held tight to the love of his future. It was a grim reminder of the pain he would feel if Emily chose not to set sail on the next big adventure of his life.

Her shivers had stopped. The brilliant orange sky transitioned into a deep purple. She said, "I always dreamed of meeting a man like you. I don't deserve you."

"I just don't want to lose you, ever," he said, pulling her close.

The sun slipped below the horizon. One-by-one, the few remaining on-lookers slowly left the lookout to escape the chill and imminent darkness. Soon, they were alone. The city lights twinkled in the growing darkness. She turned and cuddled-up against him, sliding her arms tightly around his waist.

"Don't you worry. I'm *never* letting you out of my sight." She gazed up at him for a minute and then kissed him, long and slow with passion. Her hands firmly grasped the cheeks of his buttocks pulling him tightly up against her. The kiss would have been enough, but the added encouragement of her hands aroused him.

"Excuse me, sir," said a man.

Ryan opened his eyes and looked toward the strange voice, while Emily continued kissing with no regard for the sound that had abruptly interrupted the silence. Ten-feet away stood the tall silhouette of a man. A sudden flash of light passed across Ryan's eyes. The tall man stood stiff, much like the statue of J.R., but in a unique green uniform and "Smoky Bear"-style hat.

"The park is closed," the Ranger said.

After one last kiss, Emily remained snuggled up against Ryan with her arms around his waist, seemingly indifferent to the deep voice and flash of the Ranger's white saber.

Ryan wiped the moisture from his lips with the back of his hand. "We were just about to leave," Ryan said.

"Yeah." The Ranger chuckled.

Ryan took Emily's hand as they started back to the car with the Ranger close behind. Ryan had been minutes away from popping the big question, that is, until Smokey showed up. However, the thought of a romantic dinner might make things easier.

Chapter 15

Ryan held the door for Emily, then moved around the front of the car and slipped in behind the wheel. The beam from the Ranger's flashlight ricocheted off the dash.

"Drive carefully," the Ranger said.

"Yes sir. We will."

The crunch of gravel faded as the Ranger disappeared into the darkness.

Ryan glanced at his watch—six-fifteen. Reservations were at seven. The drive down to the Hotel Del Coronado would take approximately thirty minutes. Even with the few extra minutes they had spent at the lookout, they were still on schedule.

"You sure are quiet," he said. Emily gazed out her window deep in thought. He wished he could read her mind. "Everything okay?"

"Yeah. I'm just thinking."

He started the car and pulled out onto the two-lane road, his headlights carving a path in the darkness. After a short drive, the entranceway to the Rosecrans Cemetery came into view. He relaxed the pressure on the gas. The car slowed.

The cold white stones emerged from the darkened cemetery lawns under the watchful eye of amber security lights. The lifeless remains of brave soldiers shouting their pleas to the living: "Embrace life, before it's too late!"

He thought, leaving Emily would be nothing less than a "living death". He reached and took her hand while she continued to stare out her window. She gently squeezed. Within minutes, the car plunged back into the darkness, leaving the dead behind.

Twenty minutes later, atop the San Diego-Coronado Bridge, the lights of the city cast a colorful array across the bay.

"Look how beautiful," Emily said, pointing to the hotel.

"Impressive," he said.

The spectacular view of thousands of dazzling white lights magically outlined the magnificent Victorian hotel with its cupolas and turrets rising into the sky. He knew he had made the perfect choice for a romantic evening.

Two valet attendants waited eagerly as they wheeled up to the grand hotel. Emily seemed to enjoy the attention, but not half as much as the young attendant assisting her seemed to enjoy giving it. Ryan grabbed the extra jacket and exchanged the keys for a claim ticket.

The lobby of the hotel was especially beautiful, dressed tastefully in the spirit of the season: garlands weaving down the oak banisters; wreaths of green and red; and the enormous lighted Christmas tree on Windsor Lawn reaching up toward the stars.

Dinner reservations were for the Prince of Wales Restaurant: one of the hotel's finest. After giving his last name to the hostess, she led them to a private table-for-two elegantly dressed with a white tablecloth. Their server walked up shortly after the hostess left. She greeted them and lit the single candle in the center of the table.

For the next hour, they relaxed in the lap of luxury. The cuisine, service, and presentation were beyond his expectations. Live music played in the background as they both savored the evening. Emily appeared anesthetized by the extravagant treatment.

The culmination of the four-course dinner was a dessert of warmed praline fondant, set with stone fruits of apricots, pears, and peaches, marinated in Armagnac, topped with homemade vanilla bean ice-cream.

"I hope you enjoyed your evening," the server said.

"It was wonderful," Ryan said.

"No rush. Stay as long as you like."

The server cleared the table and left a small black check folder on a silver tray with two mints.

"Thank you," Ryan said, sliding his credit card into the check folder.

"I'll be back with your receipt in a moment."

Ryan turned to meet Emily's gaze and warm smile. The flickering candle sparkled in her eyes.

"Thank you," she said. Her bare foot rubbed up against his leg. The expression on her face said it all. The date had been a big success.

The nerves in his stomach tightened. His throat went dry. He took a sip of water. Trying to make a landing on an aircraft carrier rolling with the sea had never tightened his nerves as much. In a matter of minutes, her answer to his proposal would define the course of his life.

The server returned with the check. "It's been my pleasure serving you. I must say, you make a lovely couple. I wish you both the best." They smiled.

Ryan caught his first glimpse of the bill.

Wow!

But then, he thought:

It's just money. What the heck.

He added a healthy tip and scribbled his signature.

"Would you like to take a walk?" he asked.

"Sure." Ryan held the back of her chair as she stood. "Thank you, kind sir."

How should I do this?

He looked around the room.

Maybe we should go sit in the car. No, that won't work. The valet will bring the car around and then I'll have to drive. I could wait until we get back to her place. That would give me more time to get her reaction to the day.

"Wow! Look at the tree. It's beautiful," she said.

Yeah, that's it. I'll take her over by the Christmas tree.

The breeze from the ocean put a chill in the air.

"Here, put this on," he said.

"Thank you." After slipping into the jacket, she reached around his waist while they walked. They stopped to admire the tree at the edge of the grassy lawn with the faint sound of the ocean breaking against the shore in the darkness. "Isn't it beautiful?"

"Yes, but not as beautiful as what I'm holding in my arms." Emily turned and faced him. She pulled him up tight against her. Her breasts were soft. The sweet scent of her perfume drifted to his nose. He felt her hands slide down to his buttocks, squeezing, pulling him closer. With her mouth partly open, she kissed him, slowly and tenderly. Her tongue set-off arousing sensations, signaling his heart to pump harder.

Suddenly, she pulled away. "Ryan, I need to tell you something." Her words sounded serious. A set of counter-alarms sounded: from "all ahead full" to "full stop".

No. Not the—"It's been fun, but, speech?" I haven't even had time to ask her the big question."

He interrupted. "I need to ask you something, too," he said, hoping to stall her. The thought of her dumping him was more than he could bear.

"Do you mind if I go first?" she asked, looking down briefly, then back up.

He reconsidered. "Sure, go ahead." It might save him some embarrassment, he thought.

"Ryan, I first want to say... that... this evening... this whole day... has been absolutely perfect. But more importantly, you have been the best thing that has ever happened to me." She stepped back and held his hands in hers.

The space between them felt like the Grand Canyon.

Oh boy. Here it comes. Déjà vu. Keri Hart, all over again.

"I've thought a lot about *us* today."

Which way is she going with this?

"I know we've talked about our future and that possibly, in a year or so... after you've had time to get situated in your new job, we could get together. I know how important your career is to you and I want to give you the time you need—"

This is sounding too familiar.

He interrupted, "Emily, I need to say something—"

She touched her fingers to his lips. "Wait, let me finish. I would never want to be a burden to you...."

"You will never—"

"Ryan... let me finish."

His heart dying with each word she spoke. Her tongue, like the razor sharp blade of a guillotine—the same tongue that only moments earlier had pleasured him—now threatened to sever every ounce of hope.

Don't do this. Please don't say it.

"While we were up at Point Loma watching the sunset, I decided something."

Regardless of what excuse she uses, I'll beg her to reconsider. She doesn't understand what she is saying. I know it'll work.

She said, "It was as if my inner self warned me of the future."

The whoosh of the guillotine—falling faster and faster.

She continued, "What I heard frightened me."

His heart pumped wildly with fear as each word fell from her lips.

"I knew I'd be a fool if I didn't listen to my heart."

Here it comes.

He closed his eyes.

"I realized... I can never let you go. I can't live one day without you."

He opened his eyes. "What did you say?" He held her by her arms and stepped closer to be sure he didn't miss what she had said.

"I said, I don't think I can live one day without you."

He kissed her, hugged her tight, lifting her off the ground, spinning her around.

"Ryan!" she screamed with laughter. "What are you doing?"

He lowered her to the ground. Her eyes were wide, sparkling with excitement. "I love you so much... you'll never know," he said.

Unable to contain his excitement, he reached into his pocket, pulled out a small velvet box, and held it out in front of him. Emily looked down and put both hands over her mouth, gasping. He dropped down on one knee and lifted the top to the tiny box. "Emily Anderson, will you make me the happiest man in the world? Will you marry me?"

"Yes... Yes! Yes!"

He stood and took her trembling left hand and slowly slid the solitaire diamond ring onto her finger. She held it out in front of her and admired it briefly, then jumped up on him, wrapping her legs around his waist and her arms around his neck. "I love you so much!" she said. "I'm going to make you the happiest man in the world."

"You just did."

He lowered her to the ground. Her eyes meet his. "Sailor, you ain't seen happy yet." Her voice seductive. "Now, let's go back to my apartment and celebrate." A big smile spread across her face. "Kate is gone for the weekend." She snuggled up to him and put her arms around his waist, then kissed him with intensity.

Chapter 16

As they drove away from the Del, Ryan glanced over at Emily, watching as she admired the addition on her finger. He wondered if she knew how much he loved her.

He remembered the words of his mother when he was younger. He had ask, "How will I know when the right woman comes along?" She'd said, "You'll know she's the right one because you'll feel things for her you've never felt for anyone else. She will make you feel special. You'll realize life cannot go on without her by your side." His feelings for Emily were definitely unlike any other and stronger than he'd thought possible. Like a drug, he was addicted to her.

While ascending the San Diego-Coronado Bridge, a familiar song played faintly on the radio. With Emily snuggled-up under his arm, he said, "Turn that up."

She turned up the volume, filling the car with the voice of Lionel Richie's hit song "Truly". The soft keys of the piano and his message of love made Ryan think of his love for Emily. He looked at her. "That's my song to you. I couldn't say it any better."

She rested her head on his shoulder as the music played. Her hand began slowly rubbing the inner thigh of his leg, roaming dangerously close to his crouch. His loins tightened. He looked down briefly then back to the road. He could hardly believe she would soon be his wife.

Her hand moved to his belt. With a tug, she unbuckled it, along with the hook on the top of his pants; her fingers working like a ten-legged spider. He glanced down quickly. The car swerved. "Wait!" he said. "What are you doing? I might kill us both if you do that."

"You just drive, sailor. I'll take care of the rest. After all, you are a jet pilot, aren't you? You should be able to handle a little distraction."

With his zipper down and pants spread wide, her hands were all over him. He swerved again. A passing car blew. The person in the passenger seat—a long-haired man in his thirties—hung his head out the window and yelled, "Asshole! Watch where you're going!" He flipped Ryan off as the car sped away.

"Really Emily, let's wait."

"That's twice in one day, sailor." She sat up. "When we get to my place, you are *all* mine. I'm taking you on the cruise of your life."

By the time the song ended, he had put himself back together and Emily had changed the subject. "You know where I want to have my wedding?" She asked.

"Where?"

"At the Del." As if in a world of her own, wedding fever hit her, and she couldn't stop thinking aloud. "Since I was a little girl, I've always dreamed of it. I never knew it would be this perfect. We met there; you asked me to marry you there; and now, to have my wedding there would make it all perfect. I can't wait to tell Kate. She is going to die."

His first thought was the cost, and then he realized her parents would be picking up the tab, so wherever she chose was fine with him. "That sounds great."

"I want to have it in the same place you proposed, on Windsor Lawn. How about June?"

"Sounds good to me. I'll be leaving the Navy in July and should have a class date with an airline by the end of the summer. We could—"

"I am so excited! Everything is going to be perfect. I think I'll call them tomorrow to see if they have any openings in June. No! Kate and I will drive over and talk to the wedding planners. I want to see them in person." She hugged him and kissed him on the cheek. "I could have never let you go without me. I want to be there for you, every minute. Don't you worry, we're going to get through that first year just fine."

"I don't know what I would've done if you had decided not to go. When you were talking back there... giving your little speech, I thought you were going to dump me."

"Really?"

"Yeah."

"I'm sorry baby," she said with pouty lips. "I didn't mean to scare you. I'll make it up to you." He rolled his eyes her way and chuckled.

Chapter 17

Emily put her key into the lock of her apartment door, but the door was already unlocked. She looked up at Ryan with a puzzled face as she opened the door.

He wasn't surprised to find the lights on, but he was surprised when he heard Kate's voice. "Hi guys," Kate said. She was sitting on the couch watching TV, dressed for bed. "Did you have a good time?"

Emily crossed the room with her hands hidden behind her back. Standing in front of Kate, she drew her left hand out, fingers extended, palm down.

"Oh... my... Gosh!" Kate said. She looked over at Ryan and back to Emily, then jumped up from the couch and put both arms around Emily. "Congratulations! You, too, Ryan."

"Thanks," he said.

"So, when is the big day?" Kate asked.

Emily said, "We haven't set an exact date, but we're thinking sometime in June."

"A June bride," Kate said.

"Yeah," Ryan said, "I'll be leaving the Navy in July and—"

"Kate?" Emily interrupted. "Guess where we're having the wedding? You won't believe it!"

"Where?"

"The Del. The same place we met, *and* the place where he proposed. Perfect don't you think? I am so excited!"

"Sounds wonderful."

Ryan eased over by the door, sensing it was time he left. "Hey, I think I'll take off. It's getting late and this has been a big day."

Emily walked over to him and wrapped her arms around his waist. "I love you, sailor." She looked up into his face and pushed her bottom lip out, then whispered. "I wish you could stay." He smiled. "I'll walk you to the car."

They stood by the car a moment before Emily left him with one of her best kisses of the night. "Hey, sailor, don't forget about that cruise."

"I love you," he said. "We've got the rest of our lives. I'll call you tomorrow. You sleep tight."

"I love you, too."

* * *

Emily watched until his car was out of sight, her thoughts shifting to Kate. She knew Kate had faked her excitement about the engagement. Once she was alone with her, Kate was sure to put her on trial about marrying an "unknown", as they called men not yet established in high-income careers. They both knew marrying an "unknown" was a risky proposition and reeked of the horrid possibility of a middle-class life, having to work like a slave in some God-forsaken-dead-end job. She didn't expect Kate to understand, and as far as she cared, Kate could die an old hag.

She opened the door to the apartment. Kate was waiting, sitting on the couch with her legs folded beneath her. Emily envisioned a vulture perched on the limb of a dead tree, savoring the sweet smell of road kill.

"So, after all we've talked about you're still going to do it?" Kate asked.

"Yes, isn't he wonderful?"

"What happened to the Emily who said 'men were only good for their money'? Girl, this boy is broke. Have you lost your mind? I thought you'd at least wait until he started making some real money before you packed up and left."

Emily let Kate blab away. "You don't even love him, do you?"

"Of course I do."

"Yeah, sure. From what you've been telling me, you guys are going to be broke for several years. Emily, I know you too well, and to be honest, I just wonder if you'll be able to make it. I'll give it a month, tops, if that long. I just don't know what has gotten into you."

Emily couldn't hold back. "If you'll remember, I did say one of the options was to marry for love and hope for the money. Well, I think he's worth the chance. Anyway, haven't you heard how much money airline pilots make? In a few years, we'll be doing great. And just think… we'll be able to travel the world for free. And besides, he has some money saved… and there *is* a thing called credit? Not to mention, I'm not getting any younger. You know as well as I do, most of the guys in this part of the world are nothing but lazy slobs looking for the next wave—absolutely no ambition. Ryan is totally different. He has a plan… and besides, he really loves me. As long as he's happy, he'll give me what I want. And I think I know how to make him happy."

"Whatever, but I think you're making a *big* mistake."

Emily held her hand out admiring her ring. "If it doesn't work out… I'll just divorce him."

Chapter 18

December 29, 1983—7:15 p.m.
Laguna Beach, California

Keri pulled into the driveway of her Laguna Beach condo. Without her dad's help, buying a condo in Laguna Beach on a flight attendant's salary would have been impossible. She and her dad agreed it would be their little secret. If Barbara Ann found out, she would surely unleash her fiery vindictive rhetoric: "I told you so. You should have listened to your mother. You're wasting your life. I didn't raise you to be a servant." Keri had heard it *too* many times.

The news of her taking a job as a flight attendant and leaving Buckhead had sent her mother into a rage. She threatened that she would *never* find a decent man while working as a servant flitting all over the place. Her mother urged her to return to Buckhead. She tempted her with the leisurely life offered only to those in high society and the promise of the brightest and most promising men Atlanta had to offer—a fairy tale she now found repulsive. The thought of ending up in a loveless marriage built on wealth and vanity was enough to confirm her strong desire to move as far away from her mother, and Buckhead, as possible.

Unlike her mother, her dad supported her desire to leave Buckhead and encouraged her to spend some time seeing the world. He thought the experience would be good for her. In addition, he'd made sure she was not burdened by financial concerns.

She smiled when she remembered her dad's timely call only days after she had received the upsetting letter from Ryan. Her dad confessed his approval of Ryan and hoped one day they might end up together. He encouraged her not to give up and reminded her that life is always filled with surprises.

As she parked her car, the sight of her Christmas wreath on the front door of her condo reminded her of the promise she'd made herself; before her next trip, all signs of the holidays would be boxed-up and put away. She was sure she would have more energy tomorrow, but for now she was exhausted.

The five-and-a-half hours of whining passengers had worn her to a frazzle—not to mention having to listen to a fellow flight attendant brag incessantly about her engagement and upcoming wedding to "Mr. Wonderful". To top it off, a traffic jam in the southbound lanes of the 405 added thirty minutes to her commute home.

She walked to her mailbox to find it stuffed with the usual junk mail and bills. The postman had wrapped a *Victoria's Secret* magazine around the entire contents and secured it with a rubber band. Normally, she would have sifted out the junk mail before reaching her front door, but the only thing on her mind was a hot bath.

After hearing the dreadful news of Ryan being in a relationship, she begged the airline to cancel her July transfer to the West Coast. She'd convinced herself that running after Ryan was a ridiculous idea—especially after his cold response to her letter. The company had suggested she find another Miami-based flight attendant who was willing to take her transfer to LA. If not, she would be required to fill the slot.

After posting notes on company bulletin boards and spreading the word to everyone she knew, she finally found a young flight attendant, Wendi, who was homesick for California and eager to take her place. But before the swap was official, Wendi's hometown boyfriend asked her to marry him. She accepted and quit the airline.

Keri begged the airline for more time. A one-month extension was granted, but her second search for a replacement produced no volunteers. In mid September, Keri had packed up and headed west.

Her spirit lifted when Bill met her at the door. He sat patiently, looking up, waiting for her acknowledgment; his tail giving an occasional nervous wiggle.

"Hey, little buddy!" She bent over and rubbed his head causing him to burst into a flurry of excitement.

She tossed her keys on the kitchen counter and unloaded the mail. Bill followed her to the sliding-glass door and bolted into the backyard as it opened. She was thankful for the arrangement she had with her neighbors to help care for Bill. They treated him as their own when she was out of town.

Without breaking stride, she headed to her bedroom, peeling off layers as she went. Ridding herself of the uniform skin—like a molting arthropod—brought her one step closer to her real identity, rather than, "Oh Miss". Down to her bra and panties, her thoughts focused on the wonderful feeling of immersing her tired body into a hot bath.

She adjusted the temperature of the running water. Steam rose from the tub, engulfing the bathroom in a cloud of mist. While the tub filled, she pulled the dirty items from her suitcase, removed her bra and panties, and placed them all in the hamper. Accompanied by soft music and a stress-relieving lavender candle, she felt the pieces of her world falling back into place.

She pinned her hair up, turned off the water and stepped into the tub. The warmth sent a soothing charge throughout her body, relaxing her down to her core. With only her head above water, she let her mind and body unwind with the soft music and stimulation of the pleasant fragrance.

I hope Ryan is happy. I wonder if he thinks about me anymore?

A side of her wanted to jump out of the tub and race off to Del Mar, find him and do whatever was necessary to convince him he couldn't live another day without her. However, a safer, more practical boring side of her had released the idea of it all long before she ever stepped foot in California; trusting he would be happy with Miss Whoever.

Why do you keep doing this to yourself? Get over him. You know he's over you. And besides, he's probably married by now.

She stepped out of the tub, toweled off, and applied a liberal amount of her favorite body moisturizing lotion over her smooth skin before slipping into her most comfortable robe and slippers.

Entering the den, she heard a whimper and spotted Bill waiting for her to return. "I'm coming, little buddy." When she slid the door back, he ran in, hovering around her legs, following her every step.

She made a hot cup of herbal tea, took the mail and curled-up on the couch. Bill jumped up beside her. Flipping through the assorted bills, an envelope with a handwritten address caught her eye. Seeing the name "Martha Mitchell" in the upper left corner of the envelope made her smile.

Chapter 19

A letter from Martha always cheered her up, but more importantly, Martha was her lifeline to Ryan. Although he had not responded to the letter she'd sent him back in May, he must know by now she was living in California. She had specifically mentioned in the letter that his mother would have her address after she moved. It was hard to imagine why he had waited so long to contact her. Hopefully, Martha's letter would answer some of her questions. Her heart raced as she tore open the envelope.

Perhaps he is on a multi-month deployment with the Navy. That would make sense why he hasn't contacted me. Martha would know.

She pulled the folded note from the envelope.

December 23, 1983

Dear Keri,

> *I hope all is going well. I miss you. I wanted to write you as soon as I heard. Ryan is getting married...*

She stopped. "Married? No!" Her body reacted uncontrollably. Her throat tightened. Tears swelled in her eyes, burning, blurring her vision. She couldn't hold it back. Consumed by the ache in her heart she burst out crying. The pain penetrated to the very center of her being, deep down to the most sensitive area of her life.

Why, God, why?

Bill, close by her side, whimpered, releasing an occasional bark. The finality of the word "married" robbed her of all hope. Like a death, the possibility—the hope—of them ever being together was gone.

Several minutes passed before she could think clearly. Sniffling, she wiped the tears from her eyes and cheeks. Bill sat up and placed his paw on her leg. She patted him on the head. "I'll be okay, little buddy. At least I've still got you."

Although Ryan had mentioned in his letter that he and "this woman" had *talked* about marriage, she remained in a state of denial that it would happen this soon, if ever. Questions flooded her thoughts.

Where did he meet her? What kind of girl is she? Does he really love her?

So many questions.

How could God let this happen?

She wanted to talk to Ryan, to ask him why, before he made a huge mistake. Nobody could love him the way she did. She wanted to understand.

It's just not fair.

She refocused on Martha's letter.

> *I can only imagine how this news makes you feel. It was a surprise to me, too. I know how much you care for him...*

Reading the words...

> *I know how much you care for him...*

...ambushed her emotions, causing her to burst out again. A fresh stream of tears raced down her cheeks. She quickly wiped them away, blinking to clear her eyes. She continued to read.

> *I know how much you care for him, but you must know that God must have someone better for you.*

She thought, how could Martha say God has someone better for me? She knows how much I love Ryan. She knows we were meant to be together. She continued reading.

> *The girl he has asked to marry him lives in San Diego. I have never met her. This is the first I have heard of his even dating her. He has not been in contact with me for some time. I must tell you that I received the news with mixed feelings. I tried to sound happy for him, but wondered why he never mentioned this girl to me. It doesn't sound like Ryan.*

She sensed the hurt in Martha's words.
Poor Martha, she must be disappointed.
Ryan's lack of communication probably hurt her more than the surprise announcement of his marrying a woman she'd never met.

> *The wedding is set for Saturday, June 16th, in San Diego, at the Hotel Del Coronado.*

"June? That's six months from now."
One side of her said: There is still time. He's not married yet. You can stop him. Go to him now while there's still time.
The other side—the side she had grown to hate—said: He's gone. Let him go. Be happy for him. There's someone else for you. Get on with your life.
It was an emotional game of tug-of-war tearing at her heart, both sides pulling equally, keeping her from acting— unable to pursue Ryan and unable to get on with her life. Like a deer standing in the middle of a dark road, frozen, staring at the on-coming headlights of a Mac truck, unable to step aside; her dreams were about to be flattened forever. She read on...

I want you to be there with me. I know it will be hard for you, but please, I want you to come to the wedding. Do it for me.

I love you,
Martha

How could she possibly watch the man she loved marry another woman? The image of the two of them standing at the altar, giving themselves to each other, made her feel abandoned and alone. She loved Martha and would do anything in the world for her, but how could she attend Ryan's wedding?

She dropped the letter, buried her face in her hands and cried.

Chapter 20

The Wedding
Saturday, June 16, 1984—7:15 p.m.
The Hotel Del Coronado, San Diego, California

Since hearing the news of Ryan's engagement, Keri had written and mailed him five letters. He had either read the letters and trashed them, or never received them. She found it hard to believe that none of her five attempts had reached him. If the letters had not been delivered, the post office would have surely returned them to the return address on the envelope.

By the time she'd written the third letter, it was obvious that he must have received at least one of them, read it, and chosen not to contact her. Her last two attempts sounded more like desperate pleas—cries from her heart—telling him how much she loved him and needed to see him, or talk to him.

The daily struggle in her heart continued, tugging in opposite directions, one side telling her to go find him; the other side growing more embarrassed, regretting she had ever written the first letter. She knew he had loved her at one time, but if he still loved her, he would have contacted her. Time ran out.

Keri arrived at the Hotel Del Coronado alone. She wore a cute sleeveless mid thigh-length fitted dress. It was the only dress she owned that was black, and black was the only color she felt appropriate for the occasion.

She asked the concierge, "Can you direct me to the Mitchell wedding? I believe it is being held on Windsor Lawn."

The concierge pointed toward the back of the lobby. "Just through those open doors and onto the patio. You can't miss it."

"Thank you."

Perched on the patio, she gazed-out over Windsor Lawn extending from the beautiful Victorian hotel out toward the

Pacific Ocean. The gathering of guests resembled a look-alike contest for the cast of the television soap series *Dynasty,* or *Dallas.* Women with their big hair, shoulder pads, and loads of sparkling jewelry, decorated the lawn in a colorful sea of fuchsia pink, sea green, purple, royal blue, and red.

Beyond the crowd were rows of evenly spaced white chairs atop a manicured green lawn; the Pacific Ocean in the distance. Potted pink hydrangeas hung from strategically placed stands. Then, her eyes followed a carpet of pink rose petals to the altar; the place where Ryan and Emily would soon be exchanging their vows. She imagined a magnificent sunset as they kissed their first time as husband and wife. It made her want to vomit.

What am I doing here?

Her attention was drawn to an elderly woman in the crowd, waving both arms in the air, calling her name. It was Martha Mitchell. Keri felt comforted by her welcoming smile, but embarrassed by the attention of heads turned in her direction.

She left the patio and made her way through the crowd to Martha.

"There you are." Martha said. "I am so glad you came. It's been *too* long. Come here and give me a hug." Martha's unrestrained excitement caused those standing near to stop and observe, perhaps wondering why the groom's mother was making such a fuss over her.

After a big hug, Martha took her hand and led her away from the crowd. She turned and faced Keri, looking into her eyes. She knew Martha had an unobstructed view of her broken heart. In a concerned tone, Martha asked, "How is my baby doing?"

Keri forced a slight smile. "I'm okay."

Martha tilted her head down and lifted her eyebrows. "Are you sure?"

"Really Martha, everything is great." Silence followed. Martha just stared, as if she knew Keri was lying. "Okay, maybe it's not *great*, but I'll be okay, honest."

"Have you talked with Ryan?" Martha asked.

Shivers ran up her neck at the thought of talking to him. "Today? Here?" She quickly glanced from side-to-side, checking to see if Ryan might be near. "No. Not yet... I mean no."

"Dear, it's all going to be okay. I know how you must feel, but like I've told you, God has everything under control. You must believe that."

At the moment, she found Martha's confidence in the promise of a brighter tomorrow hard to accept. If God had everything under control, why wasn't *she* the one exchanging vows with Ryan tonight? She knew Martha loved her and only meant the best, so she let it go. In need of a diversion, she said, "I've missed you so much."

"Oh, Dear. You are so sweet."

Keri hugged her again and then stepped back to get a full look at her. "You look great."

"Thank you."

"I should be the one asking how *you* are doing with all this?"

"Considering the circumstances... just fine."

Without thinking, Keri peppered her with questions. "How is he doing? Do you think he's going to be happy? Have you met this girl yet?" Realizing her anxious flurry of questions, she said, "Listen to me. I must sound like some pitiful wretch."

Martha leaned close and whispered, "Remember, I feel the same way."

While she chatted with Martha, her eyes constantly darted about the crowded lawn in hopes of spotting Ryan. She even wondered if she would recognize him after all the years.

I can't walk up to him now. What would I say?

The embarrassing thought hit her of him reading what she had written in her last two letters, telling him how much she loved him, and how she knew they were meant for each other.

God, I wish I hadn't been so stupid!

Then she spotted him. Her heart fluttered. He was turned to the side talking to some guests.

She tried to remain calm. Her throat tightened, cutting off air while her heart pounded on her chest from the inside. She felt weak in the legs. Her body trembled.

Get a hold of yourself.

Martha said, "Oh, there's Ryan. Would you like me to go get him?"

"Not now. He looks busy. I'll talk to him later."

"Darlin', I understand."

"Thank you." She felt relieved. "He looks great. Tell me, Martha, is he happy?"

Martha hesitated. "To be honest, I really don't know. From the little I've seen, Emily shows him a lot of attention, but she just doesn't seem like his type to me."

Keri breathed deep and slowly exhaled—her heart still racing. "What do you mean?"

"She's definitely a beautiful woman, but I'm not too sure there's much behind that pretty face of hers."

"Yeah, I know the type." She felt the blood returning to her face and the trembling stopped. She hoped Ryan had not been tricked by the likes of a Jezebel.

"That's what he liked most about you. You weren't like the rest. Of course I already knew that."

"You're sweet." Keri reached out and held Martha's hand.

"I may be judging her, too soon, but there's just something that doesn't feel right. I can only hope that Ryan didn't let his heart deceive him. I've always tried to warn him that if he didn't guard his heart, some cute little girl, who was only interested in herself and what *she* wanted, was going to come along and lead him into a trap." She turned to Keri. "And that goes for you, too. Don't ever compromise when it comes to marriage."

"Martha, you don't have to worry about me, and I'm sure Emily is a sweet girl and will make Ryan happy." Keri had to lie. She didn't want Martha to worry—she was worried enough for the both of them. She looked over where Ryan had been standing. He was gone. Her eyes searched the crowd.

There he is! I need to talk to him. I'll know if he loves her by the way he acts toward me. If I don't, I'll never have another chance.

Martha took her hand. "Keri, I want you to do me a big favor."

"Anything." She kept her eyes on Ryan.

"Sit by me during the wedding."

"What?" Shocked, she turned to Martha. "But I'm not family. I couldn't do that. I'll just sit with the guests. Maybe they can seat me in the row right behind you."

"No." She held both of Keri's hands forcing her to keep eye contact. "I want you to sit right by my side. As far as I'm concerned, you are family."

"I don't know, Martha." Keri looked for Ryan.

Where is he? I can't lose him now. There's not much time.

"If you don't want to see an old woman get upset and make a scene, then you better plan on putting your pretty little self in the chair beside me."

"Martha... I don't know."

"Well, I do. And you're sitting with me."

Keri hesitated briefly, but knowing she really didn't have a choice, she said, "Okay, if you insist."

"Now that that's settled, let's get on with the show."

Keri took one last look for Ryan. Most of the guests had made their way to the seating area. He was gone. Even if she'd found him, Martha had her arm laced in hers so tight, she would never get away.

Martha pulled one of the groomsmen over and instructed, "Young man, I want you to take this lovely young lady to her seat and..." she said, pulling on the usher's arm encouraging him to lean down, whispering in his ear, "be sure she is sitting in the seat right beside where you plan to seat me. Do you understand?"

"Yes, ma'am."

"Good."

The usher looked at Keri and offered his arm. Keri put her arm in his as they walked slowly down the aisle toward the front row.

"So, are you related to Ryan?" he asked.

"Just a close friend."

"He didn't tell me he had relatives that were models. You are a model aren't you?"

"Not hardly." She blushed at the comment. "Mrs. Mitchell and I are just good friends, and she insisted that I sit with her. To be honest, it's a bit embarrassing."

"It's just a wedding," he said. "We'll pretend you're his sister. Nobody will know." He stopped beside the first row and released Keri's arm. "Just between you and me, there's no way Ryan could ever have a sister as good-looking as you are. It's just not in the gene pool."

"Thank you," Keri said.

"No problem. Now be sure to wait for me when the wedding is over. I'll be back for you."

She looked up at him for the first time. "Okay."

Before he left, he whispered, "Oh, I forgot to introduce myself. My name is Rex Dean. I'm a good friend of Ryan's."

"My name is Keri Hart. Nice to meet you."

Even with her thoughts muddled, she couldn't help noticing his striking appearance. Blue eyes, sandy blond hair, and a killer smile. If only for a moment, she forgot about the wedding, the front row, Martha, and even Ryan.

Chapter 21

Like an out of body experience, Keri sat paralyzed and helpless. Only minutes remained until the man she loved would be married to another woman.

She wanted to yell out: *Stop the wedding! It's not right! Ryan, you can't marry this woman! I love you! I have always loved you!*

But her thoughts went the way of all thoughts—unheard—while Ryan and his soon-to-be wife stood side-by-side, their backs to the crowd, like two plastic figures atop a wedding cake.

She imagined herself standing beside Ryan. The feeling of his eyes looking deep into her soul, expressing his love for her, made her drift into a "happy place".

For a moment, the proceedings of the wedding became meaningless, like the frames of a silent film flickering past, until the minister's deep voice jolted her back into the present. "Dear friends, Ryan and Emily wish to recite their vows."

Facing each other, Ryan began, "I, Ryan, take you, Emily Anderson, to be my wife, my constant friend, my faithful partner, and my love, from this day forward. In the presence of God, our family and friends, I offer you my solemn vow to be your faithful partner in sickness and in health, in good times and in bad, and in joy as well as in sorrow. With every sunset and every sunrise, I will be reminded of the importance of each day, and how it can only be lived once. It is my desire that my love for you will grow deeper than the mind can understand. I promise to love you unconditionally, to honor and respect you, to laugh with you and cry with you, for as long as we both shall live."

As Ryan recited his vows, Keri clung to each word as though they were meant for her. If only for a brief time, her heart swelled with joy. Her fantasy abruptly ended with the high-pitched voice of a woman.

"I, Emily Anderson, take you, Ryan Mitchell, to be my husband, my partner in life, and my one true love. I will cherish our union and love you more each day than I did the day before. I will trust you and respect you, laugh with you and cry with you, love you faithfully through good times and bad, regardless of the obstacles we may face together. I give you my hand, my heart, and my love from this day forward, for as long as we both may live."

Keri turned her head away in disgust; the thought of Emily's words bringing a wave of nausea to her stomach. She breathed deep and exhaled, trying to hold back the urge to vomit.

I can't believe this is happening. Not now!

She didn't know which would be more embarrassing: jumping up and running down the aisle, hoping not to explode before she reached the grassy lawn beyond the seating area, or lowering her head and releasing the contents of her stomach at Martha's feet?

She closed her eyes, praying the queasiness would pass. When she opened her eyes, she located Emily's parents seated across the aisle on the front row. Her mother was a pitiful sight, frail and wrinkled, looking to be in her eighties, but probably not more than sixty. She looked as though she had been released from a nursing home or rehab center for the sole purpose of attending her daughter's wedding. Her father was at least a hundred pounds overweight and appeared to be drunk. His eyes were frozen on the distant sky as though he cared less about the most important day in his daughter's life.

She turned back to the ceremony when she heard Ryan and Emily reciting in unison. "In the presence of God and our friends, I take you to be my partner in life, promising to love you, so long as we both shall live."

This is all wrong!

After exchanging rings, the pastor had them face the crowd and pronounced them, Mr. and Mrs. Ryan Mitchell, followed with the words, "You may kiss the bride."

Wait!

She swiveled her head around and saw nothing but blank stares on the faces of those watching.

Aren't you supposed to ask if anyone objects?

Ryan and Emily kissed as the organ bellowed out Mendelssohn's *Wedding March*. Arm-in-arm, they turned and faced the crowd. With her eyes locked on Ryan's face, studying his every expression, Keri's heart jumped when she caught him glance her way. He smiled. She smiled back, thinking he'd noticed her. But his smile was directed at Martha. She realized she was invisible to him; undoubtedly the last person in the world he would expect to see at his wedding.

Ryan, please look at me.

If he broadened his field of view just an inch to the right, he'd see her, but instead he turned to Emily and smiled. They glided down the grassy aisle headed for the reception in the beautifully decorated Crown Room of the Del. As he passed, she felt more alone than ever. She'd lost him.

Chapter 22

Twenty minutes later, family and friends stood in the traditional receiving line, anxious for an opportunity to extend their heart-felt congratulations to the newlyweds. Rex, of course, was first in line. He cordially greeted Emily's parents before standing in front of Emily.

"Well, you know the custom," he said reaching for Emily's hands. She glanced over at Ryan and back to Rex. "I'm finally going to get that kiss," Rex said.

Ryan watched as Rex moved face to face with his new bride. Unlike the traditional peck on the lips he'd expected, Rex indulged himself with a full, open-mouth kiss. At first, Emily stood frozen, but within seconds, she was fully engaged, her tongue painting his lips and the inside of his mouth.

"Okay, Rex, that's enough." Ryan pushed on Rex's shoulder encouraging him to break it off.

After one last kiss, Rex pulled Emily close and whispered into her ear loud enough for Ryan to hear, "I'll be here when you get tired of wading around in the shallow water with that little shrimp… if you know what I mean." Rex glanced over at Ryan, giving him a sly smile and then winked at Emily.

"Rex, you are so bad," Emily said. She laced her arm around Ryan. Her cheeks red with embarrassment.

"I'll see you kids later," Rex said, then walked away.

Ryan stared down at Emily with a bewildered look.

"What?" she asked. "It was just a kiss." She rolled her eyes.

What he had witnessed was more than a kiss, and there was no doubt that Emily had enjoyed it—even encouraged it. The steady line of guests kept Ryan from laboring over the disgusting image of Rex making out with his new wife.

His gaze turned to the next guest in line. In near disbelief—like an apparition of a lost loved-one from a past life—he froze.

"Hi Ryan. Remember me?"

"Keri Hart! I can't believe it's you! I can't believe you came."

His heart raced. Unsure of what to say, his thoughts ricocheted through time, from that night in her driveway to the day he opened her disappointing letter, over a year ago; the letter telling him that she and some guy named Bill were talking about marriage.

He reached his hands out toward her. "Come here and give me a hug." She smiled big as she stepped past Emily to hug him. Her body up against his felt different from Emily's— smaller, but familiar. It had been a long time. He released her and met her gaze; her brown eyes sending him confirmation that she was happy to see him.

Why would she just show up at my wedding?

"How have you been?" he asked.

"I'm doing great."

For a brief moment, he'd lost himself in her presence. The sound of Emily's voice brought him back to reality. "Honey, don't you want to introduce me to your friend?" Emily asked, sounding a little perturbed.

He turned to Emily. "Oh, I'm sorry, this is Keri Hart. We're old friends." He quickly turned back to Keri.

"Nice to meet you, Keri," Emily said, then laced her arm around Ryan's, as though she were locking him at a safe distance from his "old friend".

"Congratulations to both of you," Keri said.

Ryan asked, "Have you seen Mom?"

"Yes. As a matter of fact, she's the reason I'm here. When she told me about the wedding, there was no way I was going to let her come all this way and me not see her. I love her so much."

His heart sank. He'd subconsciously wanted to believe that Keri had come to see him, instead of his mom. He knew it was wrong, but, in a way, he hoped that she still cared about him.

"Well, I'm glad you came," he said. "So, are you still a flight attendant."

"Coffee, tea, or me," she said.

Everyone laughed.

"I'm based in LA and live up in Laguna Beach."

"That sounds great." His calm response masked the sudden rush he had after hearing she was living only an hour away. The last he'd heard, she was based in Miami and living in Fort Lauderdale. "I'm waiting to hear from a couple of airlines myself," Ryan said. "Who knows, one day, we might even be working together… for the same airline."

"That would be great," she said. "I'll keep an eye out for you."

"So, how long have you been in California?"

"Don't you remember… my letter?" she asked.

"Oh… yes," he said, sounding a bit puzzled. He did remember the letter, but he didn't remember anything about California.

Emily tugged on his arm, causing him to lose his balance. He had so many questions for Keri but knew Emily's patience was growing thin. "So, how's Bill doing?" Ryan glanced at Emily. She didn't look too happy with the way the conversation was going. Asking about Bill might calm her down.

"Bill? Oh, Bill. He's great," Keri said. "I don't know what I would do without him."

"Sounds like you two are close," Ryan said. "I'll bet he misses you when you travel."

"Yeah, it's pretty hard on him, but you should see him when I get home. Most of the time he is standing at the door, waiting. The minute I open it, he jumps all over me. He is so cute."

"Emily looked up at Ryan and said, "That's the way I'll be, Honey. I'll be standing at the door waiting, ready to jump all over you." She shot an evil glance over at Keri.

Knowing his time with Keri was up, he said, "Listen, I'll get your address from Mom and let you know which airline I end up working for."

"Okay. That would be great. I'd better be going. I have an early flight tomorrow. I wish you guys the best." She hugged Ryan, one more time, and then looked at Emily. "I hope you know what you've got here. Be sure to take care of him. He's special."

"Don't you worry, I'll take *good* care of him," she said in a seductive voice. "You can count on that." She reached up and kissed him on the lips, as though she were saying, He's mine, get your own.

Chapter 23

Keri wanted to run and hide. Staying for the reception would only result in more pain. As she walked away, she replayed every second of her time with Ryan. If only it could have been longer, and *without* his new bride hovering over him like a vulture. Seeing another woman clinging to him was enough to make her want to puke, and hearing them call each other "Honey" was more than she could handle. It was wrong, all wrong.

However, the thought of Ryan one day working for the same airline offered some compensation. *If* he did land a job with her airline, and *if* he were based in LA, they would definitely fly together—without *her*. At least then, she would be able to get to know him again. Even if he *was* married, they could be friends.

Suddenly, the most baffling part of the entire conversation hit her. Why had he acted so surprised when she mentioned that she lived in California? She'd not only written it in the first letter she sent him back in May, but in each of the five letters she'd sent him since she moved to California. She was sure he must have seen her return address on the envelope. It didn't make sense. He acted so weird. It must have been Emily.

I doubt he has told her about us.

Before she left, she stopped to tell Martha good-bye. "Martha, I need to go."

"Oh Dear, can't you stay a bit longer?" Martha took Keri's hands in hers. "We haven't had enough time to catch up. How are your parents?"

"They're fine… or at least that's what dad tells me."

"Is Barbara Ann still upset about you moving away from Buckhead? From what I remember, she had your life pretty much mapped out."

"I think what upset her most was when I took the job as a flight attendant." Keri paused, reflecting on the horrible day when she told her mom. "In general, we just didn't agree on the direction my life was headed. She'll get over it."

"What about your dad?"

"He's been my savior. I couldn't have made it without him. Other than you, he's the only one that understands. I love him so much, and I know he loves me."

"Your father is a wise man."

"Martha, I wanted to tell you what he said. He told me he has always thought highly of Ryan and secretly hoped we would end up together—but that was before Ryan and Emily were engaged."

Martha nodded. "Me, too, Dear. Me, too. Like I told you, your father is a wise man. It's obvious he wants the best for you. I know he would do anything to give you the desires of your heart. We both must continue to believe that God has a wonderful plan for your life. Now is not the time to lose your faith. When you think of how much your earthly father loves you, just remember that your Heavenly Father loves you much, much more."

"I know." Keri hugged Martha. "I really need to go."

"Are you sure? The Crown Room is absolutely gorgeous. You should at least take a peek."

"I'm sure it is, but I really must go."

"Okay then, but promise me you will keep in touch."

"I promise. I love you."

"I love you, too, Darlin'. Take care of yourself."

"I will."

Coming to Ryan's wedding had been difficult enough, but staying for the reception would be stupid. She hurried to her car.

As Keri reached to unlock her car door, a voice called out. "Keri!"

She turned. "Oh, hi, Rex."

"That was some wedding," he said, walking up a little winded.

"Yeah, it was beautiful."

"Listen, I was wondering if you might let me take you out for dinner sometime. I figured since we're both good friends with Ryan, and probably going to be seeing more of each other, we should get better acquainted."

"I don't think I'll be seeing much of Ryan." She turned to unlock her door.

"Sure you will," he said. "You never stop keeping up with old friends."

"Rex, you're thoughtful, but you have no idea… it's a long story and it's getting late. I've got to fly early tomorrow and need to get home."

"Okay. I'll tell you what, let's just forget about Ryan. Let me take you out for dinner because I want to hear all about the airline biz. After I leave the Navy, I'll be going with the airlines. Plus, I can tell you stuff about Ryan I know will make you laugh. I probably know him better than anyone does. I promise to make it worth your time. What do you say?"

When she heard the part about learning more about Ryan, she reconsidered. The opportunity to get answers to her questions was hard to turn down. "Okay. That would be great. I could use a good laugh."

"Fantastic! We can call it a 'Ryan Roast'." They both laughed. "Next Saturday sound okay?"

"That sounds good." She dug a pen out of her purse and jotted down her number. "Just give me a call next week and I'll give you directions to my place."

"Sounds great. Talk to you soon."

She drove off.

The drive back to Laguna Beach gave her time to think. She verbalized her thoughts aloud, as if she were talking to an imaginary passenger seated beside her. "I just attended Ryan's wedding. Can you believe that? His wedding!" She continued in disbelief. "That means he's *married*. Married!" The words "wedding" and "married" resonated a feeling of finality, much like the word death.

In her mind, she replayed the slow kiss Emily had given Ryan—right in front of her face. It sickened her. She imagined Ryan holding her, sleeping with her, giving himself to her. "It's all wrong! It'll never work!"

Driving faster and faster, she slammed her palm against the steering wheel. "Why, Ryan? Why?" The pain was unbearable. She wanted it all to be a bad dream, but it wasn't.

The image of Ryan kissing Emily at the altar popped into her head. Her anger grew. "I waited! Why couldn't you?"

A sharp pain shot through her chest; she started gasping for breath.

Heart attack? I'm having a heart attack!

She clutched her chest; the car swerved. Within seconds, the pain in her chest rocketed up into her throat, tears bursting from her eyes uncontrollably. With her body trembling, she wailed; the car speeding down the freeway. Her vision obscured by her watery eyes, she instinctively reached and flipped on the windshield wipers. Realizing the danger, she pulled to the shoulder of the road and braked to a stop. Sitting alone on the side of I-5, cars whizzing by, her wipers screeching back and forth across a dry windshield, she cried.

Married or not, she had to know the truth. Rex Dean had the answers she needed. A thought brought a glimmer of hope. Two things she knew for sure: Over fifty percent of all marriages end in divorce, and Ryan Mitchell still had feelings for her.

Chapter 24

"Give me two dates," Rex Dean said, as he splashed cologne on his face, "and I'll have her eating out of my hand."

He glided through his condo lip-syncing and whistling along as the stereo blared-out *Quando, Quando, Quando (Tell Me When), After the Lovin',* and other tunes by his hero, the crooning heartthrob, Englebert Humperdinck; Hump; the Humpster; or the name he most identified with: the "Rex of Romance". In his mind, it was no coincidence that Humperdinck had been tagged with the name "Rex"; it was fate.

He had to admit, Ryan's little sweetie had blossomed quite nicely since her high school days. He never expected that the little peach from Georgia would turn into such a babe. The minute he laid eyes on her he knew she would be his next project, and thanks to Ryan, it should be easy pickin'.

One last glance in the mirror, continuing to lip-sync the Humpster, and out the door he strode. Behind the wheel of his Porsche, he sped off to Laguna Beach to work his magic on Keri.

* * *

Keri knew her motivations were purely selfish, but Rex Dean had the information she needed. The Ryan she knew would have *never* married a girl like Emily, and to get closure, she needed to know why.

Crazy thoughts filled her head all week: Ryan and Emily on their honeymoon in Hawaii; basking in the sun beneath towering palms; sipping Mai Tai's by the pool; romantic dinners at sunset; and then, the repulsive memory of Emily's voice: "Don't you worry, I'll take good care of him."

Keri feared for Ryan. She remembered a National Geographic TV special where a male and female praying mantis were placed in a jar. After mating, the male, in alarm, tried to escape. While he pawed at the glass, the female grabbed him, bit off his front tarsus, consumed his tibia and femur, and then gnawed out his eyes. The narrator calmly stated that it was only an accident if the male ever escapes alive from the embraces of his partner.

She couldn't just sit there and let Ryan be eaten by some blond bug.

The doorbell rang. She checked herself in the mirror before opening the door.

Remember, it's not a date. It's a meeting. Use him, then lose him.

"Hello, Rex." She'd forgotten how attractive he was, especially now, dressed in casual clothes instead of the rented monkey suit, and taller than she had remembered. At any other time, she might have entertained romantic possibilities. She quickly reminded herself:

He's merely an informant, nothing more. Use him, then lose him, that's the plan.

"Wow!" Rex said.

"What?"

"Oh, I'm sorry. It's just... you're so stunning in that outfit. Or..." His probing eyes locked on hers. A chill tingled its way up her spine. "maybe it's your eyes. I don't remember them being brown... and beautiful."

"Thank you."

Is he for real?

She waited to see if his eyes might wander. Him, a head taller, and her in a V-neck top revealing a bit more cleavage than she had planned, she expected his eyes to dart below her neck. They didn't.

"Are you ready to go?"

"I'm ready." She closed and locked the door, and they walked to his car. After assisting her into the passenger seat, he moved around the front of the car.

Impressive. The perfect gentleman.

Before starting the engine, he said, "I know a great place up in Newport Beach. You'll love it. It's called *The Cannery*. Great atmosphere… and the food is fantastic."

"Sounds good to me."

She had heard of the place from a coworker—nice but pricy. *The Cannery* was an upscale waterfront seafood restaurant originally built as a commercial fish cannery in 1921. The location on the Rhine Channel, between 30th Street and Lido Park Drive, offered a natural charm and seaside ambiance; a perfect postcard scene of weathered boardwalks, gleaming yachts, and gently bobbing sailboats.

"Guess what?" Rex said.

"What?"

"I got my acceptance letter today with the airlines."

"Fantastic!"

"Better yet, it looks like we're *all* going to be working together. You, me, and Ryan. Your airline picked us both up."

"Ryan, too?"

"Yes. We even have the same class date, August 20th."

Hearing "Ryan, too", ignited more crazy thoughts: flights together; private conversations; layovers—all without Emily.

I shouldn't be thinking like this.

"Where would you like to be based?"

"I'm definitely coming back to the West Coast."

"What about Ryan? Is he… or, I should say, are *they* planning to move back to the West Coast?"

"Ryan doesn't know about his acceptance yet."

"How did you find out?"

"Oh… I opened his mail. If he calls, I can tell him the good news."

"So, you think they will eventually move back to California?"

"I doubt it. Emily is all charged up about Texas. She *thinks* she wants to travel and see the world."

"Really?" She gazed out the window at the ocean and the distant horizon as they sped north on the Pacific Coast Highway. The sun was only minutes from disappearing behind the thin line separating the sky from the ocean. Somewhere far beyond that line were the Hawaiian Islands.

He's over there—with Emily.

"Penny for your thoughts," Rex said.

"What did you mean by Emily 'thinks' she wants to travel?"

"Emily doesn't know what she wants."

"What makes you the expert on what Emily wants?"

"I've practically lived with her for the last six months. Remember, Ryan *is* my roommate. In some ways, I probably know more about Emily than he does."

"Maybe she's put some thought into it and knows what she wants."

"Emily? Think? Are you kidding?" He snorted. "Emily is your classical dumb blond: an empty shell."

"Interesting." Rex had confirmed Keri's initial impression of Emily: air-head. That's why she couldn't believe Ryan had fallen for her. What was he thinking?

* * *

Rex felt empowered. The music of the Humpster played in his mind: *After the Lovin'*.

This is going to be easier than I thought.

Straight from the pages of *Gone with the Wind*, he would become the perfect gentleman that every Southern woman dreams about, removing any suspicion of his motives.

Next, he would paint Emily as man's most feared predator, allowing him to bond with Keri and her obvious concern for Ryan. With her guard down and someone nearby she could confide in, the trap would be set.

All he had to do then was pluck the little peach from her worried branch after assuring her Ryan would never leave Emily, regardless of how she treated him.

Easy as one, two, three—perfect gentleman; paint the predator; pluck the peach. The trick was not to hang around too long. The minute she starts to show any signs of attachment would be his queue to dump her and move on.

As the car rolled into the restaurant parking lot, two valets rushed to meet them. While one young man assisted Keri, Rex exchanged greetings with the other one, handing him the keys to the Porsche.

A brass plate by the door to the restaurant was engraved with the words, "DRESS CODE".

Keri looked down at her white slacks, navy V-neck top and sandals and hesitated. "Am I dressed okay?"

"You're fine." He reached in front of her and took hold of the brass door handle to the large wooden door. "After you." He smiled.

"Thank you."

The receptionist stood behind a lectern. A small brass lamp illuminated the seating chart. After a casual greeting, Rex leaned over the lectern and pointed to a particular table on the seating diagram. "Is my usual table available tonight?" A ten-dollar bill fell from his hand to the lectern.

"I believe it is." She smiled. "Follow me." The hostess seated them by the window overlooking the harbor filled with extravagant yachts.

Keri glanced out and noticed two men aboard a yacht dressed in uniforms: white shirts, navy slacks and ties, epaulets with gold stripes on their shoulders; apparently the crew, waiting for their wealthy owners to return from dinner. It reminded her of her privileged life growing up: chartered jets, limousine rides, shopping trips to New York, and family vacations to Europe. She learned the power of money at an early age—both to provide pleasure and inflict pain.

Just as mind-altering drugs have the ability to strip a person of their true identity while robbing them of their souls, the abundance and abuse of money has the power to do likewise. It was a lesson she learned best while watching her mother operate in her grandiloquent and boastful style. For Barbara Ann, the measure of a person was determined *not* by their character, but by their status and standing in society. Her mother's twisted view of life had ultimately cost Keri a life of happiness with the man she loved—her soul mate.

As she grew older, Keri longed for a life free from any association with the pompous arrogance her mother embraced so dearly. Instead, she hoped to emulate the life of her dear friend, Martha Mitchell. Ryan's mother lived a simple life, but had a profound understanding of the essence of humanity: love, strength, determination, and persistence when dealing with adversity. She lived her life quietly and without fanfare, always available to contribute to the lives of others. From Martha's strength of heart, Keri found enormous amounts of personal inspiration.

The soft music and dimly lit dining room relaxed her. The glassy calm water in the harbor mirrored the lights from restaurants, shops, and yachts standing ready in the harbor.

The menu offered delightful selections of seafood and beef. She decided on a macadamia nut crusted northern Halibut with a tropical pineapple relish and mint-champagne sauce. Rex chose the wood-broiled Pacific Swordfish, mashed potatoes, and seeded mustard sauce.

"You sure know how to pick your restaurants," she said.

"This is one of my favorites. I always look forward to coming here when I'm in the area. I hope I'll be in the area more often." He cut her a smile.

Keri put the white cloth napkin in her lap and took a sip of wine. "What do you think Ryan will do? I mean..." looking down, pretending to adjust the napkin in her lap, "long term? I know you said he plans to start out in Texas."

"I don't think it's a matter of what *Ryan* wants."

"What do you mean?" she asked, unable to hide her concern.

Rex reached over and held one end of the hot bread the waiter had just delivered. Making two slices in the small loaf, he took one for himself.

"I think it's going to depend on his new bride and what *she* wants," he said. With his knife, he scooped a healthy portion of the soft butter from the dish beside the bread loaf and smeared it on the bread. "To be honest, I don't think she's gonna last in Texas. She's too much like me. California blood runs in her veins."

"What do you predict will happen?"

"I'd give her a year, two tops."

"Until what?"

"Till they... or she is back in California."

"What do you mean 'or she'?"

"You'd have to know Emily." He took a bite of the soft buttered bread. "She's not the kind to be told what to do."

"You don't think she'd *leave* him, do you?"

"No telling. The poor girl has never stepped one foot out of California her entire life. I can't wait to see how she reacts to her first Texas summer." He laughed.

"Well, if she truly loves him, I don't see how she could even *think* about leaving him."

"I'm not so sure she loves Ryan as much as he loves her."

"Surely Ryan wouldn't marry someone that didn't love him."

"I'm not saying she doesn't love him, after all, how can anybody know if someone loves them, or not."

"You can tell by the way a person acts toward you."

"Hmm. So, I guess if some dude is kind, sensitive, attentive, and always showers you with gifts, and flowers, you would take that to mean he *loves* you?"

"No. It's more than that. I can't explain it, but I would know." She felt awkward—almost threatened—trying to defend her beliefs about love. She needed to change the subject. "Anyway, why was Ryan in such a hurry to get married?"

Rex said, "Ryan is grade-A husband material. He's the type that is destined to marry, sooner or later."

"The type?"

"Needy. The entire time I've known him, almost six years now, he has always been a little awkward around women. I can't imagine why. He's a nice looking guy. I just think it's his background. Based on what he's told me, he never dated much in high school. And at the Naval Academy, well, from what I hear, the best you can do there is a one-night stand with one of the local girls, or you might get lucky with a faculty member's daughter; although now I hear they let women attend."

"So, you think the only reason he fell for Emily was because she happened to be there at the right time?"

"He never liked dating much. Emily made it *easy* for him." He laughed.

"What's so funny?"

"Just thinking about the word 'easy' in the same sentence with 'Emily' makes me laugh."

"You saying Emily was easy—as in sexually?"

"Well, let's just say, she's no Emily Post."

"Funny," she said, with a sarcastic tone.

"When she took after him, he didn't have a chance. But I saw right through her little game. She was looking for a ticket out of town. Sure, she likes him—may even love him—but not like he loves her. Poor boy was smitten the minute he laid eyes on her."

"So, you think Ryan really loves her?"

"Not really."

"Oh boy. I'm confused. First, you say he loves her, then you say 'not really'."

"Ryan loves what he *imagines* Emily to be, not the real Emily. I'm not even sure *Emily* knows who she is. Bottom line, I think Ryan is in for a rough ride once he sees who he really married. But if I know Ryan, he'll never leave her. He's all into the 'until death do us part' thing."

Keri was more confused than ever. The information Rex readily dished out was painful to listen to, yet, in some ways, satisfying. But she needed more—more facts. She needed to know what made Ryan lose his mind and heart. How could this girl rob him of his good senses, so quickly?

The meal came and exceeded all of her expectations. The conversation eventually drifted away from Ryan and Emily. Rex had questions about the airline. He took control of the questioning, wanting to know about schedules, layovers, and flight attendants. Keri could tell he appeared more excited about chasing skirts than flying airplanes. In a way, she was relieved. At least he wasn't interested in her.

The wonderful meal was topped off with a dessert of white chocolate crème brulees, caramelized with two sugars, topped with strawberries. After coffee, they left the restaurant and walked along the Rhine Channel.

The night was still and quiet. A full moon cast its reflection on the water. Occasional laughter and conversation echoed off the harbor's silence. Several yachts dressed with lights hosted private parties for their wealthy owners and intoxicated guests.

"What about you?" Rex turned and looked at her as they walked. "You got someone special in your life? Some rich airline captain?" He chuckled. "A good-looking girl like you probably has a different man waiting in every city, right?"

"Nope, no one special." She thought, the only one special in her life was now married.

"I don't believe my ears! We have so much in common. We both are airline people, or soon to be; we both know Ryan and Emily; we're both single and available. Sounds like fate to me."

"You're too funny." She nudged him with her elbow. "I'd probably better be getting home, and you've got a long drive ahead of you."

They strolled back to the front of the restaurant. Rex gave the valet his call tag, and, within minutes, they were on their way.

She enjoyed the evening and felt she had gained a new insight into Ryan's life, along with a new list of questions; questions she must have answers to before she could move on with her life.

Chapter 25

"Here we are," Rex said, coasting into Keri's driveway.

She turned to Rex. "Thank you for a wonderful dinner."

"My pleasure. I hope you'll let me take you out again, soon."

She paused, a little afraid to commit to another "meeting". After all, she knew she was only using him and felt a bit guilty taking advantage of him.

Then, out of the blue, he said, "Keri, I know all about you and Ryan."

"What do you mean?" Her heart raced, as if someone had discovered a deep incriminating secret about her.

"I know about your past with Ryan… in high school."

Although she had nothing to hide, the sudden and unexpected discovery that Rex knew more, possibly much more, made her feel violated. Why had he kept it a secret? Why? Her concern turned to anger. He had deceived her. The whole time, even at the wedding, he knew everything.

What a jerk!

"Who do you think you are? You *lied* to me!" She didn't know whether to be ashamed, embarrassed, or furious.

"Not exactly. I never lied to you."

"Then what do you call it?"

He raised his hand. "Calm down. Let me explain. I know you and Ryan dated for a couple of years while you were in high school. I know you guys had a *thing* for each other. That's it! I promise."

"Why didn't you tell me?"

"I had no idea you would be at the wedding. Ryan never mentioned that you were coming."

"That's because he didn't know. The only reason I was there was because of his mother; she is a very dear friend."

"Whatever. I just assumed the thing between you and him was over *long* ago—"

"There is *nothing* between us!"

"Please... Keri, it's okay. You don't have to hide it from *me*. I saw you before the wedding, craning your neck like a giraffe, following Ryan all over the place. I watched you the entire service. You did everything but stop the wedding. I've never seen someone so nervous and fidgety at a wedding before, except maybe the bride or groom. I knew you needed someone to talk to; someone who knew Ryan; someone you could trust. Who better than his roommate? I knew I was probably the only person on the face of the earth that could help you. Trust me, I didn't want to get involved, but I felt like I owed it to Ryan."

She knew that everything Rex said was true. But so what if it were? Was it a crime to have feelings for someone? It's not like she was going to stalk him. The fact that Rex—someone she hardly knew—had pulled the curtain back on her most private thoughts was embarrassing. "Why didn't you mention it earlier? Why now?

"Listen, I'm sorry. I should have told you. I know it must be hard seeing the man you once loved marry someone else, but people do change, and sometimes, for our own good, we have to let them go. You need to get on with your life."

"But earlier, you said their marriage was doomed. What's that all about?"

"I might have overdramatized it a bit. Emily is a little ditsy, but she's not all bad. And like I said, Ryan will never leave her. So, the best thing you can do is wish them good luck and move on."

Silence filled the car. Rex was right about Ryan not leaving her, or at least the Ryan she once knew, but she just couldn't understand how Ryan could have fallen for someone like her in the first place. Sure, he could have changed, *some*, but Emily was definitely not his type.

How much can a person change?

Rex offered, "Listen, if you need somebody to talk with, or just to listen, I'm always available."

"I just—"

He cut her short. "I've got an idea. Why don't you and I get together again and compare notes. You can tell me what you remember about Ryan, and I will tell you how he has changed. You'll probably see he's not even the same guy you once knew. How about next weekend? I know a great restaurant down in San Diego."

After pausing a moment, the thought of closure sold her. Rex obviously knew Ryan better than anyone. "Okay, sounds great."

Rex walked her to the door. "Listen," she said, "I'm sorry about getting upset with you. I know you were only trying to help me, and I didn't even know it. You are so sweet to even care."

"Don't even think about it. I should have told you. I just felt a little sorry for you the way things turned out."

"Listen, I have to fly Monday, but I'll be back Wednesday night. Give me a call Thursday. I'll need directions to your place in Del Mar."

"No way. I'm not going to make you drive to my place, I'll pick you up."

"Rex, that's a long way for you to drive. I can't ask you to do that."

"I wouldn't think of doing it any other way. I'll call you."

"Okay, if you insist."

They both turned at the sound of a muffled bark coming from inside her condo. "That must be Bill," Rex said.

She looked back to Rex. "How did you know I had a dog named, Bill?"

"Oh... ah... Ryan told me. He said you named him after the Naval Academy's mascot. I thought that was a nice touch."

I knew it! Ryan did get my letter.

A wave of depression rolled over her heart. "Another one of my weak moments, I guess."

"Don't you worry. Everything is going to be fine. After next weekend, you'll feel like a new woman."

"That would be great. Listen, thank you again for everything. And I'm sorry for jumping all over you. I just didn't know."

"No problem. All I want to do is help. I know how tough these things can be. I've had my share of heartbreaks... but that's a story for another day."

"Don't tell me you've been dumped, too?"

"I told you we had a lot in common." They laughed. "Her name was Kate. I'll have to tell you about it someday. I'd better be going."

"Thanks, Rex."

"No problem. I'll call you."

From inside her condo, she heard the throaty growl of the Porsche vaporize into the night. She felt a little embarrassed for the way she had acted but found it hard to accept that Ryan had changed *that* much. She hoped, one day, she would be able to repay Rex for all he was doing to help her.

Bill jumped up, demanding a rub. "Hey little fellow. I missed you."

If Rex knew about Bill, he probably read the letter I wrote Ryan. He and Ryan probably talked about it. That's what friends do. I wonder what Ryan said? Rex must know everything. I'm finally going to get to the bottom of this.

Chapter 26

Rex maneuvered his Porsche down Interstate 5, weaving through traffic like an Olympic downhill skier on a gold-medal slalom run. With his right arm stretched out behind Keri and left elbow propped up on the door, he negotiated his way through traffic using only a two-finger grip on the wheel.

Keri clutched the door handle, her feet pressing hard against the floor, hoping her corpse-like stiffness and eyes as wide as headlights would send a signal to Rex to slow down. Meanwhile, she prayed.

"Am I driving too fast for you?" he asked in a relaxed voice.

"A little." She leaned over and gasped slightly, with widening eyes, seeing the needle on the speedometer well above one hundred miles per hour.

"If it bothers you, I'll slow'er down a little," he called out over the roar of the engine.

"That would be nice."

As their speed synchronized with the flow of traffic, she relaxed her grip on the door handle and eased off the pressure of her foot pushing against the floor.

"I hope you won't think I'm being too forward, but I thought we would go back to my place in Del Mar. That way, we won't have to spend so much time in the car."

After the thrilling drive down the freeway, the thought of not being a crash dummy the rest of the evening sounded like a good idea.

"I didn't know you were a cook and a race car driver." She turned and gave him a sly grin.

He chuckled. "Yeah. I like to think I am—a cook, that is. But I'll let you be the judge." He grinned.

"Your place sounds like a good idea," she said.

"Great!"

She realized that "my place" was also Ryan's place. Although he was gone, the thought of being there brought their worlds closer together. "When are Ryan and Emily due back from their honeymoon?"

"Not until tomorrow. We'll have the whole place to ourselves." An awkward silence followed until he added, "Don't worry. I'm harmless."

"I'm not. Worried, that is... not harmless. I mean, I *am* harmless, but I'm also not worried. Wow! Listen to me."

Rex burst out laughing. "I think I get it."

The life Rex enjoyed was not typical of most young Navy officers. Off duty, he presented an image typical of a high-rolling young real estate broker, lawyer, or maybe even an up-and-coming plastic surgeon seeing how many lipos and implants he could squeeze in before tee time.

His condo was located in the hottest section of Del Mar along the beach north of Fifteenth Street; an area considered a fantasyland of architectural dream houses flying colorful flags fronting a wide sandy beach.

Del Mar is a Southern California beach town offering a rural yet sophisticated feel. The famous Del Mar racetrack, "where the turf meets the surf", is home to thoroughbred racing in a laid-back and fun-loving style. Bordering the Pacific Ocean, with its dramatic coastline views, is the world famous Torrey Pines Golf Course; truly a golfer's paradise.

Rex opened the door to his condo and extended his hand for Keri to go in.

"I love your place," she said.

"Thanks." He tossed his keys on the small table by the front door. "It's not where I want to spend the rest of my life, but it works for now... good location."

He walked over and opened the blinds, revealing a stunning view of the ocean and a beautiful sunset in the making. He slid back the glass door to the balcony.

Keri stepped out and took a deep breath. She could hear the sound of the surf breaking on the shore. "It's beautiful!" The captivating view of the sky beginning its daily transformation of colors from bright blue to eventual darkness with wonderful reds and oranges was breathtaking.

"Yeah. There's nothing like a California sunset."

She stood between Rex and the panoramic view, her arms resting on the railing of the balcony. "You are so lucky to have a view like this."

"I sure am... especially now that you are in it," he said. She turned and smiled, as to thank him for the compliment, and then returned to the view. "I'm going to take care of a few last minute details in the kitchen."

"Do you need any help?"

"No. You stay out here. These sunsets are beautiful but they don't last long. Enjoy it."

Staring out at the ocean, her thoughts moved beyond the horizon and the two-thousand miles of ocean separating her from Ryan. Regret ambushed her, reminding her of her many mistakes and missed opportunities. It started with her mother. She should have never listened to her.

It's all wrong. I should be the one in Hawaii—not Emily.

Her second mistake was not going after him once she moved to California, or sooner. Why hadn't she at least *tried* to stop him from making the most horrible mistake of his life?

Now he's over there—with her—and I'm here, alone.

The beauty of the sunset and the warm feeling of just knowing he was out there made her grasp for the impossible. She closed her eyes and recalled the details of his face from the night she'd talked with him at the wedding. His hair, his eyes, his smile, his lips; everything about him was so beautiful; so perfect.

God, why did you let this happen?

"You getting hungry?" Rex called from the kitchen.

"Starving."

The faint light against the sky faded into black as the sun made its final plunge below the horizon—just as her fantasy was melting into her memory, saved for another day.

She headed back inside. Smelling the food made her aware of her hunger. She took a seat in one of the bar chairs overlooking the kitchen. "I'm impressed," she said.

While out on the balcony, Rex had been busy on the grill. He placed a plate on the counter with two grilled Halibut steaks. "I remember how much you said you liked the Halibut at *The Cannery* last weekend, so I decided to see if I could top their chef. Oh, by the way, it's one of Ryan's favorites. I got the recipe from him."

"Ryan cooks?"

"I don't think he could start a restaurant, but he has a few favorites."

Keri picked up an index card lying on the counter. She recognized Ryan's handwriting. "So, is this the recipe?"

"Yep. Simple enough, even for me."

She read aloud, "Marinate for four hours using soy sauce, ginger, brown sugar, garlic and mustard. Sounds easy enough. Can't wait to taste it."

Rex pulled a large bowl of mixed green salad from the refrigerator along with a small bowl of grated cheese. A pot of rice simmered on the stove.

"Let me help you." Keri walked around the bar into the kitchen. Two plates had already been pulled from the cabinet and placed on the counter.

He pointed to the drawer at the end of the counter. "If you'll grab us some silverware, glasses, and a couple of napkins, I'll put it on the plates."

He lifted the lid off the steaming rice and laid it aside. Holding one plate, he picked up the large spoon, scooped a couple of spoonfuls of rice from the pot, and spread them on the plates. He then placed the steaks on top of the beds of rice.

Keri filled two bowls with salad and set the table. "Looks like we're ready," she said.

He walked over to the table with the two plates, steam rising from the rice. After putting the plates down they both took a seat.

Rex looked across the table at Keri as he placed his napkin in his lap. "Dig in."

She picked up her fork and started to break off a piece of the filet. "It looks wonderful. I'm really impressed." After taking a minute to enjoy her first bite, she said, "It's delicious. Give my regards to the chef."

"Thank you, I will."

"Is Emily a good cook?" She wondered if the woman Ryan married knew her way around the kitchen.

"Are you kidding? She has trouble reading the directions on a TV dinner. But who knows, after a few months, with a little supervision, of course, I'll bet she'll be able to pour a mean can of soup."

"Poor Ryan."

"Don't worry, he's a survivor. He'll be fine."

Emily sounded so wrong for Ryan. Keri knew she could have given him so much more.

Why, Ryan? What were you thinking?

Keri said, "So, when are we going to compare notes… you know… about the old and new Ryan."

"Sure. You go first."

"I was thinking, maybe, you could start by describing the *new* Ryan. I'll tell you when I hear something that doesn't sound like the Ryan I once knew." She knew if she started, Rex might use what she said to fabricate a false image of Ryan. He'd already lied once. Plus, she didn't want to bare her soul about her wonderful memories of Ryan.

After taking a sip, Rex put his glass down. He asked matter-of-factly, "Keri, do you still love Ryan?"

The directness of his question caught her off guard. She looked down at her plate and pushed some rice around with her fork. "I don't know. Part of me wants to, but I know I can't. He's married." She lifted her head. "Rex, I just need to know why? Why would he marry someone like Emily? They're nothing alike."

"Keri, Ryan is not the same person you knew in high school."

"In what ways?"

"By the time I met him, he had finished the Naval Academy. Based on what he told me about the way he grew up, and about you, trust me, Ryan Mitchell has changed."

"What did he tell you about me?" She wanted every detail.

"For starters, he told me you were a sweet girl." He paused, taking another bite of fish.

"Is that all, a 'sweet girl'?"

Rex put his fork down, propped his elbows on the table, and laced his fingers together as he continued chewing. "He told me you were *too* good. I believe his exact words were 'a goody-goody'."

"What is that suppose to mean?" The pitch in her voice raised an octave.

"I believe you know what it means. Remember me telling you how Ryan was socially uncomfortable around girls and didn't like dating?"

"Yeah."

"Well, there's more to it than that."

"Like what?" Keri hung on his every word.

"Although he didn't like dating or being around women he didn't know, at least not at first, he felt the best way to correct the problem was to immerse himself into his fears."

"So, you're saying he dated more to overcome his fear of women."

"In a way."

"What are you trying to say, Rex? Just say it. I'm tired of your not being upfront with me—last weekend, and now this. Quit messing with my mind! I want to know the truth."

"Okay, calm down. I just hate to see you get hurt."

"Look, how can I get hurt any more than I already have? Ryan is married, for God's sake. I just want closure."

"Keri, I hate to be blunt, but Ryan is an animal when it comes to women. It's all he talks about. Before he found Emily, he used to constantly drag me around trying to pick-up girls. Being shut-up like a lab rat for four years probably did it to him."

"Ryan, an animal? How can a person change that much?" she asked. "I find it hard to believe."

"Time has a way of changing a person. I know I've changed, and I'm sure you have, too." Rex looked down humbly as he pushed the rice on his plate into a neat pile. "I'm just glad I'm over all that. I really like Ryan, but I'll have to say, he and I are like night and day. I guess I'm probably more like the old Ryan you knew than he is."

Maybe he wasn't the man she first fell in love with years ago, but in her wildest imaginations she couldn't see Ryan Mitchell as a skirt-chasing womanizer. No way. She stared off into the distance, thinking.

"Penny for your thoughts," Rex said.

"Oh, it's nothing."

"Come on… spill it. You need to get it out."

"I just remember a letter I sent Ryan trying to get back in touch with him… it's really nothing."

Rex rolled his eyes and nodded his head. "I think I know the letter you are referring to."

"You knew about the letter?"

"The letter where you talked about Bill and how you named him after the academy goat?

"Did you read it? Let me guess… you opened Ryan's mail for him?"

"Not this time. He beat me to it." Rex chuckled.

"What *don't* you know about me?"

"Hey, I just happened to be there when he opened the letter. That's when he told me about you and how it seemed like a million years ago. I told him he should at least call you."

"You did?"

"Absolutely! I mean… really. He at least owed you that much, especially after you poured your heart out in all those letters."

"You knew about the other letters, too? So, I assume you read them."

"Ah… I only saw the first one. Ryan just mentioned the others. He decided not to respond to them because he was afraid you might get the wrong idea if he kept writing you."

"He told you that?"

"Let's face it, at the time he was hot on Emily. Why would he want to keep you hanging on? He figured if he didn't respond, you would just go away."

"He said that?"

"I'm sorry Keri, but it is what it is."

"It embarrasses me to think about what I said in all those letters. After he mentioned he had met someone, I had to go and write him back; telling him how my heart was broken and that I always thought we would end up together. Then when he didn't respond, I kept writing. How pitiful I must have sounded." She didn't know whether to cry or scream.

"That's why, when I saw you at the wedding, I felt I could help. I knew once you learned the truth, you'd be over him. I also knew that I was the only person in the world that could save you from yourself. If I didn't do something, I knew you would spend the rest of your life locked in an emotional prison. I really didn't have a choice."

She stared at Rex in amazement.

Is this guy for real?

"I had no idea about Ryan… about him turning into this… *animal*. I guess he could have changed some. I mean, look at who he married. If what you say is true, she's perfect for him."

"Yeah, like I've said, you just need to move on."

For the first time, she started to see Rex in a different light. Maybe he did care about her. The more she thought about it, the *old* Ryan would have never fallen for someone like Emily. She knew she had to let him go.

He's married. He has Emily. I don't need him.
"Do you know what?" she asked.
"What?"
"I wasn't too sure about you when we first met." She looked at him and smiled.
"In what way?"
"I'm not sure."
"So, how do you feel now?"
"Better." Her smile grew. Everything Rex had done hit her at once. "Thank you."
"No problem. I only did what I had to do. You're going to be fine. You just need to bury the past and move on with your life."
They quietly continued to eat the last of their dinner. She finally had the closure she had longed for, thanks to Rex. But she also started to feel something else—something she had not counted on. She no longer saw Rex as a messenger or human conduit for information, but a caring friend, maybe more.
"You keep eating. I'm just going to get something else to drink," he said, rising from his seat. "Can I get you anything?"
"No. I'm fine." She watched him walk away. In her thoughts, she recalled the details of the limited time she had spent with him, all the things he had said, and the way he had acted toward her. He had treated her with respect and attentiveness. He listened to her questions and offered caring responses about Ryan. He knew she had feelings for Ryan, yet he still offered his friendship. Never once had she felt his motives were selfish.
She studied him as he approached the table. Their eyes connected. "What are you thinking about?" he asked. "You look like you're in deep thought."
"Oh nothing, I'm just thinking about how good it feels to finally be free." She smiled.
"I'm happy for you."

She took her napkin from her lap and dabbed it on her lips before placing it neatly underneath the corner of her plate. "That was excellent."

"Did you get enough to eat?" he asked.

"Yes. Thank you."

He reached over and took her plate. "Here, let me get that out of your way." He stacked it on top of his plate and moved them both aside. She checked her watch.

"You don't need to rush off, do you?" he asked.

"It's almost nine o'clock, and you have at least two hours of driving ahead of you."

"Are you kidding? Don't you remember? I'm not only a good cook, but a race car driver, too." They both laughed.

"If you don't mind, maybe I should get you to take me back now." She stood up.

"If you insist." As she reached for the stacked plates on the table, he said, "No... I'll get that later."

"Are you sure?"

"Yes."

"Do you mind if I use your bathroom before we go?"

"Sure. Why don't you use Ryan's bathroom? I'll run to the other one." He pointed, showing her the way. "It's just down the hall."

"Okay."

She turned on the bathroom light and closed the door. She instantly detected the masculine fragrances of shaving cream and men's cologne. The thought of Ryan having—as recently as two weeks ago—stood where she was standing, in some strange way connected her to him.

She gazed at the woman on the other side of the glass—the reversed image of herself. It was the perfect metaphor of her life. The masculine fragrances of his bathroom were common to her. She imagined standing beside him, admiring his tall masculine frame next to her with a towel wrapped around his waist just out of the shower, preparing to shave. The woman on the other side of the glass should have been her. She quickly dismissed the ridiculous illusion and used the toilet.

After washing her hands, her eyes caught the reflection of a white terrycloth robe hanging on the back of the door behind her. She turned and reached for it and pulled it close to her face. She closed her eyes and breathed in, deep and slow, filling her lungs. It smelled of a fresh scent, possibly the lingering fragrance of the soap he'd used during his last shower mixed with the familiar scent of his body oils that the years had surprisingly not taken from her senses. She clung to his robe as though the mere physical contact with it brought them together, one last time. She knew the soft robe she was holding would soon be wrapped around his body—something she longed for herself.

Opening her eyes, she released her grip on the robe and backed away. The robe hung limp, empty, on the hook. Ryan was gone. He belonged to another woman. She knew the best way she could show her love for him was to let him go. God obviously had other plans for her life. She left the bathroom and returned to the den.

"You ready?" Rex asked as she walked back into the den.

"More than ever."

Chapter 27

Rex took it slow and easy on the drive back to Laguna Beach. Flanked by the ocean to their left, a brilliantly-full moon spread its shine across the water.

In the darkness of the car, her thoughts wandered between her past with Ryan and her new—yet evolving—relationship with Rex. A new door had opened. She wondered if the feelings in her heart could be trusted.

Rex wheeled up into her driveway and coasted to a stop, reached down and turned the ignition off. Silence surrounded them. He twisted slightly in his seat and looked her way. His shadowy face was made visible by the outside houselights.

"I'd like to see you again," he said.

"Aren't you leaving for Texas soon?"

"Not for several weeks."

"Well then, just call me. I'll look forward to it."

"Great!" He patted the top of the steering wheel with his left hand, opened his door and moved around to her side. When he arrived, she had already opened the door and was starting to stand. They strolled to the front door.

Butterflies took flight in her stomach as they approached the porch. She wondered if he would try to kiss her. If he did, she was ready.

Once she reached the door, she turned toward him. For a moment, they stood facing each other. She wanted him to kiss her. He stepped closer. She felt his hands move around to her back. The kiss was soft and slow. She pulled back just enough to look into his eyes. She kissed him again, but longer this time. Her body tingled as his hands gently moved up her back. He pulled his head away, hugged her gently, and stepped back. He took her hands in his and took a deep breath, exhaling slowly.

"Thank you for a wonderful evening," he said. "I can't wait to see you again."

"Me, too." She smiled.

"I'll call you," he said. He stepped away and turned to head to his car.

"Okay. Be careful driving home." She turned, unlocked the door, and went inside. She latched the door behind her and stood listening until the engine of the Porsche faded in the distance. She felt satisfied. She turned off the porch light.

Rex had done more than provide her with the information she needed to get closure, he had given her a new life and a new hope. She began to imagine herself with Rex. He was everything she had wanted Ryan to be, and more.

God sure does work in mysterious ways.

* * *

Rex sped away feeling on top of the world. He owned the night, and now, it looked like he owned the little peach from Georgia. "Yeah, baby!"

He popped in a cassette tape and cranked up the volume. The Humpster bellowed out his tunes of romance while Rex joined in, holding his pretend microphone up to his mouth, imagining his being onstage singing to thousands of swooning women.

Knowing the little peach was "in the bag", he needed to celebrate. One of his favorite spots, the Watford Hotel & Resort, Monarch Beach, was only a few miles up the road in Laguna Niguel: a luxury resort hotel on the coast, a great bar, and on a Saturday night at nine forty-five, a nightlife that guaranteed plenty of available women.

Chapter 28

Ryan spent months planning the perfect honeymoon: a seven-day stay in the beautiful Sheraton Maui Resort on Kaanapali Beach. After looking at several destinations, nothing compared to Hawaii. He booked a newlywed package that included everything: hotel, car rental, food, sight-seeing trips, and more. The only drawback, it was nonrefundable.

The first two days exceeded all of his expectations, but on day three his dreamy honeymoon in paradise began unraveling when Emily started her period and was bedridden with severe menstrual cramps—explaining her snappy attitude on the flight over. Laid up in bed, she became bored, whining to be back in California. As she put it, she was tired of "lounging around and doing nothing".

By the time she was up and about, thanks to a "swim with the sharks" TV special, she refused to go anywhere near the water, convinced her bleeding would draw sharks. He tried to be understanding but with her constant complaining about being weak and her generally bitchy attitude, sharks didn't sound like such a bad idea.

After doing everything possible to entertain her, he finally gave in and negotiated to leave two days early on the Friday night red-eye back to Los Angeles. The sudden change in plans cost him two days of his honeymoon special, plus the cost of two full-fare coach tickets to LAX. If he had it to do over, he would have packed up on day three when she first complained. For all practical purposes, that's when the honeymoon ended.

After flying all night, they arrived back in California early Saturday morning and spent most of the day in bed, sleeping.

Sunday morning, first thing, they stopped by the condo in Del Mar to see Rex and check the mail. Ryan hoped to find his letter of acceptance from the airlines. He had applied with two companies, both of which had given him a verbal indication they were interested. Depending on the airline, he knew they would either be moving to Dallas or Atlanta. He had an apartment on hold in Texas and if the Atlanta-based airline hired him, they planned to stay with his mother until they could find their own place. Emily was hoping for Dallas, mostly because she wasn't too keen on getting to know Martha Mitchell.

When they opened the door to the condo, things appeared quiet. "Rex must be out for a run or at the gym," Ryan said.

"I think he's already had his workout," Emily said, holding up a red-laced bra she picked up off the back of the couch. A closer observation revealed a trail of clothes leading to Rex's bedroom, including the bra's matching bikini bottoms.

Rex slithered out of his bedroom looking like road kill. He stood naked, except for a pair of boxer shorts. "Well, well, the newlyweds are home. I didn't expect to see you two until tomorrow."

"For God sake, Rex, put some clothes on," Ryan said.

"Emily doesn't mind. After being with you, I'm sure she's dying to see what a real man looks like."

"What happened to you? You look like crap," Emily said.

A woman's voice groaned from the bedroom, "Rexy, come back to bed?"

He pulled the bedroom door closed. "So, Emily, did you take good care of my buddy on his honeymoon?" He smiled seductively.

"Where's the mail?" Ryan asked.

"Over on the counter. Hey Dude, I'll save you the trouble. We're both going to the Big 'D'."

"Yes!" Emily screamed. She ran over to Ryan and wrapped her arms around him. "We're going to Dallas. I'm so excited! When can we leave?"

"Honey, calm down. I told you, we're leaving Friday.

Ryan pulled the letter from the already opened envelope and read it. "When is your class date? Mine is August 20th."

"Same," Rex said.

"You mean we're in the same class?"

"Yep."

"That's great!"

Ryan folded the letter and slid it back into the envelope. "So, when are you leaving?"

"I'm not in a big hurry. I'll probably wait and leave the first of August. I need to take care of a few things around here before I go."

"That reminds me." Ryan turned to Emily. "I need to call and confirm our apartment in Texas and let them know we'll be arriving on July 1st. They were nice enough to hold a one-bedroom for me until Wednesday."

"Dude? One bedroom?" He raised his hands. "Where am I going to sleep?"

"Rex, you're full of it."

"Hey, that's okay. I don't mind sleeping between you two."

Ryan turned to Emily. "Honey, let me run to the bathroom before we go."

* * *

When Ryan headed for the bathroom, Rex eased over closer to Emily. She couldn't help but notice that his boxers were not doing the best job of hiding his manhood.

"So, you cut your honeymoon a little short," Rex said. "What's wrong, did you miss me?"

"Rex, get real. I'm married."

He ran his hand slowly down her left arm, pausing to adjust the solitaire diamond on her finger. "That didn't seem to stop you from enjoying our little going away kiss at the wedding." He moved closer and whispered. "Emily, why don't you just admit it. You want me, and you know it."

"Have you lost your mind?" She stepped back. "Ryan might see you. Why don't you go take care of little miss prissy pants."

"Oh, how sweet." He chuckled. "You're jealous, that's it." Rex eased away at the sound of a toilet flushing. "Don't you worry, when we get to Texas there will be plenty of opportunities." He winked at her.

Ryan emerged from the bathroom moving at a quick pace. "Rex, I'll call you tomorrow and we can head over to the base."

"Sounds good, Brah." Ryan turned to leave, but Emily delayed long enough for Rex to lock eyes with her. "I'll see *you* in Texas."

* * *

The drive back to her parent's house was quiet. Emily knew Ryan was busy going over a mental checklist of every hour, of every day, for the upcoming week. Her mind, free to roam, wandered off into forbidden places.

The scene back in the apartment was her first stop. If she did make herself available, would Rex *really* risk sleeping with her? Surely not, she thought. He would never jeopardize his friendship with Ryan.

She took another step into her fantasy and asked herself, if alone with Rex, what would *she* do? She closed her eyes. Her mind recalled the image of him in his boxers: tanned, rock hard abs, and...

"How big does it need to be?" Ryan asked.

"What? How big? What are you talking about?"

"The truck. Do you think an eighteen footer is too big?"

"How should I know?" The last thing she wanted to think about was a truck.

"Sometime tomorrow, we need to sit down and look at what we plan to take with us."

"Yeah, sure. Whatever."

Ryan turned and looked at her. "I thought you were excited about all this?"

"I am. I just have a headache. I guess I'm still hung over from the trip. I'll feel better tomorrow."

"You looked like you were in another world. Are you sure you're okay?" Ryan reached over and massaged the back of her neck.

"I'll be fine. I was just thinking about what it's going to be like living in Texas, just the two of us."

And Rex.

"It'll be great." He put his hand back on the wheel. "Just like your friend J.R.: A whole new world of exciting opportunities await."

"Yeah." The thought of Rex lingered. Something about him intrigued her.

Chapter 29

Ryan knew the move to Texas would be Emily's first trip east of the California state line. Having spent her entire life in Southern California, his primary focus for the next thirty days would be to help his new bride mentally prepare for the inevitable culture shock he knew was imminent. Trying to explain Texas to a person who had spent their entire life in beautiful Southern California would be hard enough, but trying to describe Texas in the middle of the summer—there were no words.

By the end of business on Wednesday he had officially resigned from the Navy, sold his old car, and—with Rex's help—had everything organized and ready to load into the eighteen-foot rental truck he had reserved to pick up the next morning. They planned on spending most of Thursday loading and launch-out on the three-day drive to Texas early Friday morning.

When the moving truck wheeled into the driveway, it must not have dawned on Emily that with one truck and one car she would be expected to drive her car behind the truck. Once she put two and two together, she screamed. "I am not driving all the way to Texas—alone!"

Although they had reviewed the plan at least a thousand times, for some reason she hadn't made the connection.

After an intense twenty minutes of arguing, realizing he was losing valuable time, and Emily was not about to budge, Ryan returned the truck to the rental company and swapped it for the largest trailer the car could pull. Emily's parents agreed to store the things they couldn't fit into the trailer.

He woke early Friday morning, slipped out of bed, and headed for the kitchen. He hoped a strong cup of coffee would help prepare him for Emily. So far, married life had not been what he'd imagined. The honeymoon was a disaster, and—since they returned—they argued at least daily about something. The thought of being locked up in a car with her for twenty-two hours was daunting, at best.

He was sipping his coffee, contemplating the details of the next month, when Emily bounced into the kitchen as excited as a four-year-old at Christmas.

"Good morning, Sweetie," she said. "Are you ready for our great adventure?"

"Ready to go." The change in her attitude amazed him. He was afraid to question it—so he didn't. He only hoped it would last until they reached Texas.

The cross-country continued to find Emily excited and playful. She sang, laughed, and marveled at the Arizona desert as they rolled along the barren freeways. She dreamed out loud about their future and how wonderfully happy they would be. Each motel stop became a romantic rendezvous—glorious nights and early morning surprises made up for the sexless "honeymoon from hell". Each morning she was up early, eager to grab a quick breakfast and hit the road, like some trucker being paid by the load.

Ryan felt satisfied on the surface, but—like a sailor might sense a storm brewing by the smell of the air, or the way animals scurry about in fear when there appears to be no sign of visible danger—he had his concerns.

It all started when the dusty car and loaded-down trailer finally rolled up in front of the apartment complex in Bedford, Texas. Emily's first words let him know he was in trouble.

"Is this it?" she asked.

"I'm sure it's not as bad as it looks," he lied.

During the next few days, the *idea* of Texas was replaced with reality. The small one-bedroom apartment he had rented, sight unseen, primarily because of location and price, was smaller and older than he had imagined. Located beside a major freeway interchange, the merciless hum of traffic and occasional diesel horns blaring at all times of the day and night, cut through the paper-thin walls and poorly sealed windows like a knife through hot butter. The air-condition compressor ran constantly, grinding and thumping like a jet engine trying to overcome the hellish summer heat. But even the compressor wasn't loud enough to drown out the barking dog on one side, and the bawling baby on the other.

With the air-conditioner set on MAX COLD, the temperature in the apartment seldom dropped below seventy-five. Thank God there was a pool.

Emily quickly grew homesick for California. She didn't know a soul and once school started, Ryan's training schedule robbed her of his full attention. She soon grew cold and distant toward him. No longer did she dote on him as she once did. Her bubbly, cheerful, fun-loving attitude vaporized with the heat, replaced by constant flurries of negative comments and complaints.

She drew inward becoming despondent, always teetering on the edge of depression. Ryan bore the steadily growing burden of challenges and pressure from his school and from his new wife's growing bitterness and unhappiness with her new life. Each week of the five-week-long training program presented Ryan with new challenges, mostly at home.

Always there to offer his support and encouragement, Rex would say, "If she gives you any crap, just dump her. Send her packing back to her momma where she belongs."

For Rex, being in Dallas—a major flight attendant training base for the airline—offered many opportunities. Like shooting fish in a barrel, he found the big-haired Southern speaking women from Texas an interesting novelty and a relatively easy challenge. "Picking up cowgirls at the local saloon," as he often bragged, "is about as easy as it gets."

With one week left in training, assignments were out. Ryan approached the bulletin board where a piece of paper hung listing the names of each student and their initial assignments.

Dallas was his first choice but knew it was highly unlikely. Only on occasion were new-hires assigned anywhere other than

New York. Practically all the available slots at the better bases were taken by those pilots who had already "done their time" in New York. However, with each class, one or two of the better assignments did slip through.

He heard the groans and expected expletives as pilots located their names and assignments. He was searching the list at a distance, far enough to satisfy any eye exam, when he heard a "Yes!" rise from among the huddle. Everyone turned to see who might have been blessed by the gods in crew planning.

Rex stood beaming. "I got it! Yes!" His arms were raised as if he had won first place in an Olympic marathon. "LA here I come!"

When the crowd thinned, Ryan's eyes zoomed back to the list: MITCHELL – LGA (New York). He sighed. Studying the list, he noticed one other new-hire had been assigned ORD (Chicago), but everyone else, except Rex, was headed to New York.

His thoughts turned to Emily. Although she was aware of the strong possibility of his being assigned temporarily to New York, he was concerned about how she would react when she put two and two together, realizing she would be spending *at least* the next six months in Dallas—alone. He should have never mentioned the *possibility* of his being assigned to Dallas.

He grabbed Rex by the arm. "I'm going to New York."

"Yeah. I saw it. Sorry, Dude," he said, not sounding too concerned; obviously still basking in the thought of his returning to California.

"Thanks for the sympathy."

"I'll bet Emily's going to be one pissed-off female."

Rex had been around the apartment enough to witness the slow transformation in Emily's behavior. He even witnessed a few of her little tantrums.

"Dude, when are you planning to hit her with the news?"

"I guess when I get home."

"Good idea. I definitely wouldn't call her. You want me to come over? My being there might keep her from going ballistic."

"Thanks, but I don't exactly think you being there to tell her about your LA assignment would be a good thing."

"I guess you're right. She might want to pack up and come with me."

Ryan scowled at Rex's comment. "This is not the time for jokes. I've got a crisis on my hands."

"Sorry Dude. Let me know if there's anything I can do. I gotta run. I need to make a few phone calls back home and tell everybody the good news."

"Yeah, you do that," Ryan said. He knew Emily was going to have a melt-down even though they had discussed the unlikelihood of a Dallas assignment many times.

The short drive to the apartment was a blur as his mind played out ways to tell her the news and how she might react. There was no easy way to do it.

He pulled into the apartment parking lot. Being mid-afternoon, spaces were plentiful. Within seconds after turning off the ignition, the boiling heat engulfed the interior of his car. He opened the car door, greeted by an even stronger blast of heat.

He wondered what mood he would find her in? Possibly she'd be relaxing in the pool, but more than likely, he'd find her in front of the TV watching her depressing melodramatic soap operas. It's where she spent most weekday afternoons. He argued that filling her brain with such trash only made it worse. She defended her addiction with the comment, "I'll have you know, these shows are the only glimpse of freedom I have outside this God-forsaken place you dumped me."

The logic of her rationalizations worried him the most. The little he had watched these daytime serial dramas had proven to reveal nothing more than is presented in any typical paperback romance novel. The story lines all weave intricate, convoluted, sometimes confusing tales of characters who have affairs, meet mysterious strangers, fall in love, and are swept off their feet by dashing, yet treacherous lovers. They sneak around engaging in adulterous affairs keeping their audiences returning to find out who is sleeping with whom; who has betrayed whom; who is having whose baby; and so on. He didn't understand how she could feed her mind and emotions this type of garbage and not be affected in a negative way.

Cooped-up for a month with little outlet for exercise, she started to look bloated. Seeing her lounging around the pool in her bikini no longer gave him the thrill it once had. It amazed him how she was able to put on so much weight in such a short period of time. She must have been starving herself while they dated.

Since they'd been in Texas, she hardly ever wore make-up, and, except for her occasional morning outing to the local shopping mall, her uniform for the day consisted of either a T-shirt with gym shorts, or a T-shirt over a bathing suit.

The door to the apartment opened into a small foyer separated from the den. The sound of the squeaky door was muffled by the steady hum of the air-conditioner's fan. After closing the door, he heard a woman's pleading voice. "I don't love him anymore. Our marriage means nothing to me. I love you."

With the shades drawn, in an attempt to knock-off a few degrees of heat, the apartment was likened to a movie theater. Emily sat curled up on the couch, engrossed in the lives of her "TV people" as though they were her beloved friends.

He glanced around the apartment seeing that no attempt had been made to tidy up the place since he last saw it at 5:00 a.m. Dishes were piled-up in the sink from the previous night's meal. The coffee pot from breakfast sat half-full, and an opened carton of milk looked to be souring on the counter. The stale smell of dirty laundry mixed with the odor of old garbage made him want to gag. He noticed a soda can and an opened bag of chips on the end table beside Emily.

He walked through the darkened room unnoticed. "Did you have a good day?" he asked with a forced enthusiasm.

Without as much as a simple turn of her head in his direction, she offered, "Is that possible?" Her voice so faint, it could barely be heard over the breathy romantic dialogue of the beautiful young woman on TV, pleading with her lover to leave his wife and take her with him.

Ryan made his way into the narrow kitchen flipping on the light switch. "Is that necessary," she said.

He lifted the carton of milk to find it half-empty and slightly warm, as he suspected. The contents of the refrigerator showed the need for a trip to the grocery store.

He emptied the cold remains of the morning coffee grounds and began washing the dishes. The cold water felt soothing.

Within a matter of fifteen minutes, the kitchen was clean and neat with everything put away. He wiped the counters with a damp dishtowel then tied off the full garbage bag, replacing it with a new one. He glanced at the TV to see the credits running accompanied by the somber music signaling an end to another day of afternoon sex and seduction. He felt there was no better time to drop the bomb.

"We got our assignments today," he said.

She seemed to show interest getting up from the couch. "What did you get? Dallas I hope. Please... tell me you got Dallas."

"I told you Dallas would be a long shot."

"New York?" she asked. He nodded. "I should have known!" She flopped back down on the couch.

He walked over and sat beside her. "Listen, it won't be that bad. It's just six months, and then I should be able to get back to Dallas," he said, trying to sound confident.

"Ryan," she tilted her head. "Let's get real. Look at me. Do you think I'm going to last six months in this hellhole?"

Those were thoughts he had entertained more than once. "We can make it. Maybe if you get a job, like we had originally planned, you could make some friends and get your mind on something positive. You *know* we could use the money."

"I've tried." Her gaze returned to the TV as though seeking sympathy from one of her friends.

"I'll help you. I have a week off after I finish school. We can spend it together, job hunting. There's got to be something out there you would like to do."

His mood changed to one of compassion sprinkled with affection. "Emily, I love you. I know we can make this work. It's going to all work out just like you imagined. Everything is going to be fine. The hard part is over, and it's only six months."

"Okay. But only if you promise to help. I just don't like looking by myself."

His sensitivity must have triggered something. "Listen, I have one more week and then my check-ride. After that, I'm all yours."

She took one of his hands. "Ryan, do you really think things are going to work out?"

"I know they are! Trust me. Everything is going to be fine. You'll see." He kissed her. She smiled.

The week passed quickly. Emily had even started to show signs of personal revival in her attitude. She began jogging and exercising in the gym at the apartment complex which resulted in her taking more pride in the appearance of the apartment. The idea of a new life must have given her a fresh start.

The week they spent job hunting turned out to be a needed breath of fresh air for their marriage. Intimacy and the physical contact they both craved returned. They jogged together in the mornings, had coffee at a local coffeehouse, and spent the remainder of the day pursuing leads.

On Thursday, as Ryan shuffled through the mail, a letter caught his eye. Addressed to "Resident", he almost tossed it, but the quality of the envelope and professional presentation intrigued him.

Dear Resident:

Career opportunities await as "Excalibur Homes", a regional homebuilder and subsidiary of an Atlanta-based national conglomerate, expands into the Metroplex.

Consider this your invitation to stop by and see what we have to offer. We are looking for smart, aggressive, and professionally minded leaders to join our team in the Dallas-Fort Worth area. Six-figure salaries possible. Sales and non-sales positions are available.

Sincerely,

Donald Towers
V.P. of Sales, Southwestern Division

"Hey honey, look at this," Ryan said.

Peering over Ryan's shoulder, Emily read the letter silently. "Do you think I can do that?"

"Are you kidding? It sounds perfect... and look at that." He pointed to "Six-figure salaries possible."

"I guess we can go check it out tomorrow."

After meeting with Donald Towers, he offered Emily a position as the sales manager for one of their residential developments. "You are just what we were looking for," he told her. She accepted.

The base pay, not including the possible commissions, exceeded Ryan's and her expectations—a giant boost to her confidence. Ryan found it hard to believe that she was able to land such a lucrative job with no previous experience in real estate. He also found it strange that Mr. Towers asked very little, if anything, about her past work experience. It was as though all he was looking for was a pretty face.

With the new job came a new outlook on life for Emily. All Ryan had to do now was survive the next six months of separation and pray that Emily could hang on until he could get an assignment back to Dallas. However, based on what he had seen so far—the honeymoon; the move; and only six weeks in Dallas—the next six months were guaranteed to be full of surprises.

Chapter 30

Keri sat by the phone in her Laguna Beach condo waiting anxiously for Rex to call. The chances of his being assigned to the West Coast—a very senior base—was highly unlikely, but God owed her.

Regardless of his initial assignment, Rex would eventually return to the West Coast, but she needed him in her life now, more than ever.

The phone rang…

"Hello," she said.

"LA here I come! I'm coming home!"

"You got it? Fantastic!" Keri tried to contain her excitement, but she couldn't. "I am so happy for you—"

He interrupted, "For us."

"Yes, for us!" she agreed.

Thank you, God.

She had missed him and needed him. "When will you be coming home?"

Home. That feels good.

"I only have one more week of training, then a week off before I start flying."

For the first time, stability was returning to her life. Rex had given her hope and a reason to move on.

Sounding a bit somber, Rex interjected, "Ryan's assignment didn't turn out so well."

"Where's he going?"

"New York."

"How is he taking it?"

"Ryan's good. It's not him, it's Emily; She's the one that almost lost it."

"What do you mean 'lost it'?" Her voice rose with curiosity.

"Ryan and I both knew she would freak—possibly leave him—if they tagged him for New York. But somehow he was able to encourage her to pull herself together. She's fine now. She found a great job and is stoked."

"That's good."

"Yeah. That guy is amazing."

Keri sensed a tug on her heart. Ryan was an amazing guy, but that was not what caused her heart to jump; it was hearing that Ryan was having trouble with Emily. One side of her—the selfish dark side—hoped it was the beginning signs of a marriage headed for divorce, while the other side of her knew Ryan would do whatever was necessary to make his marriage work.

Thanks to Rex, she now realized that she and Ryan were not meant to be. She was happy for him and wished him the best, but she had fallen for Rex.

"That's great. Well, hurry up and get home. I can't wait to see you."

"Me, too." Rex hesitated, then said, "Keri?"

"Yes?" She sensed a change in his voice. He sounded serious.

"I love you," he said.

She hadn't expected it. Hearing his words, 'I love you', opened a part of her heart she had not yet opened to him.

"I love you, too, Rex." Her response felt so natural. With three simple words, she felt their relationship jump to a new level—simple, but powerful words able to synchronize two hearts in commitment to each other.

* * *

After hanging up, Rex felt a surge of power.

Yes! Right where I want her. Shouldn't be too much longer, now. The good ones always take a little more time.

Good ones, he thought. Unlike the other women he'd been with, this one was different. Most of his relationships were short: a night; a week; at most, a month—any longer and there was the risk of the woman becoming "clingy and demanding".

And when it came to living together, a female roommate totally violated his principles. Experience had taught him that romance often dies when lovers become roommates. Sleeping together for sex is quite a different commitment than sleeping together for rest. However, he wasn't sure if the little peach might be worth making an exception. What did he have to lose? It's not like he'd have to stop seeing other women.

Speaking of other women...

It was Friday night, and he didn't want to keep the cowgirls waiting. Time to celebrate. A quick shower; grab a bite to eat; then mozy on down to the local saloon and herd up a lost calf, or two.

Giddy up cowboy!

Chapter 31

With school complete, Rex flew back to California and insisted, without much resistance from Keri, they celebrate at *The Cannery*—the location of their first date.

During dinner, the conversation centered on how their relationship had grown in ways neither of them had anticipated. She embarrassingly told him of her initial reluctance to date him but assured him of how thankful she was now that she had. He looked into her eyes and shared with her how attracted he had been to her from the moment he took her arm and walked her down the aisle at Ryan's wedding.

Her heart raced the entire evening like a schoolgirl experiencing her first crush. She felt satisfied when she was with him, never wanting their time together to end.

While driving home from the restaurant, she felt a closeness to him she had not felt before. Thoughts concerning the future pushed into her mind. She fantasized about becoming Mrs. Rex Dean. She liked it.

Keri Dean.

Her body grew warm. She gazed over at him, wondering when, or if, the relationship would become more intimate. Up until now, the extent of their physical involvement had been limited to heavy kissing. Since Rex didn't appear to be a run-of-the-mill horny guy looking for a one-night stand, a few subtle hints or flirtatious suggestions might be needed if she wanted the relationship to progress to the next level—something she'd been careful *not* to do, so far. Secretly, she hoped he would stay the night and make love to her.

After easing into the driveway, they sat for a moment. The silence aroused her. "Would you like to come in?" she asked.

"I don't know. It's getting kind of late and I haven't even unpacked."

Maybe he's not ready. I'm sure he's tired and needs some time alone.

Rex opened his door. "Let me walk you to the door, and then I'd better head out."

Before he left, he asked, "Are you off tomorrow?"

"Yes," she said, hopeful he would suggest they spend the day together.

"Great. I'll give you a call."

He sounded tired. She put her arms around him and pulled him close. "You must be worn out from training."

"Yeah, it was exhausting... all that studying. But, the hardest part was being away from you. I missed you so much."

She pulled back and gazed into his eyes. "You are so sweet. I love you."

"I love you, too." He kissed her tenderly on the lips. She felt his body up against her. The kiss grew as his hands explored her back. She wanted him more than ever.

She wanted to say, *Please, Rex, stay with me tonight.*

If only she had the nerve to tell him how she felt.

Chapter 32

April 1985
Dallas, Texas

Emily blossomed during the eight months Ryan spent in New York. Within two months after he left, she'd risen from Sales Manager of one of Excalibur's residential developments, to Director of Sales for the entire Dallas-Fort Worth Metroplex area: eleven projects with over five-thousand residential units.

Her performance quickly gained the attention of both the management executives at Excalibur and their parent company in Atlanta. She attended monthly sales meetings in Atlanta and one national awards banquet, which included a ride on the corporate jet and a private dinner with the CEO of the parent company.

Two months before Ryan's transfer back to Dallas, he and Emily signed the papers on their first home located in one of Excalibur's better neighborhoods. They were able to buy it at a significant discount because of her employment with the company.

Although Ryan's probationary salary paled in comparison to Emily's six-figure paycheck, on his return to Dallas and after close scrutiny of their personal finances—which Emily had been managing while he was away—revealed frightening results. Where he had expected to see large surpluses, he instead found less than a thousand dollars in their checking account and numerous credit card balances totaling multiple thousands.

A closer examination produced pages and pages of charges for impulsive purchases: household furnishings, restaurant charges, fine-retail-clothing boutiques, and more.

She must be banking her paycheck in a private account.

In the days that followed, he learned that if he ever challenged her concerning their finances, she was quick to snap at him like a Rottweiler defending a prize bone. She'd made it perfectly clear, except for the mortgage payment, "The money I make is mine to do with as I please," she would say.

With the financial problems came more heated arguments, killing any lingering hope of intimacy between them. Ryan felt like a cornered rat staring up at a coiled viper, its forked tongue darting in and out, testing the air as it prepared to strike.

The next strike came in the form of car payments. With multiple credit card accounts maxed to their limits and their checking account short on cash, needed auto repairs forced them to dump their older cars for two new ones—both financed.

Alone, he stared out the kitchen window.

A beautiful house, two new cars, and good jobs. Why do I feel broke?

Any thought of saving for retirement or realizing his dream of starting a family—thanks to Emily and the tens-of-thousands of dollars of debt she'd accumulated—remained just that: a dream.

His only fragment of hope resided in the fact that within a few months he would complete his year of probation. The increase in his salary would allow him to manage the basic household expenses without Emily's help.

He breathed an exasperating breath, exhaling slowly. With a sip of coffee and help from the refreshing rays of the morning sun, he surrendered to the circumstances of the life he had been dealt. After all, *How could it get any worse?* Then the phone rang.

"Is this Ryan Mitchell?" asked the voice at the other end.

"Yes." Placing his coffee cup down on the kitchen counter, he glanced at the digital clock on the microwave: 10:47. Emily had left for work two hours earlier.

"I don't mean to alarm you. My name is Dr. Wilson. I'm your mother's doctor, here in Atlanta." The doctor's voice was calm and professional. "She listed you as a medical contact."

"Is everything okay?" Ryan asked.

"Your mother just left my office. Everything is fine. However, I felt prompted to advise you as soon as possible about your mother's condition."

"What kind of condition? I thought you said everything was fine."

"She has been having trouble with her memory. Her supervisor at work encouraged her to make an appointment with her doctor. After meeting with your mother, I believe she has early signs of Alzheimer's disease."

"Are you sure?"

"You need to understand, there is no definite way to diagnose the disease," Doctor Wilson said. "The only way to know positively is after a person dies. During the autopsy, the brain tissue can be tested for the presence of plaques and tangles which is our only positive sign the disease exist. All we can offer now, as doctors, is to make a diagnosis of probability."

His voice sounded like an older man, possibly in his late fifties or early sixties. His manner was caring and patient.

"There *are* tests that can be conducted at specialized centers capable of diagnosing the disease correctly ninety percent of the time, but the behavior of a person is the most revealing test."

"What indications make you believe she has the disease?"

"While we visited, I asked her a few basic things about her life—her family, her work, the names of people she worked with, and her children. The red light went off when she hesitated while trying to tell me your name—only a few seconds—but long enough to cause me some concern. She also had difficulty remembering her telephone number and a few other things."

"What do you recommend?"

"I believe you are her only living relative."

"Yes."

"It's early, but you'll probably need to be thinking about making arrangements for her care. More than likely, her employer will, at some point, ask her to stop working."

"How fast does this type of thing progress?"

"It varies from person to person. On average, Alzheimer patients live from eight to ten years after they are diagnosed, though the disease can last for as long as twenty years or more," he said.

"But my mother is still relatively young. I thought this sort of thing only happened to folks much older than her."

"Based on statistics, the disease usually begins after the age of sixty and is more likely to occur in women than men. And you're right; it is more prevalent in older people. Only about five percent of men and women between sixty-five and seventy-four have it, but it attacks nearly half of those eighty-five and older."

"Well, Doctor Wilson, I appreciate your call. I am off for a couple of days. I think I will fly over to Atlanta tomorrow and visit with Mom."

"I think that would be a great idea. Call my office if I can be of help."

"Thank you, again." Ryan hung-up.

He stood staring out the bay window in the kitchen admiring the new flower beds Emily had recently hired a landscaper to put in. All of his problems seemed insignificant, except one: money. How much would it cost to care for his mother? What would Emily say about having her move in with them? These were real concerns.

His mother couldn't survive alone without her job, and she was too young to apply for Medicaid. He had no choice; he and Emily would have to find a way to make it work. There was no one else.

Already living hand-to-mouth, hiring a full-time professional caregiver in Atlanta was out of the question. His only choice would be to move her to Dallas. Emily would have to understand the seriousness of the situation and be willing to help. It would take a coordinated effort and huge sacrifice, on his *and* Emily's part, to make it work. As the disease worsened, they would need to adjust their work schedules so someone would be home to watch her. Emily might even have to quit working.

We can't afford to lose Emily's income, not now, especially after what she has done.

Each attempt he made to mentally construct a logical plan of attack took him down another path filled with more problems and concerns; a mine field of unknowns he didn't want to consider.

Regardless of what he decided, one thing was for certain, Emily would be home in a matter of hours. Breaking the news to her was certain to uncork a whole new set of difficulties.

Chapter 33

That afternoon, Ryan stood in the garage as Emily's car pulled into the driveway. Their eyes met without any further greeting. Emily turned off the car, opened the door, and stepped out. As she walked toward the house, for a moment, he remembered the playful, fun-loving girl he had fallen madly in love with less than two years ago.

"What's wrong with you?" she asked. Her brash tone quickly vaporized his memories.

Although he and Emily were emotionally disconnected, a stranger could have detected Ryan's pain.

"It's my mother. I received a call from her doctor in Atlanta. He thinks she has Alzheimer's."

She strode past him in disinterested silence, opened the door, and went into the kitchen. He followed her.

"Isn't that the thing where you go crazy or something?" Her response seemed distant and cold. Emily hardly knew his mother. The one and only time they met was at the wedding.

"Not really. It has more to do with a person's ability to remember. It's a form of dementia." He closed the door behind him.

She put her purse on the counter, opened the refrigerator, and grabbed a bottle of water. "So, what's going to happen to her?" She twisted the top off the plastic bottle and took a seat at the kitchen table.

"That's what we need to talk about." Ryan pulled out a chair and sat down.

She raised her eyebrows and shrugged her shoulders. "We're talking, aren't we?" She flipped through the first few letters in the stack of mail on the table, taking a drink from the bottle of water.

"Emily. This is serious. We're going to have to make some big decisions soon."

"What? Is she about to die or something?" She looked up at Ryan, showing little concern in her face.

It was obvious she felt no differently for his mother than she would a stranger. He couldn't decide if it was her lack of concern for his mother, or her lack of sensitivity to him that hurt the most. Tired of fighting his emotions, he decided to tell her the facts and be done with it.

"Alzheimer's does shorten a person's life, but the most difficult aspects of the disease are how it affects a person while they are living," he explained. "As the disease progresses, it robs the victim of their ability to care for themselves. This is where we come in."

"I hope you're not thinking we're going to pay someone to take care of your mother."

"Listen, it's obvious we can't afford to pay for professional care, but she's too young to qualify for Medicaid. That's why when she's forced to stop working, she has to move in with us." He braced for the emotional explosion.

"What!" With raised eyebrows, she leaned toward him and poked her index finger hard against the table with each word she spoke. "Your mother is *not* moving into this house! Do you hear me? Not... I repeat... NOT moving into this house!"

"Calm down," he said, leaning away from her, holding up the palms of both hands. "It's not something that's going to happen immediately—"

She slapped the table with her palm, "Listen to me! It's not something that is going to happen—EVER!"

"Emily, it's inevitable!" His voice tone grew louder. "It's just a matter of time. And when the time comes, I don't see that I have a choice."

She stood quickly, sending her chair flying backwards. Putting both hands on the table, leaning down, her eyes boring into his like lasers. "Here's the only choice you have. It's either me, or her! I don't have the time or the patience to be somebody's nurse, and the last thing I'm planning to do is spend my hard-earned money to take care of your mother. What has she ever done for us?"

"If I had the money it would be a different situation, but I don't." He paused. "Thanks to you."

"Oh! So, now you're saying it's my fault we have a nice house, drive new cars, and a descent life! Well, if I had left it up to you, do you know what we'd have? Nothing! I'd still be living in some dumpy apartment, driving a broken down car, and praying I could make it to the grocery store and back without the piece of junk breaking down on me." She leaned down and picked up the chair she had sent flying.

Grocery store? When did going to the grocery store ever concern her?

"Please, Emily, I don't want to argue with you. I just want to do what's right for my mother. We're going to have to make some decisions soon. To be honest, I don't think we have many options. We can either scale down to the point where we can pay someone else to care for her in Atlanta, or we can keep everything the way it is, for as long as we can, and move her in with us."

"Well, I'm not 'scaling down' and I'm not giving up my lifestyle, either, so it looks like your only decision is who you want to live with: me or your crazy mother." She shoved her chair up against the table and walked away.

His biggest question was how long could his mother continue to work?

Hopefully, long enough for Emily to get used to the idea of her moving in with them.

Chapter 34

When Ryan woke the next morning, Emily was gone.

He'd heard her stirring earlier, but instead of taking a chance and subjecting himself to more of her verbal abuse, he played opossum and eventually dozed off. When he heard the kitchen door to the garage slam closed, he knew it was safe to get up.

Today he planned to hop a flight to Atlanta and visit his mother. He wanted to see for himself if Dr. Wilson was right about her memory. If Wilson was right and his mother was in the beginning stages of Alzheimer's, he needed to have a plan. He couldn't worry about Emily; he didn't have a choice.

After he showered, dressed, and packed a bag, he headed to the DFW airport. Flights between Dallas and Atlanta ran frequently. Even with the one-hour time change, he figured he would be in Atlanta by noon. He wanted to be there when she came home from work.

* * *

With his window down, the sound of gravel crunched beneath the tires on his rental car as it rolled slowly up the driveway.

To his surprise, his mom was sitting on the front porch. He glanced at his watch: two o'clock. When he walked up on the porch, she greeted him with a big smile and open arms. "Ryan! What are you doing here? You should have warned me you were coming."

"I wanted to surprise you." She looked great. They hugged and then he joined her, sitting in the familiar high-backed wooden rocker next to the swing.

"Can I get you some iced tea?" she asked.

"No, I'm fine. How are you feeling?"

Sounding surprised he would ask, she said, "Me? Never felt better."

"I thought you would be at work."

"I decided to take the day off. I sure am glad I did now that you are here."

The swing slowly glided back and forth, hanging by chains mounted in the ceiling of the porch. Crossed at the ankles, her feet rhythmically motored the swing like a metronome set at its slowest speed.

Beneath her cooking apron she wore a dress with a flower pattern. "You been cooking?" Her apron was a dead give-away something tasty was in the oven.

"Your favorite," she said with a smile. "Apple pie, just the way you like it."

Ryan smiled. He could almost smell the pie baking and imagined how it would taste, piled high with vanilla ice cream. It had been a long time since he had eaten anything home cooked.

"I can't tell you how good that sounds," he said.

"Well, you can eat the whole pie all by yourself. And if you want more, I'll bake you another one. How about that?" She took a sip of her sweet tea.

"Makes me feel like I'm eighteen again."

"So tell me, how are you and Keri doing?"

"You mean Emily?" He corrected her.

This must be what Dr. Wilson was talking about.

"Oh yes, Emily. Of course. What was I thinking?"

"We're doing fine," he lied.

As long as we don't talk to each other.

"She wrote me."

"She did?" Shocked by her words, he asked, "What did she say?" He could not imagine why Emily would write his mother.

"She told me how much she enjoyed being a flight attendant." Her eyes widened and she asked, "Do you two ever fly together?"

Her confusion alarmed him, but for now, he decided to play along. "No. We rarely fly together."

"That's too bad."

"Yeah."

Unexpected thoughts entered his mind: thoughts of Keri and what it would be like to fly with her—to be married to her. The sound of her name stirred-up long-forgotten emotions. For a moment his thoughts drifted into the past. Hearing his mom talk about her, and the old wooden rocker—the swing where he had spent many evenings with Keri—brought back feelings that only being home could have given him—good ones.

Then he remembered Keri's letter and the shocking news that she had met someone; an airline pilot named Bill. The thought was like a steel wall suddenly dropping, dividing his pleasurable thoughts from the painful challenges ahead of him. Reality slapped him back into the present when he thought of Emily and the reason he had come to Atlanta.

He had no doubts, now, that he would need to start working on a plan to move his mother to Dallas. Based on Dr. Wilson's professional opinion, and what he was seeing, he probably had six months, maybe less.

"How long can you stay?" she asked. "You know I want you to stay as long as you can."

"Mom, I received a call from Doctor Wilson."

"*My* Doctor Wilson?"

"Yes."

"He is such a sweet man." She looked off at the tall oak in the front yard, as a squirrel scratched its way up the bark. "Why would Doctor Wilson call you?"

"He told me about your condition. He suggested I visit with you."

"Oh, that. It's really nothing to worry about. I'm just getting old, and like all old folks, we just forget things now and then." The swing continued to glide with her gentle push.

"He says you have the beginning signs of Alzheimer's." Ryan sat quietly.

She glanced down at the floor and then back at Ryan; like he'd discovered something she'd been hiding.

"It's really nothing you need to worry about. I'm sure I'll be fine; just a part of getting old." She tried to laugh, but instead, her eyes grew watery. "I started forgetting a few things that I knew I should remember. And then last Sunday..." She chuckled. "I woke up, dressed, and drove to work like I always do." She turned and looked at Ryan. Tears spilled from her eyes. "The store is closed on Sundays. It frightened me a little, that's all. It's normally little things and doesn't happen all the time, but I never know when." She took a tissue from the pocket of her apron and blotted her watery eyes and dried her cheeks.

Ryan moved over to the swing and put his arm around her. "It's going to be okay. That's why I'm here. I want you to think about moving to Dallas and living with us."

"I don't want to be a bother to anyone."

"You're not a bother," he comforted her. "I'm the one coming out smelling like a rose. Just think of all those apple pies I'll get to eat." They both laughed.

"What about Keri? Do you think she would mind having her old friend around the house?"

"Not at all, Mom. I'm sure she'll be thrilled."

As he lied, the image of Emily pounding on the table, issuing her ultimatum—"Your mother is not moving into this house!" —screamed in his head. Not to mention the thought of how she would react the first time his mother called her "Keri".

He didn't know whether to cry or laugh out loud. What he did know was he loved his mother. He only hoped, when it came down to it, Emily wouldn't make him choose.

After spending the night and tanking-up on his mom's home-cooking, he started back to the airport. The quiet drive through familiar residential streets reminded him of the years he spent growing up. He always loved the change of seasons: the smell of azaleas and honeysuckle; freshly mowed lawns and budding pink and white dogwoods beneath towering oaks.

He felt good about his mom. Except for her continuing to think he was married to Keri, she appeared to be fine. She should be okay for at least six months, but when he thought about Emily, six months didn't seem long enough.

He continued to think about the logistics surrounding the move. She didn't have much in the way of material possessions, but he would need to sell what he could. Paying for storage was out of the question. He could convert the spare bedroom and bath into a small apartment. The details poured into his head, mixed with imagined responses from Emily.

After exiting the freeway, large signs directed him around the airport's perimeter road toward the rental car return area. He mindlessly glanced into a passing car

That woman looked exactly like Keri! And the man with her... he could have passed for Rex Dean's twin brother! Impossible. That's great! Now I'm hallucinating. Hearing Mom talk about Keri must have really messed with my mind... but, Rex? With Keri? I am going crazy.

The mere thought of Emily washed his mind clear of any momentary fantasies of Keri, returning him to his uncomfortable reality. In a matter of hours all hell would break loose when he presented Emily with the news—like it or not—Mom is moving in.

Chapter 35

Keri was dying for Rex to meet her parents, especially her mother. She knew if Rex could win the approval of her mother, her dad would follow. So far, her mother's receptiveness to verbal descriptions of Rex had been encouraging.

Rex, however, knew very little about Keri's parents or her past and was not that excited about making the trip to Atlanta. During the nine months they had dated, she had purposefully avoided conversations that might lead them into talking about her parents' affluence. She wanted Rex to love *her*, not her money, or better said her parent's money.

They arrived in Atlanta about noon. Keri opted for a rental car, knowing that her mother hated to drive in Atlanta traffic and especially hated the congestion at the Hartsfield Airport. The last thing she wanted was for Rex to see her mother in a tizzy.

After picking up the car, she navigated clear of the rental car parking lot and onto the perimeter road. For some strange reason, her eyes followed an approaching Ford sedan. As it grew closer, she locked-in on the man behind the wheel. In a matter of seconds, the car passed and was gone, but not before she was able to get a clear shot of the man's face.

That man looked exactly like Ryan Mitchell.

A rush of electrical currents swept through her body. She glanced at Rex to her right. He was staring out his side window. Her heart swelled in her chest. Underneath her calm exterior, a part of her was tugging for her to turn around and chase the car. Her eyes searched for a place to reverse directions.

A traffic light ahead. I can make a U-turn. The turn arrow is green. What will I tell Rex?

But before she could act, the traffic light was behind her. She questioned her stupidity. Even if it were Ryan, how crazy would it be to run after him? The urge quietly left, but her thoughts continued.

What would he be doing here? Visiting his mother, maybe? I could call her. Have you lost your mind?

A minute passed; more thoughts arrived.

Is this the way my life is going to be? Am I always going to be looking for Ryan Mitchell in every man I see?

Forty-minutes later, she turned onto West Paces Ferry Road. She couldn't hide it from Rex any longer, they were in Buckhead; the place she called home.

"Stately homes and gardens make Buckhead the Beverly Hills of Atlanta," the magazine articles had recently stated.

She noticed Rex come alive; pivoting his head from left to right, seemingly intrigued by the elegant homes nestled into large wooded lots.

"Pretty, isn't it?" Keri asked.

"I had no idea this place existed. So, which one is yours?" He chuckled.

"A few more minutes and we'll be there."

"Well, don't disappoint me."

* * *

Turning off West Paces Ferry and down Habersham Road, Rex admired the collection of early to mid-20th century architectural styled homes: from Georgian and Tudor to Italianate and Greek Revival. Magnolias and pink and white dogwoods bloomed against shadowy-green lawns featuring beds of flowering azaleas.

The idea of making a trip "all the way back to Atlanta," as he'd told Keri, "was not necessary". After all, they were only dating. In his eyes, the formality of "meeting the parents" was normally reserved for those with more serious intentions, like marriage. He was definitely not thinking "marriage", and he for sure didn't need her parent's approval to sleep with their daughter. Therefore, as far as he was concerned, making the journey to Atlanta was a big waste of time.

But his interest changed while cruising down the quiet tree-lined streets of Buckhead. Landscaped traffic islands at neighborhood intersections flashed the colors of spring. Southern mansions spread out atop rolling green lawns conjured up thoughts of *Gone with the Wind.* He wondered if slavery still existed in the South. Keri's parents might even have household servants: maids, butlers, cooks.

I had no idea my little peach was rich! Dude, I hit the jackpot!

The more he saw, the more he liked.

Her folks must be loaded. Sweet!

The unthinkable suddenly became thinkable, and once he saw her parents, he would know for sure. If they showed the level of affection and concern for their "little girl" he expected, it was a done deal.

This is when marriage makes sense.

* * *

Keri slowed, turned into a driveway and rolled through an opened wrought-iron gate. The winding drive cut through an immaculately manicured lawn beneath towering pines and up to the front of a large Georgian style home.

She felt the nerves in her stomach tighten as she pulled to a stop. Two thoughts replayed in her head: how would her mother react to Rex, and what would Rex think after the weekend was over.

"Wow!" Rex said. "Is this where you call home?"

"Well, it's my parent's home."

"Dude! The South has, *definitely*, risen again." Then, with his best Southern accent, he said, "Why, Miss Scarlett, you should have told me about you-alls plantation in Buckhead."

She looked at him with a grin. "My mother will definitely love you if you can keep that up."

Keri's mom popped out of the front door of the large white Georgian before Keri had time to switch off the ignition. She plastered Rex with a big Southern hug and stepped back, still holding his hands and keeping her gaze fixed on his face. "Darlin', I think you've got a keeper."

"Mom!" Keri said, sounding a bit embarrassed.

"Rex, I am so glad to finally meet you, though, I think I could have picked you out of a crowd from Keri's description."

"I have also been looking forward to meeting you and Mr. Hart. Keri is a very special woman and I knew she must have wonderful parents. I can already see I was right." He leaned closer to Keri's mother and said, "And to be honest, Mrs. Hart, I would have never imagined Keri's mother to be so young."

"You're sweet," her mom said.

Rex turned and looked up at the house towering over him. "I love your home, Mrs. Hart. It's my first trip to Buckhead and I was just telling Keri how beautiful this area is."

"Rex, please... call me Barb." She smiled. "Would you like a quick tour?"

Rex glanced over at Keri.

"Mom, don't you think we should get our bags inside first?"

"Heavens no! I'll have James take care of them, Dear. He knows which rooms ya'll will be staying in."

She took Rex by the arm. "Now let me show you the house."

"That would be great, Mrs. Hart... I mean, Barb." She gave Rex a smile of approval.

Keri could see that her mother found Rex to be quite the toy. She followed them into the house and listened as her mother guided Rex through the ten-thousand square foot house like a tour director at a museum. She ended her tour in the guest room where Rex would be staying. "I hope this will be okay," she said.

"It's perfect, Barb," Rex said.

"Mr. Hart will be home soon and dinner will be served at six sharp." She turned to Keri. "Now Sugah, you know your father."

"Yes, I know. He doesn't like to be kept waiting."

"Keri, why don't you show Rex the garden or take him on a walk? You still have an hour or so before dinner. I need to see if I can help Nora Jean in the kitchen."

"We'll be fine," Keri said, "And don't you worry, I'll take good care of Rex."

After her mom left, Rex said, "Your mom is wonderful."

"She can be, when she wants to."

"What about your dad? Sounds like he rules around here."

"He's all business, sorta hard to read until you get to know him, but don't let him intimidate you."

"Not a problem."

Her dad had a gift for sizing up people within minutes after he'd met them, and he was seldom wrong. She knew once he met Rex, he would instantly see the wonderful qualities that she had fallen in love with.

"You should have seen him before his heart surgery. Since then, he has calmed down considerably."

"When was his surgery?"

"Six years next month... seems like forever ago, but he has been doing great."

"Amazing what they can do."

"Yeah. We would have lost him if it hadn't been for the surgery."

* * *

Once her dad arrived, he and Rex exchanged a manly handshake and a few minutes of casual conversation. Rex found Keri's dad easy to talk to and not the least bit intimidating, as Keri had warned. They made their way to the dining room while Nora Jean, the Hart's maid, served the table.

Dinner conversation centered mostly on Keri's life in California and how she and Rex had met. The more Rex talked about his life—his parent's home in La Jolla, his attending the University of Southern California, and his recent earnings from real estate ventures—the more Keri's mom smiled. She appeared to be impressed. The fact that he was not a true-blue Southerner didn't seem to be a factor. Her dad showed no emotion.

Throughout dinner, Rex grew more and more comfortable, especially enjoying the attention he was receiving from Mrs. Hart. She laughed at all of his jokes and hung on his every word as he told stories about his life growing up in California. Mr. Hart held a stern face, rarely cracking a smile. Knowing that Mrs. Hart held the keys to the kingdom, Rex disregarded the old man's lack of interest.

Rex felt it was all too perfect. After seeing the big picture, the little peach he'd plucked was juicier than he'd imagined. He had her mother eating out of his hand; her old man's ticker was ready to seize at any moment; and the palatial Southern estate, rivaling Tara in *Gone with the Wind*, was ripe for the picking. If he played his cards right, it could all be his in a matter of a few years, and just in time.

The stories of his lucrative real estate deals had all been lies. In actuality, Rex had lost hundreds of thousands of dollars of his dad's money sprinkled among speculative stock purchases, bad real estate ventures, gambling, and frivolous exotic car deals. His dad had recently become so furious at Rex's numerous blunders that he threatened to cut him out of his will all together. Rex knew the days of leaching off his parents were over and wouldn't be surprised if they willed him a mere token of their wealth when they died, leaving the balance to charity.

After dessert, Rex stood and said, "Mr. and Mrs. Hart, you have a lovely home, and I would like to thank you for having me this weekend. But the main reason I wanted to meet with you was to tell you in person that I am in love with your daughter."

Keri's mother gasped.

Rex turned to Keri seated beside him. "Keri, I know this might come as a surprise, but I wouldn't ask if I didn't think you felt the same way about me as I do about you." He reached down and took her hand. "Keri, will you marry me and make me the happiest man in the world?"

Chapter 36

Ryan's flight from Atlanta touched down in Dallas, Saturday afternoon about three o'clock. Each mile of the short drive home twisted his gut like a rubber band.

Emily would be waiting, and the thought of telling her what he had decided made him want to puke. If the threats she had made Thursday night were real, it could mean the end to his marriage.

As the garage door opened, the sight of Emily's car wrenched his nerves, one last time. He sighed.

I might as well get this over with.

He entered the house through the garage door leading into the kitchen. He noticed Emily's purse parked in its usual place. The smell of roast cooking in the oven hit him first, followed by the sound of soft music coming from the in-ceiling speakers of the whole-house sound system. He walked into the den and stopped, stunned by what he saw. Candles flickered on the mantle above the fireplace, the carpet was freshly vacuumed, and every pillow was perfectly placed.

He cautiously made his way up the stairs to the master bedroom. The thought crossed his mind that she might not have expected him to return home today. What would he do if he caught another man in the house?

He eased the door open. Emily met him with a smile and said, "Hi, Honey. How was your trip?"

Honey?

She was barefoot wearing tight white jeans and a black V-neck camisole top—beautiful, sexy, and braless. She reached up and kissed him on the lips.

"Fine. I guess." It would have made more sense if he had found her in bed with another man.

"Listen, I know you're tired and probably famished. Let me go check on dinner while you change into something more comfortable."

Unsure how to respond, he quietly did as she suggested.

He wondered if she was even aware that he had been to Atlanta to see his mom. He couldn't remember if he mentioned it to her. It didn't matter. What *did* matter was how she would react when he broke the news to her that his mom would be moving in with them in a few months.

He walked into the kitchen and asked, "What's the occasion?"

She stopped what she was doing and walked over to him. "Ryan, I need to apologize for the way I reacted when you told me about your poor mother. I feel awful."

"Ah… sure. That's okay."

"No! It's not okay. I've thought about it, and if your mother needs us, we need to do everything we can to help her. If that means her moving in with us, then that's what we'll do."

"What made you change your mind?"

"You."

"What do you mean 'you'? What did I do?"

"It's not anything you did, it's just that I love you so much. I can't stand the thought of ever hurting you. I know how much you love your mother. It's time I got to know her better—especially since there might not be much time. We need to do everything we can to make her life as comfortable and happy as possible."

Hearing her words made him forget anything she had previously said or done. He pulled her close and hugged her. "Emily, I love you more than you will ever know." With her arms wrapped around him, her head up against his chest, he heard a muffled whimper. "What's wrong?"

She sniffled, then said, "Can you ever forgive me? I've been such a witch these last few months. It must be the stress from my work and all the traveling."

"Listen, it's going to be fine. *We're* going to be fine—all three of us."

"I needed to hear that," she said, wiping the tears from her cheek. "What about your mom?"

"She's fine. We have plenty of time to decide what to do. For now, let's just focus on us."

"That sounds good." She kissed him and then said, "I'm so lucky to have you." She gazed up into his eyes with a seductive grin; a look he hadn't seen in a long time. "I think somebody might get lucky tonight."

"What about dinner?"

She reached over and turned off the oven. "Who said you couldn't have dessert first?" She took his hand and led him to the bedroom.

* * *

Emily planned to make their reunion a night Ryan would never forget. Starting tonight, she wanted him to know, beyond a shadow of a doubt, that she was madly in love with him and willing to sacrifice anything and everything to make him happy. She was even willing to cook. After all, she knew the way to a man's heart was through his stomach, but more importantly, the way to a man's wallet was sex, and Ryan was no different than any other man—dogs, all of them.

While Ryan was visiting his mother in Atlanta, Emily had come to the conclusion that their marriage was dead, and she needed to move on with her life. All the crap with his mother happened at the perfect time.

Her career was booming and she was more than able to provide for herself. In addition, she had been offered a lucrative job in Atlanta as the vice president in charge of residential real estate for the southeastern division of the corporation that owned Excalibur Homes. The president had personally hired her with the intentions of her working closely with him on future development projects. How could she turn it down?

But before she dumped him, she had a few things she needed to take care of; she called it her financial insurance plan.

Chapter 37

Rex beamed a smile at Keri, then asked, "Keri, will you marry me and make me the happiest man in the world?"

She felt flushed and totally surprised, but excited and tingly all over. Without having to think, she said, "Yes!" Then jumped up and wrapped her arms around him.

"Not so fast!" Her father's stern voice blared out. "Son, you might be able to fool these women, but I see your game. If you've come here thinking I'm going to give you my blessings to marry my daughter after only spending a couple of hours with you, you're sadly mistaken."

"Sir, I—" Rex attempted to speak.

"Daddy! What are you doing?"

Barb turned to her husband. "Ronald!" Reserving his full name for when she was angry. "This is Keri's decision. Can't you see that your daughter is in love? Please, don't spoil it for her." She turned to Keri. "Honey, it's going to be okay. Your father just needs some time."

"You are so right, Barb. I need some time," he said. "Some time to check this young man out before I consent to letting him marry my daughter."

"Mom? Please! Do something with dad."

Barb said, "Ronald, could I talk with you alone?"

"That's okay, Mrs. Hart," Rex said, "We'll just wait in the den." Rex urged Keri to follow him.

Once in the den, Keri hugged Rex and said, "Don't listen to my dad. He acts like that when he is not in complete control. He can be a real ass. My mom will take care of him." Keri and Rex made faces at each other as they listened to the heated debate in the adjacent room.

"Ronald, I don't know what your problem is, but you are NOT going to ruin this special night for your daughter! You should be happy for her."

"The boy is a player. He's no good. Can't you see it? Or are you just as blind as she is?"

"What are you talking about? Rex is a wonderful young man, and Keri loves him. Don't you trust your daughter?"

"Are you kidding? Keri couldn't see the real Rex, even if she wanted to, and by the looks of it, neither can you. Amazing! What is it with you women? He was groping Keri right in front of our eyes. I can only imagine what he does when they are alone."

"For God's sake, Ronald, they are two adults in love. What do you expect?"

"I expect a little respect!"

Keri peeked into the dining room just in time to see her mom deliver her final ultimatum to her dad.

Barb stood, leaned in close, and said in a normal but firm tone, "Let me tell you what you can expect. Either you will change your tune, or I will make your life a living nightmare. And if you don't think I can do it, just try me."

* * *

Without responding, Ronald rose, calmly left the dining room, and headed for the den. It was clearly a waste of time to argue with his wife. If she approved of Rex, there *would* be a wedding. He planned to make sure Rex knew exactly how he felt.

He approached Rex and Keri. "Keri, would you excuse us for a moment?"

"No! I'm staying with Rex."

"It's okay," Rex said. "Let me talk with your father, alone."

She reluctantly moved away and back into the dining room.

Before Ronald had a chance to speak, Rex said, "Mr. Hart, I think once we spend a little time together—"

"Rex, I'm not stupid. You forget, I'm a man, too, and I can see through your little game. As you have probably assessed, I'm a very wealthy man, but my daughter is, by far, the most valuable thing in my life. I'm not about to stand by and watch some *surfer dude* come along and ruin her life."

"Sir, I promise you, I have no intentions—"

He raised his hand. "I don't need to hear any more. When it comes to other people's intentions, I spend my life reading between the lines. As for you—"

Rex spoke his mind, respectfully, but firmly, "Sir, I love your daughter, and you know you can't stop Keri and me from getting married."

"No, son, you're right, I can't stop you from marrying my daughter, and if my wife has her way, she will ensure Keri doesn't have to elope. But I just want you to know that I'm on to you." He turned and looked toward the dining room, then back. "I just don't understand why Keri can't see you for who you really are."

"Mr. Hart, I'm not the monster you make me out to be. I'm perfectly safe, and I love your daughter."

Ronald silently stared at Rex for a moment, then said, "Son, face it, you know you're not ready to take on the responsibility of providing for a wife."

"Sir, I would have agreed with you before I met your daughter, but Keri is an exceptional woman."

"How much?" Ronald asked.

"Excuse me?"

Ronald lowered his voice and continued, "How much will it take for you to walk away... forget you ever met Keri."

"Are you offering me a bribe?"

"Call it what you like."

"Sir, I can't believe you would think I could put a value on the woman I want to spend the rest of my life with."

"Oh, come on Rex. You know you don't love her. So, what's your price... five thousand, ten thousand... twenty? Just name it."

"I can't believe this."

"Believe it! And believe this: regardless of how this plays out, if you ever hurt my daughter, I will hurt you—a hundred fold."

"I'm out of here." Rex turned and headed for the dining room.

"Keri, I'm leaving. I can't stay here. Your father just tried to pay me to dump you."

"What!" Keri turned to her mom, her face twisted in torment. "Mom, do something with him!"

Rex started for the stairs, "I'll just grab my bag and be out of here. It shouldn't be a problem finding a hotel. Keri, I can pick you up in the morning and we can fly back together on the first flight."

"Rex, please don't go," Barb said.

"Mrs. Hart, thank you for your hospitality, but I think it would be better if I did."

"I'm going with you," Keri said.

Ronald stood silently, leaning up against the door frame between the dining room and den, thinking. It obviously wasn't going to be easy, but he loved his daughter and wasn't about to let some "dude" from California ruin her life.

Keri turned and burned a stare into his face. "You are disgusting!"

He knew Keri didn't mean it; if she could only see past the smooth exterior of this creep, she would understand.

"Keri, I only want the best for you, and trust me, I have my doubts about this one."

"Ahhhhhhh!" Keri screamed through clenched teeth. "Unbelievable!"

In the business world, when it came to people, Ronald Hart had dealt with much tougher situations than this. He had learned that in conflicts, when someone is pulling against you, sometimes the best solution is not to resist, but to go with the pull. This results in the opposition losing their balance, making the negotiation process easier. It was apparent that the smooth-talker from California had blinded Keri *and* his wife. The last thing he needed to do was enter into a long protracted tug of war with two women, trying to convince them of the deception buried deep within their hearts. For now, he planned to go with the pull.

* * *

Rex slipped off to retrieve his bag from the guest bedroom, smiling all the way. Keri's mom loved him, and that's all that mattered. Her dad's little stunt to buy him off was tempting, but he knew there was a much bigger prize waiting, once he was officially "family". With her mom eating out of his hand, and a time-bomb in her old man's chest, the future looked bright.

Chapter 38

April 1986
New York City

It was Monday, April 21st. The wedding Keri had dreamed about since she was a little girl was only a week away. Her mother had done a masterful job of pulling the reins in on her father, and though he continued to show a cautious acceptance of Rex, as his soon-to-be son-in-law, he could not stop the wheels of fate.

Keri's mother made sure Atlanta would never forget her daughter's wedding, especially the high-society types. Her effort rivaled that of any corporate marketing blitz. A close friend who worked at the *Atlanta Journal* helped her coordinate the campaign. In every Sunday edition of the *Journal,* during September and October, she'd featured the upcoming wedding with a big splash filled with impressive photographs and background information on Keri and Rex.

Several posh Atlanta retail stores, popular among the upper-class clientele for their bridal registries, also planned to use poster-size pictures of Keri dressed in her bridal attire in conjunction with store promotions and announcements of new lines of china. She capitalized on every possible opportunity to ensure that her daughter's name took front billing among the local gossip buzz.

After saturating the local markets, she broadened her campaign by submitting articles of interest for brides-to-be— *How to Plan a Dream Wedding; The Perfect Wedding*; *Make Your Dreams Come True*—to the national magazines, *Modern Bride* and *Elegant Bride,* with photographs featuring Keri and Rex. Senior editors were quick to print her submissions after seeing the sizable contributions sent with each article.

Even the date for the wedding was strategically selected: Saturday, April 26th. April ensured the full effect of the magnificent beauty of budding azaleas, blooming dogwoods and magnolias.

Her mother's desire for a fairy-tale wedding had even led her to research the 1981 wedding of Prince Charles and Lady Diana Spencer. Unable to match the scale and grandeur of such a royal celebration, she felt victory of sorts by touting the fact— mostly among her gossiping socialite acquaintances—that the guest list to her daughter's wedding would easily surpass the 3,500 in attendance at St. Paul's Cathedral.

Keri had one last trip with the airline before starting a two-week vacation. On Tuesday morning, after her trip, she'd fly to Atlanta and begin the pre-wedding festivities: luncheons, shopping, and last-minute details. Rex would join her on Thursday, two days before the wedding. She and Rex had both arranged to take the week off after their wedding for a wonderful honeymoon in the Cayman Islands.

* * *

The elevator doors opened in the lobby of the Park Central Hotel in New York City. Although she had not ordered the eight thirty wake-up call, seeing the beautiful day made her thankful the hotel had made the mistake.

She paused briefly and scanned the lobby, checking to see if she recognized anyone from her crew. In addition to the unscheduled wake-up call—strange but not uncommon—a message with a man's voice simply said, "Keri, I'll meet you in the lobby at nine thirty." She didn't recognize the voice, but did remember mentioning to both pilots that they were welcome to join her the following morning for a walk. After scanning the lobby, preferring to spend the day alone, she quickly continued out the front doors of the hotel onto 7th Avenue.

Located directly across from Carnegie Hall in Midtown, the hotel offered airline crews a great location from which to explore the city on foot: Central Park, three blocks to the north; Times Square a few blocks south; and the Theatre District and Rockefeller Center only a short walk away.

She always enjoyed New York layovers, especially in the spring. She breathed in the morning air. A slight chill of wind rushed across her face. The forecast promised a near perfect day with temperatures in the mid sixties. The cloudless morning sky gave way to the warmth of the sun as it slowly dissolved the shadows from the towering skyscrapers.

She paused briefly drawing in the warm morning sun. After a relaxing walk in the park, she planned to grab a take-out lunch from one of her favorite delis and head over to her dad's condo on the Upper East Side. The luxury condo sat empty most of the time, as it was primarily used to entertain business associates. Surprisingly, her dad had mailed her the key at the beginning of the month and offered for her to use the place the next time she was on one of her New York layovers; a little "pre-wedding gift" he wanted to give her.

She glanced down at her watch: nine thirty-five. With her pick-up to the airport not until three thirty, she looked forward to spending some time alone reflecting on the exciting changes ahead of her. She was only days away from becoming, Mrs. Rex Dean.

Hello, Mrs. Dean. Hi, my name is Keri Dean. She liked it.

Walking north on 7th Avenue toward Central Park, she stopped after only a few steps. A man exchanging money with a street-side vendor for one of his bagels caught her attention. He was dressed in jeans, tennis shoes, and a light blue knit shirt underneath a navy sweater—much like most tourist or pilots. She moved closer. "Ryan?"

Ryan Mitchell turned after hearing his name. His smile was immediate and pleasant. "Keri! How are you doing?" He gave her an innocent hug.

"Great! How about you?" She stepped back. Even though it had been almost two years, with her life finally on track, she was ambushed on the spot by galloping horses in her chest and knees wanting to buckle. She was certain he noticed the instant paleness in her face. What did she expect? He was the first man she ever loved—and still loved.

"Doing good. What a coincidence to be laying over here on the same day."

"Yeah. Amazing."

She nervously pushed through her attack pretending everything was normal. "So, how's Emily?"

He paused, looking away as though searching for the right words. "She's good." He quickly redirected the conversation back to Keri. "You still enjoying California?"

"Yeah. I especially *love* the weather... and there's so much to do," she said. "How is Emily adjusting to Texas?" Keri knew if she didn't focus on Emily, the conversation was certain to go in directions she hoped to avoid.

He folded the paper bag around his bagel. "She wasn't too fond of it at first, but I think she's slowly accepting it."

"I can understand why she might have issues with Texas, especially the heat."

He stepped aside to let a man place an order with the street vendor. "Listen, I was planning to take a walk up to Central Park. I'd love for you to join me. It would give us a chance to catch up on things."

She stared at him for a moment weighing her emotions.

What things do we need to catch up on?

Just seeing him was hard enough. Only days before her wedding, the last thing she needed was to stir up feelings for a man she could easily love again.

He continued, "I need to tell you the latest about Mom."

The mention of his mother made her decision easier. She loved Martha Mitchell and had lost touch with her during the last year. "Is she okay?" she asked.

"She's fine, but it looks like there are some challenges ahead for us all."

I'll just walk with him for a while. After he tells me about Martha, I'll make up an excuse to leave.

"I was headed to the park, myself. I really do want to hear about Martha." They both started walking slowly toward the park.

As they walked, she found herself taking in everything about him. Every few steps, the crowded sidewalk caused him to brush up against her, and occasionally he took her arm, guiding her through the crowd.

The chance of seeing anyone they knew was remote. Just the two of them, alone in a city far from the lives they'd left behind, gave way for feelings of guilt which she quickly suppressed. She compromised—he's a married man; I'm getting married in a week; we're just friends.

"Mom's doctor called me just a few months ago. He said she had the beginning signs of Alzheimer's."

"Oh no," she said, putting her hand on his arm.

"After spending a couple of days with her, I decided we had about six months until she would need full-time care."

"I am so sorry," she said. "I didn't know. That explains why she hasn't written me back for some time."

They crossed 57th Street with a crowd of people.

Keri continued, "I was afraid something might be wrong. She was always good about writing, ever since..." She trailed off, but thought ...*the wedding.*

They stopped briefly on the corner of 7th and Central Park South (59th Street) waiting for the traffic light to change. They walked across the street and along the sidewalk leading into the park.

As if they entered another world, the cool air beneath the canopy of trees and grassy lawns invited them to relax. Rollerbladers, joggers, and bikers glided by on the smooth asphalt. The clip-clop of horse's hooves pulling carriages replaced blaring horns and screeching tires. The sounds of the city grew muffled and less noticeable the farther they walked into the park. A refuge from the chaotic city life: 843 acres stretching from 59th Street to 110th Street.

As they walked, he continued to talk about his mother. "You won't believe what she said."

"What?"

"While I was visiting her, she wanted to know if you and I ever flew together at the airline."

"That's understandable; after all, she knows I'm a flight attendant."

"But that's not what she meant. She thinks you are Emily."

Keri's eyes widened. "You mean she thinks..." she trailed off.

Ryan nodded. "Yep. She thinks I married you, rather than Emily. Or she thinks Emily is you... or... well, you know what I mean."

"How do you know for sure that's what she meant?"

"She specifically asked me if, *Keri*, liked living in Texas... with me." He turned to her and smiled.

"What did Emily say?"

He contained a chuckle. "I thought it might be best to keep that as my little secret... at least for now. I'm sure she'll find out once Mom moves in with us."

"When do you plan to move her?"

"I'm leaving on Saturday the 27th. I've got a break in my schedule."

It hit her.

He's going to be in Buckhead the day I'm getting married! Should I tell him?

Her mother had warned her *not* to tell Ryan about the wedding. It would only create unnecessary complications, both for him and herself.

Parts of her wanted to tell him the truth—the honest part; the engaged soon-to-be-married part. But another part of her— the still-in-love-with Ryan Mitchell part wanted nothing to do with the truth; all it wanted was to spend one last day with the first man she'd ever loved—alone. She knew that once this day ended, she would go back to Rex and the new life that awaited her, and Ryan would return to Emily and his life, but for now, she just wanted to be with Ryan. Just talk.

"Are you okay?" Ryan asked.

"Ah, yeah... I'm fine," she stammered. "Why do you ask?"

"You just look like you might have seen a ghost."

"I felt a little queasy for a minute. I'm okay, now. Maybe I'd better sit down."

They took a seat on a nearby park bench. "Are you sure you're okay?"

"I'm fine, really. So, you're moving Martha to Texas next Saturday?"

As they talked, Keri's mind darted into forbidden areas, especially for a woman only days away from walking down the aisle with another man. She struggled with her thoughts, but finally compromised that, if only for one last day, she would enjoy the time she had with him; to freely talk with him without the worry of Emily's piercing eyes. She would not deny herself this one last unrestricted pleasure.

As if they strolled along a deserted beach, waves of emotions pounded against her heart while her mind struggled to stay focused on reality. She knew the dangers of allowing her heart to loiter too long within forbidden fantasies, but regardless of her measured restraint, she would never stop loving this man.

Within the moments of silence, as the tide of emotions drew back, reality surfaced its ugly head to remind her that Ryan and Emily were happily married and within a few days she would become, Mrs. Rex Dean. She loved Rex and he loved her; that's what was important.

There's nothing wrong with talking to an old friend?

For the next few hours, Ryan was hers to enjoy.

Chapter 39

Ryan had a prearranged three forty-five pick-up from the hotel to the airport. His flight was scheduled to depart JFK at five forty putting him back in Dallas at nine. He was planning to drive to Atlanta first thing in the morning. Since his fact-finding visit with his mother, six months ago, he'd taken care of all the details for the move.

Emily had made a remarkable turnaround and seemed to be ready for Martha to move in. In a way, she had been *too* good. She never complained and, even with her busy work schedule, always kept the house in perfect order. Very seldom did she travel on business trips when he was in town. But something just didn't feel right.

Visiting with Keri flooded him with memories from the past, good ones. She brought alive a part of him that he had forgotten existed. As they talked about his mother, Keri's concern and love connected them in a special way; something he didn't have with Emily. Maybe that was what felt so strange about Emily's sudden turnaround. She claimed to be eager about his mother moving in, but seemed distant and disconnected whenever he wanted to talk about the details.

Emily had told him that she had cleared her schedule for the entire first week his mother would be with them. But when he approached her with questions about decisions they needed to make, she would say something, like, "Honey, do whatever you think is right. She's your mother."

While he was with Keri, except for small talk, talking about Emily made him uneasy. The last thing he wanted to do was waste time reliving the misery of his first year of marriage, and he was sure Keri didn't want to hear it. He knew the time he had with Keri would be short and probably his last for a while. If the hotel had not given him the bogus wake-up call, along with the strange message on his phone, he might have missed her.

After looking down at the ring finger of her left hand, he noticed it was bare: no wedding band and no engagement ring.

What about Bill. I thought they were hot and heavy. Maybe she left it in the room safe.

He started to ask but stopped. He decided it might be best if he let her initiate any conversation about her love life.

"You hungry?" Ryan asked.

"I guess I could eat something," she said.

"Let me buy you lunch." He held out the bag he'd been carrying since they met in front of the hotel. "I'll share."

* * *

"I've got a better idea," she said. She hadn't planned to have lunch with him, but didn't want to leave him, either. It was just one day, only a few hours, she might as well make the most of it. After all, when would she ever have the chance to see him again, alone?

"I know where there's a great little deli over between Madison and Park Avenues. That is... if you don't mind walking a couple of blocks."

"Sounds great." He held up his bag once more. "And if we get lost, we've always got my bagel." They laughed.

"The place is called Delmonico Gourmet Food Market. They've got just about everything from salads to gourmet specialty sandwiches, and the prices are very reasonable." She checked her watch. "It's just a little after eleven, so we should beat most of the lunch crowd."

As they walked, her previous nervousness was replaced with a comfortable familiarity. The talk about his mother and the memories of the years—before their lives had taken them down separate paths—reconnected her to him.

"So, how far is this place?" Ryan asked, jokingly.

She reached over and playfully squeezed him on his side. It was a habit from the past; something she'd done many times before. She always teased him that one day, his God-given lean and muscular physique was going to grow a pair of love handles if he wasn't careful. Instead, this time she said, "The walk will do you good." And as in the past, there was still nothing to grab; after all the years, not an ounce of fat.

"I should have seen that coming." He chuckled. "Hopefully, I won't pass out."

They crossed Madison Avenue beneath the shadows of towering buildings, the cool winds swirled through the streets. The smell of fresh bread and pizza filled the air.

"Here it is," she said. He reached for the door, holding it open while she entered, following her close behind.

Ryan ordered the grilled chicken breast sandwich from the "Specialty Sandwiches" menu. It came with roasted peppers, basil oil, and red lettuce on crusty ciabatta bread. He also added a bowl of Manhattan clam chowder. Keri ordered from the "Create Your Own Salad" menu: a grilled chicken and asparagus salad with mandarin oranges and roasted peppers topped with a mandarin vinaigrette dressing.

When Keri started to pull some money from her pocket, Ryan reached over and said, "No, I'm taking care of this. I told you I'd buy you lunch."

"I can't let you do that—"

"I insist." He quickly produced a credit card and handed it to the cashier.

Keri stepped back. "I really didn't want you to buy my lunch... but thank you, you're sweet to do that."

"My pleasure."

The cashier swiped the card through the card reader and paused waiting for approval. "Your card was disapproved." With an impatient look, the cashier tried to return the card to Ryan.

"That's impossible. Please try it again," Ryan insisted. He glanced over at Keri, giving her a surprised look.

After swiping the card a second time and waiting for a brief moment, the cashier rolled his eyes and handed the card back to Ryan.

"That's strange." He reached in his pocket and produced a twenty-dollar bill. "Here, that should work." He turned to Keri and shrugged.

After settling with the cashier, Ryan looked around for a place to sit. Not liking what he saw, he said, "How about we head back to the park for a picnic?"

Keri paused. She had originally planned to grab lunch and take a cab up to her father's condo, spending the rest of the afternoon relaxing. But that was before she'd met Ryan.

Amid blaring alarms within her subconscious, warning her not to do it, she said, "I've got a better idea."

Chapter 40

While Ryan and Keri ordered take-out from the Delmonico Gourmet Food Market in New York, Rex sped north on the PCH at eight forty-five, West Coast time.

Morning rush traffic in Laguna Beach had subsided assuring him that making his nine o'clock appointment with Bob Stickler in Newport Beach would be a piece of cake.

After clearing the last traffic light in north Laguna, he reached up, tweaked the volume on his radar detector, popped in some tunes, and let the Porsche stretch its legs. The open coastal highway offered an unrestricted view of the ocean and no traffic lights.

With Keri coming home tonight and the wedding only a week away, he knew that if he didn't see Stickler now, it would be weeks before he could even think about scheduling another appointment. He had already procrastinated too long.

As he drove, he thought about what it would be like to be a married man. The thought of marrying into money had its perks, and he definitely had no objections to the idea of having sex with a gorgeous woman whenever he liked, but he wondered if being with the same woman could satisfy him.

For a moment he felt guilty not telling Keri about his appointment with Stickler, but he knew she would never understand. Married was one thing, but there was no way he was going to have kids, even though he had lied and told Keri he would.

He wheeled into the parking lot in front of Stickler's office and exited the Porsche. As he reached for the front door, he glanced down at his watch and smiled: 8:59.

The waiting area was empty. He noticed an extremely overweight woman seated behind a waist-high counter to the right of the door. He guessed her to be in her late fifties.

"Mr. Dean, you finally made it," the woman said in a deep, raspy voice. "I hope you weren't having second thoughts?"

"Not hardly."

As he stepped up to the counter, the woman's appearance startled him. Her thin red hair was matted to the top of her balding head with some sort of gel or glue, and her eyes were caked so thick with black mascara that she looked like a raccoon. Her fire-engine red lipstick looked like it had been applied in the dark while driving down a bumpy road. He tried not to stare.

"Well, you certainly did cut it close. Aren't you getting married next week?"

"Yeah, next Saturday."

"She sure is a lucky woman." She laughed.

"What's so funny?"

"I just realized what I said. "Cut it close... get it? Cut... *it.*" Her painted-on, hairless eyebrows rose to the middle of her wide forehead.

"Yeah, I get it," he faked a smile.

Man, this woman is creepy.

"I promise I'll be careful and hopefully, I won't... 'cut *it*, too close'." She laughed again, but this time with an added snort.

He faked another smile as he signed the roster.

"Dr. Stickler will be with you in a moment, but you can come on back, and I'll get you prepped."

"You?"

"Don't worry, I haven't cut one off yet," she chuckled, "but there's always a first time for everything." She rolled her eyes. "Just kidding."

The woman struggled to lift her large body from the chair, releasing a couple of hacking coughs and a few other sounds he couldn't identify. Sweat beaded on her forehead. He cringed at the thought of her touching him.

"Follow me," she said.

"You are a nurse, aren't you?" he asked, glancing down at her name tag. The letters R and N were engraved below a small caduceus: a winged staff with two snakes wrapped around it. Her name: Rosie Bonner.

"Yep, I sure am... certified, registered and good to go... snip, snip." Pretending her fingers were scissors, she cut through the air. Another scare ran through his mind when he saw her fingernails.

"What happened to Sara?" He'd expected Stickler's personal nurse, Sara, to be the one doing the "prepping". Sara was a hot-looking blond in her early thirties, and if anyone was going to be giving "the boys" a bath and a shave, he at least wanted it to be someone like her. Dr. Stickler had given him the option of shaving his scrotum at home or letting them do it for him, once he arrived at the office. After seeing Sara, he'd opted for the full-service treatment—something he now regretted.

"Sara took the day off. I only work part-time for Dr. Stickler. I'm pretty much retired." She glanced over at him as she hobbled down the narrow hallway to the exam room. "I'm also single." A smile spread across her round face. "My name is Rosie."

There was nothing he could say.

"About all I do now is prep for the vasectomies. I'm the best." Rosie smiled big, baring her yellowed teeth. The foul stench of her tobacco breath drifted up his nose.

"Here's your exam room." She handed him what looked like a small disposable tablecloth with sleeves. "Once you undress, put this on. I'll be back in a minute." She left and pulled the door closed.

The thin backless gown was little more than a paper rag. After undressing, he slipped it on and attempted to tie the back closed but decided to let it just hang on his shoulders. He took a seat on the edge of the exam table.

The sound of a hacking cough announced the return of the redhead. "Don't you look cute," she said. "You can go ahead and lie down on the table, prop your feet up, and spread your legs, good and wide, so I can get at everything." She looked his way and shot him a smile.

I must be crazy.

She walked over to the sink, washed her hands, snapping on a pair of thin rubber gloves. Then she plopped down on a small stainless-steel stool and rolled over beneath the tent formed by the gown draped over his spread legs, putting her eye level with his manhood.

"Oh my, aren't we a big boy?" she asked.

Flat on his back, the sight of Rosie was hidden by the gown. His only knowledge of her being in the room was the sound of her wheezing and occasional comments.

He tried to imagine Nurse Sara being between his legs, rather than the redhead. He stared at the ceiling and tuned in on the buzz of a bad ballast in a fluorescent light fixture, hoping to drown out the wheezing.

"Here we go," she said. "Be real still, and I'll try not to... *cut it*." She laughed and coughed.

He flinched at the sound of a pop and buzz as she fired-up the barber-style hair clippers.

In a serious tone, she said, "Okay, now here is where we don't want to move around too much."

He only hoped she wouldn't have one of her coughing spells while she was working. In less than ten minutes, the buzz of the clippers stopped. Seconds later, he felt Rosie's hand lift his penis followed by a warm, moist sensation on his scrotum.

Sara, Sara, Sara.

He tried to picture the beautiful blond nurse.

"Hmmm, looks like we're starting to enjoy ourselves," she said. "I told you I was good."

Beautiful Sara.

"Well now, looks like the big boy wants to stand up all by himself," she said excitedly.

He couldn't help it, but if the fondling continued much longer, he might lose it. Then he felt her wrap his entire package in a soft towel, followed by a gentle, steady buffing of his stiff prick, while rubbing his scrotum dry.

That was all it took. The train left the station; the point of no return. He groaned, his eyelids twitched, his upper lip quivered as waves of pulsing pleasure riveted through his body.

"Oops," the redhead said, "looks like we had a little accident. That's okay, it happens all the time." He felt her continue rubbing his pulsing prick until it was completely flaccid. "There we go, all done. Good boy."

She rolled back on the stool, stretched the gloves from her hands and tossed them in a stainless steel trash can by the sink.

"Everything looks good. Let me get the doctor. She left the room and closed the door.

Dr. Stickler was all business, and the procedure only took about twenty minutes using a local anesthetic. Stickler told him the anesthetic would last for about an hour, long enough for him to stop by a local pharmacy, pick up his pain relievers, and drive home.

Keri would be arriving late tonight from her trip and leaving early tomorrow morning for Atlanta, so he shouldn't have any trouble hiding it from her.

In about four to six weeks, he would return to Dr. Stickler for a follow-up visit to ensure that his semen was sperm free. Until then, he'd need to continue using a condom since the birth control pill gave Keri headaches. In a couple of months, he would finally be able to enjoy sex without using protection and without the worry of Keri becoming pregnant. She would just have to deal with it.

Chapter 41

Keri knew that inviting Ryan to her dad's empty Upper East Side condo might not be the best idea, but her life was about to change, forever. This would be the last time she would be with him, alone. Not that she planned to do anything wrong, she just hated to see the day end.

While a part of her screamed-out to do as Ryan suggested—take the food and go have a picnic in the park—another part of her screamed louder to invite him to the condo.

"I was just thinking... we could grab a cab and head over to my dad's condo. It's not far from here, and I know you've always wanted to see it."

"Does he mind?"

"Not at all, he even gave me a key," she said. "He hardly ever uses the place, except for business. Most of the time it just sits empty."

"In that case, yeah, I'd love to see it."

They walked out of the deli onto 59th Street, hailed a cab, and after sliding into the backseat, Keri leaned up and told the driver the address. She then slipped back next to Ryan as the yellow cab sped away.

As they continued north on Park Avenue into the depths of the prestigious Upper East Side, her mind raced ahead. She played-out what it would be like to be totally alone with Ryan. She only wished the circumstances were different.

* * *

Ryan remembered Keri mentioning her dad's place in New York, back when they dated in high school. He always wished he could see it.

On layovers, he had taken many long walks in the Upper East Side area, but he never was exactly sure where it was located.

The area from 59th street to 96th street, between Central Park and the East River was noted for having some of the most luxurious and expensive residences in the world. It was a place where New York's rich are shrouded behind thick walls, guarded by uniformed-doormen with ermine collars; where children go to elite private schools, and the subway stations even seem cleaner.

As chronicled by Tom Wolfe in his novel, *Bonfire of the Vanities*, it is an area touting a "who's who" list of retail stores, art galleries, museums, restaurants, and expensive boutiques: Tiffany, Louis Vuitton, Chanel, Gucci, Christie's, Sotheby's, the Guggenheim, and FAO Schwartz. He had heard it even surpassed the Ginza in Tokyo as the most expensive retail area in the world.

The cost of being a part of this world was staggering, and Keri's dad had a place in the middle of it all; the ultimate in opulence. He couldn't wait to finally see it.

Keri leaned up and pointed, telling the cabdriver where to pull over. Ryan couldn't help stealing a look at the curves of her figure; his eyes rapidly scanning from top to bottom, while his thoughts danced with infatuation.

Don't even think about it. You're married.

As the cab changed lanes and headed toward the curb, Ryan's mind changed gears. No longer was he thinking about the condo, but about Keri and being alone with her. He wondered if she felt the same way. He brushed the thought away, rationalizing that women think differently than men. Perhaps his initial excitement to see the condo had masked a deeper desire to be alone with her.

We'll go have lunch, I'll take a quick look at the place, and then we'll leave. It's perfectly safe.

They exited the cab.

Chapter 42

Back in Dallas, Emily scurried around the house taking care of last minute details. Ryan was due in that night, and he would be leaving early tomorrow morning driving to Atlanta. The two-day drive would put him in Atlanta sometime on Thursday. After spending the rest of the week packing, he and his mother would start the trip back to Texas on Sunday, arriving in Dallas late Monday.

With the sink full of dirty dishes, the bed unmade, and the house a wreck, wearing only her bra and panties, she moved quickly from the bathroom to her dressing closet. She selected a flowing dress with a plunging neckline.

This ought to do it.

After slipping into the dress, she checked herself in the mirror and then grabbed three pairs of shoes that she knew would work with the dress. She needed to hurry. She could decide later which pair to wear.

After one last look around the bedroom, she rushed downstairs to the kitchen, rummaged through a drawer for a pen.

Where is a pen when you need one?

A second drawer produced the pen. She took the notepad by the phone and began to write:

Ryan,

I know the house is a wreck...

Chapter 43

When Keri opened the door, she could tell that Ryan was impressed. He walked from the marble-floored foyer into the large and elegantly decorated den. "This is unbelievable," he said, as he stood taking it all in.

"Would you like something to drink?" Keri asked. She put the sacks of food on the kitchen table and checked the refrigerator for drinks. The state-of-the-art gourmet kitchen opened to the den.

"Water's fine."

Keri took two Waterford crystal footed beverage glasses from behind the glassed cabinet doors and filled them with ice and water. She then set the table with colorful place mats, matching cloth napkins, and sterling flatware. Taking Ryan's grilled chicken sandwich, she heated it slightly in the microwave and transferred it, and her salad, onto elegant bone-china dinner plates. When she had finished, her creative presentation looked like a wonderfully prepared home-cooked meal.

"Lunch is ready," she said.

Ryan walked into the kitchen, paused and stared at what she had done. "Wow! Where's the magician?" He looked at Keri. "This doesn't look like a deli meal to me."

"I just thought it would be nice if we took advantage of what was here."

"Well, I'm impressed. When this day began, I never would have guessed I'd be eating a deli sandwich on bone china, drinking from a cut-crystal glass in a multi-million dollar condo on the Upper East Side. The best I was hoping for was my own park bench where I could chomp down my dry bagel." They both laughed.

"As the old cliché goes, 'It's not what you know, it's who you know," she said.

The ambiance of their luxurious surroundings and seeing Ryan happy made her forget she was on a layover with the airline. Instead, it was more like a date, or, better yet, a dinner at home.

But when he lifted the glass to his mouth, seeing the gold band on his left ring finger reminded her that he belonged to someone else.

After finishing lunch, she asked, "Would you like for me to give you the grand tour?"

"Sure."

The condo had a spectacular layout with five bedrooms, superb entertaining spaces, and terraces offering spectacular views of the city. All the baths were top-of-the line with polished nickel fittings, bowed wood cabinets, and marble floors.

After giving him a tour, she stopped at the large window overlooking Park Avenue. Beautiful, isn't it?" she asked.

"Magnificent. So, if you say your father rarely comes here, why doesn't he sell the place?"

"He uses it for business while he's in New York."

"Must be nice."

"This is only one of the places he owns."

"Really?"

"He has a place in London, Hawaii, Colorado, and even a place in California."

"Wow."

Isolated from the street noise some twenty-five floors below, they continued to stare out the window. Ryan appeared mesmerized by the view. The contrast of the busy city below and the quiet of the apartment made her sense the protected privacy they shared.

Several minutes passed with only the sound of their breathing. Her body tingled with a rush of warmth.

I wish this day would never end.

Unexpectedly, he slowly turned and looked at her, his eyes looking deep into her soul. Time seemed to stop. With each second, she sensed a battle raging wildly within her, growing in intensity; a battle between mind and emotions—right and wrong.

Her grip on restraint was slipping as the rhythmic gait of her heart was spurred-on with each second of his alluring stare. She knew it was too late. She willfully released all restraint and fell into the void between right and wrong, waiting, willing, and wanting.

She took his hand and brought it up to her face, pressing his warm palm against her cheek. She closed her eyes. She felt his other hand on the opposite side of her face gently push a strand of hair behind her ear. His gentle touch set off a rush of sensations throughout her body. Her smooth flesh tightened as millions of tiny blood vessels and glands throughout her epidermal layering constricted erecting legions of protective goose bumps.

When she released him, he brushed the back of his hand against her face as if he were touching delicate porcelain. The feeling of his touch was soothing. With his finger, he traced around her eyes, nose and then slowly over her lips and down to her chin. Her unrestrained submission to his touch encouraged him. He softly kissed her neck, her cheek, her eyelids, and she felt the moisture of his mouth linger wherever his lips had touched.

"Oh Ryan," she responded with a breathy whisper.

As though she were suspended between worlds of black and white, the pleasure of her passion paralyzed her ability to clarify right from wrong. A world of gray engulfed her like a warm ocean. Her mind had no thought of the past or future, only the present.

She opened her eyes. He slowly brought his lips to hers; softly kissing only her upper lip, then the lower. It was their first kiss after many years. It felt good.

He always was a good kisser.

She wanted more.

Her hands found their way around his waist. She stepped in close, bringing their bodies together. She felt his firmness.

He held her head carefully and tenderly between his warm hands and kissed her again—lips parting—letting the kiss slowly grow. Her body exploded with sensations. She felt like she was floating.

The years of wanting to be with him dissolved in the passion of the moment. With every fiber in her body exploding with desire, she trembled, a weakness in her legs.

* * *

Ryan couldn't believe this was happening. The moment she took his hand and moved it to her face, he knew there was no way he could resist. With his body exploding with desire, all logic, all restraint, and every ounce of willpower within him surrendered to the love he'd harbored deep within his heart for her. After all the years of wanting her, they were finally together.

He had never stopped loving her and felt foolish for ever believing that Emily would somehow be able to fill the hole Keri had left in his heart.

His mind told him that what he was doing, and about to do, was wrong—it was adultery, but in another place, somewhere deep within his heart, he believed it was right. After today, he and Keri would never be together again. He was married to Emily, and Keri would soon be with Bill. But today they were together. They had each other and, if only for this one day, nothing else mattered.

She took his hand and led him through an open door and into the master bedroom. He willfully followed. Once in the bedroom, Ryan asked, "Keri, are you sure?"

She put her finger up against his lips. "For today, we belong to each other. If only this once."

Chapter 44

Ryan's flight touched down at the DFW Airport at eight forty-seven that night, a few minutes ahead of schedule. He was not the same man he was when he took off for New York two days ago. Being with Keri had changed him. She was all he could think about. As if a corpse had risen from the grave, his heart was beating with new life. He had fallen in love with her all over again.

After taxiing the big jet to the gate and completing the necessary checklist, he left the cockpit and stood at the entry door greeting passengers. When the last passenger deplaned, he said good-bye to the crew, grabbed his kit bag and suitcase, and headed for the terminal.

His mind began its subconscious transition back to the familiar routines of home, except this time, it was different. The life that awaited him was not the same life he had left two days earlier. How could he face Emily after what he had done?

Although guilt pressed hard against his conscience, it paled in comparison to what he had experienced during the last twelve hours; something that he had only dreamed of: the sincere love of a woman, but not just any woman.

How can something so wrong, feel so right?

He needed to be alone, and the last person he wanted to see was Emily. He would be leaving for Atlanta in the morning to pack up his mom's things and move her to Texas. The two-day drive was just what he needed. It would give him time to think about what had happened in New York.

He glanced at his watch: fifteen past nine. His only hope of avoiding Emily was to arrive after she'd gone to bed.

Once in the terminal, he stopped by a bookstore and browsed the magazine racks trying to kill time. He blindly flipped through a couple of magazines with no interest. His eyes floated over the rack: automotive, sports, money, cooking, bridal...

The woman modeling the wedding dress on the cover of *Modern Bride* caught his eye.

That looks like Keri.

He pulled the issue from the rack for a closer look.

What an amazing resemblance! That woman could pass for her twin.

He knew it was impossible that Keri would have her picture on the cover of a major magazine and definitely not in a wedding gown.

I must be going crazy.

He remembered the time he thought he had seen her in Atlanta in a passing car. Both times, now and then, he'd had her on his mind.

He checked his watch again: nine thirty-five. By the time he dropped his kit bag off in Operations, made his way to the employee parking lot and drove home, it would be well past ten. Hopefully, he could slip in the house, and Emily would already be in bed. Then he could wake up early and hit the road before she woke.

When he pulled into the driveway, the house was dark.

Good, she's probably asleep.

But when the garage door rolled up, her car was not there; relieved that he wouldn't have to face her, but curious as to where she might be. Before he'd left for New York, she had said nothing about being gone when he returned.

He pulled his car into the garage, grabbed his bags and went into the house. When he flipped on the kitchen light, the sight of the kitchen along with the rank smell from the overflowing trash can stunned him. Dishes caked with food filled the sink. He lifted the top to a pizza box on the counter revealing four cold slices.

He thought, Emily must have had a relapse from the Suzie-Homemaker role she had adopted over the last few months.

He knew he couldn't sleep with the kitchen in such a mess, but he first had to change out of his uniform. The rest of the house resembled the kitchen. The bed was unmade and wet towels were on the floor in the bathroom.

He changed into a pair of shorts and headed back to the kitchen. It took him about fifteen minutes to stick the dishes in the dishwasher and take out the trash.

As he was cleaning off the counters, he noticed a hand-written note from Emily.

Ryan,

> *I know the house is a wreck, just like my life would have been if I'd hung around here much longer. I thought it would work, but I guess I either lost the love I once had for you or never really had it in the first place. I probably could have stayed with you if you hadn't broken all your promises and, basically, lied to me.*
>
> *I decided that you'll never be able to give me what I need, and I don't intend on working the rest of my life, like some slave. I was stupid to have ever believed you in the first place. Plus, you are never home, and I told you if you ever brought your mother here, I was leaving.*
>
> *My car is at the airport. I won't be needing it. You'll be hearing from my lawyer.*

Emily

* * *

While Ryan tried to make sense of the note, Emily was 750 miles away settling into her new life in Atlanta. Her flight had arrived at the Hartsfield Airport late that afternoon. She was met by a limo driver and taken to her new home: a large, newly-remodeled luxury apartment in one of downtown Atlanta's best areas.

As a vice president and special assistant to the president, she had been given a lucrative salary, benefits, and the car of her choice. But she didn't come to Atlanta to pursue a career; it was a man she was after, a very wealthy man.

In her numerous trips to the company's headquarters, she and the president had become close. Although he was a married man and much older, she knew that in time, she would become the new, Mrs. Ronald Hart.

Chapter 45

After tossing and turning all night, Ryan couldn't take it any longer; his thoughts ricocheting between his mother, Emily, and Keri. Trying to sleep was a waste of time.

The digital clock on the nightstand glowed: 4:50 a.m.

He pulled himself out of bed, took a shower, repacked his suitcase and grabbed a quick bite to eat. With a fresh mug of coffee, he launched off for Atlanta.

Until reading Emily's note, he had envisioned his drive would be a twelve-hour struggle for answers, mostly filled with compromise and acceptance of life's reality. But now, thanks to his coincidental rendezvous with Keri—a divine appointment, of sorts—Emily's departure had freed him to dream of his first love. His newfound hope was anchored by his mother's words from long ago. "I believed when two souls are meant to be together, nothing can keep them separated. Eventually they will find each other."

As the morning sun pushed above the horizon and the caffeine started to kick in, instead of taking two-days to make the 782 mile drive, he decided to drive nonstop. Arriving late Monday night would give him a full day on Tuesday to start packing up his mom. In her state of mind, he expected to run into a few surprises once he started negotiating with her what she could and could not take back to Texas.

More than anything, he wanted to talk to Keri, to tell her about Emily. He knew she would be excited to hear the news. Hopefully, his mom had Keri's telephone number, if not, he would be forced to call her parent's home before he returned to Dallas on Sunday. The thought of possibly having to speak to Keri's mom wrenched his gut.

Sleep deprived and thirteen hours later, Ryan rolled into the driveway of his mother's small rental house. He peeled himself from the driver's seat, stood by the car, and stretched.

Finally.

He knew his mom would be surprised to see him a day early.

He slipped in through the back door leading into the kitchen. When she heard the door, she turned from the stove and rushed over to him. "Ryan!"

"Hi, Mom." She wrapped her arms around him in a big hug. "Sure smells good in here. Look at all this food! It looks like you've been cooking all day."

"Well, my memory may be going but I still remember how to cook. I fixed all your favorites, including an apple pie."

His eyes caught the lattice-top pie on the counter. "Wow! I can't wait."

"I'll bet you're exhausted. How long was the drive?" She reached behind her and pulled the strings holding her apron.

"Yeah, I'm beat." He glanced up at the wall clock. "Counting the stops, it took me exactly thirteen hours."

"Poor boy. Are you hungry? Let me fix you something to eat. How about a fresh turkey sandwich?" She reached for the refrigerator door. "I know how you love Thanksgiving, so I decided to cook you a turkey." She pulled a whole turkey from the fridge.

"Mom! I can't believe you."

"Why not? I planned a big meal for your arrival tomorrow, but, since you are already here, you can start on it now. I also figured we'd need sandwiches for our trip to Dallas."

The sight of all the home-cooked food and attention from his mother was just what he needed.

She carved the turkey and stacked it high on fresh wheat bread. After adding some lettuce, she placed it on a plate and poured him a glass of milk.

"You look good," he said.

"I feel great. How's Keri?" she asked.

He paused.

Let it go. It's not worth trying to explain.

"She's fine."

In time, he knew he would be faced with the impossible task of trying to help his mom understand, but for now, he couldn't deal with it.

Wouldn't it be weird if Keri and I get together? Then she would never have to know. He chuckled.

"What's so funny?"

"Oh, nothing. I just thought about how much food you cooked, just for the two of us."

"Well, look at you. Somebody needs to feed you. I'm going to have to talk to Keri when I get to Dallas. I thought I'd taught her better."

"Mom, I'm fine, really."

After eating, he helped her clean up the kitchen and then said, "I think I'll hit the sack, I'm exhausted."

"I put fresh sheets on your bed and clean towels in the bathroom, if you need anything, just let me know."

"Thanks, Mom." He hugged her, took his bag, and headed for his old bedroom. After a hot shower, he collapsed.

The next morning, he awoke to the smell of breakfast cooking. When he entered the kitchen, his mom greeted him with a hug. "You look much better," she said. "Did you sleep well?"

"Yes, I needed that. I feel great." The aroma of fresh coffee brewing, biscuits in the oven, and cheese grits made him smile. "Mom, you are amazing. Look at all this food."

"Help yourself to some coffee," she said.

He poured himself a cup, adding milk and a packet of artificial sweetener. "After breakfast, I'll run down to the *U-Haul* place and pick up the trailer I reserved. They weren't expecting me until this afternoon, but hopefully I can pick it up early."

"I've already boxed up most of my things, so it shouldn't take us all week."

Ryan knew better. He would have to recheck each box, ensuring she hadn't packed anything that wasn't absolutely essential. What they didn't take he planned to haul-off to *Good Will* or the trash.

He took a sip of coffee. "We can spend today going through everything. We have today, Friday, and Saturday; that should give us plenty of time." He would need every minute of it, especially with her condition.

The one item he desperately wanted to find was Keri's telephone number in California. He realized he couldn't ask his mom because she thought Keri lived with him, and talking to Barbara Ann was the last thing he wanted to do. Unless a miracle had somehow changed the bitter woman, he was pretty sure she still hated him. Even if he did call her, she would probably refuse to give him her number, making up some lame excuse.

Mom never throws anything away. I'll bet she has every letter Keri has written her hidden in a shoebox, somewhere.

By late Saturday afternoon, the meticulous job of sorting through every detail of his mom's life was complete. With the trailer stuffed tight with boxes, her favorite overstuffed chair, and a rocker which she refused to part with, he convinced her to donate the remaining furniture to *Good Will*. They arranged for a pick up Sunday morning so they could use the beds their last night.

After an exhaustive search of every box and every address book he could find, all that turned up was Keri's old address in Fort Lauderdale—nothing for California. He remembered Keri telling him in New York she hadn't heard from his mom since the wedding. Perhaps, his mom truly believed—more than she didn't—that he and Keri were married and living in Texas.

He had no choice but to call the Hart's house. If he was lucky, Mr. Hart would answer, or possibly Nora Jean, the maid. He and Nora Jean got along great—especially after his dad died and Barbara Ann started treating him like trash. Then again, Nora Jean was probably more afraid of the wrath of Barbara

Ann than she would have been of the conic masks and white robes of the Ku Klux Klan.

On his first attempt no one answered. He decided against leaving a message on the recorder. Several more tries that night were also unsuccessful.

When Ryan awoke Sunday morning, his mom had prepared breakfast and was busy making turkey sandwiches. After eating breakfast and washing the dishes, they packed the last few boxes and loaded them in the back seat of the car.

The *Good Will* truck arrived right on time. Two large men quickly disassembled the beds, loaded them onto their truck, and were off in less than an hour. The little house was completely empty.

"Are you ready to go," he asked.

"I'm ready," she said.

He locked the door and helped his mom into the front seat of the car. "Mom, I forgot to unplug your phone. I'll be back in a second." He closed her car door and hustled back to the house. He had left the phone in the kitchen on purpose, still plugged in. He needed to call Keri's house, one last time.

After dialing and listening to three unanswered rings, Keri's mother answered, "Hello."

"Mrs. Hart, this is Ryan Mitchell—"

"Well, hello Ryan!" She sounded excited, but he knew differently. "It's been a long time. What's going on with you? Did you ever leave the Army?"

"Yes, ma'am, I left the *Navy* a couple of years ago. I'm working for the airlines now—"

"How nice. You know, Keri is also with the airlines."

"Is that right?" He wanted to make it as short as possible; get the number and go. "Well, I called to see if you might have her telephone number?"

"Of course I do, but why in the world would *you* want to contact them."

He thought, *'them'?*

She continued, "Besides, they won't be back in California for at least another week."

Perplexed, he said, "I'm not sure I know what you're talking about. Who is 'them'?"

"Oh Darlin'... you must not know... I'm sorry. Keri is on her honeymoon. Her wedding was just last night, and I must say, it was spectacular. You should have seen her, she was absolutely gorgeous."

He couldn't speak. While his heart raced, his mind rewound to the day he'd spent with Keri in New York. In a matter of seconds, he scanned a mental tape of every minute, but found nothing, not even a hint. She had said nothing about Bill, or anyone else. She was engaged and said nothing.

Why? Why didn't she tell me?

Then it hit him.

She must have been afraid that if I knew she was getting married I wouldn't have had anything to do with her. She wanted us to be together. I knew it! She still loves me. If only I'd known about Emily sooner.

"Ryan, are you still there?"

He no longer needed Mrs. Hart's help. He was too late.

"Ah... yes, ma'am, I'm still here."

"Ryan, Keri is very happy, and I think it would probably be best if you didn't contact her. I think you understand."

"Yeah, I understand," he said sarcastically.

"I knew you would, Dear." Sounding very social, she said, "Now Darlin', be sure and stop by sometime, we would love to—"

He jerked the chord from the wall. "Don't hold your breath! I'll bet you're happy now! You finally got your way."

When he returned to the car, his mother asked, "Is anything wrong? Your face is beet red."

His heart was racing from anger and regret. If he had been within arm's reach of Keri's mom, with her little uppity attitude, he would have backhanded her into next week. None of this would have happened if it hadn't been for her. He took a deep breath and exhaled. After a short pause, he forced a smile and said, "Everything is fine, Mom."

"Are you sure?"

He looked at the sincere concern in her face.

How will I ever explain this to her... probably won't have to.

"I'm positive... everything is fine," he lied.

Things could not be any further from *fine*. He'd committed adultery with a woman his mother thinks he is married to; his wife just left him; and the woman he loves—and who he now knows loves him—is on her honeymoon with some guy named, Bill.

He pulled out of the driveway and onto the road with the trailer in tow. "Mom, it looks like it's just you and me... just like old times."

She reached over and patted him on the shoulder. He glanced at her and then back at the road. "Ryan, it's all going to be alright."

"I know."

But he didn't know. All he did know was he loved Keri and that she loved him. He couldn't rest until he talked with her. He wanted Keri to know that Emily had left him.

Chapter 46

On the return trip to Dallas, Ryan stopped in Vicksburg, Mississippi. He wanted to surprise his mom. He had made reservations at a bed and breakfast located in Vicksburg's historic garden district overlooking the Mississippi River. The fifteen-bedroom inn was a true Southern mansion built in the late 1800s and recently converted to a bed and breakfast. It turned out that his mom was thrilled. Vicksburg, being located half way between Atlanta and Dallas, made for the perfect stop on the easy two-day trip, putting them in Dallas late Monday afternoon.

"We're home," he said, as he backed the trailer into the driveway. Once parked, he switched off the ignition. "Welcome to Texas."

"You have a beautiful home," his mother said.

"I think you'll like it. Let me show you around."

"Okay."

She appeared to be happy. The trip from Atlanta could not have gone smoother. He enjoyed reminiscing about old times. She talked about the past with a surprising clarity, but it was the more recent events that made her stumble.

He was thankful that she had only alluded to Keri twice during the two-day trip: once, when she asked if she would be home when they arrived; and a second time, when she asked if he and Keri had talked about starting a family, anytime soon.

After touring her through the house, he headed back outside to start unloading the trailer, but first, he unloaded the weeks-worth of mail from the mailbox. A casual flip through the stack of mail caused his heart to pump a few extra beats with the sight of each bill or bank statement.

To keep from misplacing the bills, he decided to drop the mail off inside before starting to unpack. Once in the kitchen, he quickly rifled through the mail, tossing the junk mail in the trash. He anxiously ripped open the bankcard statements, afraid of what he might find. With the unfolding of each statement, blood rushed to his face. "What the..."

All five statements showed balances equal to their individual card limits: $10,000; $12,000; $6,000; $5,000; and $15,000. "Emily!" It didn't take him but a second to know what she'd done.

"Is everything okay," his mother asked. "Who is Emily?"

Chapter 47

Keri and Rex arrived back at their Laguna Beach condo, refreshed, tanned, and married. After a trip to the grocery store, Keri planned to start the wash, cook dinner, and settle in.

More than once during her honeymoon, she had thought about Ryan and his mother. She imagined Martha Mitchell adjusting to her new life with Ryan and Emily and hoped she would be happy.

"Martha thinks I married Ryan." She smiled.

Wish I could see the look on Emily's face when she finds out.

Keri returned from the grocery store and found a scribbled note on the kitchen counter.

Keri,

Back in a few.

Love,
Rex

While putting away the groceries, the phone rang. "Hello."

"Keri..." She heard her dad take a worried breath.

"Dad? Is everything okay?"

"Keri, I have bad news. Your mother was in a terrible accident last night, and... she didn't make it."

"What?" She struggled to grasp the reality of what her dad had just told her. "What happened?"

"She was coming home on West Paces Ferry Road when a drunk driver in a pick-up truck crossed into her lane and hit her head-on. She passed away early this morning."

"Dad, are you okay? What can I do?" He was alone. She needed to be with him. She was the only family he had.

"Darling, there is nothing you can do. I'll be fine."

"Dad, I'll catch the first flight out in the morning. Don't worry about picking me up at the airport, I'll rent a car."

"Are you sure?"

"I think it would be easier that way. You're going to be busy with all the details for the funeral. I should be there by three or four tomorrow afternoon."

They spoke briefly before hanging up. The thought of her mother's death saddened her, but, surprisingly, she didn't cry.

Her mind raced, reaching for something that might anchor her in the real world.

I've got so much to do. I need to get a load of wash in, unpack, fix something for dinner, and I should get to bed early... but first, I need to take a bath.

Suddenly, reality blindsided her.

She's gone—her voice, her smile, her touch. I'll never see her again. We will never talk again.

Keri's legs weakened. She collapsed to the couch, bursting into tears, sobbing uncontrollably. Regret and guilt invaded her memory. Scenes of her and her mom arguing flashed through her mind; about things that really didn't matter. It all seemed so useless, now that she was gone.

She heard the back door close. "Keri, I'm home," Rex called out. "What's for dinner?" With her face buried in her hands, she felt Rex sit beside her. Putting his arm around her, he said, "Babe, what's wrong?"

"It's Mom." She forced the news out, wiping her eyes with the back of her hand. "She was killed last night in a car accident."

"Oh honey, I'm sorry." He held her.

"I can't believe this happened," she said.

"I know—"

"Some drunk crossed over into her lane and hit her head-on."

"Babe, I am so sorry." He said, "Life is not fair."

Sniffling, she whimpered, "I know." In the midst of her grief when Rex said, *Life is not fair* she thought of Ryan. It was as if everything "not fair" in her life, rushed into her mind. Possibly a subliminal coping mechanism for dealing with her stress and grief; the brain's way of diluting the trauma.

He leaned in and kissed her on the cheek. "Honey, why don't you run up and take a hot bath, it will make you feel better. I'll take care of dinner."

She sensed the distinct smell of alcohol on his breath. "Have you been drinking?"

"What makes you think that?" She moved closer and sniffed his breath.

"Because you reek with the smell of booze!" She jumped up in anger. "I don't believe you! You're no better than the drunk that murdered my mother!"

"Babe, I just had a couple of drinks."

"Bad timing, Rex!" she said as she stormed off.

The remainder of the evening flashed by. Drained of emotion, after bathing, she packed for her trip then fell asleep without eating.

She woke at six, showered, dressed, and slipped out without waking Rex. When she arrived at the airport, the flight she had planned to take canceled because of a mechanical problem.

The airline rebooked the passengers on the next flight making it impossible for any standbys to be accommodated. With any luck, she could catch the flight that departed in two hours which was scheduled to arrive in Atlanta at five-fifteen.

That's going to put me in the middle of rush traffic.

She needed to call her dad and tell him she would be late.

Chapter 48

When Emily Anderson arrived at work, the office was buzzing with the news about the death of Ronald Hart's wife. She immediately rushed to his house.

As his special assistant, she knew he would be contacting her soon, but her interest went far beyond her professional responsibilities. With his wife now out of the way, Emily needed to be sure Ronald knew she was there for him.

When he opened the door, she said, "I just heard. I knew you would need some help."

"Yes." He stepped aside. "Come in. Your timing was perfect. I was just on my way out."

When he closed the door, she turned and gazed up into his eyes. "Is there anything I can do?"

"Would you mind staying at the house today? There are some details I need to attend to, and it would be nice if someone, other than the help, were here to answer the phone."

"Certainly." She followed him through the kitchen and into the garage.

After sliding into his car, he reached up and pressed a button starting the electric garage door up, then started the engine. "I'm expecting my daughter this afternoon. Other than her, there's no other family."

She bent over, resting her hands on her thighs, thankful she had worn her favorite red dress with its deep plunging neckline. As she'd hoped, his eyes stole a quick look at her cleavage. "I'm here for you," she said. "Just let me know what you want me to do."

He met her gaze. "For the next few weeks, we need to be discreet. In time, we will be free to do as we please, most people will even expect it."

"Anything you say."

He reached his hand out of the car window and up to the side of her head and gently pushing a strand of hair behind her ear. "All I want is for you to be happy," he said.

"I couldn't be happier, and don't you worry, everything is going to work out fine."

"I know." He took her hand and kissed the back of it. "Thank you for being here."

She leaned in and kissed him softly on the cheek then stepped away from the car.

As he backed out of the garage, she watched him leave.

I can't wait to see Keri's face when she finds out about me and her dad.

She smiled and waved to Ronald one last time before the garage door rolled down.

* * *

Ronald paused, smiling at the beautiful young blond in the red dress as the metal curtain rolled down touching softly against the high gloss finish of the polyurethane coated floor.

The vision of the young woman was slow to fade from his thoughts. Any man his age would die to have such a woman beckoning his affection.

He reached for the shifter located between the two plush leather seats, pulled it into "drive", then slowly maneuvered the luxury sedan around the circular drive that cut through the perfectly manicured lawn beneath towering oaks. Once at the end of the long drive and through the iron gate, he checked both ways and drove onto Habersham Road.

Neither his late wife nor his daughter knew of his threatening health concerns that had risen since his bypass surgery, six years ago. His condition, diagnosed as ischemic cardiomyopathy—an enlarged heart—had been the result of his coronary artery disease.

Recent episodes of chest pains and shortness of breath had driven him to visit his cardiologist. Tests revealed that since his bypass surgery, his heart had enlarged considerably along with increased coronary damage—both conditions untreatable by medical or surgical means.

Because his health and age put him in a high risk category for a heart transplant, his doctor had been forced to deliver the sad news: he had less than a year to live.

He had enticed the young blond to Atlanta with promises of marriage and a life of financial security, something he'd hoped his daughter would be slow to discover. But now, Keri was coming to Atlanta. This was not the way he had planned it. He needed more time. His biggest concern was how she would react once she learned that the young blond he was entertaining was none other than, Emily Mitchell.

As for now, he would make a quick stop by the funeral home and then visit with his good friend and lawyer, Philip Darby. Phil had worked with him closely during the past year structuring a will that accounted for every possible variable, including his plans for the young Emily Mitchell.

The unexpected death of his wife, though tragic, required that he accelerate his plan ahead of schedule. Time was of the essence.

Chapter 49

With the payphone receiver pressed against her ear, Keri anxiously waited for her dad to answer; her chest growing tighter with each unanswered ring.

Come on, Dad, pick up, pick up, pick up. Where are you?

She scanned the crowded terminal: a businessman worried about his connection; a mother calming her sleep-deprived infant; a middle-aged woman nervously biting her nails—Keri assumed either nicotine-starved or a white-knuckled flyer.

"Hello." A strange woman's voice answered.

Surprised, she said, "Ah... this is Keri Hart, is my father there?"

"Oh, hi, Keri. Your dad is not here at the moment, but he mentioned that you would be arriving this afternoon."

"That's what I called about. I wanted to let him know that I will be arriving later than planned... hopefully by six or seven."

"I'll tell him."

Keri paused, then asked, "Who is this?"

There was a moment of awkward silence, and then the woman said, "That's too bad about your mother... I mean the drunk. It's terrible that she had to go like that. But in a way, I guess it was a good thing."

Her comment caught Keri off guard. "Excuse me?"

"I mean, your dad really didn't love her anymore."

"What's that suppose to mean? Are you saying just because my father didn't love my mother, that she might as well be dead? Who are you?"

"No, not really. It's just a good thing she doesn't have to live with the pain of knowing her husband is in love with another woman. It's easier this way... for everyone."

"Everyone?" Keri said angrily, "And how do you know so much about my dad?"

"Oh, I've known your dad for some time. He and I have grown very close over the last year. Listen, I know he wants to tell you himself, but considering the circumstances, I guess I could go ahead. Your dad and I are in love and plan to be married soon."

"Married! That's impossible!" Heads turned her way and stared. Keri pulled the receiver away from her ear and yelled into the phone, "Who are you?"

"Keri, I know with everything happening so suddenly, you have good reason to be upset, but I'm sure once we get to know each other—"

"In your dreams!" She slammed the receiver down. Her mind spinning like a top.

Dad, how could you do this? How could you do this to Mom? To me? Why? I thought we were close?

Her dad must have been seeing this woman before her mom died... for at least a year, maybe longer.

He's probably glad Mom is dead. That's disgusting!

She suddenly saw no reason for going to Atlanta. She was only going to comfort her dad. It looked like he already had that area covered.

As far as she was concerned, he, along with his little skank, could rot. Now that her mom was dead, that woman would be moving into his house—the house Keri once called home. She never wanted to see him, or that woman, as long as she lived.

* * *

When she returned home, it was almost eleven o'clock. Rex was gone.

She spent the rest of the day trying to piece together her life; to make sense of all the confusion. Her mother was dead, her father had betrayed her, and her husband was not there when she needed him most. She needed someone to talk with that would understand. If only...

At five o'clock, the phone rang. "Hello."

"Keri, are you okay?"

The sound of his voice sickened her. Her first thought was to hang up, but she didn't. "Dad, how could you do it?"

"Keri, let me explain."

"Explain? Explain what? I think I've heard about all I want to hear. You make me sick!"

"It's not like you think—"

"How can you say that? I talked to that woman. She told me everything."

"Keri—"

"I guess you're happy now. Mom is dead! Now you can get on with your life. You and your little—"

"Please, Keri—"

"Don't expect to see me at the funeral, and do me a favor... leave me alone. I never want to see you, or that woman, as long as I live." She slammed the phone down and then cried.

The next morning, Keri rolled over and noticed that Rex had stayed out all night. She checked his schedule. He wasn't due to fly out for two days.

Chapter 50

One month later—May 1986

Driving south on the 405 from LAX, Keri felt unusually tired. It had been a routine trip to New York and back, but she was exhausted.

She expected Rex would be home since his trip was scheduled to arrive at noon. They each had three days off. It would be the first time since the honeymoon that they had been at home together for more than one night.

Her body had been acting strange. She thought the slight tinge of nausea she had experienced in New York might have been from the pizza she had eaten for dinner. But combined with her sore breasts and being almost a week late starting her period, she suspected something else. She placed her hand on her belly.

Could I be pregnant?

Before they got married, she and Rex had talked about having children, but not this soon. When the conversation came up, Rex was always excited about the idea, but wanted to wait a year or so. He had said he thought it would be good for their marriage if they waited. She thought back to the honeymoon and remembered how careful Rex had been to use protection. However, there was once, while they were in the whirlpool tub, that he hadn't.

It only takes one, she thought. *One strong swimmer.*

The fastest way to know for sure was to stop and pick up a self-pregnancy tester. She remembered a pharmacy near her house. This way, she and Rex could find out together, tonight. Although it was unexpected and earlier than planned, she knew he would be just as excited as she was; that is, if she was pregnant.

When she arrived home, Rex was not there. In a way, she was glad. It would give her time to take a quiet bath and unwind a bit before he returned. The thought of shedding her uniform, a warm bath, and slipping into something comfortable sounded wonderful.

Anxious to be ready when Rex returned, she rushed the bath. While toweling off, she noticed his doc kit was not by his sink nor was his suitcase in the spot where he normally parked it after a trip.

I thought he was due in hours ago.

She checked his schedule, then called the airline to check arrivals. She was right. His flight landed on schedule. She glanced at her watch: 4:45.

She convinced herself that administering the self-pregnancy test before he arrived would not be all that bad. It might even be a good thing. After all, when it comes down to it, men just want the facts: yes or no.

She tore open the box and removed the contents. Interested in exactly how the test worked and how accurate it was, she took time to read the enclosed pamphlet.

She learned that a pregnancy can be detected within days of conception, but the test is ninety-nine percent accurate when used on or after the day of your expected period. For her, it had been five days since the date she'd expected her period.

After the test, she anxiously waited the required minutes, staring at the little stick. Right before her eyes, the color band appeared, bright. Her heart fluttered with excitement. There was no doubt now, she was pregnant.

She pulled her shirt up and looked at her flat stomach. Soon, she would be waddling like many of the pregnant women she had envied. A warmth rushed to her face. Thoughts of being a mother filled her with joy.

Her attention was quickly diverted when she heard the sound of the back door opening.

That must be Rex!

Chapter 51

With Mrs. Hart six feet under, Emily decided it was time to turn the heat up on Ronald Hart. Three weeks had been long enough. It was time to end the gossip and introduce the next Mrs. Ronald Hart to the Buckhead social network; mostly made up of gossipy-old women who could care less whether the Hart woman was dead or alive. Up until now, Emily had been nothing more than a sacrificial lamb to the gossip gods. As *they* put it: "Ronald Hart's young little blond *friend*".

Things were about to change—big time.

When she approached Ronald to discuss the idea of moving in, he surprisingly beat her to the punch. Not only did he suggest she leave her apartment, he rolled out the red carpet by offering to help her resolve her divorce with Ryan. "I have a great lawyer," he'd said. "He can take care of everything very quickly." From the beginning, all Ronald ever wanted to do was take care of her. She thought, finally, someone appreciated her.

Although anxious to become Mrs. Ronald Hart, one thing about Ronald puzzled her. Since they had been dating, he had not made the first sexual advance toward her. He hugged her and kissed her occasionally, mostly on the forehead or cheek, but was always the perfect gentleman, almost fatherly. He seemed to be completely satisfied simply by her company and the attention she gave him. In a way, she liked it. The thought of sleeping with the old geezer sent chills up her spine. She wondered if he would change once she moved in.

Chapter 52

Ryan didn't waste any time assessing the financial damage left in the wake of Emily's departure. After all the monthly bills and statements hit, with the help of a budget counselor, he was able to put together a survival plan. The bare-bones plan allowed him enough to eat, pay the mortgage, cover the basic utilities, and the minimums due on all the debts. Short of a boost in his income or some form of miracle, he was looking at a debt prison for at least the next five years.

What he needed was a good lawyer, but that took money—money he didn't have. Besides, no lawyer in his right mind, after doing a credit check, would be willing to take him on as a client.

Even though the advances Emily had taken on the bank cards were on joint accounts, the divorce should bring everything to the table, unless the little con had already squandered the money.

His financial nightmare was further compounded by the need to care for his confused mother. He'd temporarily hired a neighbor's high school daughter to watch her while he was on trips. But once the summer ended and school started, he would have to come up with another plan.

He found his escape—his happy place—in thinking about Keri. He replayed that day in New York until his mental tape seemed to blur between reality and what he'd imagined happened. With each day, the hope of ever seeing her again grew more remote. For the time being, the idea of finding her would have to be postponed. He had no money and little time. After all, she had her life with Bill.

Chapter 53

"I'm home," Rex called out, as he closed the door. He looked up to see Keri coming down the stairs.

"I missed you. Where have you been? I thought your flight landed at noon."

"I had to give the guy I was working with a ride home. Dude didn't tell me he lives on the other side of the airport until we were in the parking lot."

"What happened to his car?"

"It was in the shop. Something about his wife dropped him off and she had forgotten she needed to pick him up... blah, blah, blah... you know the story; good old Rex comes to the rescue."

He hugged her and gave her a peck on the lips. "So, how did your first trip go?"

"Good." A smile tugged at the corner of her lips.

"What's up?"

She took his hand, led him into the den and sat on the couch. For a brief moment, she gazed into his eyes. "I've got some good news."

He smiled. "Well... give it up."

She placed his hand on her stomach.

"What?" He looked down at her stomach and then back up to her face. She was blushing and smiling. His eyes widened. "No!"

She's not...

She smiled and nodded. "Yes. I'm pregnant."

"No! You can't be!" He jerked his hand away. "It's impossible!" He jumped up from the couch.

"What's wrong? I know it's not exactly like we planned, but I thought you'd be excited."

"Excited! Oh yeah, I'm friggin thrilled to death!"

"I don't understand."

"What's to understand? You're pregnant." All he could think about was Dr. Stickler and the obnoxious red head. This was not suppose to happen. Just to make sure, he'd used a condom every time he had sex.

This can't be happening!

"You said you wanted to start our family." Tears spilled from her eyes.

"It's too soon. We're not ready."

"Rex, why are you so mad?" He started to leave. "Where are you going?"

"I need to be alone!" He left the house, slamming the door behind him.

He remembered the redhead saying, "Now you will still need to use protection when you have sex until we get a clear sample."

He racked his brain trying to remember every time they had sex. He was positive he had always used a condom. Then he remembered the one time on the honeymoon in the tub; he was drunk.

Just my luck.

Chapter 54

One year later—April 1987

As the jet streaked through the cloudless sky somewhere over California on descent for landing at Orange County's John Wayne Airport, Ryan stared down at the ground through the small window beside his cramped passenger seat.

The past year had been one ginormous emotional roller coaster ride; his biggest high being the day he spent with Keri Hart in New York. By any measure, he knew the world—and God—would judge him severely for what they had done that day. But in hindsight, he had no guilt, only remorse for not having told her how much he loved her before it was too late.

Then the bottom fell out. If he had only known about Emily—the real Emily. It was exactly what his mother had warned him about during their many Sunday morning talks. She'd said, "I pray that, over the years, you will learn how to listen to your heart; to know it and trust it before some cute little girl comes along and sweeps you off your feet. The kind of girl that's only thinking about one thing—herself!"

How could I have been so stupid? I should have seen it from the beginning.

But at the time, he interpreted her advice as nothing more than an overly protective mother's worried concern for her son. Never before had her words meant so much.

Although Emily's reckless abandonment had left him on the throes of financial ruin, her departure had freed him to pursue the only woman he had ever truly loved; someone he now believed to be his soul mate. But learning of the news of Keri's marriage sent him into a freefall for the depths of despair.

After he'd returned to Texas with his mother, the first few months passed slowly, with the days of each week spread thinly between work and caring for his disoriented mother.

At the time, he knew that until the divorce was finalized with Emily, he would remain buried beneath suffocating debt payments. A leap of progress was made when he located a hungry divorce lawyer willing to receive payment for his services after the settlement was complete.

Once contacted, Emily's lawyer stepped forward surprisingly eager to finalize the divorce. After the required sixty-day waiting period, the two lawyers negotiated an acceptable agreement within a few months.

Emily agreed to take full responsibility for all of the debts she had run-up, to split any equity gains they received from the sale of their house, and accepted a small cash settlement for the remaining property they jointly owned.

Ryan found Emily's change in character odd, but he was not about to question it. He suspected that her willingness to let go so easily was because she had attached herself to a fresh host victim, much like a tick on a dog's back.

It took a few more months to sell the house, after which, he and his mom moved into a rental house. When it was all over, the debts were cleared, the lawyer was paid, and Ryan had a new lease on life.

Amid the tumultuous year, he longed to talk with Keri. A recent attempt to contact her parents in Atlanta, hoping to find her number, met with surprising news. The maid answered and informed him of the tragic death of Mrs. Hart, shortly after Keri's wedding, and that Mr. Hart was in intensive care following a recent heart attack.

When he queried the maid for more information about Keri, she replied, "Mr. Ryan, all I know is that she is married now and living in California. That's all I know."

The airline had no record of anyone by the name "Keri Hart" being employed. He assumed that she must have either quit or changed her last name to her married name.

He strained to recall if Keri had mentioned Bill's last name in the letter she'd sent him. He remembered her saying he was a pilot, but couldn't remember if she'd mentioned the airline. Finding a pilot by the name of "Bill", even if he knew the airline, would have been impossible.

Maybe I still have the letter.

He paused a brief moment, then dismissed the thought after having no clue where to look.

With his airline rapidly expanding, he felt it was the perfect time to transfer to the West Coast. His seniority at the LA crew base would offer him a better schedule, translating into more control over his life; something he desperately needed with his mother's worsening condition.

He knew it wouldn't be long until she would need professional care and after contacting the Alzheimer's Foundation of America, he learned of a wonderful facility in Orange County.

The only person he knew in California was his old Navy buddy, Rex Dean. He hadn't seen him or talked with him since they finished their initial training at the airline. He knew Rex was based in LA, and after a quick call to the LAX flight office he was able to locate his number. Once the admin assistant learned of Ryan's possible transfer to the base, and that he and Rex were old friends, she referenced Rex's bid line and passed along his days off.

When he called Rex to tell him that he was considering moving to California and interested in coming out for a visit, at first, Rex sounded strangely reluctant to help. However, after they'd exchanged a few stories from the past, he not only offered to help, but also invited him sailing, over for dinner, and before the conversation had ended, he insisted that he spend the night at his place.

* * *

Rex popped the tailgate up on his Jeep Cherokee parked in the driveway of his Laguna Beach condo. He tossed a small ice chest in the back, then glanced down at his watch: ten past eleven.

Ryan's flight should be on the ground by now.

He knew the day would eventually come, but when he'd picked up the phone last Monday and heard Ryan Mitchell's voice, it caught him completely off guard—especially when Ryan mentioned his plans to transfer to LA, and that he wanted to come out for a visit.

But during the conversation, he thought, why not? He could take him sailing, which would be the perfect opportunity to ease the news on him. After a few beers at dinner, they would all be laughing about it.

While loading the car, he replayed in his mind how Keri's reaction had made it so easy.

* * *

"Who was that, Honey?"

Rex turned to see her walking into the room. "Nobody."

"I heard you talking to someone."

"Oh that. Just an old Navy buddy."

"Did I hear you mention something about going sailing?"

Rex moved around Keri and toward the kitchen. "Yeah, I told him we should go sailing this weekend."

"That sounds nice. If he's married, we can make it a foursome."

"No!"

Keri recoiled at his sharp reaction.

"What I mean is, no, he's not married."

"Are you okay? You're acting kinda weird."

"I'm fine. It's just... hearing the poor dude's story put me on edge. His ex ripped him a new one after a wicked divorce."

"I'm sorry. Maybe we should have him over for dinner. I'm sure he could use a good home-cooked meal." Keri turned when she heard the baby cry.

"Yeah, I'm sure he would like that," Rex said.

"Well, be sure to invite him over." The cry grew louder pulling her away.

* * *

Although Keri's pregnancy had almost driven Rex crazy, nothing could have prepared him for the sleepless nights and siren-like screams once the little terror was freed from the womb. But now that the baby was three months old, life showed signs of returning to normal. He slept through most nights and Keri was working again.

Since Rex never intended on being in the baby business, when it came to baby duty, he had his limits. He refused to be left alone with the kid, and he wasn't about to touch one of those stinky diapers. "That's why God made women," he would say. At first, he reluctantly agreed to hire a nanny but later admitted that it had been money well spent. It freed him from worrying about Keri's work schedule and allowed him to come and go as he pleased.

Ryan's flight was scheduled to land around ten o'clock. To ensure that Keri would be gone when he arrived, he sent her to the grocery store to pick up some steaks and beer.

The plan was for he and Ryan to spend the afternoon sailing while Keri prepared dinner for him and "one of his old Navy buddies". Keri always jumped at the opportunity to do a little entertaining. This time, he figured, it was his turn to bring the entertainment to her. After all, he owed her a surprise for having ambushed him with the news that she was pregnant.

Chapter 55

Flat on his back, Ronald Hart stared up at the acoustical-tiled ceiling from his bed in Piedmont Hospital's coronary care unit (CCU), while sophisticated computers continuously monitored his vital signs. The only sound: a rhythmic and welcomed beep coming from the cardiac monitor.

Oxygen flowed into his nose through the two prongs of the nasal cannula with an intravenous line in his arm; ready for administering periodic pain relievers or other life-saving drugs.

The antiseptic smell, harsh lighting, and stiff furniture of the drab hospital room were a vast contrast to the luxury of his Buckhead estate.

A light knock on the partially opened door was followed by a familiar voice. "I wish you had called to let me know you were planning another party down here," Philip Darby said, as he eased into the room.

A smile tugged at the corner of Ronald's mouth. "Invitations are going out this afternoon."

Philip moved to the side of his bed. "How are you doing, buddy? Any pain?"

"No, they have me pretty doped up." He turned and gazed up at Phil. "Phil, I think this one might be it."

"Nonsense."

Weak and sedated, Ronald lifted his hand to Phil's arm. "Tell me... is everything in place."

"Everything is finished. All the pieces are falling into place beautifully."

"Phil, how do you think she will remember me?"

"First of all, you're not going anywhere soon." He took Ronald's hand. "Ron, she loves you, and I know how much you love her; that's all that matters."

"I just want her to be happy."

"I know you do."

"I want her to have the life I didn't. She deserves it after what she has been through."

"Trust me, you can rest assured that her life is going to be wonderful."

"I hope so. I just wish I could live to see it."

Philip Darby placed Ronald's hand back on top of his chest. "Look at you; you'll probably be playing racquetball next week. But for now, you need your rest. I'll be back tomorrow." He turned to leave, stopping at the door. "Now you be sure and let me know if they let you go home... and Ron, take it easy on those young nurses."

Ronald grinned at him, giving him a thumbs-up sign.

* * *

Emily pulled the BMW luxury sedan into a handicapped parking slot in front of the hospital. She quickly marched through the electric doors and to the elevator. She paced impatiently until the doors opened.

She had become very comfortable living in the Hart house during the last year, bossing the help around, acting as if she owned the place.

Ronald Hart's illness had been the best thing that had ever happened to her. With his constant assurance that she would be taken care of after his death, she felt empowered in a way only possible with great wealth.

When the elevator doors opened, she hurried down the hallway to his room. She needed to make it quick. Her hair appointment was in less than an hour.

She paused briefly, took a deep breath and exhaled slowly before pushing the heavy wooden door open. She eased up to the side of his bed. White sheets and a thin blanket, pulled to his chest, encased his slender body like a corpse.

When she took the frail hand of the sixty-five-year old man, he opened his eyes and smiled at her. "Emily."

She forced a smile, leaned down and kissed his forehead. "How are you feeling?"

"Well, I don't think I am up for a marathon, at least not today."

"I wanted to stop by to see if you needed anything, or if I can do anything for you."

"Emily, you have been so good to me. I'm sorry this had to happen."

She put a finger to his lips. "Don't think like that. You're coming home soon, and you're going to be fine," she lied. His doctor had told her there was not much they could do. He needed a new heart, but his age, medical condition, and a lack of donors ruled out the option of a transplant.

He smiled, "There is something you can do for me."

"Anything."

"Do you see the envelope over on the table?" He rolled his eyes toward the nightstand beside the bed.

"Yes."

"I want you to take it and put it somewhere safe. Don't open it now."

"When do I open it?"

He gazed up into her eyes. After a brief moment, he said, "When this thing finally beats me, I want you to open it, but not until then."

She stared at the envelope wondering what might be inside. "Okay."

"Promise me you won't open it until..."

"Sure, I promise."

"Good." He closed his eyes, seemingly very tired.

"I better go. You need your rest." She leaned over and kissed him again. "I'll be back in the morning." He didn't respond. She left the room, anxious to join the living. Hospitals and sick people creeped her out.

Once in the car, she took the envelope and tore it open, pulling the single piece of paper out. She sat quietly and read it.

Dear Emily,

There will not be a funeral. I have no existing family, except for a daughter who has all but disowned me. In a way, you are the only family I have.

Philip Darby, my lawyer, will contact you within a day or so after my death. He has been instructed to give you a package. The package will contain my ashes. I hope this does not make you uncomfortable, but I felt I could count on you to do me this last favor.

I arranged for my corporate jet to fly you to California where I would like you to disperse my ashes off the coast of Newport Harbor. Arrangements for a yacht have been made.

A limo will pick you up at the Orange County Airport, and hotel accommodations have been made for a week's stay at the Watford Hotel & Resort near Dana Point. They will be expecting you. You will have an open account, and all of your expenses will be taken care of.

I want this to be a time for you to relax and celebrate. I don't want you to mourn my death. You are a beautiful woman with a long life ahead of you. I want you to start it in style.

When you return to Atlanta, Mr. Darby will contact you with the details of the final reading of my will. I would like for you to attend.

Love,
Ron

Emily lifted her head. "Thank you."
Looks like I've got some shopping to do.

Chapter 56

As the jet descended for landing, Ryan gazed down at the California real estate—growing larger by the minute. Flight attendants scurried up and down the narrow aisle ensuring seatbacks were up and tray tables were stowed.

Once on the ground and clear of the runway, the jet lumbered to the gate where anxious passengers were finally freed from their cramped confines.

Ryan maneuvered his way through the bustling crowd and onto the escalator leading down into the dungeon of baggage carousels and nicotine-starved passengers.

After checking in at the rental car counter and completing the necessary paperwork, he headed to the adjoining covered garage to pick up his car. The attendant checked his paperwork and then offered directions to Laguna Beach.

With the ocean only a few miles away, the air felt clean and fresh, circulating beneath a cloudless blue sky. Tall palms with their feathery tops lined the street, evenly spaced, like sentinels standing guard over the tropical oasis.

Waiting at a traffic light, he breathed deep as the fragrance of lilac drifted in through his open window. He'd forgotten the stunning array of floral beauty that flourished in the tropical climate of Southern California: hibiscus, bougainvillea, and his favorite, bird-of-paradise plants—frozen in flight—filled the median with their marvelous combination of distinctive shape and brilliant color. The sight, smell, and feel of it all left no doubt of his being in a place often referred to as "paradise".

* * *

Less than thirty minutes later—11:25—Ryan pulled up in front of Rex Dean's condo. A Jeep Cherokee was parked in the driveway with the tailgate up. A small ice chest and a black sports bag had been loaded in the rear.

As he unfolded his tall frame from the small rental, he heard Rex call out, "Hey Buddy! How's it going?" He greeted him with the same big smile he'd remembered; a smile that had melted the hearts of women all over the world.

Barefoot wearing navy shorts with a tight fitting white cotton shirt, his California tan made it obvious that he spent most of his days outdoors. A pair of sunglasses rested on top of his head, partly hidden in his thick, wavy blond hair.

"Couldn't be better," Ryan said.

Rex ignored Ryan's extended hand and instead locked him up in a manly hug with a few firm pats on the back.

"So, you finally came to your senses and decided to move to paradise?"

"I'm thinking about it."

"Dude, you're going to love it. The weather, the ocean... and the *chicks*." He winked. "Just doesn't get any better than this."

The sound and inflection in his voice rang with a familiar resonance.

The same old Rex, still on the prowl.

"Sounds great," Ryan said.

"Hey, Dude, if you don't mind, how about moving your piece out on the curb... better yet, park it across the street. It'll save us from doing it later."

"Sure, no problem."

After repositioning the rental, they jumped in the Cherokee and took off for Newport Harbor. "Boy, it's good to see you," Rex said reaching over and patting Ryan on the shoulder.

"Same here."

"Hey, sorry to hear about Emily."

"Thanks. I'm just glad it's over."

"Well, once you get moved back out here, you'll forget all about that skank." Rex looked at him with wide eyes. "Dude, you're prime, and I know just the chick for you."

"Thanks... but no thanks. If I remember correctly, it was you who pointed me to Emily."

"Yeah, bummer. But, Dude, I've changed. You're looking at the new and much improved Rexter."

"Oh yeah?"

"Totally."

"I'll believe it when I see it." Ryan turned with an expression of comical disbelief. "This time, I need proof."

"Trust me, before sunset, you'll have your proof."

"What, may I asked, caused this metamorphosis? Did you finally meet a woman that was able to tame your wild side?"

He glanced over at Ryan and smiled. "All I'm going to say is that you're in for the shock of your life."

"Is that so?"

Rex wheeled into the small parking lot of the sailing club, parked and quickly exited the Cherokee. "I'll be back in a second."

Ryan stepped out of the car and gazed out over the harbor. Mast protruded from the numerous boats like pins from a watery pincushion. The club had a nice selection of boats in the nineteen to thirty-two foot range.

His gaze lifted beyond the club boats and across the harbor. *Wow!*

Huge boats were docked in front of unbelievable water-front mansions; some of the most expensive real estate in the world.

The quiet was broken by the gentle throbbing of a diesel engine, as a beautifully restored Kettenberg graced the harbor with its smooth curves and low sheer. The polished wooden hull with its fine entry displayed the craftsmanship of an era gone by.

In contrast, a large yacht—at least a sixty footer—maybe more—was making its way slowly through the harbor. He knew that yachts that size would be priced in excess of a million dollars.

As he admired the sleek lines and smooth curves of the luxury yacht, his eyes zeroed-in on the curves of the two busty women in their tiny bikinis perched on its bow. Then he noticed two men up in the flybridge talking. It amazed him how young the two couples appeared to be.

"You ready to go?" Rex asked, as he stepped up behind him.

"You bet."

Lifting the tailgate, Rex grabbed the small ice chest in one hand and black bag in the other.

"Here, let me get that." Ryan said, reaching for the bag.

"We'll be in the thirty-foot Catalina." Rex slammed the tailgate closed.

They walked down the steps to the dock. Ryan couldn't help but chuckle when he noticed the name given to their boat. Written in script on the stern, it said: "Easy Come, Easy Go".

I can identify with that.

They loaded the boat and prepared the sails. Rex cranked the diesel while Ryan untied the rope on the bow and cast off.

Once away from the docks and in the harbor, Ryan took the helm while Rex raised the main sail. Positioned directly into the wind, the ruffling of the trailing edge of the sail let them know that the need for the diesel would be short-lived.

Next, Rex unrolled the jib and used the winch to draw it tight. With the sails made ready, Ryan turned the tiller slightly and with a pop, the stiff breeze filled the large canvas.

"Kill the engine," Rex said.

Ryan reached down and turned the key off to the engine. The sound of water slapped against the hull as they moved gracefully under the power of the wind against their sails.

Ryan looked up at the trailing edge of the main sail and the wind indicator mounted on the top of the mast. He adjusted the tiller slightly to maximize the angle of the wind against the main sail.

Off the bow, the yacht he had seen earlier had reversed course in the harbor and was approaching on their port side. It looked much larger and more impressive up close: definitely, Italian made.

The powerful twin diesels purred, twisting the props beneath the surface of the water churning a small, white, foamy wake to its rear.

The two buxom beauties were still perched on the front deck, like hood ornaments on a fine car. The closer view confirmed Ryan's earlier observation: they were young, probably in their late twenties.

Ryan's lustful gaze was quickly tempered by what he knew existed behind the veil of their perfectly sculptured bodies. More than likely, it was not the men the women were after, but their money; like vultures, perched, and ready to swoop down on the dead and rotting flesh of a carcass. If given enough time, the two predators would surely mount their unsuspecting victims like road kill on some deserted highway, stripping them of the booty that was the extent of their manhood, leaving the two hormone-charged studs with little more than a painful memory.

Ryan's attention quickly snapped to the bow of the sailboat when he noticed that Rex had removed his shirt and blue shorts, standing proud, wearing nothing but a canary yellow Speedo-style swimsuit and sunglasses.

With his manhood bulging like an arched banana, Rex waved at the girls as their boat passed only feet away, totally ignoring the men. The girls waved back, giggling.

"What a pair of hotties!" Rex called out.

Ryan cringed knowing that Rex's voice had echoed off the water like a loudspeaker into the harbor. They passed close

enough to have shaken hands. The men stared down angrily
from their elevated tower.

"Hey Buddy!" Rex called back to Ryan. "See what I mean?
We need to get us some of that!"

Ryan stood frozen at the tiller in total embarrassment. He
smiled and tipped his head at the girls as the yacht powered by.
He could see that they were amused with Rex's bold outburst of
testosterone.

The men were also waving, or more like jabbing, with only
the middle finger of their raised hand.

Rex made his way back to the cockpit. "Rex!" Ryan
whispered strongly. "You're going to get us shot."

"Dude, calm down. There's nothing wrong with looking,"
he calmly responded. Quickly changing his tone, he said, "Did
you see those two babes? They were unbelievable! Dude, don't
you just love California?"

They continued through the harbor toward the jetties, the
yacht almost out of sight, moving in the opposite direction.

Based on the short time he had spent with Rex and what he
had seen so far, Ryan couldn't wait to hear what Rex had meant
when he'd said, "I've changed." He looked at him in that
ridiculous-looking bathing suit.

Only Rex.

"So, Buddy, tell me about this *miraculous* change in your
life." He expected him to say something lame, like, he'd
stopped dating women younger than he was, or, possibly, he no
longer went to bed with a woman unless he knew her last name.

The thirty-foot Catalina glided through the calm water
abeam the jetties leading to the open Pacific.

"I'm married," Rex said.

Ryan stared at Rex, dumbfounded. The words didn't fit.
"You! Married?"

Rex smiled and said, "Dude, I told you you'd be surprised."

"Rex Dean, married? When did this happen?" Ryan asked,
his face twisted between a look of shock and amazement.

Rex glanced up briefly, then back. "Been about a year."

Sounding slightly angry, Ryan asked, "Why didn't you tell me?"

Rex snapped back. "Dude, I called your house and told Emily. She was quick to drop the news that your mom was very sick. Her exact words were that she was "on her deathbed". I decided you didn't need to be bothered with my wedding. I figured you had your hands full, and from the sound of it, it didn't sound like your mom was your only problem."

"Yeah, you can say that again," Ryan said under his breath. "Rex, she lied to you. My mom *is* sick, but she's not exactly on her deathbed. She has Alzheimer's.

"Sorry, Dude. For whatever reason, she really blew off on me. If I'd only known—"

"There's no way you could have known. That's just one example of what my life has been like with that little twit."

For a brief moment, Rex reflected on his conversation that day with Emily. It didn't go exactly like he had told Ryan. For starters, Emily had called him.

She said she had been looking through some old pictures and wanted to see how things were going. Rex knew she wanted more than that; she wanted him. But for the first time in his life, he had to say no to a woman. After he told her about Keri, she acted as if she already knew. It didn't seem to faze her that he was married.

"Hey, if it makes you feel any better, you didn't miss much, really... no big deal. It was a small wedding," he lied.

"What do you mean, 'no big deal'? It's a very big deal. This is front-page news. I can see it now," Ryan made quotes in the air with the two fingers on each hand as he said, "confirmed bachelor, tamed."

Rex was relieved that Ryan had lightened up a bit. The news about his being married was finally out, but he knew what was next: Ryan would want a name. But he wasn't about to go there. How would he explain that one? And the baby?

Rex looked over at him and smiled. "Well, it's not like I said I would *never* get married. If I remember correctly, I always told you that when the right girl came along, I might give it a try."

The sails tightened and the boat tilted as they moved clear of the jetties and into the blue Pacific. The bow cut through the rolling waves sending a salty spray into the air.

"Well, all I can say is this woman must be something special. I can't wait to meet her."

They exchanged a few light-hearted comments and shared funny stories about Rex and his many women. As the day progressed, Ryan seemed to grow more accepting of the idea that Rex was married. Then, it started.

"So, how did you two meet?"

"She's a flight attendant."

"Does she work for us?"

"Yeah." Rex waited for him to ask for her name.

"Just one question," Ryan asked jokingly, "what about the old Rex who always said, one woman would never be enough?"

Rex laughed. "Yeah, we were wild and crazy back then... or at least I was. This girl is different. After leaving the Navy, I started thinking I should settle down, maybe even one day have a little Rexter or Rexann."

"Now that would really be hard to believe: Rex Dean, a daddy. I just hope it's not a boy."

Rex knew he couldn't tell him about the kid. After all, he didn't want to ruin *all* the surprises.

"Well I'm happy for you. Can't wait to meet her. So, have you told her about all the crazy times we had together in the Navy, or are you leaving that job up to me?"

Rex stared at the Newport coast. In a monotone voice he replied, "She knows all about us."

"That's good. I don't want her thinking that I was a bad influence on you." They both laughed.

Chapter 57

When Keri entered her condo, she paused briefly listening to the almost eerie quietness. Then she realized the nanny had taken the baby for a stroll.

She placed the bags of groceries on the kitchen counter, wondering which one of Rex's Navy buddies would be joining them tonight. Several names crossed her mind.

Since she had returned to work, there had been little time in her busy schedule for socializing. Tonight, she looked forward to relaxing, maybe having a glass or two of wine. The baby should be asleep by dinnertime, and the nanny would be there to watch him.

She pulled the steaks from the plastic grocery bag and placed them on the counter. Her eyes glanced into the den and caught the blinking red light on the answering machine. After putting the steaks in the refrigerator, she rounded the corner into the den and pressed the play button on the recorder.

She didn't recognize the man's voice.

"Keri, this is Philip Darby, your father's lawyer. Please give me a call at your earliest convenience..."

Hearing the words "your father" sent a rush of blood to her face. Anything to do with her father could wait. Probably one of his tricks to make contact with her. It wasn't the first time he had tried to call since their last conversation over a year ago.

She replayed the message, jotting down the number and the name, Darby, and left it on a scratch pad by the phone. She would have to call him later; the boys would be home soon and she wanted everything to be ready.

Chapter 58

It was four thirty when they returned to the dock. They secured the boat, loaded the car, and Rex signed out with the young girl in the front office.

The afternoon sun was dropping toward the horizon as they headed south on the coast highway. Rex steered the conversation away from his marriage and to Ryan's plans. Ryan updated him on his mother's condition; the scare he had when he discovered how Emily had tried to ruin him; and his excitement about moving to California and starting over.

Minutes from the condo, Rex thought he'd made it, until Ryan asked, "Do you remember my old girlfriend, Keri Hart?"

"Ah... yeah," Rex mumbled.

"If you remember, she's the one that ran off with some guy named, Bill. Actually, I think she ended up marrying the guy."

Rex goosed the accelerator, hoping to shorten the few miles that remained. He couldn't tell him now, he could only brace for the impact, letting the cards fall where they may. Give it a few days, weeks, months, whatever, and hopefully it would all be history. Ryan would accept it, and life could return to normal. Or would he?

Rex needed a stiff drink—or two, or three—if he was going to make it through this night.

"I was hoping I could look her up, you know, just as a friend."

Rex pressed harder on the accelerator and remained quiet, only offering an occasional grunt. Ryan seemed to be happy talking to himself.

"I called her house in Buckhead, but the maid told me that her mom had passed away and her dad was laid up in the hospital from a recent heart attack. Can't say I was too broken up about her mom... she was a real piece of work, if you know what I mean."

"Yeah, Dude. Believe me, I know what you mean," he said.

"But her dad was my hero. I always admired that man."

Rex perked up.

...her dad... hospital... heart attack.

"Dude, when did you call her house?"

"A few days before I called you... maybe a week ago. Why?"

The wheels started turning. The old man was finally going to kick it. Rex smiled. Keri was the only surviving relative, and he was her husband.

Awesome!

"What are you smiling about?" Ryan asked.

"Oh nothing." He hid the smile. "Here we are. I hope you're hungry."

* * *

Rex parked the Cherokee, promptly exited and headed for the front door. Ryan followed closely behind.

With one hand on the doorknob, Rex paused and turned to Ryan. "Let's surprise her."

"You never told me her name," Ryan whispered.

Rex ignored him, twisting the knob slowly and very carefully easing the door open.

Once inside, Ryan sensed a warm, inviting atmosphere: soft background music, candles flickered on the mantle above the fireplace, the aroma of food—possibly bread baking.

Through the cutout separating the kitchen from the dining room, he could see the back of a woman. She stood about five six, her shoulder-length brunette hair pulled back into a ponytail. She wore a red tank top.

They tiptoed closer passing a table set with three bright yellow place mats and matching linen napkins. A cut glass vase filled with fresh flowers stood in the center of the table.

Rex turned, lifting his finger to his lips, "Shhhh." Slightly crouched, he crept slowly toward the kitchen.

As more of the woman came into view, Ryan could see her tight white shorts and softly-bronzed skin. Apron strings tied off at the mid of her back, hung loose. He'd imagined a taller woman, possibly blond.

Rex eased up behind her, slipped his arms around her waist, hugged her, and kissed her on the neck. Then he stepped aside.

The woman turned. Ryan found himself frozen in space, staring at the woman, as if on a carousel whirling at top speed while the details of the surrounding world smeared into a ghostly blur. For an undetermined period of seconds, seeming like minutes, the fourth dimension—time—slowed to paralytic proportions. Like an astronaut moving lethargically on the lunar surface of the moon.

Catapulted into a head-on collision with reality, his subconscious ejected her name from his mouth.

"Keri!"

"Ryan!"

They both stood staring; his mind struggling to join the shattered pieces of the puzzle that connected him to his past, and Keri; the letter and some guy named, Bill; the day in New York at her dad's condo; the short conversation with Mrs. Hart while in Atlanta; and now, *REX!*

Almost simultaneously, they turned to Rex.

He shrugged, and said, "Surprise!"

Chapter 59

Emily boarded a Gulfstream jet parked on the tarmac at Fulton County's Charlie Brown Airport, headed for California.

Ronald's diseased heart had finally surrendered to a cardiac arrest three days earlier. She never returned to see him after learning of his last wishes. Philip Darby had contacted her with the news of his death and, as the letter had promised, delivered the package containing Ronald's ashes.

Not to be burdened with the ridiculous hassle of disposing of the old man's ashes, she had instructed the limo driver to make a quick detour behind a local strip mall near the airport where she tossed what were presumably the cremains of Ronald Hart into a dumpster.

The young copilot greeted Emily, pulled the cabin door closed and returned to the cockpit. Within minutes, the sleek private jet taxied to the runway and took off.

Wrapped in luxury, sipping on a glass of champagne, she stared out at the Atlanta skyline as the Earth slipped away.

Thank you Ronnie.

She thought, from here on out, only the best, starting with a week-long vacation at the fabulous oceanfront, Watford Hotel & Resort on Monarch Beach, compliments of the late Ronald Hart.

After a year filled with emotional stress, "celebrate" is exactly what she intended to do: sleep late, breakfast and lunch by the pool, daily pampering at the resort spa, cocktails and relaxing dinners. Upon her return to Atlanta and after the reading of Ronald's will, she expected her new life would be much the same.

Chapter 60

With his eyes locked on Rex, Ryan belted out, "What! You two are married?"

"Can I fix anyone a drink?" Rex said. "Beer? Glass of wine, maybe?" With no response, he held up a finger. "I think I'll have a beer."

Keri untied her apron, slipped it off and tossed it on the counter. "Yes, we're married." She turned to Rex, her brow furrowed, shooting him an evil look. "I wish Rex had told me that *you* were 'one of his old Navy buddies'."

"When?" Ryan searched for words. "I mean, how long?"

"We've got plenty of time to fill you in on all the details," she said, sending Rex another scowled look.

Rex jumped in, "Dude, I wanted to tell you, but knew how much you liked surprises."

Taking a deep breath, Ryan said, "I'll have to say, I'm more than surprised." He met Keri's gaze. She was the same beautiful woman he remembered—except married. For a brief moment, it seemed her eyes were telegraphing something that was in direct conflict to the casual flippancy in her voice.

"Oh come here and give me a hug," Keri stepped up to Ryan and hugged him, then stepped back. "You look great. So, how's Emily?"

"Honey," Rex said, "remember? The phone call?"

She hesitated for a moment, then turned to Ryan with a sad expression and said, "Oh God... Ryan, I'm so sorry." She shot Rex another one of her piercing looks. "I just remembered Rex saying 'his old Navy buddy' had gone through a bad divorce. But again, he failed to mention it was you."

"Hey, Buddy, you sure I can't get you a beer?"

"Yeah, I think I will."

Putting her hands together, Keri said, "Well, it looks like we have a lot to talk about over dinner, speaking of which, is almost ready." She looked at Ryan through eyes he couldn't decode. "Ryan, I hope you're hungry."

"Everything looks and smells wonderful. Could I use your bathroom to wash up?"

"Sure. It's just down the hall and to your right," she said, pointing the way.

Once in the small bathroom, he turned on the water and looked at himself in the mirror.

How can this be happening?

He leaned over and put his wrist under the cool water trying to bring his body temperature back to normal. His underarms were damp; his brow wet with perspiration.

What is going on? Rex and Keri are complete opposites. How in the world could Keri have ever fallen for a guy like, Rex?

It was one thing to believe that opposites attract, but he knew the only way Rex would have ever been able to land a woman like, Keri, was if he had masqueraded as someone he wasn't, something Ryan knew Rex was notorious for doing.

I can't wait to hear this story.

After splashing some water on his face, he took the small hand towel hanging on the rack beside the sink and dried his face and hands. He had found her and lost her in the same day again.

He took a deep breath and exhaled. With one last look in the mirror, his mind spinning in a thousand directions, he turned, opened the door, and headed back toward the kitchen.

* * *

When Keri finally put two and two together, remembering that Rex had said his old Navy buddy had gone through a bad divorce, she realized that Ryan must no longer be married to Emily. An ache stabbed deep into her heart.

Her next words floundered from her lips, "Oh God..." but she'd caught herself and finished with, "Ryan, I'm so sorry." But in that instant, her mind had raced back to New York. She had wanted to say, "Oh God, why didn't you tell me?"

He had mentioned nothing. If he had been having problems, why didn't he say so?

Then she knew why. Ryan would have never left his wife, regardless of the state of the marriage. The pain in her heart wrenched tighter. Poor, Ryan, he must have been suffering.

She regretted not telling him of her impending wedding. If she had only known about Emily—if Ryan had only known about her wedding—things would be different.

What now?

Ryan returned from the bathroom. "What would you like to drink with dinner?" Keri asked.

"Just keep the beer flowing," Ryan said. "I think I'm going to need it."

Their eyes met. She couldn't hide the pain buried deep within her heart. Words were not necessary. Her obvious longing to share her many regrets would have to wait.

* * *

After sitting down to eat, Rex kicked off the conversation. "Dude, you won't believe how Keri and I met..." Five minutes later, he finished his emotionless recollection of the events, "...and then we were married in Atlanta."

Keri made no attempt to interject or add to the story. Her refrain told Ryan that many details were left out; details that would only further separate the two of them from the fantasy they secretly embraced.

If only he could be alone with her; to hold her in his arms like he had in New York; to hear her sweet words telling him how much she loved him.

His mind ran wild with scenarios of what the night might bring. After Rex went to bed, she might suggest that they stay up and talk. Sitting beside her on the couch, he imagined her hand reaching for his as they consoled each other. An innocent embrace leads to an accidental kiss, unleashing pent-up passions. The kiss grows, their restraint weakens. She leads him to the guest bedroom where they satisfy the cravings of their deepest desires.

"Babe, Ryan says he's moving out here. Right, Buddy?"

"Yeah, I'm seriously looking into it. I think I can get more help for my mom out here."

About to take a sip of wine from her glass, Keri immediately stopped and looked at Ryan. "Ryan, I am so sorry," she said, setting her glass back down. "With all the surprises, I completely forgot to ask about Martha."

"That's okay. She's been doing as expected. There's a fantastic center right here in Laguna Beach that specializes with Alzheimer's patients. It's nationally recognized."

"That sounds fantastic," Keri said. "I would love to see her again. It's been so long, and she's always meant the world to me. Do you think she'll remember who I am?"

"They say memory of things long ago often stay intact right up to the end. I wouldn't be surprised if she calls your name out the minute she sees you."

"I miss her so much." Keri's voice full of compassion.

For a moment, Ryan felt a connection with her on a deeper level, almost like family. He remembered how hard it had been to avoid his mother's many questions about Keri, especially when she referred to her as his wife. He knew how much his mother loved Keri. He couldn't tell her now, but, even with his mother's condition worsening, Keri was the one person she talked about most.

As the evening progressed, in the lulls between conversations, he struggled to piece together the events from the past. It made sense, now, when he had attempted to locate Keri through the airline, why they had no record of her, and why there had been no listing for her in the Laguna Beach directory; she had changed her last name to Dean.

Then he wondered what happened to Bill, making a mental note to move that to the top of his list of questions to ask her, once they were alone.

The mind numbing effects of the alcohol eased his eagerness to connect the dots from the past, instead, he found the present more stimulating.

Each time he stole a glance of Keri, he was reminded of how stupid he was to have ever let her get away. Surely, she didn't love Rex, and, after his display in the harbor today, it was still obvious the only person Rex loved was himself.

"So, Dude, how long before you get your butt out here?" Rex asked.

"I'm hoping to hear from the center soon. Mom's on a waiting list for the next available opening. They told me it shouldn't be long."

Keri said, "If there's anything you need, you just let me know." She reached for the breadbasket and pushed back from the table. "Let me get you some hot bread."

"Hey, Buddy," Rex said, pausing as he hurriedly drained the last swallow of warm beer from his bottle, waving it in Keri's direction. "Hey, Baby, do you mind?"

"Sure," she replied. "Ryan, can I get you one?"

"No thanks, I'm fine."

Ryan lost count how many times Rex had ordered Keri to fetch him a beer from the kitchen. At one point, he felt it might have been easier to fill an ice chest and stick it by Rex's chair.

Besides her numerous trips to the kitchen, Ryan noticed that she had made several trips upstairs. All she had said was, "Excuse me, I'll be back in a moment." It seemed like a long way to go to the bathroom, considering the master bedroom was downstairs. But thanks to the beer buzz and Rex's constant string of stories about "the good old days", he hadn't given it much thought.

"So, Dude," Rex continued, "what time you shoving off tomorrow?"

Keri returned with a chilled bottle of beer and handed it to Rex, then started to clear the table. Ryan quickly rose to help.

Rex snapped, "Hey Dude, sit! She'll get it. That's what I married her for." Rex laughed.

Keri shot him a sneer, then turned to Ryan and smiled. "Thanks Ryan, but I'll get it. I'm used to it. You and Rex visit."

"I planned to head to the airport first thing. The flights all look good. Shouldn't be a problem getting a seat. I've got a trip Monday."

Rex said, "Let's move into the den." He rose to his feet and stumbled over to the couch. "Dude, could I ask a huge favor?"

"Sure, anything."

"I've got a turn-around to Dallas out of LAX in the morning at seven, and Keri has a three-day out of Orange County at eleven. We've been trying to get her car in the shop for a month. You know how it is, both of us coming and going at different times, we just keep putting it off. If you could give her a ride to the airport in the morning, I could take care of her car while she's out of town. It'd be a big help." He raised his bottle taking another slug.

"No problem. Consider it done."

"Hey thanks, Brah, you're the best." Rex slurred.

Keri joined them in the den. Ryan stood when she entered the room. "Are you sure you don't need any help in the kitchen?" Ryan offered.

"You're sweet, but it's all done. Only took a second to load the dishwasher."

She placed her hand on his arm and said, "Listen, thank you so much for taking me to the airport in the morning."

"What time do we need to leave?"

"My sign-in is at ten... so, how about we leave at eight forty-five. That should give us plenty of time. We won't have to rush."

"Sounds great." Ryan quickly did the math. He knew the drive to the airport would only take, at most, twenty minutes, more likely fifteen. That would give them at least an hour to talk, not counting the drive time.

"Well, I guess it's time to call it a night," Keri said.

Ryan glanced down at Rex, slumped on the couch, his eyes half closed. "Looks like some of us had better hurry, or we might not make it." He turned to Keri. "Thank you for everything, the meal was wonderful."

"Let me help Rex to the bedroom, and then I'll show you to your room."

Rex blurted out, "I don't need any help!" He rose slowly to his feet. "I'm just a little buzzed. I think I can make it a few feet to the bedroom. But first, let me give my good buddy a hug."

After finding his balance, he leaned over and draped his arms around Ryan's shoulders. "Goodnight, Buddy." He patted him on the back.

"Thanks for everything, Rex. I enjoyed the sailing."

"We'll have to do it again."

As Rex stammered off toward the downstairs bedroom, Keri turned to Ryan. "Your room is up the stairs and to the right."

He smiled, "Shouldn't be that hard, but first I need to run out to the car and grab my bag."

"Okay." After a short pause, she said, "We can talk tomorrow."

He met her gaze. "I think that would be good. As you can probably imagine, I have a few questions."

"Yes, and rightfully so." Keri stood only a foot in front of him. He looked at her face and into her big brown eyes.

She stepped in close and hugged him. Her soft body pressed against his chest. The fragrance of her perfume, fresh and recently applied, filled his senses. She lingered for a brief moment as her hand rubbed slowly across his back.

He wondered what she must be thinking. He felt comforted, confused, frustrated, and mad, all at the same time.

After releasing him, she paused briefly, gazing up into his eyes. "Tomorrow we can talk," she said. "I'm sorry. I never wanted to hurt you." Anxiety flickered in her expression, as if she was remembering something painful.

What should I do? We're alone. Should I suggest we talk now? Should I hug her again?

"It's okay." He stepped back and smiled. "Tomorrow." He knew with certainty that he still loved her, even though they could never be together.

After retrieving his bag and finding his room, he brushed his teeth, slipped into a pair of boxers, and hurried to bed, thinking sleep would free his mind from his many unanswered questions. He set the digital clock on the nightstand for seven.

But how could he sleep knowing that she was downstairs. He wrestled with forbidden fantasies instead of counting sheep like he knew he should. What would he do if she left her drunken husband and offered to slip into his bed?

Go to sleep!

Her warm body next to his?

Ryan, GO TO SLEEP!

The harder he tried, the more awake he felt.

Then, he heard a sound outside his door. He lifted his head, stretched his eyes wide, and stared through the darkened room, straining in the direction of the partially opened door. Nothing. He laid back and closed his eyes.

Next, the thought of being alone with her in the morning spun his mind in a new direction. Rex would be out the door by five—three and a half hours before Keri would need to leave for the airport. Three and a half hours. That's a long time. Just the two of them, alone.

Come on! For God's sake Ryan, go to sleep!

MIKE COE

With his eyes closed, he begged the sleep fairies to rescue him from his mind and whisk him into Neverland. Finally, he began to drift in and out of sleep. The night raced on.

At one point, he opened his eyes. The green glow of the digital clock on the nightstand stared back—2:12.

He mumbled, "I've got to get some sleep".

Then, unsure if he were awake or asleep, he thought he heard a sound. Not the creaking of steps or the squeak of a door hinge, but an unexpected sound, more like the muffled whimper of a baby. He listened harder, but nothing.

Silence once again filled every corner of the darkened room and finally, his mind released him into a deep sleep.

Chapter 61

A blast of annoying beeps jolted Ryan from a deep sleep. He quickly reached for the awful noise. Once the alarm clock was silenced, he rolled over on his back, took a deep cleansing breath, and exhaled.

Where am I?

When the debilitating grogginess cleared, he remembered.

"Keri!"

Her name released a rush of adrenaline through his veins. He glanced at the clock—7:01.

He sprang out of bed and headed to the bathroom. He wondered if she was awake.

He cranked up the shower and slipped out of his boxers. Once the water temperature tested right, he stepped in. The heat and pressure of the water stimulated the nerves in his skin encouraging blood flow, while sending rejuvenating impulses deep into the core of his body.

The clean fresh aroma of the soap entered his limbic system—the part of the brain responsible for moods, emotions and memory. Though sleep deprived, he felt invigorated.

After showering, he shaved, brushed his teeth, and then gargled with spearmint mouthwash.

While dressing, he heard activity downstairs and caught a whiff of bacon cooking. The nerves in his stomach tightened.

At the bottom of the stairs, he heard a voice coming from the kitchen... then another. Through the cutout, he saw Keri standing beside another woman... and Rex.

Rex walked out of the kitchen and into the den. "Hey Buddy, you hungry?"

Surprise in his voice, he said, "I thought you had to work."

"I got up last night to go to the bathroom, actually early this morning... about two. I knew I'd never make it to work, so I called in sick."

"Yeah, I must admit, you looked pretty bad last night."

"Totally slammed, Dude."

"Do you still need me to take Keri to the airport?"

"If you don't mind, that would be great."

"No problem. I'm going that way anyway."

Keri entered the den from the kitchen. "Good morning, Ryan." She beamed a smile his way. With her hair pinned on top of her head, she wore a light pink robe. "Did you rest well?"

"Great," he lied.

The strange woman eased out of the kitchen and stood next to Keri. "Ryan, this is Sara."

His eyes zeroed in, not on the attractive young woman, but on the baby she held in her arms.

No! Don't tell me...

Ryan glanced at Rex, then back at the baby.

"And this is David." Keri reached and took the tiny three-month-old baby from Sara. His little legs stiffened inside the blue jumper as a big smile spread across his face.

David who?

And then she said it, "Our little David. Isn't he adorable?"

"Yes, but—"

"Dude," Rex interrupted, "we just couldn't tell you last night."

"All I can say is, wow!" Then, it hit him: Keri must have married Rex because she was pregnant.

That's it! She never would have married him, otherwise.

It made perfect sense.

"Can I get you some coffee?" Rex asked.

"That'd be great."

Rex called out from the kitchen. "How do you take it?"

Keri answered for him, "One sweetener and a little milk, not cream but milk." She looked at Ryan and smiled. "Right?"

He nodded. "You got it. Amazing that you remembered."

"I guess some things never change."

"Yeah, some things—"

"You want to hold him?"

"Ah..." he hesitated.

"Sure you do." Keri stepped over and placed the little baby in Ryan's arms.

He looked down as little David smiled big, giggled, and stretched his legs. "He is so cute." Ryan extended his pinky finger. David latched on to it. "He's strong, too."

What a coincidence that she named him David. David is my middle name.

Keri stood close and gently brushed the baby's light brown silky hair, admiring her son. His bright blue eyes stared up at Ryan, curiously searching his face, then over at Keri. A big smile broke across his face followed by a laugh. "I think he likes you."

"Here, I better give him back to you before I break him." He handed little David back to Keri.

"Ryan, why don't you grab something to eat while I finish getting ready. I made grits, bacon, and eggs. Help yourself. Give me about twenty minutes and I'll be ready." Keri carefully passed the baby to Sara.

"Take your time."

He watched her walk away. From the look of her, he never would have guessed she had delivered a baby only a few months ago.

Rex returned from the kitchen and handed him a mug of steaming coffee. "Dude, it's been great seeing you again. Sorry about all the surprises."

"Yeah... It's gonna take a little time to soak in." He took the coffee from Rex.

"It's cool. We're all family. Listen, I'm stoked about you getting out here. It's gonna be like old times."

"Yeah, I can't wait." Ryan faked a smile while looking at Rex.

You're married to Keri, my Keri. She had your baby, and you think it's going to be like old times? What planet are you living on?

Rex continued, "And when you get out here, I'm going to hook you up with some hot babes. Man, I envy you. Your life is going to be sweet."

He motioned Ryan over to the breakfast table. "Help yourself." Rex stepped back into the kitchen.

"Thanks," Ryan said, taking a seat. "So, tell me, how is it being a daddy? Hard seeing the Rexter married, much less with a child."

Rex returned with a plate and joined him at the table. He leaned in and said in low voice, "Just between me and you... it's not exactly what I had planned."

"What do you mean?" Ryan took a bite of toast.

"Dude, the last thing I wanted was a kid."

"But Rex, your son is fantastic. How could you not be happy?"

"Easy for you to say, but you have no idea what a kid does to your sex life."

Ryan swelled with jealousy thinking about Rex's situation: married to Keri and a beautiful son. It should have been his life. He knew he had no right to be thinking such a thing, but he couldn't help it.

Rex continued, "Since the kid was born, she's always too tired. And now that she has started working again... well, frap, she's always noodled. When we do have sex, she just lays there. I might as well be humping a corpse."

Ryan took a sip of coffee and then said, "If having a child was such a big deal, you should have been more careful. Didn't you guys use protection?"

Rex scooted his chair over toward Ryan a bit, checked the adjacent room again, and then leaned in. In a low voice, he said, "I even got snipped."

Ryan recoiled with surprise. "A vasectomy? When?"

"Shhhh... not so loud." Rex looked over his shoulder. "That's the problem. I should have done it earlier. I waited until the week before the wedding. The doc said it might take several weeks before I was 'good to go'."

"Does Keri know?"

"Dude... be real. And I'd appreciate it if you wouldn't tell her."

"So, you had a vasectomy the week before your wedding without telling your soon-to-be wife? On top of that, after the doctor's warning, you still had sex without either of you using anything?"

"There might have been a couple of times... I think... I'm not exactly sure. I might have been a little loaded."

"What about Keri?"

"If you mean, was she drunk, too? You must be kidding. She hardly drinks at all, and if she does, it's only an occasional glass of wine. I don't think she's ever been the least bit tipsy."

"She must have known you weren't using protection."

"Keri wanted kids, and... well, the thing is... I had sorta told her before we married, that I did too. She could have thought I was doing it on purpose... or, who knows, she could have reminded me, and I was too drunk to understand."

Ryan stopped eating. "Let me get this straight. You had a vasectomy without telling Keri, knowing that she wanted children. Then, at some point in the future, after Keri was unable to become pregnant, you would conveniently learn that you had a low sperm count, or, better yet, to your surprise, you were sterile."

Rex pushed his chair back, raised his eyebrows, and smiled. "Genius plan, don't you think?"

"Are you kidding? You deceived your wife. You lied to her," Ryan said, with a stern look.

"Totally, but Dude, what's the big deal? She got her baby in the end."

MIKE COE

Ryan shook his head as he stood and took his plate to the kitchen."

Something Keri had said earlier, hit him. As she had taken the little baby from Sara, he recalled her words, "And this is David... *our* little David..."

Is it possible?

"Okay, I'm ready," Keri said. Dressed in her company uniform, she crossed the room to where the men were standing. The dark navy skirt and white blouse fit close to her body complimenting her figure. The air filled with the familiar fragrance of her perfume.

Ryan watched, disgusted, as Rex gave her a quick hug and a peck on the lips, more aware now of his insincerity.

They walked to the front door. Sara and the baby followed behind. Keri said her good-byes to Sara and the baby, kissing little David on the forehead and tickling his tummy. "Mommy's going to miss you."

Rex gave Keri another peck on the lips. "Have a good trip, Babe," he said. "I'll see you in a couple of days."

Ryan reached to shake hands with Rex, and, to his surprise, instead of the expected hug, Rex extended his hand. "Hurry-up and get your ass out here."

"Can't wait," Ryan replied, still feeling the unresolved tension. "Here let me get those." Ryan took Keri's bags.

Ryan turned as he walked to the car, glancing over his shoulder. Rex stood in the doorway, Sara beside him holding little David in her arms.

After the door closed, he couldn't help but think, knowing what he knew now, how Rex could ever be trusted. He had always known it, but now it had become personal.

Chapter 62

Ryan tossed the bags into the trunk of the small rental and moved with Keri to the passenger side. He held the door while she slipped in. Once seated, she looked up at him and smiled.

As he walked around to the driver's side, he glanced in through the front windshield and met her gaze. This would be the first time they had been alone since their unexpected rendezvous in New York, a year ago.

Once in the car, the awkward silence seethed with anticipation. He put the key in the ignition and started the car. Neither of them spoke. He hoped that she would be the first to break the eerie silence. Instead, she stared out the passenger window as if she were cataloging her memories. He left her alone with her thoughts.

He checked his side mirror for oncoming traffic then pulled out and drove away. The silence grew stronger with each minute. From the main road, he entered the on-ramp to Highway 73: the toll road to John Wayne Airport.

He heard a sniffle and saw that she was holding a tissue in her hand.

"Are you okay? She turned her head. Tears filled her eyes.

"I'm sorry." Trying to smile, she carefully blotted the tears. "I didn't want you to see me like this."

"What's wrong?"

She took a deep cleansing breath. "It's been hard. I don't know if I should get into it now." She pulled the visor down looking more closely at her eyes in the small mirror, wiping mascara from her tear-stained cheeks.

"Remember, I'm a good listener," he offered, not sure what was upsetting her but glad they were talking.

She looked at him and smiled. "Yes, I remember. First of all, I need to tell you I'm so sorry about last night."

He wanted to comment but refrained.

"I know that must have been awkward for you." She paused.

Again, he let her talk without interrupting.

"I had no idea. But to be honest, after the shock left me I can't tell you how happy I was to see you."

He felt her stare and turned. For a brief moment, their eyes connected, leaving him with an uncomfortable, yet welcomed tightening in his chest. "Why, Rex?" he asked.

"He approached me after your wedding and asked me out."

"And you went out with him? Just like that?"

"At the time, I had so many unanswered questions about you. Rex was your best friend. Who better to find out about you than from your best friend?"

"So, you sorta, used Rex?"

"In a way..." she trailed off, making another check of her make-up.

"But why Rex, of all people?"

"Rex came along when I was at my lowest. Once I found out that he was close to you, I guess I felt that being with him would, in a way, let me be with you." She sniffled as she touched the tissue to the corner of her eye. "I know it sounds crazy, but for me, at that time, Rex was all that was left of you."

"Hmmm... interesting," he said.

"I wanted so badly to be the one that you loved. I wanted to love you back. The main reason I moved out to California was to see if maybe we could get back together. I had no idea about Emily until your mother wrote me a letter telling me about the wedding.

In time, Rex convinced me that I needed to move on; to let you go. Reluctantly, I did just that. I wanted you to be happy. Up until that point, Rex had only been a friend to me. But once I realized that you were gone I started looking at Rex differently. I guess you could call it the classic rebound."

She paused briefly. With harshness, she said, "But I know now that he was a wolf in sheep's clothing, and I was a stupid little lamb. I really screwed up."

He released a chuckle. "Talk about stupid, I'm the poster child."

"Whatever happened to Emily?"

"Oh, you'll love this: the night I returned home from New York, I discovered that she had taken off." He glanced over at her. "Perfect timing, huh?"

"I'd say."

"But she was kind enough to leave me a parting gift, although I didn't discover it until I returned from Atlanta."

"What's that?"

"She took advances on all of our credit cards—maxing them out—leaving me holding a truck-load of debt."

"No!"

"Yeah, she must have been working on the little scheme for months. It buried me for almost a year and would have been much longer if her lawyer—during the divorce settlement—for some miraculous reason, hadn't agreed that she would take care of the debts."

"Where did she go?"

"The best I could find out, she ran off with some rich guy that owned the company where she worked. Listening to her lawyer describe him, the guy must have been old enough to be her father."

"That's sad."

"Well, I hope she finds what she's looking for. I'm just glad to be rid of her."

He exited the toll road toward John Wayne Airport.

"When Emily finally left me, all I could think about was you—us. I desperately wanted to talk to you. While I was in Atlanta moving my mother, I called your house, and your mother informed me"—sarcasm bathing his words—"that I had just missed your wedding, and that you were on your honeymoon."

"If I had only known about Emily," she said.

"Would it have made a difference? I mean, would you have still married Rex?"

"If I had known there was the slightest hope for us, I would have *never* married Rex, or anyone." She pulled a pair of sunglasses from her purse and slipped them on.

"Speaking of 'anyone', whatever happened to Bill?"

"Poor Bill, he ran out in front of a car and was killed."

"How tragic," Ryan said. He had heard of joggers being hit while running too close to the road.

"Yeah, I never could break him of chasing cars."

Ryan whipped his head around. "What?"

With the visor pulled down, her left hand lifted her glasses, making a quick check of her makeup. She had not seen the startled look on Ryan's face.

"Yeah, I always feared he would get hit. That's why I never let him out of the house without being on a leash." She flipped the visor up and turned to Ryan. "What's wrong?"

"I thought Bill was the guy you almost married! The pilot. Remember? You told me about him in your letter."

"What are you talking about? Bill was my dog—"

"Your dog!"

"I told you in the first letter I sent you. I told you that I named him after the Naval Academy's mascot, Bill, the goat. Seeing him, reminded me to think of you."

Ryan pulled up in front of the terminal building on the top level, put the car in park, and turned to Keri. In a serious tone, he asked, "Do you remember what you said in that letter?"

"I told you about the little Westie I bought and that I named him Bill. I also told you that I was transferring to California. I hoped we could be friends but would understand if you felt it would be too stressful."

She looked off in thought then reached up and wiped a tear from her cheek that had rolled from behind her glasses. "I also said that I had thought we would one day be together, but I would never stand in the way of your happiness, and that I couldn't wait to meet the girl that had won your heart."

"Wait a minute! What made you think there was a girl?" Without giving her a chance to respond, he continued, "At the time I wrote, I wasn't even dating anyone. I barely had time for myself. When I called Mom to wish her a happy birthday, that's when she gave me your address. I wrote to tell you I was leaving the Navy and wanted to find out if you were dating anyone. Mom said she was pretty sure you were still single. I put my number in the letter hoping you would call. You never did."

"Ryan, the only thing you said in your letter, about seeing me, was when you mentioned that you hoped I would come to your wedding."

"What?" His face twisted with disbelief.

"Later, after I heard you were marrying Emily, I assumed she was the woman in the letter."

"That's impossible! At the time I sent the letter, I hadn't even *met* Emily!" He paused. "Something weird is going on." He shifted in the seat, turning more toward her. "Keri, all this time, I never stopped loving you and realize now what a jerk I was for not writing to you more. I always remembered you telling me that if it was meant to be, nothing could stop us from eventually getting together. All those years I was in the Navy, I clung to those words. Then, when I received your letter telling me you were seriously in love with some guy named, *Bill*— who I now know was a dog—I gave up on us."

"Ryan, this is crazy."

"I know. The letters. The past. Us. You being married. None of it makes sense."

They stared at each other for a long moment. "What's going on?" Keri asked.

After a brief silence, Ryan asked, "What did you mean when you said 'the first letter'? I only got one letter from you."

"Ryan, I sent you five more letters after I moved to California. I guess the last two must have *really* scared you. By then I was desperate. I poured my heart out, thinking I could somehow stop you from marrying Emily."

"Keri, I never got any of those letters!"

"What? How could that be? How could the post office lose five of my letters?"

His mind quickly sorted the time line of events. He remembered Rex's words after he'd read the only letter he knew of, "She's no good for you." Then he remembered how excited Rex had been about taking him out to look for girls. He also recalled how interested Rex had suddenly become in checking the mail. He'd said he was waiting to hear from some of the airlines he'd written.

"I think I know," he said.

"What?"

"Rex. That's what."

She took in his words. Her eyes widened. "No! You don't think he—"

He nodded. "Yep. I think our friend Rex pulled a fast one on us."

An officer appeared beside the car. "Excuse me. You're going to have to move this car."

"Yes sir." Ryan pushed the car door open, trying not to hit the officer. He stood a head taller than the cop. "Let me get her bags out of the trunk and I'll be on my way."

"Make it fast. You've been sitting here too long already." The officer walked off to police more cars standing two-deep against the curb.

Ryan pulled Keri's bags from the trunk. "I'll meet you on the other side of security by gate nine," he said.

"Okay."

He drove off to return the rental car, and she headed for the terminal. Wheeling the car through the underground parking garage, he couldn't stop thinking about what Rex had done and how he'd done it.

How could he live with himself?

A simple little prank had altered the entire course of his life. He wondered what would have possibly happened if Rex had not done what he did. Would he and Keri be happily married? Would they have a son named David?

Chapter 63

"That was fast," Keri said, seeing Ryan approach her after clearing security.

"So, where do you want to sit?" he asked.

"My flight departs from gate ten."

Ryan looked up at the electronic board displaying arrival and departure flights for the different airlines. "You know what?"

"What?"

"It just dawned on me. I'll be flying on your flight back to Dallas."

"That's great!"

"What position are you working?"

"First."

"In that case, I'll see if they have any openings in first."

He looked out through the wall of glass to the jet bridge. The plane wasn't there. "Looks like we've got some time to talk," he said.

"I talked with the agent before you came, and she said the plane would be a little late. It's coming out of Dallas and was delayed because of the weather."

After scanning the seating area next to the gate check-in, he motioned with his head. "Let's sit over there. We'll be out-of-the-way."

From where they were sitting he had a clear view of the jet bridge through the large plate-glass window. He knew that once the plane pulled up to the bridge it would still take another ten to fifteen minutes to unload the passengers.

Ryan started, "I can't believe Rex—"

Keri quickly interrupted, "Ryan, there is something else. I think Rex is running around on me."

"What?" Sounding alarmed.

"I think Rex is seeing another woman."

"Are you sure?" All he could think about was the day in the harbor and the way Rex had acted.

"I'm not sure *who* it is or even if it's only one woman. As far as I know, he could be screwing the nanny, as we speak."

"Sara?"

"Yeah."

"When did you start suspecting all this?"

"Pretty much, right after we were married. I remember once when he was supposed to be on a three-day trip, I found his company ID on his dresser. When I asked him about it, he said he had managed to slip by without it. You and I both know that would have been impossible. And on a regular basis, he comes home from his trips late."

"What do you mean by 'late'?"

"For example, a few weeks ago, his sequence showed him landing at LAX around noon, but he didn't get home until six that night."

"What did he say?"

"That particular time he said he had to give the pilot he was working with a ride home, and that he'd gotten tied up in traffic."

"What's to say he wasn't telling the truth?"

"Maybe. But it has happened more than a couple of times. He always has a different excuse."

Pushing his lips together tight in frustration, he said, "I wish I could have warned you about Rex. I don't understand *why* he ever got married."

She reached over and took his hand, putting it in hers. "I am so sorry. Can you ever forgive me?"

"Listen, it's not your fault. If Rex hadn't screwed around with our lives none of this would have ever happened."

She gazed deep into his eyes. "Ryan, seeing you again has given me hope." His heart gave a giant unexpected thump in his chest. "I just don't want to lose you again."

"Keri. There's nothing I want more than to be with you. But unless you know for certain that Rex is messing around on you, you can't just leave him because we all-of-a-sudden realize that we both made mistakes. Have you confronted him about this? I mean have you specifically told him what you think he's doing?"

"No. I can't prove it, but trust me, a woman knows when a man is not there—so to speak—and Rex is definitely somewhere else."

"Well, I have to confront him about the letters," he said.

The rest of Keri's crew approached, dressed in their dark blue company uniforms, each pulling a roller bag. Ryan introduced himself.

As they were talking, the agent for the flight appeared and told the crew the plane was on the ground and that she wanted to board the passengers as soon as possible. After Keri acknowledged the agent and agreed to help rush the boarding, the agent scurried off.

Through the window, the plane could be seen pulling up to the jet bridge. "Keri, we'll see you on board," one of the flight attendants said. "Take your time."

"Okay. I'll be there in a second."

When Keri turned back to face him, he said, "Keri, did you know about Rex's vasectomy?"

"His what?"

"Rex told me that he had a vasectomy the week before your wedding."

"That's impossible! I mean... if he had a vasectomy, then how could I have gotten pregnant?"

Ryan explained, "After a vasectomy it can sometimes take a few weeks, or even a month, before it is completely safe to have sex without using protection. And as you know, it only takes one strong swimmer."

They held each other's gaze for a moment. He spoke slowly, each word hanging in midair before falling softly. "Keri, there is a slight possibility that—"

With widened eyes and a face full of hope, she said, "Do you think it's possible? I mean... if Rex had a vasectomy before we were married then it *is* completely possible, isn't it?" Her eyes widened further. "Do you know what this means?" She placed her hand on his arm. "Oh Ryan, you can't imagine how many times I've wished it was true."

"I know, but it's not for sure. Have you ever looked at the exact dates?"

"Not that closely. I just figured it had to be Rex."

The agent appeared again, peering over-the-top of her half-glasses, frustrated, stressed, and frazzled. She said, "Do you think you could help me out here? We're already late enough as it is," she said.

"I'm sorry. I'm coming." Keri turned to Ryan. "I've got to go."

"We can talk later. I'll see you on board."

"Okay."

He took her by the arm. "Listen, everything is going to be fine."

"Thanks. I needed to hear that. I'll see you on board," she said.

* * *

After boarding the plane and storing her bags, Keri began preparing the first-class galley. She couldn't stop thinking about the possibility that little David's real father might be Ryan. It made her want to see David, to examine his features. Perhaps she'd not noticed that David had Ryan's eyes, his mouth, or his ears. She wanted to believe it was true.

Chapter 64

"Next," the agent called out impatiently.

Caught in a daydream filled with *what ifs*, Ryan popped back into reality, his eyes meeting the glare of the gate agent. He quickly stepped up to the ticket counter, presented his company ID, and asked sheepishly, "Are there any seats open in first?"

Her head down, the agent continued typing as a thin smirk formed on her face. In less than a minute, he heard the familiar clicking of the ticket printer. Without any exchange of words, the agent reached over, took the ticket from the printer, and slapped it down on the counter with his ID.

"Next," she called out, peering over the top of her reading glasses and beyond Ryan. Ryan glanced down at his ticket— "6A": a first-class window seat.

"Thank you," he said.

"You can board now." She faked a smile and motioned to the next passenger in line.

After making his way down the jet bridge, he saw Keri standing in the galley. When he stepped on board, her eyes quickly checked the seat assignment on his ticket. A smile spread across her face. "Welcome aboard, Mr. Mitchell."

"Thank you, ma'am."

Ryan settled into the spacious leather seat and tucked a small carry-on bag under the seat in front of him. A moment later, Keri approached with two cups of coffee. After handing one cup to the gentleman in the aisle seat next to Ryan, she offered the second cup to Ryan. "One sweetener, milk, not cream but milk. Right?"

"Right," he replied, taking the coffee.

The last few passengers trickled on-board, and the agent closed the entry door to the plane. After a short taxi, the jet thundered down the runway and into the cloudless blue sky.

Ryan reclined his seat, and for the next few hours, enjoyed observing Keri glide among the first-class passengers, occasionally catching her shoot him a smile or a wink. She seemed as lovely as ever. Thoughts of the life that could have been filled his mind just before he drifted off to sleep.

He woke realizing the plane was beginning its descent for Dallas. The memory of his dream was fresh in his mind, a dream of he and Keri married with two small children, still madly in love.

He glanced over the top of the passenger seat in front of him toward the front of the cabin. He saw Keri in the galley stowing a service cart. Reality rushed back into his thoughts.

Keri is married. She has a child.

The captain's voice crackled over the PA. "Ladies and gentlemen, this is the captain, may I have your attention. A line of weather has developed between the Dallas-Fort Worth Airport and us. Because of our fuel we are unable to hold, but instead will be diverting to Oklahoma City. By the time we land and refuel we should be able to depart and continue to Dallas. Thank you for your patience. At this time I'd like to have the flight attendants prepare for landing."

The divert went just as outlined by the captain. They landed, refueled, and were off again, all within an hour. The trip down to Dallas from Oklahoma City was quick. The thunderstorms had moved across the airfield leaving clear weather behind.

While deplaning at Dallas, Keri said, "Ryan, I'm sorry we didn't have more time to talk. I was so busy."

"That's okay. I think I dozed off."

"Wait for me in the terminal. I want to say good-bye."

"I'll be out front by the gate," he said. "I need to check the computer, anyway."

After checking to confirm his departure time for his trip going out the next day, he pulled up Keri's sequence to discover that she had been reassigned to return to Orange County. The delay caused by the divert had turned her three day trip into a one-day "turn-around".

Concerned about how she would get home once she landed in California, he quickly remembered that Rex had been taken off of his trip and would be there to pick her up.

He felt a hand on his shoulder. "Ryan, we never finished our conversation," she said.

"Look," he said, staring down at the computer screen.

"What?"

He tapped his finger against the glass monitor. "You've been reassigned." She leaned in close, her hand still on his shoulder. He could smell her sweet scent. "Looks like our divert caused you to misconnect with your trip to New York. They've got you working back to Orange County." He glanced over at the gate to his left. "That's your flight over there, and it looks like they're already boarding."

"I couldn't be happier." She moved around in front of him.

"How's that?"

"I get to see my little David," her voice quickly changing from drippy sweet to attack mode, "plus, Mr. Dean has some explaining to do."

"Are you sure? Don't you want to wait until I can come out?"

"The sooner the better."

"Okay, but promise me you'll call me right after you finish talking with him. I'd like to know what he says before I call him, myself."

"Oh I will, but when I get done with him there might not be anything left for you to chew on. I even suspect that he'll probably be calling you to beg your forgiveness."

"Does me a lot of good now." Their eyes met.

"Ryan," she said with tender empathy, "you know I will always love you... don't you?"

"Yes."

She hugged him, then stepped back. "There's something else we need to find out—immediately," she said.

"What's that?"

"About little David."

"How do we do that? You expect Rex to come running when we ask him for a DNA test?" he asked, his words bathed in sarcasm.

"I think there is another way, but we need to know the blood types of all four of us: you, me, Rex, and little David."

"So, how do you propose getting Rex to agree to a blood test? Or were you thinking of, somehow, drawing blood from him involuntarily?"

"I'm not sure we even need his blood."

"How's that?"

"I once worked with a flight attendant that had this same sort of thing happen to her. If I remember correctly, she said that although blood type alone cannot determine the biological father, it *can*, however, eliminate a person as being the father."

"How?"

"Every person has one of four blood types: O, A, B, or AB. With David's and my blood types, there are only certain possibilities for his biological father."

Excitedly, Ryan said, "So, you're saying with David's, yours, and Rex's blood types, we can know if Rex is *not* the father?"

"Exactly!"

"That means if you had my blood type, you could *also* tell if I was not the father."

"Yes, but even if your blood type shows that you could be the father, we will still need to know about Rex to rule him out. And even though I have only been with two men—you and Rex—there is always the chance that both of you have blood types that would work. That's when we'll need a DNA test."

He looked away in thought, then said, "Well, it should be easy to find out Rex's blood type."

"How?"

"Do you happen to know where his dog tags are?"

"Ryan, you're confused." She chuckled. "Bill was the dog, not Rex."

"Funny. But I'm talking about his military ID tags. They're referred to as dog tags. Military regulations require that every person in the military wear them. They're used to identify service members who have died or been wounded in the line of duty. They're little aluminum tags worn on chains around the neck."

"Now that you mention it, I do remember them. But I'm not sure where they would be." She thought. "The only place they could be is with some of his military things in a box he keeps in his dresser drawer. I'll look when I get home. But what is so important about the tags."

"Those little tags might give us the answer we're looking for."

"How?"

"Each tag is embossed with the soldiers name, social security number, branch of service, religion, and blood type."

She added, "And I can call my gynecologist to get mine and David's blood types."

"Great. Just so you know, my blood type is A-positive. So, all we need now is blood types for you, David, and Rex," he said. "But what then? How do we determine which blood types do not work together?"

"There's a chart. I'm sure my doctor will have one."

He looked over at the gate next door. The agent was waving for Keri to come over. "You'd better go. We'll talk later."

"Okay. I'll call you when I find out something."

"Sounds good."

As she rushed away, she glanced back over her shoulder at him and smiled. He never had the chance to ask her little

David's full name. All he knew was David, *something*, Dean. When he reached to pick up his carry-on, his eyes locked on the luggage tag: "RYAN D. MITCHELL".

He thought, Ryan *David* Mitchell. He picked up the bag and moved through the crowded terminal. "David... Mitchell," he said in a low voice as he walked. Pride swelled in his chest.

Chapter 65

When Keri arrived, the flight crew for the trip back to Orange County was already on-board. "Hi, I'm Keri," she said as she stepped aboard.

The lead flight attendant, busily setting up the first-class galley, shot her a cursory glance and said, "I'm Susan. Amanda and Candice are in the back."

"The agent is sending them down," Keri said. Susan didn't reply. "You guys LA based?"

"Yep." Susan quipped, continuing to work.

"I was headed to New York until our flight diverted on the way in. Turned my three-day trip into a turn."

Nothing from Susan.

"Boy, things sure are screwed up out there. Glad I'm not an agent." Susan didn't respond. "At least now I get to go home and be with my little boy."

Still nothing from Susan.

Keri turned at the sound of passengers coming down the jet-bridge. "Here they come. I'll talk to you later," she lied.

She made her way down the narrow aisle, her roller-bag in tow. One of the other flight attendants met her. The girl smiled, stepping between rows of seats to let Keri pass. "Hi, I'm Amanda." An attractive brunette in her early thirties.

"I'm Keri. Looks like I'll be working with you back to Orange County."

"Great. You LA-based?"

"Yeah."

Amanda motioned with her eyes toward the rear of the plane. "That's Candice." Keri glanced back at the young blond. Amanda chuckled. "I'll warn you now. She's a real piece of work." Keri returned a puzzled look. "You'll see. Gotta go."

Amanda slipped back into the aisle and headed toward the front of the airplane.

The young blond, about five three, wore the optional polyester uniform dress instead of the traditional blue skirt and white blouse. The polyester was considered too clingy and revealing by some flight attendants, but, by the looks of it, this girl considered "clingy and revealing" to be a good thing. Altered like a surgical glove, the lines of her bra and thin side-bands of her thong looked as if they were shrink-wrapped beneath the navy-blue polyester. She was thin yet miraculously big breasted—no doubt the work of a good plastic surgeon.

"You must be Candice."

"Oh hi. Call me Candi... everybody does." Hearing her high-pitched voice completed the package. "Don't tell me," she said picking up a small piece of computer paper. "You must be Lisa."

"No, I'm Keri."

"Oh. Wow. Bummer. You're supposed to be Lisa. Not that I even knew Lisa, but she was just on the crew list. Whatever."

"I was re-assigned. I guess I'll be taking Lisa's place."

"That's totally cool. Well, I'm Candi... or did I already say that? Whatever. Anyway, glad to meet you."

As passengers filled the cabin, struggling to stow their carry-on luggage and shoe-horn themselves into their cramped seats, Candi began her show.

She paraded up and down the aisle, squeezing between passengers with her hands raised, as though she were practicing solo half-turns from her Latin Salsa dance class, the hem-line of her dress rising well above her thigh. The men couldn't keep their eyes off her, especially when she made her overextended reaches into overhead bins to adjust luggage or retrieve a blanket or pillow.

After takeoff, Keri and Candi started a beverage service in coach. Candi chattered nonstop, only taking time to flirt with male passengers.

"So, where do you live?" Keri asked.

"I live in San Diego. What about you?"

"Laguna Beach."

"Awesome. I love Laguna Beach. That's where my boyfriend lives."

"How long have you guys been dating?"

"About a year. He's like, the best. He's a pilot."

"Does he fly for us?"

"Yeah. He's like, soooo hot. I'll have to be honest with you..." She leaned over the cart and whispered quietly, "He is like, so unbelievable... like, you know what I mean?" She winked at Keri.

Keri faked a smile. "I guess."

"I mean, like, he makes me want to do things that, like, I've only dreamed about." She rolled her eyes while her tongue slowly swept across her top lip. "Mmmm, he is totally delicious."

"Interesting." Keri was caught off guard by her openness, not to mention her obnoxious overuse of the word "like". "You living with this guy?"

"No. Not yet. He's married."

"Oh really?"

Great! A homewrecker. This is exactly the type of skank I would imagine Rex to be running around with.

"I know what you're thinking, but it's totally okay. He doesn't love her, and he's like, leaving her soon."

"Did he tell you this?"

"Like, duh. Do you think I would be with him if he hadn't? Like, really. Give me a break."

"Well, you never can tell about some guys."

"I can totally tell, he is like, *so,* in love with me. Sometimes he will even pop by my place on his way home after a trip. He says all he thinks about is me and can't go home until he sees me." She rolled her head. "Isn't that just, too sweet?"

Keri didn't answer. Nothing, so far, sounded "sweet" about this jerk.

Candi leaned closer and whispered to Keri, "I think I'm pregnant." She pulled back and smiled big. "I missed my period... and I *never* miss my period. That's why I'm, like, pretty sure I'm pregnant. I guess I should get one of those little thingies to make sure."

Keri just stared, not sure how to respond. This "thingy" she was working with was, *like*, from another planet.

"Oh, it's totally cool. My boyfriend loves children, and he said that once he leaves his wife, we're going to have lots and lots of children. We both love kids... and, like, I'm still a kid at heart. I can't wait to be a mommy."

The thought of this woman being responsible for a child was plain scary. "Does your boyfriend know you're pregnant?"

"Not yet. But he, like, never uses a condom—you know, like, when we do it—so I'm sure he'll be excited to hear the news."

This guy must really be a piece of work.

He's married, having sex with this little slut on the side, without using protection, and now he's gotten her pregnant.

Keri asked, "So, what does this guy look like?"

"He's totally hot. You can see for yourself. He's meeting me when we land. I'm like, soooo stoked! I'm gonna stay with him, like, for a couple of days. You'll have to meet him. I just know you'll love him. He is like, the best."

"I can't wait," Keri responded, faking her excitement. She was dying to see the creep that fell for this little bimbo. It made her thankful there were still men like Ryan.

"You're so right, we, like, totally need to move-in together," Candi said.

Keri didn't remember suggesting she move in with this guy, but then again, Candi's brain wasn't her strongest attribute.

She continued, "It seems like, all we do when we're together is like, have sex nonstop." She rolled her eyes and blushed when she said, "He like, rules the bedroom. I think we've like, done it on practically every flat surface in his condo. If we moved in together, then like, maybe we would have time for other stuff... don't get me wrong, I love the sex, but you know, like, I want to get to know him in other ways, too, like, what he's into and stuff."

For the next two hours Keri listened to the nonstop graphic details of every possible romantic adventure Candi had ever had with "lover boy"; his place in Laguna; her place in San Diego; and layovers all over the country.

Keri was amazed. They had never met, yet this girl was freely telling her the erotic details between her and some horny pilot. How typical, she thought. She wondered if it was just her, or did Blondie bare her soul to every flight attendant she worked with. In a way, she started to feel embarrassed about meeting "Mr. Stud Muffin". Looking him in the face would either make her laugh-out loud, or puke.

Before landing, Candi made one last pass through the cabin ensuring that all of the tray tables were up and the seats were in their upright position for landing. But most importantly—that every man on the plane got one last look.

Once they docked at the gate and the seatbelt signs were extinguished, the passengers struggled, hurriedly, jockeying to maneuver their bags free from the tight overhead bins, and make their way to the front of the airplane.

Freshly primped, Candi emerged from the lav with a fresh coat of lip gloss, smelling like the perfume counter at some discount department store. The three of them trailed behind the last passenger, Candi leading the way.

As they emerged into the terminal, Keri almost tripped on Candi's roller bag when she dropped it and took off toward some guy standing off to the side. She had him all wrapped up in a hug before Keri could even get a look at the guy.

When they broke from their lip-lock for air, Candi moved aside, her arm laced in his, and proudly said, "Keri and Amanda, I want you to meet my boyfriend, Rex Dean."

Initially shocked and a bit dizzy, Keri quickly gained her composure. Without missing a beat, she responded in a calm voice, "How nice. Now Candice, I'd like for you to meet my *husband...* Rex Dean."

Not being too bright, Candi swiveled her head, searching for another man with the same name. Not until Rex started groping for excuses did Candi appear to catch on.

Rex begged, "Keri, it's not what you think. I love you."

"What!" Candi squealed. "What about me?"

"Not now, you little twit!" Rex scolded Candi, continuing to plead with Keri. "Please... baby, please... she means nothing to me. You're the only one I love. Don't do this. At least let me explain!"

Candi stepped between Rex and Keri, coiled like a viper. "Please, baby? I'll please baby, you!" She hauled-off and slapped him across the face. "You told me you loved me! I'm out of here."

"Thank you, my dear. I couldn't have said it better," Keri said, turning to Rex. "You'll be hearing from my lawyer. In the meantime, find somewhere else to sleep." Keri strode away with Amanda by her side.

"Are you okay?" Amanda asked, in a concerned voice.

"I've never been better." Keri said, as a smile grew on her face.

Chapter 66

Dumped by two women in one day.

Rex cruised south on the PCH toward Dana Point headed for his favorite watering hole.

This can't be happening...

It wasn't the thought of being single that bothered him; it was the fact that he now had to kiss the old man's money good-bye. His parents had pulled the plug and all he had was his airline salary. That wouldn't be so bad if it weren't for all the debt he'd racked up.

Get a-hold of yourself. You're the Rexter, remember.

He flipped the car's stereo on and hit the play button. If anyone could restore his confidence, it was his good buddy, Englebert Humperdinck. Engulfed by the drone of the Porsche's engine and the unrestricted view of the ocean, he waited expectantly for the healing words of his mentor.

Like a friend sharing words of wisdom, the crooning Humpster's voice came alive. But when Rex heard the Humpster start with *A Man Without Love,* he yelled out, "Awe, come on Hump! You can do better than that!"

He flipped to the next selection. Every tune memorized, it only took the warble of the harmonica and the first five words of *There Goes My Everything,* before Rex slammed his palm against the steering wheel and cried out, "Come on Hump! Help me out here."

He switched again. This time the Humpster bellowed out the lyrics of *Release Me.* "Better," Rex said. "But, hump... get with the program, she already dumped me." Tired of the process, he flipped back to the first selection: *A Man Without Love* and listened. By the time the Humpster had reached the chorus, Rex was singing along at the top of his voice.

* * *

"How's it going, Rex?" The bartender asked while slowly rubbing a white cloth along the top of the smooth wood surface of the massive oak bar.

"Not too good, Joe," Rex said somberly as he eased into the leather bar chair.

"What can I get you?"

"The usual... except, this time, you better make it a double. And don't go too far with that bottle."

"That bad, huh?" Joe scooped some ice into a six-ounce tumbler followed with rum and coke—mostly rum—and set the glass on top of a cocktail napkin with the imprint: *Watford Hotel & Resort, Monarch Beach*. With its elegant terraces, comfortable furnishings, manicured golf course, and spectacular elevated view of the Pacific Ocean, it made for the perfect luxury rest-stop for the wealthy.

Rex lifted his glass and took a sip, then placed it back on the small paper napkin. In the mirror expanding the entire length of the wall behind the bar, he noticed a well-dressed blond sitting alone on a small couch in the corner of the room. "Who's the hottie?" Rex asked.

"Not sure, but she's been here all week. Spends money like it's water. Big tipper."

"You seen her with anyone?"

"No. But it has been fun to watch. Every guy that walks in here tries to hit on her. So far, I haven't seen any of them score."

Rex watched in the mirror as the blond sipped on her pink-colored drink with a little umbrella shading a slice of pineapple on the rim. "She sure looks familiar."

"They all look the same to me," Joe said.

"How many umbrellas?"

"I believe that's her third."

"Perfect." Rex said, starting to feel his old self return. After slipping out of the bar chair, he pulled a thick stack of bills from his pocket, peeled off a twenty, and slapped it on the bar. "Thanks, Joe."

He took a quick glance past Joe, into the mirror. With a run of his fingers through his wavy blond hair and a forced smile at his double, he said, "Now you get to watch the Rexter do his magic."

He casually strolled over to where the woman was sitting, seconds before she turned his way.

I don't believe this.

"Emily?"

"Rex?" she said, stumbling to her feet, wrapping him in a sloppy hug. "Have a seat," she said, still holding his hands. "I can't believe it. How have you been?" Rex took a seat on the couch beside her. She continued smiling, placing one hand on his thigh.

"Good," he said. "Hey, I'm sorry things didn't—"

"Don't be," she quickly interrupted. "Everything worked out great... actually, better than great." Rex knew Emily had dumped Ryan for some rich dude, but he had no idea who the guy was. "Wow. Just look at you... handsome as ever. So, how's it going with you and Keri?"

"Ah... it's not."

"What do you mean?"

"Keri had too many issues. She sorta flipped out. Now she wants a divorce. I'm not so sure about those Southern women. Too clingy for me."

Rex glanced down at the coffee table. A paperback novel with the title "Beneath the Sheets" pictured the half-naked bodies of a man and woman wrapped in a white satin sheet. His eyes returned to meet her gaze. Still a strikingly beautiful woman.

"So, you got a girlfriend?" She gave him a sneaky smile.

He didn't want to tell her that less than an hour ago, Keri caught him with his little play toy, Candi.

"My philosophy is to love the one you're with, so, for the next few minutes, I guess you're it." They both laughed, Emily giving his thigh a soft squeeze.

"Tell me something, Rex." Her speech slurred, dragging its way to completion, while she twirled the little umbrella in her empty glass. "That day on the beach at Coronado," she said, looking down at her glass, "why did you go for my friend, Kate, instead of me?" Her gaze lifted to meet his.

"I must've been blinded by the sun." He gazed off and squinted. If I remember correctly, the sun was in my eyes that day." His tone softened. "But from what I see now, I made a big mistake." He knew that Emily was the kind of woman that quenched her thirst for acceptance with the compliments of men.

"Well, sailor, I think your ship has just come in."

"How's that?"

"You're looking at a soon-to-be very rich woman," she said proudly. "And this woman is inviting you to come aboard for the cruise of your life." She lifted her empty glass, as in a toast, then to her mouth, ice cubes sliding against her lips.

He held a salute and replied, "Aye, aye, captain. Your first mate is ready to shove off."

She laughed, then eased back on the couch and said, "You see, I only married the poor sucker for his money. Although he thought I was crazy about him, it was all about the money. He just needed a little attention; something his wife never gave him."

"What? No sex?"

"Are you kidding?" She chuckled. "The old guy had one foot in the grave. It was his heart. One night with me, and he would have surely kicked it. All I had to do was wait it out and hope his wife didn't pull a fast one. But then she had an unfortunate, but timely accident."

Rex showed alarm. "You didn't..."

"For God's sake, no! She had a head-on with a truck. Sad, but it works for me."

How cold-hearted, he thought, even by his standards. He figured it was the alcohol talking. Then it crossed his mind that Keri's mom had also been killed in a head-on.

He blew it off. "Interesting. Are you staying in the hotel?"

She reached in her purse, pulled out a plastic room key, and laid it on the coffee table. His eyes moved from the coffee table back up to her face. She lifted her eyebrows with a slight smile. He paused only briefly before reaching down to pick up the card.

Leaving the lounge, Rex looked back at the bartender. From Joe's smile, Rex knew that he had been eavesdropping on their conversation. Holding a wineglass in one hand, drying it with a white cloth, he shot Rex a wink. Rex gave him a subtle thumbs-up and a smile.

The door to the elevator opened on the third floor. Emily led him to the right, down the corridor. After passing three rooms, she stopped at the fourth door on the ocean side, slid the plastic key in-and-out, followed by a series of chirps, a click, and a green light. She pushed down on the lever opening the door to a large luxurious suite.

She walked over and opened the French doors to a balcony with a stunning view of the ocean. With her arms outstretched, she took a breath and exhaled. "Isn't this wonderful?" She turned and put her arms around Rex and gazed up into his eyes. "Just like you."

"You're too sweet," he said.

Her hands found their way down his back. She gently pulled his body up close to hers. "Tomorrow we will fly back to Atlanta and claim our prize." She kissed him softly, letting the passion grow slowly.

He enjoyed her aggressive advances. His heart pumping faster; every blood-gorged muscle in his body tightening with expectation. "I've got my prize."

She kissed him again. "So, why don't you unwrap it and see what's inside?"

"Now you're talkin' my language."

With a brazen face, she spoke to him in a poetic language. "Come, let us drink our fill of love until morning. Let's enjoy ourselves with sex!" She led him with seductive words. She charmed him with her silky smooth talk. He followed her.

The Rexter is back.

Chapter 67

Keri caught a ride home with Amanda. When she walked into the condo, Sara, the nanny, emerged from the kitchen with a shocked look on her face. "I didn't expect you home so soon," Sara said.

"It seems like this day has been filled with unexpected surprises," Keri said.

"Is everything okay?"

"Couldn't be better. Is little David asleep?"

"Yes. He went down about thirty minutes ago."

Keri needed to call Ryan. He would be leaving tomorrow on a trip, and she had to talk to him tonight.

As she lifted the receiver, before dialing his number, she noticed the notepad by the phone and the name: Philip Darby and a number. She paused, remembering the message on the answering machine.

"Keri," Sara said, "I was going to tell you, that man—Mr. Darby—has called here three times today. He wants you to call him tonight."

Keri glanced at the clock. "It's after ten on the East Coast. I'll call him first thing in the morning."

"I told him you were on a trip but assured him that you would be calling later to check on David. He left his home number and requested that you call him, regardless of the time."

Why would her father's lawyer be so eager to talk with her?

"Where is the number?"

Sara said, "It's on the next page of the notepad."

Perhaps her dad had advised his lawyer to inform her that she had been taken out of his will.

I should have known.

Remorse gripped her, squeezing her heart like a sponge. She loved her dad and hated that she had hurt him. She wanted to tell him that she was sorry. What did it matter now if he had an affair? Knowing her mother like she did, could she blame him? Keri felt it was all her fault.

Why would the lawyer be so persistent? How could it be so urgent?

Her mind searched deeper. Her mother was dead and her father's lawyer was trying to contact her. Her chest tightened with fear.

Something is wrong!

Keri made the call. Philip Darby answered after the first ring. He informed her of her father's recent death and that, before he died, he had requested that she be present for the reading of his will.

Tears spilled from her eyes. Her throat tightened. She'd waited too long. She would never be able to forgive herself for what she had done. She would never be able to tell him she was sorry. He was gone. As much as she loved her father, the thought of seeing that woman repulsed her.

Mr. Darby told her about a special video that her father had recorded, specifically for her. He said that because the video was a part of her father's will, for legal reasons, she would have to view it in his office.

The video would allow her to at least see, and hear, her father, one last time. Perhaps it would be a good thing. Partially out of guilt, but mostly because of her deep love for her father—a love that had been suppressed only because of her selfish anger—she had agreed to go. She then told Mr. Darby that she needed him to reserve a second first-class seat on the same flight. Without any questions, he said everything had been taken care of.

He informed her that two first-class reservations had been made for her and Mr. Ryan Mitchell on Delta Airlines out of John Wayne International. The flight departed at 6:45 a.m.,

Thursday, arriving Atlanta Hartsfield at 1:56 p.m. A limo would pick her up at her condo at 5:00 a.m., and another limo would be waiting for her when she arrived in Atlanta. The meeting was set-up for 3:30.

After hanging up with Mr. Darby, she paused, her mind in a fog.

How did Mr. Darby know about Ryan?

She dialed Ryan's number.

"Hello," a sweet lady's voice answered.

Before she could get a word out, she heard Ryan's voice.

"Mom, I got it. You can hang up now."

"Okay, Dear." A click followed.

"Hello," Ryan said.

"Ryan, this is Keri."

"What a pleasant surprise. Don't tell me you've already talked with Rex."

"Oh yeah... you could say that."

"What did you find out?"

"More than I needed to know."

"What?"

"I caught him red-handed. On the trip back, I worked with this little pumped-up blond who happened to be a big talker. Believe it or not, she was on her way to spend a few days with—none other than—Rex."

"No way." Disbelief in his voice.

"Yes. Without her knowing who I was, she spilled her guts for three hours, telling me all about her and Rex... and let me tell you, it was nasty."

"Are you okay?"

"It's over." Silence followed.

"Keri, are you okay? Keri?"

"Ryan, do you realize what this means?" she sniffled. "Us. We can finally be together. A family. You, me, little David, and Mom."

"Keri, I love you."

"I love you, too."

"Listen, I'm catching the first flight out in the morning."

"What about your trip. I thought you had to go to work tomorrow."

"Screw that. My trip doesn't leave until tomorrow afternoon. I'll call in sick once I get to California."

"There's something else," she said.

"What?"

"I just found out that my father passed away a couple of weeks ago."

"Oh Keri... I am so sorry. Are you okay?"

"I'm fine, but I received a call from my dad's lawyer and I'll need to fly over to Atlanta on Thursday for the reading of his will... actually it's a video. I wanted to know if you would go with me."

"Are you kidding? I'm not letting you out of my sight."

"I just didn't think I could face that woman by myself. I don't want to be alone with her in the same room. I might kill her."

"Don't you worry. I'll be right by your side. Did the lawyer mention anything about the will?"

"No. He only said that my father had made a video especially for me. As long as you are with me, I'll be fine."

"Well, you can be assured that I will be sticking to you like glue for the next hundred years. I can't wait to see what this little gold digger looks like. Maybe I'll help you cook up a scheme to kill her, and then we can takeoff with her inheritance to some romantic paradise, like in the movies, and live happily ever after."

"Ryan, what's gotten into you?" she questioned playfully.

He laughed. "You know I'm just joking."

"I know."

He said, "Well, I guess I'll let you go so you can get some sleep. It's been a tough day. I should be out there by nine, maybe earlier."

"I am so excited," she said. "I can't wait to see you. I love you so much."

"I love you, too. Did you find out anything about little David."

"After everything that has happened today, I completely forgot about that. We can do that tomorrow, together. I think it would be better that way."

"Yeah. One more thing..."

"What?"

"Where did you come up with the name David?" There was a brief silence.

"I think you know."

Chapter 68

Ryan's flight landed at the John Wayne International Airport at 8:45 a.m.

With only a carry-on, he hurried off the plane and headed to the exit on the upper level. As he passed through the electric doors and out into the crisp morning, his heart pounded hard when he locked eyes with Keri, parked, waiting patiently at the curb. A giant smile spread across her face.

Once in the car, Keri wrapped her arms around him. "I have never been so happy," she said. Then she kissed him with passion. When she pulled back, they stared momentarily into each other's eyes allowing their hearts to speak in silence what words could not say.

"God, you are beautiful," he said.

Keri smiled, brushing a tear from her cheek as she slipped back behind the wheel. She started the engine, checked her mirrors, then pulled away from the curb.

Ryan watched her every move. "God, you are beautiful," he said. "Or did I already say that?"

"Stop it." She shot him a playful smile and reached for his hand. Then in a more concerned tone, she asked, "Ryan, what do we do if you are not David's father?"

"Don't get ahead of yourself. When we get home..." he paused. "That sounds nice: 'When we get home'. I like it." He leaned over and pecked her on the cheek.

"Me, too."

"Where was I? Oh yeah... when we get home, we'll call your doctor, first thing. Then we'll look for those dog tags."

"I'm just nervous."

"Either way, it's going to be fine."

They arrived at the condo in less than twenty minutes. Once inside, Keri nervously pulled a small address book from a drawer by the phone and flipped through a few pages. "Here it is." She dialed the number then looked over at Ryan.

Ryan listened as she spoke with someone. "Hi, my name is Keri Dean," she said. "Oh, we're doing just fine. Listen, I know this might sound a bit strange, but could you possibly pull my records and tell me the blood types for my son and myself? I don't mind waiting."

Standing silently, with the phone to her ear, she stared at Ryan. In less than a minute, Keri's attention was drawn back to the phone. "So, mine is 'O' and David's is 'A'. Thank you so much."

Ryan whispered anxiously, "The chart. Ask her about the chart."

She nodded to Ryan, then quickly asked, "Oh, I almost forgot, could I ask you one more question? Is there a chart that shows compatible blood types for parents and their children? For example if a mother's blood type is 'O', and the child is 'A', then what could the possible blood types be for the father?" She listened, nodding her head. "I understand. Okay, great."

Keri held her hand over the receiver and whispered to Ryan excitedly, "She's getting the chart. It's called an ABO blood-type chart."

Her attention went back to the phone. "Yes. Let's say the mother is 'O' and the child is 'A', what are the possible blood types for the father?" She listened intently. "Okay, so the father would have to either be an 'A' or 'AB'. Are you sure? Thank you so much. Yes, we will be in next month. Thank you again. Bye."

Ryan smiled, his eyes stretched wide. "One down, one to go," he said. "That means that David's father has to be either an 'A' or an 'AB'. Anything else and he is out."

"Ryan, your blood type is A-positive. Do you realize what this means?"

"We still don't know about Rex. He has to be either an 'O' or a 'B' to prove that he is *not* David's father."

"I know, but this at least tells us that it *is* possible that you *are* David's father. Look at me," she said, holding her hand out, palm down. "I'm shaking."

He took her trembling hand. "Let's go find those dog tags."

After an exhaustive search of every possible location, the tags could not be found. "So, what now?" Keri asked.

"Do you know where Rex might be? We can call him."

She sighed, "I have absolutely no idea."

"That's okay. I guess we'll just have to wait until we get back from Atlanta."

"But I wanted to know now," she said with a sad face.

"Me, too." Ryan put his arm around Keri and kissed her on top of the head. "We'll know soon," he said, his tone lifting. He checked the time: 10:15. "Why don't we go down to the beach for a walk and grab some lunch."

She slipped her arm around his waist and hugged him. "Anything, as long as we're together."

They enjoyed the rest of the day walking on the beach in the wet sand along the ocean's edge, while stopping at times to sit and talk as they admired the beauty of the ocean and the distant horizon.

The image of the thin line of the horizon, the sky above, and the ocean below had never meant so much. They were very familiar with the concepts Martha had often alluded to— embrace the present; learn from the past; and hope in future— but now the illustration was alive.

The present was easy to embrace now that they had each other; and their future had never looked more hopeful. Trusting that God would forgive them for the mistakes of their past, they surrendered them all to the deep dark abyss of the ocean and locked them away forever—along with their feelings of betrayal, bitterness, humiliation, and hurt that others had caused. Like the birth of a new life, they had been given the gift of a fresh start.

Chapter 69

Thursday afternoon at 3:15 p.m., Ryan and Keri pulled up in front of the law office of Philip Darby.

They exited the stretched black limo and walked up the wide flagstone steps, past a large fountain encircled by a multicolored bed of petunias contrasting against the rich, green, manicured lawn.

Ryan reached and pulled the tall glass door leading into the foyer of the modernly designed law office. A nicely dressed receptionist looked up and smiled as they entered.

"My name is Keri Hart, and I'm here to see Philip Darby."

The attractive middle-aged woman answered in a drippy Southern drawl, "Yes ma'am, he's expecting you." She lifted the receiver of her phone and pressed a button on the keypad. "Mr. Darby, Keri Hart is here to see you. Yes sir. I'll tell her." Replacing the receiver, she looked up. "Mr. Darby will be out in a moment. Can I get you something to drink?"

After turning to Ryan, Keri said, "No thank you."

In less than a minute, a distinguished man in a dark suit entered the room and walked toward them with his hand extended. "Keri, I'm Phil Darby." They shook hands. "And this must be Ryan Mitchell," Darby said, reaching for Ryan's hand.

With a puzzled look, Keri asked, "How do you know Ryan?"

"For now, let's just say, I've heard about him from your father."

"Oh... okay," she said, acceptingly.

Darby was as she had envisioned: in his sixties, mostly gray hair, and every bit the Southern gentleman.

Darby lowered his voice, stepping in closer. "Keri, you are aware that you will not be alone during the viewing of your father's video message?"

"Yes," she said, glancing up at Ryan.

"The woman and her male friend are waiting in the conference room. Once we're seated, I'll begin with a short letter from your father followed by his videotaped message. After the video, you will be free to go."

"Okay," Keri replied.

She was taken by how kind he was—almost fatherly. It felt good. But, the thought of meeting the woman waiting in the conference room filled her with anxiety. She held tight to Ryan's hand.

Darby led them into the conference room. Nothing could have prepared Keri, or Ryan, for what they were about to experience.

In the center of the large room stretched a polished mahogany boardroom-style table with enough high-back leather chairs to seat at least fifteen.

As Keri and Ryan entered the room, a chair spun around. When Keri saw who it was, her heart jumped, making a thrusting attempt to escape through the rapidly narrowing passage in her throat. "Rex? What are *you* doing here?"

"Surprise!" he said with outstretched arms.

Before she had time to process Rex, the woman seated beside him swiveled around in her chair. Keri gasped with enough force to dislodge her heart from her throat, shoving it back into her chest.

Ryan and Keri sang out in unison, "Emily?"

What were the chances of Rex finding her father's little gold digger, and what were the chances of that little gold digger being Emily.

Frozen in disbelief, staring at Emily, Keri said, "You? What was my father thinking? He must have been out of his mind." She grabbed Ryan by the arm. "I'm out of here. Come on Ryan."

As they moved toward the door, Darby said, "Keri, please... wait."

She turned to hear what Darby had to say.

"I know this appears a little out of the ordinary, but you should stay and listen to what your father has to say."

She looked up at Ryan. He said, "Why not?" She smiled.

"Okay. We'll stay," she said.

"Well, now that we've all met." Darby interjected, attempting to remain professional.

Keri looked at Ryan again; their faces momentarily frozen. Then simultaneously they burst into laughter. They looked back at Emily and Rex and laughed even harder. Darby encouraged Ryan and Keri toward the table.

"Have you ever seen a more perfect couple?" Ryan said. "They truly deserve each other." Turning toward Emily he said, "You couldn't have found a more perfect companion. I am so happy for you."

"You just wait," Emily replied, "In a few minutes, we'll see who's happy for who."

Ignoring Emily, Ryan glanced at Rex and added, "Hey, Buddy, you better watch her, she's full of surprises."

"Are we ready to get started?" Darby asked. He motioned with his hand for Keri and Ryan to take a seat on the other side of the table.

Still snickering, they took their seats. Ryan leaned in and whispered to Keri, "Thanks for inviting me. This is just what I needed." He kissed her on the cheek.

Darby placed a brown envelope and a small box on the table. He removed some neatly typed documents from the envelope.

"I'm going to read a summary statement from Mr. Hart, then I'll play the video message he recorded only a few weeks before his death."

"How long is this going to take?" Emily asked impatiently.

"The videotape is approximately three minutes long," Darby replied."

"Emily, just be patient," Rex said.

"You shut-up!" she snapped. "And don't you tell me what to do."

"Okay," Darby prodded. "If we can get started now?"

"Go ahead," Emily scowled.

Darby read the words of Keri's father:

> *"The videotape that I have prepared has been transcribed and notarized. I wanted to use this format to express my emotions more clearly. I have requested that Emily and my beloved daughter Keri both be present. I have also asked the contents of the videotape, and its text version, not be viewed or read by anyone prior to this event.*
>
> *"I apologize to my good friend Phil Darby for obtaining another firm to handle this matter for me. He is aware of my desires that the information remain private until this day. After the tape has been viewed, the text version of the tape may be reviewed and filed as necessary. At this time, I would like to ask Mr. Darby to play the videotape."*

Darby placed the papers to the side.

"The old fool didn't trust anybody," Emily mumbled to herself.

"Excuse me?" Darby asked, looking over at Emily.

"Nothing. Just keep it rolling," she said, making a continuous rolling motion with her index finger. "I've got things to do."

Rex reached over to take Emily's hand in an apparent attempt to calm her. Before he touched her, she snatched her hand away and gave him a look that made him recoil in fear of being struck.

Darby took the small box, broke the seal, removed a black videotape, and inserted it into the player that was connected to the built-in projection system.

With the press of a single button on an electronic panel flush-mounted into the side of the table, a white screen at the end of the conference room lowered while the drapes closed automatically, darkening the room. With everyone's attention fixated on the white screen, Darby pressed the video play button.

Ronald Hart appeared sitting behind a large office desk in front of bookshelves that rose out of the camera frame. The view tightened, causing the image of Hart's face to grow larger.

He began to speak: "I assume Emily and Keri are both present, as I requested, and possibly, Ryan and Rex, too."

Keri leaned to Ryan and whispered, "How could he have known?"

"Keri, I first want to tell you that I love you more than you will ever know."

Keri reached for Ryan's hand under the table.

"I hope that after you've viewed this tape, you will be able to forgive me for what I believe was an understandable misinterpretation on your part.

"Emily, I'm sorry that you had to bear the brunt of my sorrow, especially during my last few months: a time when I finally accepted that I would never be able to talk with my daughter again."

"For God's sake, Ron," Emily said, shifting in her seat, "please... spare us the drama."

"First, let's talk about my estate. Mr. Darby has the documents that outline, in detail, how I wish for my estate to be distributed, but let me summarize.

"My estate consists of multiple residences, securities, and several liquid accounts, all managed by Gold Street Capital Management in Chicago. In total, my entire estate, as of this taping, is valued at roughly $100 million dollars. The real estate is free and clear and the remainder consists of cash and securities. If left in their current allocation, they should conservatively yield two hundred to two hundred and fifty thousand dollars per month.

"Did he say 'per month'?" Rex asked. "Primo," he turned to Emily and smiled.

"In regards to my estate, you might find the events that I am about to disclose hard to believe, but I trust that once you hear me out, you will better understand why I have made these decisions.

"First, Emily, you have provided me with companionship and entertainment, for this, I want to thank you. Your presence in my life also helped to reinforce my strong beliefs regarding the importance of family, although, your intentions were more than likely in diametric contradiction to their intended outcome."

Emily turned to Darby with a confused look and asked, "What is *that* supposed to mean: 'diametric contradiction'?"

Darby motioned with his eyes toward the screen and whispered, "Just watch."

"Emily, I know that you will now be able to find the life that you have longed for, and I want to wish you and Rex the best in all of your endeavors."

Emily smiled. She leaned over to Rex, sliding her arm in his, giving him a big open-mouth kiss. It never seemed to dawn on her how Ronald Hart could have known about her and Rex. She'd only gotten with him two days ago.

"Keri, I hope you will find it in your heart to forgive me for what I did and for what I am about to tell you."

Emily snickered, whispering softly to Rex, "Where's the popcorn? This is where she gets the ax." She leaned her head on Rex's shoulder.

"If I could go back, I would definitely do things differently. Keri, it would have been much easier for all of us if your mother... God rest her soul... had not been so hard to deal with."

Keri's grip tightened on Ryan's hand.

"Even as obstinate as she was, I know she loved you and only wanted the best for you. You were everything to both of us, and now, you are all that is left of our family. I hope you'll not only forgive me, but let the good memories we had together live in your heart, forever. Keri, I love you very much and have no other choice than to leave my entire estate to you."

Emily bolted to her feet and yelled-out at the projected image on the white screen as though it were alive, "What?" She quickly turned to Darby. "What did that liar say? Didn't he say for me and Rex to enjoy it all? What about my having to 'bear the sorrow'? Doesn't that mean he's giving it all to me? There must be a mistake!"

Darby pressed the pause button and reached over to Emily. "Please sit down. The tape is not over."

"This is crap!" she said.

"Honey, sit down," Rex said, reaching for her arm.

She turned to Rex with a look that would have frightened a starving Doberman away from his last bone. "What makes you think I'm your honey? A couple of nights in the sack and you think you own me? I don't think so. Get your hands off me." She sat down in a huff.

Darby pressed the play button and the tape continued.

"Emily, you must have thought that you would be the one receiving my entire estate—as I had planned. But let me explain."

"You got that right," she said, still treating the one-dimensional projection as if it were human. "After all, that's what you told me, you deceiving two-faced pig," she snapped, her voice seething with anger.

"In some ways, my master plan was designed to give everyone what they wanted or, in some cases, what they deserved. But most importantly, to give you, Keri, the opportunity to follow your heart—something your mother took from you long ago."

Keri turned and looked at Ryan, her watery eyes starting to spill tears onto her cheek.

"Actually, all I had to do was encourage the inevitable. I believe it would have all played-out the same in the end, I just didn't want to die knowing my little girl was unhappy. And Ryan, just for the record, I have always known in my heart that you and Keri would make a perfect match. I just couldn't get her mother to see past herself. It's sad, but she lived more for what people thought of her than what she really believed in."

Ronald Hart paused, appearing to hold back his emotions. "Enough of that." He sniffled. "Now Ryan, I'll have to hand it to you, you did make things a bit difficult for me when you let Rex sucker you into his little trap with those letters." He chuckled. "If it hadn't been for that, I might have been able to pull it off without you two taking the detour down Misery Lane. I just hope you both learned that with every choice in life, there are consequences—some not so pleasant. You need to be proactive and pursue what you believe is right. And for God's sake, don't let your heart deceive you. You have a head—use it. I don't mean to sound preachy, but remember, I'm dead. I can say what I think.

"You might be wondering how I did all this. First, Emily, being the classical female predator—looking for any man that would give her a life of luxury—I knew I might have difficulty. Even if I could entice a man to take her, I couldn't afford that she would ever want to go back after Ryan. That's when I decided to do it myself. I had a letter mailed to the apartment in Texas. It was designed to look like a mass-mailing. I'm sure you remember...

Dear Resident:

Career opportunities await as "Excalibur Homes", a regional homebuilder and subsidiary

> *of an Atlanta-based national conglomerate,*
> *expands into the Metroplex.*

...but it was all staged. There was only one letter. My people at
Excalibur were told to do anything necessary to hire Emily. I
knew once I smothered her with money: jet-rides to Atlanta on
the corporate jet; wining and dining; and finally an invitation to
join the company as my personal assistant, I knew she couldn't
resist.

"Emily, if I were giving you a grade, I'd have to say you
flunked 'Predatory-101' by not doing her homework." He
laughed. "If you would have done any research, at all, you
would have seen that the path to riches was definitely *not* on the
back of an airline pilot.

"Keri, you see now why I mailed you the key to my New
York condo and insisted that you take advantage of it on your
next layover. There was no doubt that when you hooked up with
Ryan the two of you would end up there. The hotel staff assured
me that they would make certain you and Ryan bumped into
each other. They had multiple backup plans just in case there
was a hitch in the street-side meeting.

"Rex, I knew you would never settle down, so finding the
right bait for you was easy. I figured a flight attendant working
for the same airline would be perfect, but it couldn't be just any
flight attendant. This girl had to be stunningly beautiful, but
more importantly, able to pull something like this off. I must
say, my people did a great job finding Candi. She was ideal for
the job—a flight attendant, a struggling wannabe actress, and
she had even done a little work on the side with a Hollywood
escort service. In addition to a large cash payment, plus a bonus
if she pulled it off, I offered to foot the bill for her to visit one of
the best plastic surgeons in LA for a few cosmetic touchups
she'd been wanting, but couldn't afford. It was a win-win for
both of us. Rex, you being the typical egotistical womanizer
that you are, I knew you would never be able to resist a cute
little thing like Candi. All I needed was for Keri to catch you

fooling around with her, and I knew that was only a matter of time. Having a few friends at the airline didn't hurt. They were nice enough to work with us to make sure that all of the 'coincidental' scheduling of flight crews took place.

"As I stated in the beginning of this message, my master plan was designed to give everyone what they wanted or, in some cases, what they deserved. Therefore, my gift to Emily is Rex. I cannot imagine two people more deserving of each other. Emily was positioned at the Watford Hotel, and thanks to the wonderful management and staff at the hotel, multiple scenarios were developed to ensure a meeting with Rex. I assume with great confidence that Emily and Rex are here today. Congratulations to both of you.

"All-in-all it was a fairly complex operation, but as they say, 'money talks'."

"Keri, I knew that once Emily was out of Ryan's life, and Rex was out of yours, you two would eventually find each other. Ryan, please forgive me for playing God with your life, but I always knew that you loved Keri, just as I know now that you will take care of my little girl. And to be honest, that's why I did all this: because I love my little girl and want her to have the desires of her heart.

"Oh. One more thing. I hope you take good care of my grandson." He winked. "Let's all hope that that day in New York turns out the way we wanted it to."

Keri's mouth dropped. "How could he have known?" She turned and looked at Ryan with amazement. Her eyes watery and her cheeks wet with tears.

The tape ended and Darby hit the button that retracted the screen and opened the drapes. Light filled the room.

"Is that it?" Emily exclaimed. "Nothing for me?" She grabbed her designer purse, storming for the door. On her way out, she yelled, "You haven't heard the last of me! Come on, Rex. Let's get out of here. I need to find a good lawyer."

Rex rose, but before he left, Ryan said, "Hey, Rex."

"What?"

"You wouldn't happen to know your blood type, would you?"

"Yeah. It's 'O-negative'. Why?"

"Just thought you'd like to know that your vasectomy is good."

"What?"

"David is not your son, he's mine."

Keri burst into tears. Ryan put his arm around her."

"Dude, not too sure how you pulled that off, but it's *definitely* the best news I've heard all day. You learned something from the Rexter, after all."

"Good luck, Rex," Ryan said. "And hey... no hard feelings."

"Yeah, sure... It happens."

Emily stuck her head back in the room. "Rex, are you coming?"

"Chill. I'm coming!" Rex shot Ryan one last look and said, "Bro, remember, I've always got your back. See you on the other side."

* * *

Darby turned to Keri, while standing in the lobby. "Keri, your dad really was a good man. He talked with me a lot over the last year. He loved you very much. I'm sure you know that."

"Yes," she said, blotting a tissue to her eye.

"He felt it would be better this way. He always had his eyes on you and wanted only the best. He knew that Ryan was the perfect man for you from the beginning."

"Thank you so much for being his friend," she said.

Darby glanced outside. "Looks like your limo is here. He'll take you to the Charlie Brown Airport where *your* personal jet will fly you back to Orange County in style. You guys go home and we can go over the details when you're ready. I think you need to be alone and digest what has happened today."

After shaking hands and saying good-bye to Mr. Darby, Ryan and Keri walked out. "Just think, Ryan. Now we can get the best care possible for Martha."

"You're so sweet to think of my mother."

"What do you mean by that?"

"I mean, thank you for including Mom in your thoughts, so quickly."

"Ryan," she stopped and grabbed him by the arm turning him toward her, "she's my Mom too, remember?"

He stared into her eyes. "I know," he said.

They looked up, after hearing the muffled voice of a woman, to see Emily, shaking her fist ranting words of revenge, "This isn't over!" The car sped off.

"Looks like they both got what they deserved," Ryan said.

"Yeah, I think they make the perfect couple." They both looked at each other. After a few seconds of silence, satisfied smiles broke out on their faces. They headed toward the waiting limo.

Chapter 70

Three months later—July 1987
The Ritz-Carlton, Laguna Niguel, California

Moments before a beautiful sunset over Monarch Bay, Keri and Ryan stood beneath a Mediterranean-styled gazebo with adobe stucco arches and red tile roof, atop a 150-foot bluff overlooking the Pacific Ocean: the perfect balance of elegance, serenity, and grace.

The unobstructed panoramic ocean view with waves crashing on the sandy beach below presented the perfect metaphor of past and future.

Powerful currents of emotions swept through the small gathering of friends as they witnessed the long-awaited and satisfying union of two soul mates.

At the conclusion of their exchange of vows, a reception was held in the Pacific Promenade Room at The Ritz.

Ryan stood before a small gathering of friends and family and said, "I would like to make a toast. Most of you know the journey that Keri and I have traveled to find each other."

He turned, looking down at Keri seated by his side. "I have learned an important lesson through it all. There is no greater gift than the gift of love, and when you find it you will be satisfied. Keri is my gift, but I feel that God has given me more than a gift; He has given me a treasure." He looked back at the people. "But more importantly, I have learned that when someone accepts the love you desire to give, you will be completely fulfilled. If you haven't yet found love, have faith and embrace the hope that you will find it tomorrow, but until then, learn to keep giving it. Your days will be brighter and the pain and regrets of yesterday will fade away faster." He lifted his glass in the air. "To love."

After several more toasts were made by friends and family, the music began to play and the guests were invited to enjoy their weekend. The invitations sent to each guest included an all-expense-paid weekend at the Ritz.

After Ryan and Keri left the Pacific Promenade, they stopped in an adjacent private room. When they entered, Martha Mitchell, dressed in an elegant evening gown that she and Keri had picked out together, turned to greet them. "There you two are. My little lovebirds," she said.

Keri hugged her and kissed her on the cheek. "Mom, you're so beautiful."

"Why, thank you Dear. And I must say, seeing you in that wedding dress reminds me of the first time you two got married."

Keri looked up at Ryan with a sympathetic but loving face, then back to Martha. "Well, we just love each other so much that we wanted to get married again."

"I think it's sweet that you wanted to renew your vows." She looked over at her nurse standing beside her, holding her six-month-old grandson in her arms. "This time, little David got to see his mommy and daddy get married. I think that's special."

Ryan hugged his mother and said, "Mom, you know Keri and I are taking a little vacation, don't you?" He knew she would probably never know they were gone, but he mentioned it out of habit and with the hidden hope that she might understand.

"That sounds wonderful. You two have fun. Don't worry about me. I'll be fine."

Keri hugged her again and then kissed David on his forehead. He smiled big. "Now you take care of your grandma for us, okay," she said, tickling his tummy.

"I almost forgot," Martha said. She reached behind her and returned with a small flat box wrapped in white wedding paper with a white bow on top. "Here, I wanted to give you something."

Keri took the gift. "Martha you shouldn't have."

"It's just a little something I thought you should have."

"Should we open it now?" Keri asked.

"Why don't you wait and open it on your vacation. I think it will mean more to both of you when you are alone."

"Thanks Mom," Ryan said. He leaned down and kissed her on the cheek. "We'd better get going."

After a change of clothes, they jumped into a stretched white limousine and sped off.

"Where are you taking me?" Keri asked.

"I thought you wanted me to surprise you."

She snuggled-up to him. "I do. But you could give me a little hint."

"Are you sure?"

"No." She snickered.

"I thought so."

After a short drive, the limo pulled up to a gate on the perimeter of the Orange County Airport. The driver spoke into a speaker box and the iron gate rolled back. They drove past small private planes and up to a private jet parked on the ramp.

"So, are *you* going to fly it?"

"Are you kidding? I'm done with that. This baby comes—batteries included."

"Batteries?"

"I mean pilots... just a joke."

As they exited the limo, the young copilot greeted them. They ascended the stairs to the cabin while the limo driver assisted the copilot with their bags.

The interior of the Gulfstream-IV was luxuriously appointed: soft, tan-hued leather seating; hand-rubbed wood inlays with Brazilian mahogany maple surfaces polished to a mirror-like sheen.

Ryan stuck his head in the cockpit and said hello to the captain and then followed Keri through the spacious cabin as she rubbed her hand along the back of the hand-stitched leather seats.

"Check out the back." He pointed to a shiny mahogany door that opened into a private sleeping quarter complete with lavatory and shower. A vase of thorn-less red roses beside the bed caught her eye.

She turned and looked at him with a seductive stare before walking over to take-in their sweet fragrance. Two small white envelopes peeked out of the stems. She slipped the card from the envelope marked "Read me first".

Ryan could see her eyes becoming watery as she read.

June 23, 1974

Dear Ryan,

I believe if we are meant to be, nothing can keep us apart. As long as I live, I will patiently wait on each sunrise and follow each sunset into tomorrow, for I believe it is the path of the sun that will lead us to our hopes and dreams. Promise me that you will never lose hope in tomorrow.

I love you,
Keri

Ryan asked, "Do you remember that?"

Speechless, she fanned her face, tears spilling from her eyes. She nodded. After a moment of silence she said, "You kept it."

"It was all I had to remember you by. Every time I saw a sunset, those words would run through my head, even when I knew I had lost you to someone else."

She turned and took the second note, but instead of reading it, she held it out, "Would you read it to me?"

He slipped the note from its envelope.

Keri,

 There are no words to express my feelings or the vastness of my love for you. If I only live this one day with you as my wife, it will have been worth the years of living without you.
 With every mile we fly westbound during the next five hours, it is my prayer that we can turn the hands of time back and begin the life that we should have started many years ago.

I love you,
Ryan

When he looked up, tears poured from her eyes. She reached for him and hugged him tight. After a minute of silence in each other's arms, they kissed.

"Mr. and Mrs. Mitchell, we will be starting-up now." The voice of the pilot filled the cabin. "If you would, please take a seat for takeoff."

"That sounds good: 'Mr. and Mrs. Mitchell'. I think I'm going to like that," Keri said.

"Me, too." He kissed her once more before leading her back into the main cabin to take their seat and buckle up.

The jet taxied to the end of the runway and thundered up and away into the silky-smooth night.

For the first hour of the trip, Ryan and Keri enjoyed the privacy and luxury of being alone while they talked and nibbled at a fruit tray filled with fresh strawberries, pineapples, and assorted cheeses.

Remembering the gift that Martha had given them, Keri went to the rear of the jet's cabin and returned with the white gift box. "Martha said we should open it when we were alone," Keri said. "I almost forgot." Ryan watched as she removed the paper and pulled a 16 x 10 frame from the box. She held the frame out in front of them so they could both see it.

Behind the glass was a familiar cross stitched scene. It was a late-afternoon beach scene, the sun three-quarters below the horizon, and the silhouette of a bird in flight headed toward the setting sun. Two empty Adirondack chairs, side-by-side, faced the ocean. Three phrases were stitched into the fabric—one below the horizon: LEARN FROM THE PAST; one on the horizon, next to the sliver of orange sun: EMBRACE THE PRESENT; the third above the horizon against a canvas of purple-blue sky: HOPE IN THE FUTURE.

They turned and looked at each other and smiled. Words were not necessary. They had both seen Martha working on the stitching, years ago, and had listened to the many life lessons she saw in the image. It had hung in the small foyer of her house since the day it was completed as a reminder to her before facing the challenges of the world outside.

The impact of the simple illustration had played a big part in the note Keri had written to Ryan the night she broke up with him. It was also the message that Ryan clung to during the years he searched for Keri. It was a message they both now knew— more than ever before—was the essence of life; something Martha Mitchell held dear.

She had always pointed out the bird in the stitching. She called it God's bird. It reminded her of how everyone is constantly flapping their wings, searching for the one thing, one place, one person that will make them happy. She'd said: *Many leave this world having never found happiness because they are confused where to look. Some will die in mid flight, others will fall into the ocean—their past—and drown.*

She believed the ocean below the horizon represents our past; the thin line of the horizon the present; and the limitless sky our future. She had taught that the finite abyss of the ocean is where our mistakes, hurts, and pains of the past must be buried, but the lessons they taught should never be forgotten.

MIKE COE

She would say: *When one stops pushing the present into the future, and instead dwells on the past, all hope is lost.*

It was a message brought to mind for Ryan while at the Naval Academy where he remembered reading Thomas Wolfe's book, *Look Homeward, Angel.* Wolf once said, "The home of every one of us is the future."

Ryan and Keri sat facing each other on a couch. Ryan reached up and tucked a strand of Keri's hair behind her ear as they talked. "Now that I'm sitting here with you," he said, "it seems like all those years of being apart never happened. It's like the pain of the past has been washed away." He let his hand rest on her shoulder, his index finger slowly tracing little circles on her neck.

She reached and took his free hand, bringing the back of it to her mouth, kissing it softly. She then placed his palm on her chest and pressed it firmly against her warm body. "Do you feel my heart? I don't know if you can feel it, but it has never been happier. It's like a new puppy jumping around in there."

He reached behind her neck and pulled her close, kissing her softly on the lips. The kiss grew as they freed their passions to explore the moistness; lips still laced with the sweetness from the fruit.

Holding each other close, they embraced the moment with anxious anticipation of what was to come—a deeper union of their bodies and souls.

Ryan reached beside the couch to a small panel and toggled a switch dimming the cabin lights to a faint glow. The steady hum of the jet's engines reassured her of the fact that they were safely cocooned and on their way to a long-awaited metamorphosis into oneness.

"So, you never told me where we are going," she said.

"I thought you liked surprises."

"I do." She paused. A smile emerged on her face. "I think I know." She cut her big brown eyes up at him.

"Oh... you do, do you? he said. "Go ahead. Take your best shot."

"We're going to Hawaii, aren't we?" He smiled. "Look at you," she said playfully. "We are, aren't we? You're taking me on a flight to paradise. How romantic." She snuggled up against his chest.

"Not exactly."

She lifted her head and met his gaze. "What do you mean?"

"Well, we *are* going to Hawaii, but as far as paradise goes... My paradise is you."

Her eyes softened. She leaned up and kissed him. "I guess dreams really do come true."

Thrusting forward, piercing the dark sky, they chased the path of the setting sun, pushing the present into the future—leaving the past behind. The journey of their hearts to find paradise had ended—the life they'd always dreamed of was just beginning.

The End

Author's Note

What often appears to destroy us is what eventually defines us and takes us to a better place.

I was inspired by one of the most popular and familiar Biblical examples of moral failure ever written. It is a story of grace, forgiveness, restoration, and hope that reminds us that God's agenda is not to crush us under his feet after we fall, but to heal us and restore us to a healthy loving relationship with Him.

David and Bathsheba: *"The following spring, the time of year when kings go to war, David sent Joab and the Israelite army to destroy the Ammonites. In the process they laid siege to the city of Rabbah. But David stayed in Jerusalem. Late one afternoon, David got up from taking his nap and was strolling on the roof of the palace. From his vantage point on the roof he saw a woman bathing. The woman was stunningly beautiful (LUST). He sent someone to find out who she was, and he was told, 'She is Bathsheba, the daughter of Eliam and the wife of Uriah the Hittite.' Then David sent for her; and when she came to the palace, he slept with her (ADULTERY). Then she returned home. Later, when Bathsheba discovered that she was pregnant, she sent a message to inform David. So David sent word to Joab: 'Send me Uriah the Hittite.'"* (2 Samuel 11:1-15 NLT)

As the story goes, David ordered Bathsheba's husband (Uriah) to be sent to the front lines of battle, then David had his troops pull back, leaving Uriah to be killed (MURDER).

David was restored and forgiven, but his actions had disastrous affects, not only on his personal life, but on the lives of others around him. After David married Bathsheba, their child was born, but quickly grew sick and died. David was constantly plagued with rebellion and personal strife from within his own house: his son raped his daughter; another son killed the son who had raped the daughter; the son who murdered the first son raised an army and tried to overthrow David's kingdom; David ended up killing that son in defense of his kingdom.

It should be noted, that although David's mistake cost him dearly, he loved Bathsheba more than any other. It only goes to prove that a marriage built on the healing grace of God—even in the face of previous moral failure—always produces a very special, intimate, bonded relationship.

We are all like David. We need God's forgiveness in our lives. David realized he could not ask for forgiveness based on his own actions. His actions were reprehensible and he was, no doubt, overwhelmed with contrition. So he asked for God's mercy based, not on his own goodness, but on God's unfailing love and great compassion. Not too many people have committed acts as bad as David's, but in spite of David's great moral collapse, God was compassionate toward him.

In *Flight to Paradise*, I merely touched on the internal struggles of the characters as they must have dealt with their moral failures. It must be assumed that Keri and Ryan dealt with these issues, much like King David, and moved forward, while Rex and Emily did not. Failing to deal with the moral failures in our life assures us that we are destined to repeat them. We must be willing to face God—and ourselves—with the same painful honesty that was David's first step toward rebuilding his life. (See Psalm 51—the greatest confession ever written).

Learn from the past; embrace the present; and hope in the future. When we stop pushing the present into the future, and instead dwell on the past, all hope is lost.

About the Author

Mike Coe was born on a Tuesday in Dothan, Alabama, two days before Thanksgiving Day. He has since celebrated with Mr. Tom Turkey on eight Thursdays (you do the math). His long Southern heritage includes a grandfather who was mayor of Dothan, and great-great and great-great-great grandfathers who served in the Confederate Army (6th Regiment Alabama Cavalry). He happily concedes that his Southern drawl is due to a genetic disposition rather than the more popular view held by most non-Southerners: a medical condition caused from constant sunstrokes and sunburns to the neck resulting in a thick tongue and a slow mind.

He married his Dothan High School sweetheart in 1977, claiming to be the first boy to kiss her at a spin-the-bottle party in the eighth grade. Promising her a life filled with travel and adventure, they went cold turkey on sweet tea and boiled peanuts and headed out to see the world. During the last thirty-three years Mike and Sue Marie have changed addresses approximately every four years (coast-to-coast and overseas), bolted-on car tags from seven different states, and been blessed with two wonderful children: David and Anna.

After college, he served six years as an Air Force pilot, five years as a corporate pilot, and twenty-one years as a commercial airline pilot with a major airline based in Washington D.C., Nashville, Chicago, Dallas, and Los Angeles. His flight experience equates to having spent over two years in the air in everything from Piper Cubs to jumbo jets and seaplanes to helicopters.

His fictional stories are derived from the real world—where we all live; stories designed to leave readers with a message of hope for a better tomorrow.

"As individuals we are uniquely defined, but within our human experiences (successes, failures, and heartaches) we are connected by a common thread."

Mike Coe

How to Order

Visit the author's website:
coebooks.com

Also available at:
amazon.com,
barnesandnoble.com,
booklocker.com,
booksamillion.com,
and others.

EBooks (instant download) available only at:
booklocker.com

* * *

To view a chapter-by-chapter photo journal and the story behind the story, visit the author's website:

coebooks.com

LaVergne, TN USA
21 June 2010
186859LV00002B/9/P